MISTRESS OF FAIRLYDEN

Also by Gwen Kirkwood

Fairlyden

MISTRESS OF FAIRLYDEN

Gwen Kirkwood

To Peggy
with best wishes
Gwen Kirkwood

HEADLINE

First published in 1991
by HEADLINE BOOK PUBLISHING PLC

10 9 8 7 6 5 4 3 2 1

British Library Cataloguing in Publication Data

Kirkwood, Gwen
Mistress of fairlyden.
I. Title
823.914

ISBN 0-7472-0434-9

Typeset by Medcalf Type Ltd, Bicester, Oxon

Printed and bound in Great Britain by
Richard Clay Ltd, Bungay, Suffolk

HEADLINE BOOK PUBLISHING PLC
Headline House
79 Great Titchfield Street
London W1P 7FN

Extract from The Cotter's Saturday Night
by Robert Burns

xviii

Then homeward all take off their sev'ral way:
The younglin cottagers retire to rest:
The parent-pair their secret homage pay,
And profer up to Heav'n the warm request
That He, who stills the raven's clam'rous nest
And decks the lily fair in flowr'y pride,
Would, in the way His wisdon sees the best,
For them and for their little ones provide;
But, chiefly, in their hearts with grace divine preside.

From scenes like these, old Scotia's grandeur springs,
That makes her love'd at home, rever'd abroad:
Princes and lords are but the breath of kings,
'An honest man's the noblest work of God;'
And certes, in fair virtue's heav'nly road,
The cottage leaves the palace far behind.
What is a lordling's pomp! a cumbrous load,
Disguising oft the wretch of human kind,
Studied in arts of hell, in wickedness refin'd!

O Scotia! my dear, my native soil!
For whom my warmest wish to Heav'n is sent!
Long may thy hardy sons of rustic toil
Be blest with health, and peace, and sweet content!
And, O! may Heaven their simple lives prevent
From luxury's contagion, weak and vile!
Then, howe'er crowns and coronets be rent,
A virtuous populace may rise the while,
And stand a wall of fire around their much-lov'd isle.

One

Sarah had just finished churning and working the butter. She hummed under her breath as she surveyed the firm, golden butter pats, each neatly patterned and lined up on the stone table. Yet it was not her work which had caused the happiness bubbling up inside her on this crisp April morning.

I feel as light-hearted as a schoolgirl, she thought with a smile, for all I shall soon be twenty-four years old.

The jingle of harness in the farmyard distracted her thoughts from what she considered to be her great age. She glanced out of the dairy window and saw Louis Whiteley leading his pair of horses to the stable for an extra feed of oats and bran. Sarah knew he had been ploughing Keeper's Field, just behind the Fairlyden steading, since the first streak of dawn crept over the horizon. She had heard the shrill cry of seagulls and seen them flying in from the Solway Firth to flock like giant snowflakes on the rich brown of the newly turned furrows. Now the sky was clear and the spring sunshine promised a fine day as Louis and his team stopped to break their fast.

'Louis!' Sarah hailed the man who had worked at Fairlyden since the year she was born. He had been a boy of thirteen then; now he was a skilled horseman with a wife and four children to support.

''Morning, Miss Sar . . . er, Mistress Fairly, what can I dae for ye?' Louis grinned sheepishly. Sarah returned his smile. It would soon be a year since her marriage to William Fairly, but she knew Louis and his wife, Janet, still thought of her as Miss Sarah. She didn't mind. She regarded Louis and Janet, and her other maid, Agnes Jamieson, as friends as well as servants, but her husband had a different view. He liked everyone to remember she was his wife.

Louis was waiting patiently.

'I would like you to harness the mare and load the cart with the rest of the corn if you please, Louis.' The man's eyebrows rose in surprise. Miss Sarah usually drove the pony and trap to the village these days, and she always harnessed it herself.

'The mare?'

'Yes. I'll take Moonbeam. I can take the butter to Mr Jardine's store first, then I'll go on to the mill with the corn. There's only a few bags left. I'll wait at the Mill House while Master Slater grinds it, then I can bring it home with me.'

She could not tell Louis that she was taking the corn as an excuse to see Beatrice Slater. She was longing to share her secret happiness with the girl who had been her dearest friend since they sat together in Dominie Campbell's schoolroom.

'I dinna expect Master Slater will be busy,' she added dryly. 'Old Mr Miller told father his mill would have closed long ago if it hadna been for one or two loyal customers like ourselves.'

'Aye, I expect he rues the day Slater became his son-in-law!' Louis agreed with feeling. 'But Master Fairly said ye werena tae take corn tae the mill anymore,' he added uneasily.

Sarah tossed her head in mild exasperation, but a mischievous smile curved her mouth.

'You know I've been going to the mill since I could toddle, Louis.'

'Aye . . . but the Master disna like Slater.'

'Well Master Fairly went to Lanark on the early train. I shall be home long before he returns. Anyway I canna imagine what harm could befall me on a drive to Muircumwell!'

Louis looked at her slender figure, standing proudly in the open door of the dairy. He guessed it was not the driving that had caused Master Fairly's concern; his wife could handle a horse and cart as well as most men. But Miss Sarah was a handsome young woman with her sparkling brown eyes and glowing cheeks, and the coil of her dark hair peeping out from the frill of a snowy cap; this morning she had a sort of inner radiance which added to her beauty. The pensive shadows which had haunted her brown eyes through most of her girlhood had disappeared.

'The Master said I was tae tak the corn tae the mill masel,' Louis persisted.

'I know you have more than enough to do, Louis, with the ploughing to finish and the oats to sow, as well as all the manure to be carted frae the midden before the turnips can be drilled.'

'Aye, there's a lot tae be done,' Louis agreed anxiously, 'especially now Master Logan has tae go tae Strathtod everyday tae attend tae his work as the new factor for the estate. I saw him riding across the glen early this morning.'

'Yes, we shall certainly miss my father's help, whether he has a lame leg or no',' Sarah agreed. 'But I'm grateful to Mr Bradshaw for offering him a chance to use his knowledge. He thought he'd never be able to earn his daily bread again after the accident with the stallion, just because he canna follow the plough and do the work he's used to doing. Now he earns more than his bread, though I'm sure he would still choose to work in the fields if he could.'

'Aye, I ken, but at least he still comes hame tae Fairlyden of an evening, and he still has his other Clydesdales tae breed from, even if he does think none o' them will ever be as guid as Logan's Lucifer!' Louis grinned. He knew how much the horses meant to Alexander Logan. He had earned a reputation as one of the most successful breeders in the district.

And at least William still likes the horses too! Sarah thought with relief. She would never admit that her husband's waning interest in the daily running of Fairlyden disappointed her.

'I shall be ready to go to Muircumwell as soon as you have finished your breakfast and loaded the cart,' she said aloud, bringing the conversation to an end and preventing Louis voicing any further objections to her proposed visit to the mill.

Sarah felt a surge of anticipation. It would be lovely to have time for a chat with Beatrice in the mill kitchen while she waited for Master Slater to grind the corn. She was longing to share her own news and hear how Beattie's friendship with Dick O'Connor was developing now that he had been released from prison.

Much as she loved her husband, Sarah felt she must defy his wishes, just for once. After all he did not disapprove of her friendship with Beatrice Slater; he knew she was not responsible for her father's terrible reputation. Beattie might even have run away from the Mill House herself, had it not been for Joseph Miller, the gentle, kindly man who was her grandfather. Then there was her mother too, driven to the brink of insanity by her husband, and in desperate need of her daughter's loving care.

Moonbeam was a steady mare and she knew every bump and dip in the track almost as well as Sarah. The load was small and Sarah took the opportunity to ride in the cart, seated on a sack of corn. She had an excellent view as they ambled between the two lines of beech trees which her father and Louis had planted some years ago when they made the new track. She marvelled at the sight of the dew-spangled spider webs still suspended daintily along the hedgerows, sparkling like diamond necklaces in the morning sun. A small flock of birds suddenly rose into the air a few yards in front, evidently startled by the sound of the iron-rimmed wheels crunching over the hard-packed earth. Linnets, Sarah thought, observing the white edges of their tail feathers.

Green buds were swelling on the hedgerows and, here and there, hazel catkins danced in the morning sunlight like miniature lambs' tails. Several clumps of primroses lifted their pale gold faces to the sun.

I'm sure I could still find at least one bunch of shy wild violets too, Sarah mused with a smile. She knew every inch of the track she had walked each day during her school days. Moonbeam needed no guidance from the reins until they reached the edge of the village so Sarah relaxed with a contented sigh. She glanced back at Fairlyden nestled in the lee of the hill. The house stood slightly higher than the farm buildings facing southwest towards the Solway and the Galloway Hills beyond. The lower building attached to one end housed the scullery and it in turn led into the dairy. The byre was adjacent to the house, while the stable was directly opposite, lower, flanked by open-fronted sheds where calves and a few bullocks were housed in winter and carts and the plough were stored. Behind the sheds the rickyard was bounded by a dry stone dyke, or as Mr Bradshaw called it, a loose stone wall, so skilfully built that it was almost indestructible. It protected the ricks from the open field and the track leading down to Strathtod. On the fourth side of the yard was the circular stone barn where the corn was flailed; there was also an assortment of other small sheds – the pig sties, the little stone shed where the ducks slept in winter, and a couple of small hen houses with pens behind.

Now that the spring is here I'll soon have the chicken coops dotted on every piece o' ground between the steading and the burn, Sarah thought with satisfaction. Already she had set the first clutch of eggs beneath a broody hen. The sale of eggs and butter was vital to the survival of the Fairlyden household, though both were extremely scarce in the cold dark days of winter. Then they were glad if they had a pig or two to sell to the bacon factory in Annan, or even a few wethers for mutton.

Sarah lifted the reins again as they skirted the walls surrounding the glebe on the edge of the village. The red sandstone of the manse glowed warmly through the trees. The Reverend Mackenzie did not come to Fairlyden so often now, Sarah reflected. The Minister was getting old. He had complained of a tightness in his chest after suffering a severe chill last winter. He talked of retiring from the manse, of leaving the shepherding of his flock to a younger man, but Sarah hoped he would not forsake his charge for a few more years. She counted him amongst her most cherished friends. She still had the cookery book, written by Mrs Isabella Beeton, which he had presented to her when she left school.

As they reached the smiddy the sound of iron on iron rang on the clear air as Sam Black fashioned a new shoe for a patient horse. The smiddy was a familiar stopping place for the horses and Moonbeam hesitated. A touch of the reins was enough to tell her this was not their destination today. On wet days farmers always took the opportunity to get their horses shod and there was usually a long queue, but today Sarah guessed there would be only two or three. She could not see Sam's customers for the angle of the wall. Further along they passed the clogger's shop.

'Good morning to you, Mr Turner,' Sarah called cheerfully to the wizened gnome of a man who was sitting in his doorway enjoying the spring sunshine as he worked. He jerked his head in greeting and mumbled through a mouthful of nails.

Unbidden, Moonbeam drew to a halt outside the Jardines' General Store and Sarah sprang nimbly from the cart. She reached for the large basket in which she had packed her butter. It seemed impossible that there could ever be anything cruel or sinister in this peaceful Scottish village; the pleasant, weathered faces of the local residents and the tranquillity of the blue and gold day added to Sarah's happy mood.

She was just finishing her business with Ray Jardine, who had recently taken over the store from his father, when the Mains of Muir trap drew up outside. Abraham Sharpe himself ambled into the store. His belly is as round as a barrel! Sarah thought as she returned his greeting with a gleam of humour in her brown eyes.

'Ye're looking real bright and happy, m'dear,' Abraham remarked almost enviously. 'I saw that husband o' yours this morning. On his way to the station again, I suppose?'

'Mmm.'

'Going to Lanark? To the McNaught's farm sale, was he?'

'I believe so.' Sarah's tone was pleasant but she never lingered to gossip in the village.

'Aye, aye! Ye're giving nothing awa' I see, an' quite right tae. But I can guess he's after buying that two-year-old filly by the stallion your step-father bred, eh . . .?' He chuckled knowingly. 'Should've gone myself!'

Sarah knew he was curious to discover William's intentions but she smiled serenely and turned towards the door.

Abraham was not so easily brushed aside however. 'Nice beast she was when I saw her at the show in the summer. Aye, says I, Sandy Logan always had an eye for a good horse. Of course,' he added wickedly, 'he had a good training, spending his youth at Mains of Muir.'

This time Sarah's indignation got the better of her discretion and she rose to the bait. 'He learned nothing at Mains of Muir that he hadna learned already frae my Grandfather Cameron in Galloway! Anyway he only worked at the Mains for a year.'

'Aye,' Abraham smiled ruefully. 'Ye're right there, lass. I was sorry tae seen him go back tae Fairlyden, and that's the truth. He always said the mares I'd bred wad never be any good. You can tell him he was right!' he added, eyeing Sarah's pink cheeks and shining hair with admiration.

'Thank you, I will.' Sarah was surprised by such unexpected frankness from the man who owned the largest farm in the parish, but then Mr Sharpe had never been vindictive towards her father, not like his wife. Few people had a good word to say for Florrie Sharpe. She had quarrelled with almost every dairymaid and ploughboy in the county. 'You will have to excuse me, Mr Sharpe. I have corn to take to the mill and I want to be back home before noon.'

'Aye, ye're a guid lass. I reckon it must be a great comfort tae Sandy, having a step-daughter like you.' He sighed. 'Florrie and me were never blessed with bairns.'

Sarah murmured noncommittally and climbed hurriedly into the cart. Since she had learned the truth about her father it embarrassed her when people referred to Alexander Logan as her step-father. She would willingly have told the world she was his own daughter, but the Reverend Mackenzie was loathe to hear her mother's name sullied by idle tongues such as Mistress Sharpe's. He felt the occupants of Fairlyden had been prey to enough malicious gossip, ever since the old Earl of Strathtod created the little farm for his mistress and his own illegitimate son, Daniel Munro, the man Sarah had believed to be her father. So she had followed the Minister's advice and told no one the truth, except her husband.

She knew she would always be grateful to her father for enlightening her so honestly. He had made no excuses; he had told her simply that Mattie Cameron had been his only love, even when she was still a young girl. Sarah still felt the warmth and security it had given her to know she was the fruit of such enduring love. She had only learned her parents' carefully guarded secret herself after the death of Lord James Fairly, her husband's half-brother. Strathtod Estate had to be sold to pay the late Earl's gambling debts; she had believed Fairlyden was secure, a place apart. She thought she had a right to inherit it as Daniel Munro's only daughter. She remembered the events so clearly.

'Ye've nae rights, lassie,' Sandy had declared despondently. 'It's part o' the Strathtod Estate and it will have tae be sold along wi' the rest.'

'But Fairlyden is my home! It belongs to the Munros!'

'Daniel Munro wasna your father, Sarah. Ye're mine – ma ain bairn . . .' Sarah knew she would never forget the anguish and uncertainty in those steady blue eyes. She had always thought of Alexander Logan as a well-loved step-father. After the initial shock his news had filled her with joy because she was no longer alone in the world; she belonged to him, and he belonged to her. She now knew her own joy had given her father immeasurable comfort, and a determination to give her as much security as he could afford.

He had had enough money saved to buy Fairlyden's house, the farm buildings, and a few acres of land, but he wanted more – for her. It was the Minister himself who had taken the unprecedented step of arranging a loan which had allowed Sandy Logan to buy fifty-two acres of land outright, as well as negotiating a lease to rent the remainder of Fairlyden's one hundred and twenty fertile acres. Both men had believed the sale of the famous stallion, Logan's Lucifer, would repay the money easily. Neither of them had foreseen the accident which had brought about the untimely death of the magnificent horse, and left her father crippled for life.

As she turned the horse and cart into the mill yard the Reverend Mackenzie's warning echoed in Sarah's mind once more.

'Evil speculations can no longer hurt the dead, they may not even hurt the living, but I advise you to keep your own counsel and consider the innocence of those children yet unborn, "even unto the third and fourth generation".'

Even such grave words could not quench Sarah's joy as she thought of the next generation – her child – hers and William's, which even now was growing within her. In her heart she knew she ought to have shared such a secret with her husband first of all . . . but she would never forget his dreadful disappointment a few months ago, when her body had rejected his seed with such devastating thoroughness. She shuddered at the memory. Sarah still felt she had failed William. He was eleven years older than her and he wanted a son so badly. This time she would make absolutely certain nothing could go wrong before she told him her news. Meanwhile she longed to share her happiness with someone and her spirits soared as she looked forward to the luxury of a chat with Beatrice, her own dear friend.

Two

Sarah concentrated on driving the cart as close as possible to the wall of the mill. She aligned it exactly beneath the small door, set high up in the wall. Edward Slater always grumbled if it was not positioned so that he could hoist the sacks up with the minimum of effort. At last she was satisfied and the mare halted obediently. Sarah scrambled down and stepped eagerly to the door of the Mill House, faintly surprised that Beatrice had not already come out to greet her. When she popped her head around the kitchen door she was disappointed to find it deserted, except for Beatrice's mother, huddled in her corner by the fire, staring morosely into space, silent as always. Sometimes Sarah wondered if Mistress Slater was as demented and oblivious to her surroundings as she appeared.

'Good morning, Mistress Slater,' she called. The woman made no effort to return her cheery greeting. She did not even raise her head. Sarah walked slowly back to the waiting cart.

The big wooden mill wheel was still and silent, in fact everything about the little mill seemed deserted except for the distant squeal of young pigs in the sties at the bottom of the yard behind the house.

'I canna wait all day! Fix the sack on if ye're wanting meal today!'

Sarah jumped, startled at the sound of Edward Slater's harsh bellow. He was glaring down at her from the little door high above the cart.

'Is the mill so busy then, Master Slater?'

Slater glowered furiously. There was scarcely any business at all, and the chit knew that well enough. He stared down at Sarah's glowing face. She had always been a proud, quick-witted, young wench, and she still had an air of innocence for all she'd been married to a Fairly since last summer. His slack lips curled. He would have knocked the pride out of her, aye and the innocence, if he'd been her husband. It had only taken him a single night to tame his own wife. She had been a proud, stupid creature, but he had taught her a lesson!

Yet nothing had ever assuaged Slater's insane jealousy, not when Joseph Miller's pretty daughter agreed to marry him, nor even when she persuaded her father to make him a partner in the mill. Over the years his resentment had simmered like a volcano. He harboured a secret fear that Jeannie still yearned for the man who had unknowingly sired her first-born, her only daughter. Slater knew Beatrice despised him, just as her mother had done, before he wreaked his revenge. Now Jeannie was no more than a haggard, demented shadow. There was nothing left of the spoiled, spirited girl who had married him in desperation, anxious only to save her pride and her parents' good name.

Sarah had climbed back on to the cart and Edward Slater watched as she struggled to fasten the first sack on to the hook which he had lowered. She looked up to tell him it was ready to hoist. He studied her upturned face insolently. He knew her eyes were brown, like Daniel Munro's, but Mattie Cameron had also had the darkest eyes Edward had ever seen, aye and the same thick dark hair. Sarah Munro, Mistress Fairly as she was now, could easily have inherited such traits from her mother, but she had a skin as fair as a lily . . . and that straight little nose, the stubborn chin . . . aye he was familiar with that. He'd seen Sandy Logan thrust out his jaw many a time when they both worked at the mill all those years ago . . .

'The bag is secured!' Sarah jerked the rope impatiently. She had always hated the way Slater seemed to scrutinise every feature of her face with his sly shifty eyes.

She repeated the routine with the next sack and waited for Slater to work the pulleys which hauled the sacks of grain on to the top floor of the mill. Only the half bag remained. She bent to fix the hook firmly, vaguely aware of Slater leaning precariously out of the door up above. He had slackened the hoisting rope excessively, even for a half sack.

'Ready,' Sarah called as she straightened up. Before she could step away from the bag of oats now fixed securely to the end of the rope, Slater's free arm had swung out in a wide arc. He stepped back swiftly and began to hoist the bag.

'Wait! Stop!' Sarah cried out in alarm. 'I'm caught up in the rope!' She struggled to free herself. The hoist did not even falter. Her knees buckled on to the half bag of corn as the rope tightened around her. She felt herself swinging, along with the bag of corn. She grabbed the rope to prevent herself falling forward and hanging upside down. 'You twisted the rope round me deliberately!' she shouted accusingly. 'Set me down at once!'

Slater laughed mirthlessly at the sight of her squirming figure dangling helplessly on the end of the rope. Sudden fear washed over Sarah. This was not just a silly trick! The bag swung above the cart. She swung with it, firmly entangled in the twisting rope! It bit into her shoulder blade, and across her stomach as the pressure increased. She was trapped! The breath was squeezed out of her as the hoist swung her skywards and she felt the burn of the rope across her body.

'My baby!' Sarah gasped in consternation. She clung desperately to the rope, her arms stretched above her head as she tried to take the strain, anxious to ease the pull of the rope across her stomach. 'Let me down! Stop playing games!' she called angrily.

'Games! Is that what ye want, eh!' Slater gloated.

Sarah gritted her teeth and held on grimly as she swung perilously near to the wall, then out into midair above the cart. She saw Slater step back out of sight. Suddenly the rope jerked, dropped fast, stopped. Sarah screamed involuntarily. Moonbeam was usually a placid mare but she was startled by the unfamiliar cry and she jumped forward, the cart jolting precariously behind her.

'Whoa! Whoa!' Slater yelled a stream of oaths. The mare quivered nervously, the cart grated against the wall of the Mill House, and came to a shivering halt in front of the kitchen window.

Sarah looked down fearfully. There was nothing but the stoney, hard-packed earth below her now. She felt sick. A terrible faintness threatened to overwhelm her. The hoist began to move slowly upwards. As she swung helplessly, a few feet beneath the small door, she saw the peculiar gleam in Slater's mean little eyes. She thought her arms would break as she clung to the rope. Sarah knew then how a mouse must feel when it was caught in the merciless claws of a hunting cat.

Slowly, tauntingly, Slater reached out a hand. Then she was being hauled roughly to safety on the top floor of the mill. Her knees wobbled. She sank weakly on to the sacks he had hauled up earlier. Her whole body felt bruised by the sting and pull of the ropes. Slater was standing over her. She raised her head. His eyes were little more than gleaming slits. There was a triumphant smirk on his slack mouth. His unkempt beard was sticky with brown saliva and Sarah's stomach heaved as she caught the evil smell of the horrible brown tobacco he always chewed; it mingled with the stench of his unwashed body. Almost as though he read her thoughts he stepped towards the open door and spat a long brown stream of tobacco juices into the clear air. He wiped the back of his filthy hand across his mouth, leaving another brown trail down his beard. Sarah controlled a desire to retch. Suddenly he moved towards her.

Every instinct alerted her to a new danger as she saw lust flare in his piggy eyes. Surely Slater could not have planned to hoist her to the top of the mill? How could he have known she would bring the corn today . . .? Unless . . . Had he watched her coming down the track from Fairlyden? Where was everybody? Beatrice? Her grandfather?

Fear gave Sarah a burst of strength. She struggled to her feet to make a dash to the trap door and the steep wooden steps which led to the floor below. Slater guessed her intention. He blocked her path. Sarah paled. Her heart was beating fast now, but she had never lacked courage. She strove to keep cool and calm.

'It is time we had a talk, Master Slater. When Louis Whiteley brings the . . .'

'Ye want tae talk, *Mistress* – Fairly?'

Sarah hated the mockery in his tone, and the peculiar emphasis he put on her marital status. She saw the horrible leer on his flabby face. 'Well here we are!' He moved quickly and grasped Sarah by the shoulders, thrusting his face closer to hers. She shrank away from him in revulsion.

'You— you smell!'

His eyes glittered dangerously.

'That, *Mistress* Fairly, isna very polite.'

'Let me go!' Sarah's fair skin coloured angrily as she struggled. She had never liked Edward Slater, but she had never had reason to fear him.

'Not sae fast now! Tell me, how d'ye like being *Mistress* Fairly. Taught ye a lesson or twae has he? Your husband . . .?' Sarah's mouth clamped shut. She wriggled impotently. 'I doubt Master William isna as much o' a man as his brother was, eh?' He peered into her face and Sarah gagged as his foul breath filled her nostrils. 'Ye've still a lot tae learn, if ye ask me!' Suddenly one hand moved from her shoulder and grasped her chin, turning her face roughly to his.

'Let me go at once! You— you will find my husband is more of a man than you bargained for!' Slater was silent; he did not release her but continued to scrutinise her, feature by feature, limb by limb. Sarah's apprehension grew. There was a peculiar glitter in his eyes now, even more alarming than lust. Everyone said Beatrice's mother was crazy, but it was her father who was acting strangely now. Sarah shuddered. Beatrice had always blamed him for her mother's condition, her silent withdrawal from the world all these years . . .

'Aye,' he sneered, 'ye've the same blood i' yer veins! I'm sure o' it!'

'Y-you're mad!' Sarah exclaimed. 'Let me go! I want to see Beatrice. Where is she?'

'She's awa' tae the smiddy wi' the auld man an' his precious mare!' He snorted contemptuously. 'There's jist we twae at the mill today, *Mistress* – Fairly!' Suddenly he moved his head and pressed his thick lips to Sarah's surprised mouth. She recoiled furiously and jerked free with a strength which surprised Slater. Sarah was tall for a woman, almost as tall as himself, and she was used to hard work. She would have darted past him and down the steps but he had her trapped in a corner and he lunged at her, sending her stumbling backwards on top of some empty sacks. He knelt beside her, staring down at her.

'Wh-what do you want with me?' she demanded angrily.

Slater ignored her question, but his eyes continued to study her.

'Aye, ye hae the same shaped mouth . . .' He tugged at the ribbons of her bonnet and pulled it roughly from her head. Sarah began to struggle but he pushed her back and grabbed a handful of hair, pulling it ruthlessly from its neat bun.

''Tis not sae dark as it used tae be when ye were a bairn at the school!' he muttered. He jerked her hair viciously and held it towards the light. ''Tis almost the colour o' Logan's now, wi' the chestnut streaks in it!' Sarah's eyes widened in surprise.

'I've aye kenned Munro wasna your father. Ye're Logan's bastard! Another one!' He jerked Sarah's hair brutally. 'Logan's your father, isn't he?'

'You're hurting me! Let me go! You're m-mad.' But Slater yanked her hair again, as though it were his enemy. The pain brought tears to Sarah's eyes and she blinked them away angrily.

'Logan is your father! Do ye hear?'

'You're hurting me!'

'Do ye hear me? Logan's your father! Isn't he, isn't he?' His stubby fingers compressed her throat. Sarah had no idea how Slater had learned the truth, but it did not matter! Nothing mattered except that she should escape from him.

'Yes,' she gasped, 'yes, Alexander Logan is my father! What is it to you . . .?'

'I'll tell ye what it has tae dae wi' me!' He shook Sarah like a rag doll. 'Logan took my woman. Mine!' Slater was almost sobbing with anger and frustration. 'Dae ye hear me? She belonged tae me, and he took her!'

Sarah stared up at him uncomprehendingly.

Slater was a madman in that moment. Everything seemed worse now that his suspicions had actually been confirmed. Logan had everything! Sinners should pay! He stared down at Sarah, at the smooth curve of her cheek, at the curve of her breast only inches from where he knelt . . . 'Ye're his flesh an' blood! I always knew it! Aye, an' I ken a bit o' the Guid Book for all I dinna gang tae the kirk! "The sins o' the father shall be visited upon the children". Ye're his! I'll see ye pay for his sins!'

Sarah trembled. It was as though something had exploded in his head and driven all sense and reason away. His eyes blazed with more than lust. Why did he hate her so? She struggled desperately, but the child she was carrying seemed to sap her strength. She felt sick and faint. The hands upon her were those of a man, but the man was possessed with a devil, and he had the devil's insane strength.

Why, oh why had she disobeyed William? Why had she come to the mill in his absence? She had been so happy – so eager to share her secret with Beattie, but she would never forgive herself if she lost her precious babe a second time; William would not forgive her either. More than anything else in the world she wanted to give him a son.

Jeannie Slater sat in her corner, half hidden by the stone fireplace which dominated the Mill House kitchen. She stared into space, seeing nothing, apparently oblivious to everything which went on around her. It was the only way she had been able to cope with a world which contained the fiend who was her husband. It was true he had almost ignored her since his bestial treatment had caused the death of her unborn child. She had almost died herself that night and Doctor Kerr had issued a grim warning to Slater. Since then Jeannie had sought refuge in a world of her own, dreaming of the past, unwilling to face the present or to consider the future . . .

Somewhere someone screamed! Or was it only in her own head? A sound from the past . . .? Yet the sudden darkening of the mill kitchen was not in her mind. Despite her constant preoccupation with unseen demons Jeannie blinked at the sight of a horse close against the window pane. It was strange; but it did not concern her; nothing concerned her anymore. She did not even venture as far as the privy at the bottom of the garden now. Beatrice looked after her; she was a good daughter. She looked after everything. Yet the horse did not move. The kitchen remained full of shadows. Jeannie did not like shadows. Why didn't Beatrice put it right? Then vaguely she remembered. Beatrice had gone with her grandfather; they had taken the mare to be shod at the smiddy. They didn't think she listened, but she did, and sometimes she remembered. So Beatrice could not come and move the horse and make the kitchen light again. Jeannie did not like the dark! She could not stand it! The drumming was starting in her head again! It came often now! Sometimes it frightened her.

In the deserted mill Sarah struggled valiantly against Edward Slater's sweating, filthy hands. An awful sickness threatened to overwhelm her, but pride and indignation gave her strength. She could not avoid his clawing fingers, his horrible face so close to her own. She could not believe this was happening. Yet Slater's intentions were painfully clear. Sarah was filled with horror and loathing. It was only a matter of time before he had her completely in his power, isolated as they were at the top of the mill. She must talk. She must make him talk. Anything to prevent him carrying out his threats. If only Beatrice would return. She would see the horse and cart. She would search for her.

'Why? Why do you hate me so?'

'Ye're his! Ye're Logan's brat.'

'What is it to you?'

'I told ye, Logan took my woman!' He gave a bark of bitter laughter. 'Now I'll take you, because ye're his! "An eye for an eye." '

'My mother was never *your* woman!'

'Not her! Mattie Cameron was deaf! Who wad want a deaf woman! Logan only married her to get his hands on Fairlyden!'

'That's not true! You . . . Oh!' Sarah gasped with pain and humiliation as he mauled her heaving breast with hard stubby fingers. Swiftly she pulled her hand free and clawed furiously at his sallow cheek, forgetting her resolve to keep calm, to talk. Slater swore violently. His eyes narrowed and Sarah shuddered at their evil gleam.

'Ye'll pay for that! It'll be a pleasure tae tame Logan's bastard, *Mistress* Fairly. When I'm done wi' ye, ye'll ken what it is tae hae a real man!' Suddenly his eyes glinted malevolently as a thought occurred to him. 'That wad be a fine revenge!' He muttered and threw back his head with a horrible gloating laugh which sent shivers through Sarah. 'Logan's daughter carrying a bairn o' mine! Aye, oh aye! Now that wad be real revenge!'

Sarah opened her mouth to tell him he was too late, but she bit back the words. There was a satanic light in Slater's eyes; he wanted to make her pay for some imaginary wrong. He might derive even greater satisfaction if he harmed her child as well. William would never forgive her if she lost his child a second time! A sob rose in her throat. She should never have come to the mill!

Perhaps if she did not struggle with Slater the child would be safe. Sarah closed her eyes and forced her body to go limp. Seconds later she screamed involuntarily as her skirts were thrust aside and Slater clutched savagely at her thigh. She kicked instinctively and heard his mocking laughter.

'Aye, I thought that might bring ye back tae life!'

Furiously she lashed out at him. She would not, could not, submit to such an animal. Sarah knew she was no match for him, but she fought against the waves of darkness which threatened to overwhelm her.

Jeannie Slater was nervous of the shadows in the darkened kitchen. She rose agitatedly from her chair. Greatly daring, she opened the door. The spring sun shone on her face. She blinked stupidly. She had liked the sunshine when she was a girl. She lifted her face to its warmth instinctively. The air was sweet and fresh. She breathed deeply and opened her eyes, seeing the world clearly for the first time in months, years even. Suddenly she felt alert, almost young and strong again. She glanced at the horse and saw the cart wedged firmly against the wall of the house. Beyond it the mill yard was empty. It was always empty these days, not as it had been when she was a girl, running up the stairs to chatter to her father. The smell of drying grain seemed to haunt her nostrils, the heat of the kiln, the white film of meal, her father like a snowman. Those long forgotten memories compelled Jeannie to leave the house, to walk once more beside the mill. She paused beneath the open door, set high in the wall. There were voices, a girl's voice . . .?

Beatrice! But no, it was not her own daughter up there. Almost of their own volition her feet took her towards the mill entrance. She could hear the water now, at the back where the great wheel turned. She moved inside, seeing the machinery, the wheels and cogs, axles which drove the heavy stones on the floor above. Jeannie had always liked to watch the stones, slowly grinding the grain. Like a sleepwalker she climbed the wooden stairs to the floor above. The stones were still. She felt disappointed, like a child deprived of a treat. The grain must be stored in the loft, waiting for her father. She heard a sudden thud, a scuffling noise. Slowly Jeannie began to mount the ladder in the far corner; her breath came in little gusts but she ignored the tightness in her chest. She was half way up when she heard the scream. Something seemed to crack inside her head, and then her brain cleared. She felt alive! Beattie's friend was up there with Slater! All Jeannie's fears evaporated in that moment. There was only anger – anger which had smouldered deep within the dull spiritless being she had become.

'Let her go!' Jeannie's voice was little more than a rasping croak by the time she reached the top of the ladder and emerged through the trap door set in the floor.

Edward Slater stared incredulously. His limbs froze. Was he seeing a ghost?

To Sarah the voice seemed a great distance away. She forced her eyes to focus but her brain could not believe. To her certain knowledge Jeannie had never left the house for the past five years, much less climbed a flight of stairs.

Jeannie felt a great sense of disappointment. The loft was empty except for the two bags of grain. There was no warmth rising from the kiln, no piles of dried grain, no groats waiting to be pounded by the heavy stones below. Only the hoist was as she remembered it, when her father had lifted the heavy sacks. There was the wooden drum in the rafters, the two ropes, the belts and pulley. She moved over the floor towards Slater.

Her staring eyes unnerved him.

'Wh-what are ye doing? How did ye get up here?' He still half believed she was an unholy spectre.

Jeannie looked down at him, kneeling on the floor beside the girl. Sarah felt the blood flowing back into her brain. Slowly her mind began to function clearly. She struggled to sit up but Slater reacted instinctively, knocking her flat with a hard slap from the back of his hand. For a second her senses reeled again.

'Leave her be!' Jeannie commanded harshly, without any trace of fear. Her brain felt cool and clear, oh so clear. 'Is't not enough to force your lecherous body on oor ain innocent bairn . . .?

'*Oor* bairn?' Slater almost screamed with rage. 'Your bitch o' a daughter is no bairn o' mine, an' weel ye ken that! Get back tae your corner, ye blethering idiot!'

He spoke to his wife as though she were a hound, Sarah thought. Carefully she edged a little way away from him then suddenly, with all her strength, she pushed him sideways, catching him off balance, sending him sprawling onto his back on the dusty floor. Swiftly she seized her advantage, scrambling to her feet, but even as she darted to Jeannie's side he was hauling himself to his knees and blocking their path to the hole in the floor, to the ladder, their only means of escape.

'He— he is insane!' she gasped. 'He says my father took his woman. He says I must pay for . . .'

'He did! Logan had his way wi' her! Ask her!' Slater fixed his glittering eyes on his own wife. Sarah gasped.

'Sandy? Aye, Sandy Logan . . .' Jeannie sighed softly. Then she looked at Sarah. 'Your faither? Aye . . . aye, he wad be . . .' Sarah saw a strange expression in her blue eyes. They were no longer vacant.

'I am proud to have Alexander Logan for a father,' Sarah muttered, lifting her head defiantly. 'My parents loved each other!'

She could not know that Jeannie had suspected the truth long ago, even when she was a child, playing in the mill yard with Beatrice while her mother collected the Fairlyden meal. Jeannie had recognised Sarah's faintly crooked smile and her habit of pulling her right earlobe when she was deep in thought. It was a mannerism which had once been all too familiar when Sandy Logan and Joseph Miller held their discussions over the mill table in those far off evenings of Jeannie's happy girlhood.

So Slater had guessed, had he? Now he wanted more revenge. He wanted to hurt and humiliate the lassie because she was Sandy's. He had never been man enough to confront Alexander Logan face to face with his petty jealousies, Jeannie realised with contempt. Instead he had forced himself on Beatrice. Aagh! That had grieved Jeannie sorely. But he would not have his way this time.

Slater believed his wife was too frail to be any hindrance. He took a menacing step towards Sarah. The evil smirk on his sallow face filled her with revulsion. She stepped back involuntarily and felt the dusty cobwebs tangle in her hair from the sloping roof. He would not trap her against the wall again. She eyed the trap door only a few feet behind Slater. She thrust out her chin defiantly. He would not take her without a fight.

But it was his wife who moved so unexpectedly. She grabbed one of the ropes and pulled it swiftly towards her. It was the one with the heavy iron hook on the end.

'Stay away from her!' Jeannie's voice wavered; she could feel the drumming in her head again, but her blue eyes blazed with hatred as she glared at her husband across the dusty floor of the mill. Slater hesitated, frowning.

'Get out o' ma way, woman!' His face registered his sullen frustration. 'Ye'll pay for this! Ye're my wife, remember?'

'Keep back or I'll send this hook through your skull!' Jeannie retorted, and her voice held a steely determination which astonished Slater after her years of cowed, perpetual silence.

'Ye're mad!' he taunted.

Sarah listened, but her eyes darted around the loft seeking some means to help Jeannie overpower her husband, at least long enough for them to make their escape down the precarious ladder. Slater was the one who was mad, she was sure of it now. She glanced at Beattie's mother. The poor passive creature she had known seemed to have vanished; her blue eyes burned with hatred.

Jeannie was clutching the sharp hook on the end of the rope, pulling it back, ready to send it skimming through the air at her husband's head. They both saw fear in Slater's eyes. He was a coward!

He's afraid o' me! Jeannie thought triumphantly. Her, his weak, crazy wife. The woman he had despised, aye and humiliated all these years. His threats had all been empty bluster, to force her to submit to him. Jeannie felt a great surge of power. She stepped forward, her eyes glittering in her white face.

'Ye're nothing but a craven worm, Slater!' As she spoke she grasped the iron hook tightly and took another step towards the man whose name she bore.

Sarah held her breath. Suddenly she knew Beattie's mother was not crazy at all. Mistress Slater knew exactly what she was doing. Had she not played in the mill throughout her childhood?

'Ye— ye're out o' yer mind. Let go o' that hook!' Slater's voice was a whine.

In reply Jeannie lifted her arm and aimed the hook at his sallow, sweating face. She took another step forward, revelling in her brief spell of power. There was a pain in her chest, right through to her shoulder blades. She guessed the unaccustomed exertion of climbing the stairs had brought it on. Doctor Kerr had warned her she must have no excitement. Oh, but it was worth it, just to see the fear in Slater's hateful, piggy eyes, and on his clammy face; the devil had tormented her and made her life a living hell. He had degraded her beloved Beattie, ruined her . . . Jeannie was barely aware of moving forward, brandishing the hook.

'Let go! Leave . . .' Slater stepped backwards. He had forgotten the gaping mouth of the trap door as he took one more step. Sarah cringed as she heard his fearful scream. There was a loud crack as he hit the wooden ladder before landing on the floor below with a sickening thud.

Three

There was an awful silence in the mill. Sarah glanced at Jeannie Slater and saw the stunned expression in her eyes, and the ominous blue shadow around her mouth. They had to get out of here before Edward Slater regained his senses.

'Come,' she murmured hoarsely and held out her arm to Beattie's mother, 'we must get down the ladder.' But Jeannie shook her head faintly.

'Must rest . . .' She slumped awkwardly on to a bag of oats. Her face was grey, her blue eyes had a glassy stare which alarmed Sarah. She moved to the ladder and peered through the trap door, wondering how long they dare linger.

'Dear God!' she gasped hoarsely. 'I— I think he's dead . . .'

'Dead . . .?' Jeannie's vacant eyes kindled with a feverish glitter, but it was beyond her to rise and see for herself.

'His neck . . . He— he's lying at a peculiar angle,' Sarah faltered. 'I— I must go down to him.' She shuddered. She wanted to vomit.

Even before she reached the bottom of the ladder, Sarah knew that Edward Slater had departed from this world he had regarded through such jaundiced eyes. Her limbs felt leaden as she climbed back to the top floor. She glanced at Jeannie and sat down heavily beside her.

'He is dead,' she whispered huskily, stifling the threatening nausea once more. She felt drained, exhausted; her whole body felt as though it had been beaten and she guessed the ropes had left their marks on her back and stomach. But she must think. She must get the doctor. She frowned at the woman slumped beside her. Right now she needed help to get Beattie's mother back into the house. Beattie! She would have to tell Beattie.

Suddenly Jeannie shattered the tense silence with a bark of laughter.

'I've killed him! D'ye hear? I've killed him!' She laughed again, a harsh, nerve-grating cackle.

'You didna do it! It was an accident.' But Jeannie's laughter persisted in great harsh gulps and sobs until her energy was spent and her breath came in riving gasps. Her lips were an alarming bluish purple. Sarah took her thin hands in hers and chafed them like a child's, feeling their clammy chill. At length Jeannie's breathing eased and she repeated, 'I killed him.'

'Dinna say that!' Sarah begged in alarm. 'I must get you to the house and bring the doctor, the— the constable too, I suppose . . .' Suddenly Sarah felt frightened and uncertain.

'I killed him,' Jeannie repeated like a clockwork toy.

'*Please,* Mistress Slater! Your husband is dead. Think of Beatrice.'

'I'm glad he's dead! Do ye hear me? I wanted him to die! I killed him! I killed him for Beattie.'

'No, no! You dinna realise what you're saying!' Sarah remonstrated in alarm. She wondered how she should deal with the distraught woman, but Jeannie began to talk. Her voice was firm despite her laboured breathing.

'Ye're Beattie's friend. Ye must hae kenned she hated him?'

'Yes.' Sarah's voice was little more than a whisper.

'Promise me, ye'll aye be her friend?'

'Of course I shall! Beattie is as dear to me as— as . . .'

'As a— a sister? Almost a sister . . .' Jeannie's last few words were lost in a sigh. 'I havena long now. Ye ought tae ken. Aye, ye ought tae ken Slater isna Beattie's father . . .' The drumming began in her head again and she blinked rapidly at Sarah. 'Gie me your word? Promise ye willna tell Beattie my secret, lassie!' she pleaded urgently. 'Or her ain father!' She shuddered convulsively. 'Dear God, I couldna bear it if he kenned now, after all she's suffered! He wad never forgive me!' The older woman was almost hysterical and Sarah stared at her in consternation. 'Promise me, Miss Sarah . . .?'

'I— I promise, Mistress Slater, whatever you ask! But we must get down the ladder . . .' Sarah thought Jeannie's mind had gone completely with the shock of her husband's death. She would have promised anything in that moment to keep her calm. But Jeannie gripped Sarah's fingers with astonishing strength.

'Slater forced his way into Beattie's chamber. He wanted revenge because she wasna his. He was jealous. Aah ma puir wee Beattie! Ma puir bairn. She needs ye, Miss Sarah, for her friend . . . I'm glad he's dead! I'm glad I killed him!'

'Hush,' Sarah soothed anxiously. 'He fell. You must remember that. He fell.' The blue eyes looked earnestly back at her and Jeannie nodded like an obedient child.

'I haena long.' The drumming in her head increased; her breath came in little spurts. '. . . Can't get down the ladder. Dick . . .' Jeannie gasped painfully, '. . . at the pigs. A sow— farrowing. He's a good man.' She closed her eyes and Sarah held her own breath, waiting tensely. Suddenly the pale face crumpled like a child's, but her voice was strong.

'She loves Dick O'Connor. He isna a bad man, for all he fought wi' the Earl o' Strathtod. He was vile: he took Dick's ain sister! Slater's vile! Beattie was innocent, I tell ye! He forced her!' The breath rattled in her thin chest.

'I'll call for Dick,' Sarah said soothingly.

'Wait! Promise me! Ye'll— keep— my secret!'

'Yes, Mistress Slater, I promise,' Sarah agreed patiently.

It was silent in the loft except for the sound of Jeannie's laboured breathing. Sarah looked down at the thin hands clinging to her own. She tried to free herself, but Jeannie's grasp tightened, though she had begun to shake.

'I must tell ye . . .' she whispered huskily. Slowly, but clearly, she began to talk, her voice low and intense. 'Slater was aye jealous o' Sandy Logan, frae the minute he came tae work at ma faither's mill.' The blue eyes held a faraway look. Sarah stiffened. 'Sandy disna ken. It wasna his blame. I wanted him, but 'twas aye Mattie Cameron he loved, even when she married Munro. Drunk he was, my Sandy, on her wedding day! Senseless! Still he called her name.' She choked. Sarah sat tensely, her mind reeling. Jeannie pushed herself away suddenly.

'I— I dinna understand,' Sarah faltered. 'Sandy Logan is my father! He canna be Beattie's father! C— can he . . .?'

'Whisht! Aah whisht,' Jeannie pleaded fearfully. 'They must never ken! Never!'

Sarah was alarmed by the high thin wail of distress and for a second she thought Jeannie's heart had failed when she collapsed into her arms. But the blue eyes opened again and the anxiety and pleading in them wrung Sarah's heart.

'Ye mustna tell Beattie, or Sandy,' she gasped. 'Promise me!'

Sarah hesitated. 'But surely they have a right to know . . .?'

'No! Promise me, please . . .?' Jeannie grew agitated.

'I— I canna believe it . . .' Sarah muttered uncertainly, then, 'Aye, aye – I promise,' she agreed quickly, seeing the older woman's awful agitation. She was rewarded by Jeannie's sigh of relief. She lay as meekly as a child in Sarah's arms for several minutes and Sarah gazed around the silent loft helplessly, unable to move, her mind seething with questions.

Then, as though refreshed by the brief rest, or by the relief of unburdening herself at last, Jeannie began to talk of the past. Sometimes her voice was no more than a whisper, and there were many pauses while she summoned her strength, but Sarah listened to the story of Jeannie Miller's unrequited love for the penniless young man who had found work at her father's mill, and favour in her father's house. Jeannie spoke of her relief and joy when Mattie Cameron, the deaf girl, married Daniel Munro, releasing Sandy from the burden of caring for her, of keeping his promise to her father. Jeannie's voice was almost inaudible as she told of Sandy Logan drowning his sorrow in drink on the night of the wedding, of Joseph Miller helping him to the Mill House in a drunken stupor, even putting him to bed. After that she was silent for so long that Sarah thought her story was ended. Then she whispered, 'I threw myself intae his arms. I— I roused him like a whore an' he didn' even ken me!' She choked on the words. 'He called her name. Not mine, never mine!' She began to sob.

'Hush now, hush . . .' Sarah soothed gently, feeling tears moisten her eyes at the older woman's poignant memories.

'Ye promised— never— tell— them.' She sagged against Sarah. 'Ye promised . . .' Jeannie's last coherent words echoed and re-echoed in Sarah's mind.

Later Sarah knew she would probably regret her promise not to tell either Beatrice or her father of their relationship to each other, and to herself, but in her heart she knew the telling of her story had brought profound relief to Jeannie's unhappy heart. Without her promise Beattie's mother would have carried her secret to the grave.

Sarah became aware of the deep rumble of a man's voice in the mill yard below. Carefully she eased Jeannie's unconscious figure on to the sacks of corn and looked down. Dick O'Connor was coaxing the patient Moonbeam to pull the cart away from the wall.

'Dick! Oh, Dick, I need you up here!' Her voice shook despite her efforts to keep calm. Dick sensed her distress. Moments later he was mounting the first flight of wooden stairs, two at a time. Sarah heard him gasp and knew he had reached Edward Slater's twisted body.

She steeled herself to move to the trap door.

'He's dead!' Dick muttered. He looked up at her and Sarah saw his stunned expression turn to consternation as he stared at her tousled hair and the bruise already darkening her temple. It did not occur to her that Dick might think she had pushed Slater to his death. He climbed the ladder and drew himself up to stand beside her.

'Mistress Slater!' His eyes rounded incredulously.

'I need help, to get her back to the house.'

'Aye.' Dick did not ask questions. Jeannie's breathing was shallow and Sarah helped to ease her up into his arms for the difficult descent down the wooden ladder, and the stairs beyond.

It was a relief to gain the sanctuary of the house. Dick carried Jeannie through to her room, and laid her gently on the bed. Sarah drew the covers over her slight figure and when she straightened she saw Dick's grim expression.

'I'll bring Doctor Kerr.' He sighed heavily. 'And the constable.' He looked keenly into Sarah's pale face, 'Ye maun tidy yer hair, Miss Sarah. An' maybe wash yer face, though ye'll no' wash awa' yon bruise I'm thinking.' He hesitated. 'Miss Sarah, the constable will ask questions.' He shuddered, remembering his own ordeal the night he attacked Lord James Fairly.

'Dinna worry, Dick,' Sarah looked at his thin, kindly face so haunted with shadows. 'I'm sure I shall be able to answer them,' she assured him, fighting down her own nervousness.

'Aye, and I dare say Slater deserved what he got, but the law isna always just,' he muttered grimly. 'Who wad believe Mistress Slater could hae climbed the steps . . .? All o' them! I dinna think she could move frae her bed now. She'll no' be much help tae ye, Miss Sarah.'

'She did help.' Sarah shivered, remembering her fear and horror.

'Master Slater tried to . . .' she shuddered and turned away from Dick's compassionate gaze. 'He— he thought Mistress Slater was a ghost, I think. He stepped back. He forgot the trap door was behind him . . .'

'Let's hope the new constable believes in ghosts then. The law will likely be on Slater's side, now that he's dead.' Dick's voice was bitter. 'Maybe it wad be better for ye no' tae speak o' any quarrel wi' him . . .'

'Maybe you're right,' Sarah muttered tightly. Unconsciously she passed a protective hand over her stomach, unaware of Dick's keen eyes watching her. She could still feel the burning sensation where the ropes had cut into her. 'He hoisted me up on a rope!'

'Hoisted ye? Tae the top o' the mill?' Dick gazed at her incredulously. 'Naebody wad believe it! And there's no' a soul tae prove it, is there?'

'No . . .' Sarah shook her head.

'Dinna say anything that you havena got to say, Miss Sarah,' Dick pleaded urgently. 'The station master tried tae tell me that, the night I attacked Lord Fairly. I didna listen, Miss Sarah. All I could think o' was Vicky, lying there, dying.' His voice shook. 'Aah, but prison is an awful place tae bide.'

When Dick had gone Sarah shuddered involuntarily, wondering if he really believed she was responsible for Slater's death. She trembled at the thought. What if the constable did not believe Slater had fallen? What if he saw the bruises on her face . . .?

'William, oh William, why didn't I listen to you?' she moaned softly. Then she pulled herself together and poured water into a bowl in the kitchen. She washed her face, then she brushed her hair out and hastily coiled it into a neat bun. There was nothing she could do about her pale face, she thought critically, peering into the tiny square of mirror on the wall. A blue bruise was already darkening her temple. With shaking hands Sarah loosened her hair again and allowed some of it to curl around her face, hiding most of the bruise. Her arms ached as though they had been pulled from their sockets, as indeed they almost had been.

Sarah's heart began to hammer in her breast when she heard voices. She was thankful to see it was Doctor Kerr who accompanied Dick.

'The constable will be here in a wee while,' Dick answered her unspoken question. 'He's awa' tae the other end o' the parish tae see a man accused o' stealing a bag o' tatties.'

'Beattie . . .?'

'She's on her way frae the smiddy. Mr Miller canna hurry.'

Sarah led Doctor Kerr through to the small room where Jeannie Slater lay unconscious, unaware that his shrewd gaze was eyeing her own pale face with concern. He had also noticed the stiff way she was moving her limbs.

'There's nothing I can do,' he said of Mistress Slater.

'But she was so alert! So . . .' She told him how Jeannie had ascended not only the wooden steps, but also the ladder, to the top floor of the mill.

'Sometimes, shortly before the end, patients are given a sudden burst of strength, Miss Sarah. Aah, I beg your pardon, lassie.' The old doctor smiled apologetically, 'I am forgetting ye're Mistress Fairly now.'

'But Mistress Slater . . .? Surely there is something?'

Doctor Kerr shook his head.

'She may linger a few hours, a few days— even a few months, though I doubt if it will be so long . . .' He eyed Sarah keenly. 'What happened after she reached the top floor of the mill? I know death is upsetting, lassie, and the shock is bad for a young woman in your condition, but I'd like ye tae talk about it now, tae me, then put it right out o' your pretty head, if ye can.' Sarah's hand had moved instinctively to her stomach when Doctor Kerr mentioned her condition, confirming the suspicion Dick O'Connor had voiced to the doctor on their way back to the Mill House.

Sarah had known Doctor Kerr since the day her brother Danny was born, the day her mother died. Slowly she began to talk. She told him everything from the time of her arrival at the mill, everything except Jeannie Slater's secret. When she had finished he was silent, pulling thoughtfully at his lower lip as he considered her story.

'Dick O'Connor's right, lassie. He's a guid man and he's learned a hard lesson. Heed his advice. Leave me to deal with Constable Ross. Just answer his questions truthfully, but no more, eh?'

Sarah nodded, frowning. 'But I have done nothing wrong.'

'No, but there's naebody to confirm your story that Slater fell. It would be better if the constable didna suspect you and Slater had a disagreement. He might begin tae wonder. Why did he fall when he knew the mill so well?'

Sarah stared at Doctor Kerr in dismay. Did he, and Dick, think she had *pushed* Slater to his death?

'It was the sight of his own wife. He thought he'd seen a ghost, I think. It made him careless.' The colour drained from Sarah's face as the full implication of Slater's death began to dawn on her.

'Sit down, Mistress Fairly!' The doctor insisted urgently. 'Now drink this tea that Dick's made for you, and dinna get alarmed. Constable Ross is an earnest fellow, but he is young and inclined tae be over-zealous, that is all. I shall give him my verdict on the cause of Slater's death. I think he will accept it was an accident, unless something arouses his suspicions. He will expect ye tae be somewhat overcome. Such an event is enough to give most young ladies an attack o' the vapours. You have great courage, young woman. I hope that husband o' yours appreciates you.' Sarah knew the doctor was trying to cheer her and she smiled wanly. She did not feel very courageous.

The sound of Beatrice and old Mr Miller approaching helped her cast aside her own gnawing anxiety. Beattie had cared for her mother with tender patience for so many years. How would she react to the day's events?

* * *

When the young constable arrived at last he listened to Doctor Kerr with deference and laboriously entered his comments on Slater's death in his pocket book. He dismissed Sarah as a mere woman but she was content to be left in the background. The constable was about her own age, she guessed, though his bewhiskered countenance made him appear older at first glance. He did not yet know the village people, or its gossip, as old Constable Hardy had done and he was anxious to prove himself. He was determined not to allow the local people any opportunity to trick him. Death was a serious business however and Constable Ross was grateful for the old doctor's assistance.

He was almost ready to leave when Dick returned from the lower yard where he had been casting a careful eye on the sow and her new litter. He was cradling a minute piglet in his hands and Sarah guessed it was the weakest of the litter and needing help if it was to survive. Her face softened and for a moment the horrors of the day were forgotten as she recalled how tenderly Dick had cared for the animals at Fairlyden, how many ailing youngsters he had rescued and succoured with infinite patience before the dreadful night he had ended up in prison.

'What are you doing here, O'Connor?' Suddenly the constable assumed a steely-eyed stare. He drew himself two inches taller. His question was almost an accusation. 'I heard you were released from prison recently. Where were you when Slater met his death?' Dick drew in his breath sharply. The small piglet squealed protestingly as his hands clenched.

Doctor Kerr's eyes widened in dismay. Sarah felt the blood drain from her face and she saw Beattie's pale cheeks grow even paler, then fire with indignation.

'Dick had nothing tae dae with my father's death!' she announced fiercely. She stepped between Dick and the constable.

'Keep out of this, Miss Slater!' The constable growled warningly, 'Do not interfere with the law!'

'She is right, though, Constable,' Doctor Kerr intervened quickly, 'Dick had nothing to do with Slater's death.'

'Pardon me, Doctor!' Constable Ross interrupted coldly, 'perhaps you are not aware that O'Connor has already attempted to kill a man once. He is a known felon and you were not present when Slater actually died.'

'But I was!' Sarah announced loudly, trembling with anger at the constable's unjust accusation. 'Anyone, anyone who really knew Dick, or any of the O'Connor family, would know he could never kill deliberately, not even a fly, much less a man.'

'I'll thank you not to interrupt, madam!' The constable scowled angrily. 'O'Connor, you must accompany me. You will answer my questions,' he glared at Sarah, 'without interruption.'

'Then I must come too!' Sarah insisted, though her knees were trembling. She avoided Doctor Kerr's warning glance, but she saw the gratitude in Beattie's blue eyes, and the terrible anxiety in Dick's. 'I was there, I tell you, when Slater fell!'

'You are hysterical,' the constable declared loftily. 'No doubt it is the shock. But you had better remain here until I return. I may bring Sergeant McManus. O'Connor, come with me.'

Sarah watched the pulse beating tensely in Dick's lean jaw, she saw Beattie move towards him and take the piglet gently from his hands. She could not see the expression in their eyes but she was certain these two loved each other and her heart ached for them. She felt entirely responsible for this day's evil. She was barely aware of Doctor Kerr pressing her down on to the wooden settle, or Beattie holding out another cup of hot tea.

It was late afternoon by the time Dick returned to the Mill House. His face was drawn and pale and there was pain and bitterness in his blue eyes. He had suffered the humiliation of every conceivable question from the young constable before his superior arrived. Sergeant McManus was a kindly man and he had become adept at summing up both characters and situations in his many years of experience. Also he knew Doctor Kerr of Muircumwell well enough to realise that he would never seek to pervert justice. After reading his constable's notes and asking Dick some pertinent questions he had sent him on his way. But in his heart Dick felt he would never be free of the stigma of prison, not in Muircumwell, or Strathtod, or anywhere in this area. Even his own two brothers and his sister-in-law had greeted him coldly. He had made a secret vow that he would never trouble them with his presence again.

Maybe I should emigrate to Canada tae, he thought bitterly. He knew thousands of Scottish men and women had crossed the Atlantic to seek their fortunes, including four of Beatrice's brothers.

Despite his own fatigue and depression Dick insisted on driving Sarah back to Fairlyden with the horse and cart. Sarah felt exhausted after the hours spent at the mill, the strain of her own ordeal, the shock of Slater's death and his wife's revelations about the past. She wanted to think. If Mistress Slater had spoken the truth it meant Beattie was her half-sister; yet she could never claim her as more than a dear friend, if she kept her promise. Her thoughts revolved in circles and she was relieved when Dick ignored her feeble protest and helped her into the cart, taking up the reins himself.

'William will have returned from Lanark long since,' Sarah murmured wearily as they crossed the bridge over the burn on to Fairlyden land. She gasped suddenly. 'There would be the milking too! I'd forgotten all about it!' she exclaimed.

'Agnes and Janet Whiteley will hae managed fine,' Dick comforted, 'though I dare say they'll be getting a bit alarmed, wondering why ye're sae late, Miss Sar . . . Mistress Fairly.'

'Aye, they will. I told Louis I would be back before midday.' Sarah frowned. 'I hope Agnes made William's supper. He's always hungry after a farm sale.' She turned to Dick. 'You must be hungry too.' She felt a pang of remorse at the sight of his lean, tired face. 'I think you should return to the mill now. I'll manage now that we're over the bridge. Moonbeam knows she's on her way home to her own stable. You can see by the way she has her ears pricked.'

'Are ye ashamed tae be seen i' the company o' an ex-prisoner tae, Miss Sarah?' The bitter words were uttered almost before they had formed in Dick's mind. He regretted his outburst instantly, especially when he saw the shock and hurt in Sarah's wide brown eyes. Sarah had always been kind and understanding. She had tried to help his sister, Vicky, when she had no one to turn to. He could only guess what kind of terror she had endured at Slater's hands today, but she had kept things to herself. She hadn't hurt Beattie with tales of her father's wickedness. He saw how tired she looked too.

'I'm sorry, Miss Sarah,' he mumbled.

'I think I understand, Dick,' Sarah said carefully. 'It was wrong of Constable Ross to treat you like that. If he'd known you, he would never have jumped to such conclusions.'

'It's not only Constable Ross. Folks'll never forget I've bin in prison,' Dick declared despondently. 'Even my ain brothers are leaving the farm because o' me. They dinna want their bairns tae suffer the stain and taunts. They're going tae Newcastle. I'm thinkin' I should be the one tae gang awa', aye right awa', across the sea! I should never hae taken advantage o' auld Mr Miller's kindness.'

'Oh Dick! Surely you would not go to Canada? I told you before, there's still work for you at Fairlyden.' She thought of William so rarely at home to help Louis these days. 'Indeed we need you back at Fairlyden!'

'No! I'm sorry, Miss Sarah, but I wad aye be reminded o' the man who caused all the trouble if I worked for Mr Fairly.'

'But my husband is not like Lord James Fairly. You know that, Dick. I could not have married him if he was like that.' Sarah said reproachfully. 'Anyway he is often away at the markets, or travelling with the stallion in place of my father.'

Dick was silent. He had enjoyed working for Alexander Logan at Fairlyden. They shared a real love for the animals, and they had an eye for the good ones. Privately Dick had been dismayed when he heard that Sarah was going to marry a Fairly, even though the O'Connors had known, and respected, William since he was a boy, riding around his father's estate.

Sarah broke the silence.

'Beatrice would miss you if you went across the sea. I'm sure she cares very deeply for you, Dick.'

'I couldna ask her tae be my wife. I wadna burden her so. "She's the wife o' the man whaes been in prison," ' he mimicked. 'That's what folks wad say.'

'But you do care for her, Dick?' Sarah asked tentatively.

'Oh aye!' Dick declared fervently. 'She's a fine lassie! I've admired her ever since I first took the Fairlyden corn doon tae the mill.' He sighed, recalling happier days. 'Even then I darena hold much hope o' asking her tae marry me. I shall be thirty-nine this year; Beattie's just a slip o' a lassie.'

'She was twenty-five last month, and she's had all the responsibilities of a grown woman since she left school. Beattie needs someone kind, someone who would care for her for a change . . .' Sarah was speaking her own thoughts aloud. She could not forget Mistress Slater's revelations.

'She did seem tae like me weel enough,' Dick agreed diffidently. 'She even came tae see me, in prison, ye ken.' He shuddered, remembering. 'That gave me a bit o' hope. God kens I needed it,' he whispered hoarsely.

'I'm sure Beattie would not have visited you if she hadna cared for you, Dick.'

'Aye, I hoped 'twas so, 'specially when she asked me tae bide at the mill. But . . .' He hunched his shoulders hopelessly, 'I dinna think she— she cares enough tae want tae marry me.'

'How do you know? She was distressed when Constable Ross was so horrible to you,' Sarah reminded him gently.

'Aye, she has a tender heart. She wad be sorry for me! I dinna want sympathy! Not frae anybody. Especially no' frae Beattie!'

'It was more than sympathy! She was terribly upset when the constable took you away, Dick.'

'Ye're wrong, Miss Sarah! Beattie canna— she canna bear me tae touch her.' He muttered the last few words to himself, but Sarah heard them with dismay.

'I canna believe that!'

'It's true. I suppose it's since I've been in prison.'

'No! That would never affect Beatrice's feelings for you, Dick! I've known her all my life. She's loyal and kind. She would not turn against you, and she knows the reason why you had to go to prison.'

Some of Mistress Slater's words echoed through Sarah's mind – words she had barely heeded, even less understood, at the time – words sparked by Edward Slater's insane jealousy and resentment . . . Sarah frowned, trying to remember, to piece things together. 'Is't not enough, to force your lecherous body on oor ain innocent bairn', and later, 'Slater isna Beatrice's father . . .'

Did Beatrice herself believe Slater had ruined her for other men? Dear, sensitive Beattie. Sarah shuddered at the thought of her in Slater's power. Oh yes, she thought angrily, his very touch would be enough to make any decent girl feel unclean, aye and unwanted. Maybe Beattie was afraid, now that Dick was free again . . . free to ask her to be his wife?

'Dick, whatever it is that makes Beattie . . .' Sarah hesitated, searching for words, 'makes her draw away from you, I'm sure it has nothing to do with you being in prison . . .'

'Then what is't?' Dick asked with pathetic eagerness.

'Maybe— maybe Beattie thinks she is not— is not good enough for . . .'

'Not good enough? Beatrice!' Dick gave a harsh bark of laughter. 'She's too good! She's young and pretty, and— and perfect!'

'Aah,' Sarah groaned softly. 'None of us is that, Dick . . .' She knew Beatrice would never have considered herself perfect, but especially not if Slater had defiled her.

The horse and cart rounded the bend on to the straight stretch of track and Sarah looked up.

'Oh dear, here's William riding to meet us.'

'Aye. He'll be coming tae search for ye. Ye've been away a long time, Miss Sarah. He'll hae been worried.'

William had seen the cart now, and the two figures sitting on the front of it. He pulled his horse to a halt and waited, breathing deeply as anger vied with relief now that he knew Sarah was safe.

Sarah turned urgently to her companion.

'Please don't blame yourelf, Dick, if things don't go smoothly with Beattie. I'm sure in my heart that you mean more to her than any other man. She's shy and— and maybe she's afraid . . .'

'Afraid! Surely Beattie canna be afraid o' me? I wad never hurt her! Ye must ken that, Miss Sarah!'

'I do know, Dick, but you must know what Slater was like!' Sarah shuddered. 'Beattie had to live with him. He would make any girl afraid and she saw the way he treated her mother!' Sarah said desperately, unwilling to betray Jeannie's confidences about her own dearest friend, yet anxious to help Dick bridge the gulf between them. 'All I want is Beattie's happiness, and yours too, Dick. I know she needs you! Hold your own head high, but please, please be patient and gentle with Beatrice?'

'I will, Miss Sarah. Indeed I will, and thank ye.'

Sarah smiled at him with relief, then turned to face her husband as the cart drew level with his motionless horse.

Dick's happiness was the furthest thing from William Fairly's mind when he saw his wife riding home on the cart with him. Louis had admitted that she had been away the whole day. Now here she was, riding home with Dick O'Connor, smiling tenderly at him!

Four

As a boy William had known all the tenants on his father's estate, indeed he had been a welcome visitor in many of their homes, including the O'Connor's. He had known most of the servants at Strathtod Tower and accepted that their lives were very different from his own, but he had never treated them with contempt as his half-brother James had done. During his time in America he had learned to judge men, and women, for their courage and honesty rather than their birth. Yet now William found himself resenting his wife's warmth and friendship towards the Fairlyden servants. She worked with them, laughed with them, even wept with them. How often he had heard her praise Dick O'Connor's skills as a stockman; he knew how eagerly she would welcome him back to work at Fairlyden, especially since most of her father's attention was taken up with his work as factor. William found it increasingly difficult to control his proprietorial attitude towards his pretty young wife. He had never known jealousy in his life before, but then he had never loved anyone else as he loved Sarah.

'Where have you been?' he demanded now, frowning down at Sarah and Dick in the cart as he sat erect on his big black horse, Demon. His manner was stern. He made no effort to acknowledge Dick O'Connor. 'Agnes and Janet have finished the milking!'

'Oh, William, I've been at the mill. I went to see Beatrice but there was . . .'

'You disobeyed my instructions! We shall discuss your behaviour later. What business have you at Fairlyden, O'Connor?'

Sarah gasped. She felt humiliated by her husband's cold reception, but his hostile attitude to Dick astonished and shamed her.

'Dick was kind enough to drive me home, William.' Sarah's voice was cool now, her dark eyes sparked with indignation and twin patches of colour stained her cheeks.

William stared at her. She had always been more beautiful when she was angry, even as a child. He turned his horse and walked ahead of them for the short distance into the farmyard.

Could this be the same William who had once sought protection for Dick's family when James Fairly would have put them out of their little farm? William had counted Rory, the youngest of the O'Connors, amongst his friends on the estate.

'I— I'm sorry, Dick. I . . .'

'Your husband wad be worried.' Dick said simply, but his face was strained and tight. He suspected William Fairly considered him an unsuitable escort for his wife since he had been in prison.

There was little comfort in a farm cart and Sarah's muscles had stiffened during the drive home. She could feel the throb of the weals across her shoulders and stomach where the rope had burned her flesh, and her arms ached from her efforts to hold on to the rope and relieve the pressure on her unborn child.

William had taken his horse straight into the stable and it was Dick who jumped from the cart and helped her down. She saw the pulse beating tensely in his lean jaw, the strain in his blue eyes. He had obviously sensed William's hostility. She would never be able to persuade him to return to Fairlyden now. Her heart sank. It was true she had disobeyed her husband's wishes, but it was the first time, and it was not Dick's fault. She had committed no crime. Sarah was a young woman of spirit and her character had been formed in a hard mould. She turned as William came out of the stable.

'Master Slater is dead,' she announced baldly. 'He fell down the mill ladder. That is the reason I was delayed. There were questions to answer. I could not lea— '

'You are my wife! You should not have been in such company.' William interrupted abruptly. 'Of course there would be questions if a man died, and with an ex-prisoner living at the mill.' His statement sounded almost like an accusation. Sarah saw Dick's mouth tighten.

'It was an accident!' she gasped indignantly.

'Were you there, O'Connor?'

'No! Dick was not there!' Sarah declared, and her breast heaved with indignation. She could not understand William's manner.

'Remember Doctor Kerr's advice, Miss Sarah,' Dick warned. 'He said ye were tae rest and have no excitement for at least two days.'

'Mistress Fairly!' William corrected sharply. 'Or have you forgotten you are speaking to my wife!'

Dick's eyes widened. Master Fairly sounded almost like a jealous husband, except that a man in his position had no reason to be jealous of any man, least of all himself.

'I'll unyoke Moonbeam and leave her in the stable,' he said stiffly.

'Thank you,' Sarah's voice was husky with sudden tears. She turned away feeling unutterably weary, and bewildered. So much had happened in a single day, and William seemed too angry even to take in her news. Halfway to the house she remembered Beatrice. 'Dick . . .' she called and her voice wavered alarmingly. 'Would you tell Beatrice I shall call to see her before the funeral. Let me know if she needs my help.' Dick nodded and Sarah walked stiffly towards the house.

Dick began to lead the mare away, but William grasped his arm and dragged his eyes from Sarah's slender figure. He loved her even more now than he had when she became his bride nine months ago. He knew he had been too harsh; he had been anxious about her safety; it had been a shock to see her riding along in the company of Dick O'Connor, smiling at him so sweetly.

'Why did Doctor Kerr advise Mistress Fairly to rest?'

'She has had a terrible shock. She saw Slater fall.'

'But for two days! Did Slater harm her?' William added sharply. Dick blinked and stared at him.

'No.' He uttered the word instinctively, but he wanted to shout at William Fairly. To tell him he should have been running to his wife's side, caring for her tenderly, and then asking her these questions. Instead he straightened his shoulders and looked William in the eye. 'Slater broke his neck when he fell. Mistress Slater has had a seizure. She's like tae die too.' His words were clipped. 'That wad be shock enough for any woman, and ye must ken it's worse for one in Mistress Fairly's condition . . .'

'Condition . . .?' William broke off. Dick O'Connor was staring at him incredulously, then he turned away with a mumbled, 'I'll see tae the mare.' He led the patient Moonbeam to the stable, leaving William staring after him with a thoughtful frown on his dark, handsome face.

Sarah was exhausted by the day's events. She longed to be alone to ponder Mistress Slater's story. She could scarcely make up her mind whether Beatrice's mother had told the truth, or whether she really was completely insane. There were so many questions to be answered, and no one to answer them, unless she broke her promise and asked her father. Sarah shrank from such a thought.

Agnes Jamieson and Janet Whiteley were in the kitchen. Their faces registered relief at the sight of her. They both knew she would never miss a milking without an exceptionally good reason.

'Mercy, Miss Sarah! Ye look as though ye've seen a ghostie!' Janet exclaimed. Janet had come to Fairlyden when she married Louis Whiteley. Sarah had been nine years old at the time. She was often garrulous with the familiarity of long acquaintance, for she had witnessed Sarah's heartaches, as well as her more recent joys. Sometimes she was a little possessive, but she had a kind heart and she was genuinely fond of her young Mistress. She sensed that Sarah was too upset and exhausted to talk.

'I'll awa' hame then, now I ken ye're safe,' she said soothingly. 'Louis and Master Fairly were just aboot tae search for ye. The Master was that worried!'

Sarah nodded. 'Master Slater had an accident at the mill,' she explained wearily. 'He is dead and Mistress Slater is unconscious. That's why I'm so late. Thank you, both of you, for milking all the cows,' she added firmly, unwilling to answer their questions just now. 'Agnes, if you'll give Master Fairly his supper, I think I'll go to bed.'

Agnes's eyes widened in surprise. She had been at Fairlyden since Sarah left school; she had never known her to admit to illness in the past eleven years; she was never idle.

* * *

William already regretted his surge of anger. Could it be true that Sarah was expecting another child? he wondered. Why hadn't she confided in him? She knew how disappointed he had been the last time, and she had looked so ill she had frightened him. Doctor Kerr had said it was nature's way of casting aside an ill-formed offspring. Ill-formed indeed! William remembered how indignant he had been with the old doctor. He and Sarah were both perfectly formed and they were healthy and young; well, Sarah was young. William was conscious of his eleven years' seniority, and the weakening effect the cholera had had on him just before he returned from America.

In other circumstances Sarah would have welcomed her husband's tender apology and loving caresses with relief, for it was the first time they had been angry with each other. But she dare not risk his more intimate embraces in case he saw the marks on her body and questioned her more closely. She had been unable to see her back and shoulders but there was an angry red weal right across her stomach and already it was turning bluish yellow over a wide area. Sarah could not bring herself to tell William of her ordeal, neither could she welcome his touch until she had put Slater's groping fingers firmly out of her mind. Doctor Kerr was right. She did need to rest. She wanted to be alone, to have peace, to think. So she turned her back when William climbed into the big bed beside her. William thought she was rejecting his apology. For the first time there was a coolness between them and everyone else at Fairlyden was aware of it.

Sandy Logan attended the funeral of Edward Slater, not out of respect for the dead man, but to lend his moral support to Joseph Miller, the man who had shown his kindness and hospitality when he had first arrived at Fairlyden with scarcely a penny in his pocket. The mourners were few for Slater had not been popular. Sarah accompanied her father to the house to stay with Beatrice, but both girls knew it would have been hypocritical to make any pretence of grief.

After the funeral Sandy returned to the Mill House with Joseph and Dick. Beatrice and Sarah had prepared tea for them. It reminded Sandy a little of the old days when he had shared Joseph's table, except that the occasion was a solemn one, and the once jovial miller was now a very frail old man.

Jeannie Slater still lay in the small room off the kitchen. She had not recovered consciousness since Dick carried her down from the top of the mill after Slater's death. She clung to the slender thread of life, as though determined not to share her husband's funeral. Indeed she had long since expressed a wish that she should be laid to rest beside her mother, rather than with her husband and infant sons. Her fear and hatred of Slater extended even unto death.

It was Joseph who asked if Sandy would say a few last words to his beloved daughter.

''Tis many a year since ye joined us i' this verra kitchen at the mill. Jeannie aye admired the laddie frae the Galloway hills. Aye, she will be sorry she canna join us today, Sandy laddie.' Joseph's faded blue eyes took on a dreamy look. Sandy guessed he frequently dwelt in the past, reliving the precious memories of his dead wife and their pretty child. He was reluctant to gaze upon the ravaged and unconscious form of the vivacious girl who had once been so indulged, so spoiled, so proud of her beauty, but he did not want to offend his old friend.

Sandy's heart was filled with pity as he gazed upon the silent figure of the miller's only daughter. Her pale skin was stretched tightly over the fine bones of her face and her abundant golden curls were now mere wisps of pure white down. Her hands lay lifelessly on the coverlet, so thin that they seemed almost transparent. Almost involuntarily Sandy found himself kneeling beside the bed, taking one of those still, white hands between his own. He was scarcely aware of Joseph silently withdrawing. The old miller knew it was too late, much, much too late, but he had brought his beloved bairn her heart's desire, in the end.

Sandy had no idea how long he knelt in the small, shadowy room beside Jeannie, his forefinger gently smoothing her birdlike hand. His thoughts winged back over the years and a reminiscent smile touched his eyes as he recalled the young coquettish girl Jeannie had been when he first came to the mill. Other fleeting memories came and went.

He found his gaze wandering absently around the room. He saw the marble-topped washstand with its rose-patterned ewer and its matching bowl, the bedside table; he felt a peculiar sensation, as though he had seen it all before . . . Was this the room where he had slept the night Joseph had almost carried him back to the Mill House? The night he had been so drunk; he had had such strange dreams . . . His eyes moved slowly back to the bed – and Jeannie. His thoughts halted abruptly. He got sharply to his feet. His mind would soon be as confused as hers! Yet the feeling persisted; his brow furrowed. Mattie was the only one he had ever loved. He had dreamed of her so vividly on her wedding night, he had almost believed he held her in his arms; that was the night she married Daniel Munro; the terrible night he had got himself drunk to the gills with Sir Charles Irving. The French brandy from the Crown and Thistle had done wonderful things for his misery though, he recalled with a smile. Yet as he looked down at Jeannie's still, white face, he had the strangest feeling . . .

Sarah was surprised that her father stayed so long with Jeannie when she could not speak, or even recognise anyone. Old Joseph had settled comfortably in his chair before the fire with a satisfied sigh. In no time at all he had fallen sound asleep, with a little smile on his lips. Sarah had always liked Beattie's grandfather.

'I think it is time we went home now, Father,' she said, as soon as Sandy rejoined them. Relations were still strained between her and William so she was anxious not to displease him again. She did not notice the thoughtful look in her father's eyes, or the faintly puzzled frown which creased his brow.

Beatrice was preoccupied with her own thoughts. It troubled her that she could not grieve for her father, but Dick seemed to understand. He had not condemned her. He had been so gentle. If only she could confide in him. Her face flamed at the thought. She could not bear to seek Dick's contempt if she were to tell him the truth about Slater. She pulled her thoughts back with an effort when she saw Sarah and Sandy were ready to leave. 'Thank ye for coming, Sarah. I was glad o' your support today.' Sarah nodded. They both knew Beattie's mother could not last much longer without either food or drink and it was clear that her grandfather was feeling the strain badly.

'Wake up, Grandfather,' Beatrice murmured, shaking the old man's shoulder gently. 'Mr Logan and Sarah are leaving now.'

'Dinna disturb him, lassie,' Sandy said kindly. 'It has been a tiring day for him. It's a pity none o' your brothers could come for the funeral.'

'I was sure Joe would come,' Beattie answered with a frown. 'Especially when I wrote to tell him how ill Mother is.'

'Your grandfather told me about Eddie and Jack drowning in Canada, trying to free a log jam,' Sandy murmured sympathetically. 'I suppose the other three are still out there?'

'Bert and Jamie have moved south, intae America. They seem happy, but we dinna hear often. I've written tae them of course. Wull is the oldest now Eddie's gone, but he never bothers tae keep in . . . Grandfather!' Her tone sharpened suddenly. She was staring down at Joseph's motionless face, still with the same faint smile on his lips.

'Oh, Grandfather!' Beattie's voice was a frightened sob. Sandy and Dick O'Connor were at her side in a flash. Sarah watched helplessly.

Joseph Miller would never waken from his 'wee nap'. Sarah's heart ached for Beatrice. She had loved her grandfather dearly. After that first heart-rending sob Beattie wept silently, hiding her face against Dick O'Connor's shoulder.

Beatrice was not a superstitious girl, but when her mother died less than twenty-four hours after Joseph Miller she felt God had surely deserted her.

It was the Reverend Mackenzie who brought her comfort, reminding her of her grandfather's steadfast faith, and the many times Joseph Miller had found comfort from his bible, instilling in her his own belief that her mother would find peace at last. Beatrice knew it was true but this time her young heart was filled with grief.

Five

The spring days were turning to summer when Sarah felt the first movement of her unborn child. Her heart beat a joyous tattoo; there was a new confidence in her smile. She had been troubled by a secret fear that her visit to the mill, the day Edward Slater fell to his death, might have affected her baby. William knew nothing of the sordid details. His initial displeasure had changed to delight when Sarah confirmed that she was expecting another child. All the coolness between them had vanished.

'I pray with all my heart that I shall bear you a fine son this time, William,' she had whispered against his shoulder as he held her lovingly in his arms, knowing nothing of the painful bruises which had forced Sarah to maintain a distance between them.

'Nothing can go wrong a second time, my dearest,' he had assured her tenderly and his loving had become as gentle and considerate as in the first weeks of their marriage. William truly loved his pretty, spirited young wife, but he also longed for a son. He believed the child would provide an anchor for him at Fairlyden, a reason for striving, here in his native Scotland. He was a little dismayed at the restlessness which was stirring in him since he had regained his former health and vigour.

'I shall always be grateful to the American nuns who nursed me when I had cholera,' he had told Sarah on their wedding night. 'I think they must have known my own angel was here on earth. I shall never want to leave you again, my dearest, or Fairlyden.' He had spoken the words from his heart at the time. He knew he had been lucky to survive the dreaded cholera, but the fever had put a considerable strain on his heart and he had never expected to regain his former vitality.

Yet his health seemed to have improved almost daily since his marriage, with all the benefits of Sarah's tender care and excellent cooking. He had looked forward to travelling round the countryside with the Logan stallions, meeting breeders, finding trade, making friends.

But the stallions did not claim all his attention once the spring and early summer breeding season finished, and William found he did not derive the same deep satisfaction in the changing seasons, the toil and reward of Fairlyden's seedtime and harvest, as Sandy Logan had done. He did not share Sarah's relief and pleasure each time a cow or a sow brought forth its young in safety. William found himself yearning for the vast, untamed prairies he had glimpsed in America; he longed for the cut and thrust world of enterprising merchants, the challenge of the immense new continent. Even Strathtod, the estate he had known and loved in his youth, now seemed a small and insignificant corner of the globe, while Fairlyden was a mere speck, albeit a speck which demanded a great deal of time and daily toil if its occupants were to survive.

William had been further frustrated when an outbreak of foot and mouth disease had closed the local markets and curtailed his spasmodic dealing in cattle. The restrictions which the government had enforced in an effort to prevent the spread of the disease had led to the slaughter of thousands of cattle. While William agreed with the policy in principle, the enforced isolation increased his restlessness. He never gambled, as his half-brother had done, but he enjoyed the excitement of buying and selling, of pitting his wits against the farmers and butchers at the local markets. He bought cattle when prices seemed low. Sometimes he had to bring them home to Fairlyden and keep them until the following week, or even longer, before he could sell them again. Usually he made a profit, but not always. As soon as Sarah had heard the first rumours of the dreaded foot and mouth disease her husband's dealings had troubled her.

'Please stay at home, William,' she pleaded earnestly as the disease spread. 'Already I'm afraid in case some of your strange cattle have brought the disease to Fairlyden. I could not bear to see our own cattle slaughtered! Our bonnie wee calves being killed. I've known each one since they were born.'

William had reluctantly accepted his confinement, knowing it would ruin them and break Sarah's heart if such a disaster befell them. Even so Sarah had kept an anxious eye on all the cattle for weeks, though William sought other channels for his restless thoughts. Surprisingly he turned his attention to Dick O'Connor and Beatrice at the Muircumwell Mill. He knew he was partly responsible for Dick's stubborn refusal to return to work at Fairlyden and other farmers in the area seemed reluctant to hire a man who had been in prison. William knew Beatrice must be having a desperate struggle to survive with the few animals Joseph had left her and only two small paddocks which the miller's family had rented from the local laird for as long as anyone could remember.

'Slater seems to have lost the trade of all the local farmers, and the mill building and the machinery are very dilapidated,' he remarked to Sarah one evening after he had paid an unexpected visit to Muircumwell. 'There will never be enough trade to open the little mills again. There are mills in Annan and at many of the other ports. The railways can transport the corn and cattle cake great distances.'

'But the farmers still have to collect everything at the railway station, or pay the carters to deliver to the farms,' Sarah protested. 'Anyway the mill has always been Beatrice's home. She would not want to leave it, and where else could she live . . .?' she mused anxiously. Beatrice's situation troubled her even more whenever she thought of Jeannie Slater's story. Beatrice was more than her dearest friend now; she must be her half-sister. Several times she had been on the point of confiding in William, but in her heart she knew he would dismiss the tale as the insane ramblings of a dying woman; or he might insist that Alexander Logan should be consulted. Sarah shied away from that. It seemed such an impertinence to ask her beloved father if he could be Beatrice's father too, and she was mindful of the promise she had made to Jeannie.

'Maybe Beatrice wouldn't need to leave the mill,' William interrupted her thoughts. 'If Dick intends to help her he could take out the grinding stones and machinery and use the premises as a farmer's store. It's an idea that has been in my head for some time now. It's time farmers cooperated together a bit more in this country and Dick could lead the way. He could store seeds and scythes, grinding stones, small tools, paraffin; all the things the farmers in the parish have to bring from the towns themselves.'

'D'you really think Dick and Beattie can make a living at the mill without any corn to grind?' Sarah asked doubtfully.

'Yes, if Dick is willing to repair the mill and become a businessman. I could help him get his stores. I have met several large merchants at the markets, and I have made a lot of contacts with farmers on my travels with the stallion.'

Sarah nodded thoughtfully. William was very enthusiastic but it was the sort of business he understood from his experience as a corn merchant in America. She could not imagine Dick O'Connor being happy as a businessman – buying and selling and bargaining . . .

As soon as the government lifted the foot and mouth restrictions William returned eagerly to the markets again.

Louis's wife, Janet, grumbled openly when extra cows suddenly appeared in the byre for milking, only to disappear again in a few days, or sometimes in a few weeks. Agnes rarely complained about anything, but Sarah knew she did not enjoy the uncertain temperaments of some of these visiting cows, and Louis was at his wits' end when some of the Irish bullocks were too wild to be restrained by Fairlyden's thorny hedges. There was another problem too. When there were extra milking cows, there was more cream to make into butter. Sometimes the dairy was overflowing; every conceivable receptacle was pressed into use as a creaming pan, but it was not always possible to sell the butter, even at excessively low prices. Yet William did not seem to understand that the money he gained on the cattle was lost when his dealings upset Fairlyden's fragile economy.

'I think Agnes should take the butter to market,' he suggested one Friday when Sarah had returned looking pale and exhausted and her condition was becoming difficult to conceal, despite her voluminous dress and cape. 'You must not tire yourself, my dear,' he urged with genuine concern.

So Sarah reluctantly agreed to send Agnes to market instead. She trusted Anges well enough, but she liked to sell the butter and eggs herself. She knew without conceit that Fairlyden butter was excellent quality, both for flavour and keeping; it deserved the best prices.

At first Agnes enjoyed her small adventures on the train. Janet envied her for she rarely had an opportunity to leave Fairlyden herself now that she had four children. But as the butter became more and more difficult to sell, Agnes worried.

'I had tae bring most o' the butter hame again today,' she wailed after one particularly bad market day. 'I ken how important the prices are, Mistress Sarah, but there was ower much butter and cheese, and great baskets o' eggs. I got rid o' them eventually.' Sarah bit her lip and consoled Agnes, even while she wondered if she could have done better if she had been there herself.

'Did Mistress Sharpe manage to sell all her butter?' Sarah asked. There had long been a rivalry between the Mains and Fairlyden.

'Ach, I almost forget tae gie ye the news, Miss Sarah!' Agnes brightened visibly. 'I saw Beth, ma sister, on the train tae Annan! She had charge o' the Mains' produce today. Mistress Sharpe isn' weel! She hasna been richt for weeks, Beth says. She just wadna gie in.'

'She must be very sick today then?' Sarah frowned. Agnes's mother had been the head dairymaid at Mains of Muir since before Agnes was born. Agnes's sister, now Mrs Beth Dickson, had spent all her life in the Mains dairy too, but Mistress Sharpe had never trusted either of them to go to market.

'Aye, Beth said ma mither felt sorry for her. Terrible pains she has in her stomach. Beth reckons Mr Sharpe is fair lost wi'out her tae order him about his business. Ye'd think he wad be pleased tae hae peace frae her sharp tongue and sour face!'

'Mmm, maybe. Was Beatrice on the train?' Sarah asked, tactfully changing the subject.

'No, but Mistress McNay was taking her bit o' butter tae sell. She says Dick O'Connor and Beatrice are working terribly hard at the mill tae get it intae guid order again, but she says Dick's only happy when he's working wi' the pigs and cattle. I hope he'll like having a shop, Mistress Sarah?'

'It's not really a shop, but I hope he likes it too,' Sarah agreed fervently.

Sarah voiced her own doubts to William again that very evening.

'It will take time to get customers,' William agreed, 'but I believe Dick O'Connor would do anything to stay near your friend, Beatrice. At least they have a home. I thought the mill property belonged to Sir Simon Guillyman but apparently the Mill House and the buildings belonged to Joseph Miller?'

'Yes, but the land and the two wee paddocks belong to Sir Simon. It is an old story. One of Joseph Miller's ancestors won the house and the mill in a wager. I expect Beattie's grandfather would be disappointed when he hadna any sons to keep on the Miller name. Joe was the only one of his grandsons who was like him and he went to England to be a blacksmith. He came to Mistress Slater's funeral. Beattie says he has a wife and a nice little house. He told Beattie he and his brothers thought she deserved far more than a broken down mill, the way she had cared for them all as bairns, and then their mother and Grandfather Miller. He didna realise his father had ruined the mill trade completely and Beattie didna tell him. Joe said his two brothers in America are happily married and quite settled there. Wull Slater went with them when they went to Canada but they parted company and none of them knows where Wull is now. He's the oldest since Eddie was killed but he didna come to the funeral.'

'I don't suppose he knew if his brothers cannot contact him,' William said reasonably.

'No, but he could have kept in touch. Wull always caused trouble though, wherever he was, especially for Beattie.' Sarah sighed. 'I expect she's glad he's far away in some foreign land.'

'Once Dick has made the mill into a good storage place he will be able to stock all manner of small tools, as well as large quantities of seeds, then he can sell them locally at a profit.' William's dark eyes glowed with enthusiasm.

'I canna picture Dick as a businessman,' Sarah said slowly. 'He likes things that live and grow; he loves pigs and cows. I canna imagine him bargaining like you do at the markets.'

'I expect he will get used to it, especially if it means he and Beatrice can stay at the Mill.' Secretly he envied Dick O'Connor such an opportunity. The old mill would be an ideal place for a farmer's store; it was at the edge of Muircumwell village and well situated in the middle of a country area, yet not too far from the railway station either. This was a time for changes, even if most of the farmers couldn't see it yet.

Sarah bit her lip. 'I know Dick needs the work, and I'm glad you are taking an interest in him, William. I thought you had condemned him because he's been in prison. It's just— just that I canna see him as a storekeeper. Anyway farmers are loathe to change their ways, and they dinna have much money to spare for new ideas these days. Supposing he canna sell his stock?'

'Your father agrees that it pays to select and sow better seeds. It is nearly a century since the Society of Improvers met in Edinburgh but most farmers have never heard of the scientists and their chemical compounds – products that can make plants grow faster, or give better yields; they know nothing of improving their land, or their cattle.'

'That's not true, William!' Sarah declared indignantly. 'My Grandfather Cameron was aye draining and improving his land, and he only bred frae his own beasts, and he picked the best. My father has often told me about him. You canna say he does not know about improving things either. That's why Mr Bradshaw wanted him to be his factor at Strathtod. That's where they need improvement and all because o'—' Sarah broke off suddenly, her cheeks pink with indignation. 'I'm sorry,' she whispered. 'I didna mean . . .' But William was smiling broadly.

'I always knew you had a fighting spirit, even when you were a schoolgirl.' He grinned ruefully, 'You were pretty then, Sarah, even if you did have filthy hair and smelled like the midden . . .'

'William Fairly! You promised you would never—'

'Remind you . . .? I know my dear and I'm sorry.' His smile widened and there was a look in his dark eyes which never failed to make Sarah feel weak all over. 'You're a very pretty woman, Sarah Fairly,' he said softly, 'when the colour rises in your cheeks like soft pink roses and your eyes sparkle like black diamonds.'

'Oh, William, I didna mean to be angry. It's only because I worry so much about Beattie and Dick.'

'Well, I shall help them if I can, never fear. I have already approached some of the agents I have met at the markets. They are going to send supplies of various products as soon as the mill is ready. Everything from Dutch turnip seed to Canadian clovers, and slabs of linseed cattle cake to sacks of fish manure. We must use some of them here at Fairlyden; when neighbours see the improvements the trade at the Muircumwell Farmers' Store will increase. I expect your father will place orders for the Home Farm at Strathtod, and maybe some of the Strathtod tenants will follow his advice.'

'You've done all that for Dick? Oh William I am glad. You are a good, kind man, you always were, and I'm sorry I got so indignant.'

'Then you'll not mind if your husband snatches a kiss from his pretty wife!' William suited his actions to his words, his dark eyes as merry as a boy's.

'William!' Sarah gasped. 'Agnes might see us, or— or Janet!' But William only smiled down at her flushed cheeks.

'I hope our children are all as pretty as their mother,' he chuckled softly. Sarah pursed her lips and tried to look prim, but her eyes glowed with love as she hurried away to the dairy to collect her piggin and three-legged milking stool.

William watched her go with a smile, then he sighed. He had reacted far too harshly the night Dick had brought her home after Slater's death. He knew that now. The O'Connors had been a fine family. Most of their troubles had been caused by his own half-brother. Now Dick's parents were both dead and his two brothers had rejected him on account of his time spent in prison. But in his heart William admitted that part of his reason for helping Dick to make a success at the mill was because he did not want him at Fairlyden, associating with his own wife and children, and he knew Sarah would be horrified if she realised he harboured such thoughts.

The corn crops had filled out well despite the uncertain weather, but the showers and several heavy storms made the harvest a laboriously slow task. There were only Louis and William for the scything. Sarah was slow at binding the sheaves on account of her large bulk and the continual bending; she began to dread the constant re-stooking of the sheaves with their thistles and bedraggled bottoms. It was a great relief when the harvest was over.

It was early October and Agnes had left to catch the early train to sell the Fairlyden butter and eggs at the market. The yields of milk were decreasing, but at least the prices would be a little higher, Sarah thought with a frown. She had felt uneasy all day. A nagging pain in her back had wakened her during the night and she had barely slept. She had snatched a brief rest in her room while Agnes was away but at the sound of the returning pony and trap she rose guiltily and splashed her face with cold water from the ewer to make her feel more alert.

'What price did the butter fetch today then, Agnes?' she asked a little wearily.

'One shilling and fourpence,' Agnes announced, watching her young mistress anxiously. 'I got one and three a dozen for the eggs, but the hens were only fetching one and fourpence each and guid fat hens they were tae.'

'Oh dear, and we really must sell more of them before the winter or they'll do nothing but eat corn and grow fatter now they've stopped laying.'

'There was talk o' some stuff called margarine at the market. They say folks i' the toons are using it 'stead o' butter,' Agnes reported uncertainly. 'One o' the shopkeepers said a great ship load had come frae a country called Holland. 'Tisna true, is't Miss Sarah?'

'I don't know,' Sarah mused. 'I remember reading about a Frenchman once who was supposed to have made a substance almost like butter.' She glanced up and saw Agnes's anxious face. 'Och, nothing would ever take the place o' Fairlyden butter!' she added brightly. 'Come on, Agnes! It isn't like you to be gloomy over a bit of market gossip! The cows'll be needing to be milked whether any one buys butter or no'.'

Agnes was not fooled by Sarah's forced cheerfulness. Every week there were stories in the *Dumfries Standard* about whole families going off to America. Sarah was shocked to see her cheery maid looked like bursting into tears. 'Dinna worry, Agnes! We shall manage somehow. There's more than enough work for everybody at Fairlyden!' She sighed heavily; her unborn child was becoming a burden. 'Maybe we dinna have much money, but at least we aye have enough to eat. I hear that's more than some of the poor folks in the crowded cities can say.' But for once Agnes's face crumpled like a child's instead of resuming its usual serenity. 'Why Agnes! What's wrong?'

''Tis ma brother, Nicky!' Agnes mumbled. 'Mistress Sharpe says he'll hae tae take less wages if he wants tae bide at the Mains. He's been savin' ilka penny tae marry Sally McKie. Oh, Miss Sarah! He's threatening tae marry her an' gang awa' across the Ata . . . the ocean, all the way tae America! Beth says Mother is terrible worrit! Mr Sharpe says things are bad at the Mains. He's already tell't yin o' the young stableboys tae leave at the term, an' twae o' the maids tae!' Sarah's eyes widened. She could understand Betty Jamieson's concern. Nicky was her only son. He had been born six months after his father's death and she had had a hard struggle to rear Agnes and Beth and a baby son.

'I've heard my father say Nicky is one of the best horsemen in the area. I'm sure Mr Sharpe willna let him go for the sake of a penny or two.'

''Tis more than that— 'tis a whole shilling a week!' But Agnes's eyes had brightened. 'Mother's never forgotten how Mr Logan helped her tae keep her work and her wee hoose at the Mains, after Father wis killed! Eeh, Miss Sarah, dae ye think Mr Logan wad speak tae Mr Sharpe again? Beth says mother's breakin' her heart already, jist thinkin' aboot Nicky going sae far awa' across the sea.' Sarah nodded but she was troubled by the news. The Mains was one of the biggest farms in the area. If things were bad there what hope was there for the rest of the farmers? Her thoughts moved to her unborn child. Would it find a bleak future ahead?

All through the milking, and during the evening Sarah was plagued by her aching back, but it was not until she was wakened by a sharp stab of pain in the middle of the night that she realised her baby was making his way into the world at last. She was sure it must be a boy; it had to be a boy! William had set his heart on a son, to be called after him.

'I will leave at once!' William insisted when Sarah wakened him.

'There's no need to go 'til dawn.'

'I'll go now. Maybe I should bring Doctor Kerr?'

'Mistress Johnstone will do fine!' Sarah instructed sharply. 'I dinna need the doctor at the birthing of my babe! Do you hear me?'

'Hush, hush, Sarah,' William was alarmed by his wife's unusual asperity. 'It is not good for you to get excited. Supposing there is anything wrong? My son— our son must be perfect.'

'There's naught wrong with your son the way he has been kicking the heart out of me these past months! He is as strong as a young bull! Promise you willna bring the doctor?'

William nodded reluctantly.

As it happened there was no necessity for William's haste to summon Mistress Johnstone from her bed in the middle of the night. The baby was in no hurry to enter the world and it was almost noon before an exhausted, but triumphant, Sarah succeeded in giving birth to her first child. She lay back panting, her eyes closed, as the cheerful Mistress Johnstone lifted the slippery, wailing infant in her capable hands.

'Ye have a son, Mistress Fairly!' she declared, as proudly as if she had made the child herself. 'He's a fine . . .' Her voice trailed away.

Sarah's drooping eyelids shot open. 'Is he all right? Let me see my baby!'

'Whisht now! He's a— a fine laddie.' Mistress Johnstone soothed, but her voice was husky and she turned away and enveloped the child in a clean white towel before bringing him for Sarah's inspection.

Sarah looked down at the waxy, unbathed head with awe. This was her child! Her very own! A small, perfect miracle created by herself and William, with God's help of course. In her weary, weakened state Sarah's eyes filled with unexpected tears; joy and pride welled up in her. Love surged in her heart for her helpless infant, cradled so trustingly in her arms.

'He's perfect!' she whispered huskily.

'Aye.' Mistress Johnstone sat down heavily on the side of the bed and looked thoughtfully at Sarah's bent head. It had been a long birth and she was tired, but Mistress Fairly was a courageous young woman. She hadn't wailed or panicked like some of the young mothers she attended, even though her own mother had died in childbirth. 'The bairn will hae a' the love a guid mother can gie him, I'm sure,' she murmured. 'So he'll mak a fine laddie.' She got to her feet with an effort. 'I'll bathe him an' put him in his cradle now.' She lifted the white swathed bundle gently from Sarah's arms. 'Ye must rest, Mistress Fairly, then I'll tell Agnes tae bring ye up a wee bowl o' thin soup.' But Sarah was already sinking into the sweet oblivion of a well-earned sleep. 'Naething seems quite sae bad after a guid sleep,' Mistress Johnstone muttered uneasily under her breath.

Six

When Sarah wakened she was surprised to find the October day was almost ended. The sun was casting its last long shadows through the dormer window, before it finally disappeared over the rim of the distant hills. She raised her head lethargically. Agnes was tending the bedroom fire, sending the flames shooting up the chimney. Outside she could hear the sound of children's voices and knew that Louis's bairns were back from school.

'How could I have slept so long! Agnes, have you seen my baby? Has he cried? Has his father seen him while I slept?'

'Och, ye're awake, Miss Sarah.' Agnes felt uneasy.

'Yes, yes. You shouldna have let me sleep so long! Surely my babe— my son,' she amended proudly, 'must be ready to feed?'

'He's slept like an angel,' Agnes announced, 'but he's stirring now.'

'Then pass him to me quickly, Agnes!' Sarah could not hide her joy and excitement. 'Has— has Master Fairly not been to see him yet? Is he proud to have such a fine son?'

'Miss Sarah . . .' Agnes's plain, kindly face was flushed, but it was not just from the heat of the fire. She looked down into Sarah's shining dark eyes and her heart filled with pity.

'The Master isna in frae— frae the fields yet.' She could not tell Sarah that Master Fairly had stormed out of the house as soon as he had spoken to the midwife. Mistress Johnstone had wanted to bring the babe from his crib for the Master to see, but he had refused to look at his own son. He had ridden away on his horse at a furious pace and no one knew where he had gone.

Sarah was disappointed. She had expected William would be waiting eagerly for her to waken, eager to admire their son.

'Has my father returned frae Strathtod? Doesn't he want to see his first grandson?' Sarah demanded with uncharacteristic petulance.

'He'll be home any time now, Miss Sarah. He's sure tae come straight up tae see ye. Och now listen! He has a fine pair o' lungs to let us know he's hungry!'

'Then please pass him at once, Agnes,' Sarah grinned with delight. 'We can't keep the young Master waiting for his food, can we?'

'The young Master . . .' Agnes murmured, and Sarah wondered why she sounded so sad.

'Did you— did you ever dream of getting married, and having bairns of your own, Agnes?' she asked almost shyly. Agnes hesitated, clutching the wailing bundle briefly to her own ample bosom. Then she settled him in his mother's arms and straightened. She looked directly into Sarah's eyes.

'There was a laddie once . . . but no, Miss Sarah, I dinna want tae marry now. I reckon I'll be happy here at Fairlyden, helping ye with your ain bairns. I'm sure ye'll hae other sons – fine sons.' Sarah was too busy concentrating on feeding her firstborn to think of others, or to notice the sympathy in Agnes's eyes. The maid sighed.

Sarah must have dozed again after Agnes had laid her contented son back in his crib, all changed and sweet smelling once more. It was quite dark outside by the time she wakened to hear Agnes climbing the stairs with a bowl of clear chicken soup for her supper. Sarah felt she could have eaten a horse, but thin soup was what Mistress Johnstone had recommended as being suitable for an invalid and Agnes had obeyed the midwife's instructions to the letter. Not a grain of rice, or a piece of leek had escaped into Sarah's dish. Agnes had brought a small oil lamp instead of the candlestick which they usually used for the bedrooms, but Sarah could see quite clearly by the light of the fire. She enjoyed watching the flickering flames sending their patterns up the walls. The room looked warm and cosy from its cheery glow. Sarah sighed contentedly.

'I'm glad ye're awake, Miss Sarah. Master Logan peeped in as soon as he returned frae Strathtod, but ye were as sound asleep as the babe himself,' Agnes declared.

'And Master Fairly?'

'He's coming up as weel . . . soon as he's finished his supper.'

'His supper! Surely his son is more important!'

Agnes maintained a diplomatic silence for once.

Sarah had just finished feeding her infant son when Agnes returned to take him away, followed by William.

'Dinna take him away yet, Agnes,' Sarah insisted. 'I want to show his father what a fine son he has.'

'No!' William said tensely, and Sarah stared up in surprise at his harsh tone. 'Let— let Agnes change him,' he amended more gently. 'You are not strong enough to care for him yet.'

'I feel quite strong enough to hold my own babe and open a couple of pins!' Sarah laughed. 'This is your son William – another William Fairly.'

'No!' William almost groaned. He felt angry and confused and disappointed. This time Agnes moved out of the room and shut the bedroom door quietly behind her. She would come back later to take the child. She could not bear to see her young mistress's face when Master Fairly broke the news to her, but Agnes was certain Sarah would be far more hurt by her husband's rejection of his own child.

'I thought you were longing for a laddie?' Sarah asked in bewilderment. 'You wanted a boy, "a son named after me". That's what you said. William . . . ?' Sarah's voice was tremulous and she stretched out a hand towards her husband, beckoning him to come closer so that the light shone on his face. William took her outstretched fingers and his grip was fiercer than he knew. Sarah winced involuntarily.

'What is it? What's wrong, William . . . ?' she asked fearfully, but as he stared down into her wide anxious eyes, William Fairly found he could not speak and he cursed Mistress Johnstone for leaving him to break the news to Sarah.

'D'you not want the babe to bear your name after all?'

'No.'

Sarah looked up and saw his bleak expression and her eyes filled with unexpected tears. She blinked them away, but she felt suddenly weary and weak – and angry and confused.

'Why? Why, William? It was your heart's desire that our first bairn should be called after you!'

'Your father thinks . . . he would like us to name him Alexander.'

'B-but maybe there'll be others – or we could give him both names . . .'

'No! He is a . . . Our son is a— a cripple!'

Sarah stared at him uncomprehendingly. The words seemed to echo, and re-echo round the room.

'No!' Sarah whispered hoarsely, 'no!' Suddenly the dancing shadows on the walls had become demons. Wicked, dark, menacing!

'I dinna believe you! It canna be true!' Sarah heard her voice rise hysterically. She strove for control. She looked down at the sleeping infant snuggled in the crook of her arm. He looked so defenceless, so perfect.

Suddenly Sarah stiffened, remembering the day she had defied William; the day she went to the mill; the dreadful day Slater had hoisted her up to the very top floor like a sack of corn. The bruising from the ropes had taken weeks to disappear completely. Could her unborn child have been injured after all?

Swiftly her shaking fingers scrabbled at her son's shawl, pulling it from him almost roughly. He whimpered in protest and Sarah's heart lurched. If her son was a cripple, the fault was hers. If he needed her more, she would love him more. William gazed down at her helplessly, already ashamed of his own reaction as he saw the face of his son for the first time. Gently now Sarah eased up the long cotton nightdress and unpinned the flannel petticoats which enclosed his lower limbs for warmth. It was then she saw the tiny feet, each toe as exquisitely formed as his dimpled fingers. Her face paled. She stared down. The perfect little feet were turned towards each other, the left even more twisted than the right.

William stared miserably at his wife's bent head. He knew he had acted foolishly. The child would never run, or even walk, as other children did, but his deformity was not as bad as he had feared when Mistress Johnstone broke the news to him. He had allowed his imagination to run away with reason. In his mind the babe had become a hideous imbecile.

'Sarah . . . ?' He reached out tentatively and touched her. She looked pale, but infinitely young and lovely with her fine skin and the thick braid of her dark hair curling almost to her waist. 'Dinna touch me!' Sarah looked straight at her husband and her dark eyes were full of pain. William's heart lurched.

'Aah, Sarah – I was foolish. I-I . . .'

'I understand now,' she said and her voice was low and cold. 'Why you didna come. Why you didna wish to see— us. Why you dinna wish my babe to bear your name!'

'We shall have other sons, Sarah . . .'

'But this is our firstborn! The son we craved, and prayed for!' Sarah felt anger welling up inside her. Her husband had rejected the child she had given him. 'Please leave me.' She held her head high, despite her weariness. 'I refuse to believe that he will be a cripple, but you— you have rejected him. He will need all the love, all the care, I can give him.'

'But Sarah! I need you too.' William had meant to offer comfort, not demand it. He sensed her anger and disappointment. He had let her down when she needed him most. He felt part of her had withdrawn from him; even in his own ears his words had sounded petulant and childish. Mistress Johnstone had told him his wife had suffered a long, hard labour, without complaint, to bear him a son. 'Sarah, my dearest.' He bent over the bed and touched her temple with his lips. Sarah's head remained bowed.

'Leave me,' she commanded fiercely, striving to keep her anger under control. 'I need to be alone.'

'Very well.' William was ashamed of the relief which washed over him as he closed the door behind him. Many women would have had hysterics, or fainted, at the sight of her child's deformed limbs, he thought, but Sarah was made of sterner stuff. She would give him other sons, in time.

He would have been even more shamed had he known of Sarah's valiant struggle to control her grief and anger until she was alone. Her tears fell fast and silently, streaming down her pale face. When one fell with a soft plop onto her son's rounded cheek, he opened his eyes wide, gazing wonderingly up at her until her crying gradually ceased. Slowly and carefully she looked at her infant son, limb by limb; she marvelled at the perfection of him. Eventually she put him to her breast and he suckled strongly, kneading her soft flesh with his tiny fist, until Sarah's heart was comforted and her mind grew calm again. When he was satisfied she lay back against her pillows, cradling him in her arms. She was still gazing at the soft, dark fuzz on the crown of his head when her father entered.

Sandy Logan had never been a man to hide from an unpleasant truth. There were troubles and there were joys, and he had learned the hard way that both were better shared. He smiled directly into Sarah's eyes and there was love and kindness, and deep understanding in his own. There had been little need for words to convey the love he felt since he had summoned the courage to tell Sarah she was his own daughter. Now she saw that love extended to her son as he gently took the baby from her arms and laid him on the bed between them. He crouched down awkwardly on account of his own twisted knee. Slowly and deliberately he drew aside the layers of petticoats until he could look upon his grandson's tiny feet. One by one he took them in his big gentle hands, smoothing the soft skin, feeling the delicate bones.

'One day, maybe, men will find a way to mend God's mistakes,' he sighed softly. 'But you, my little fellow, you and I must live with our twisted limbs. Two Alexanders together, eh?' He looked up into Sarah's anxious eyes.

'D'you really want him to be named after you, Father?'

'I'd be proud! He is my first grandson.'

'Even though he will never run like other boys? Even though you will never be able to teach him to plough a fine straight furrow, as you once taught Louis Whiteley . . . ?' Sarah's voice cracked despite her determination to remain calm. Sandy's face was grave, and his blue eyes were almost stern as they rested on her.

'Sarah, make no mistake. Your son will plough a straight furrow, a straight furrow through life. That is what counts, my dear. One day ye'll be proud o' him. Have ye forgotten how bravely your— your mother faced adversity? Your son will have his measure of the Cameron courage, never fear.'

Sarah smiled wanly. Even after all these years her father could scarcely mention her mother without a tremor in his deep voice. Sarah knew he had loved Mattie more, rather than less, for her disability; not out of sympathy because she lived in a world of silence, but because she had had courage and character. Sarah looked up and met her father's blue gaze steadily.

'I shall always love my son.'

'Love him, aye,' Sandy smiled gently. 'We all need love, lassie, but never, ever, treat him differently frae other laddies. He'll learn tae deal with his ain problems, and he'll be a better man for that!'

Sarah bit her lip and looked at him doubtfully.

'Remember what I said – your son may bear the name o' Fairly, but he carries the Cameron blood in his veins. He'll never lack courage. Now,' he rose stiffly to his feet and he winced with pain, 'I'll send Agnes up to make young Alexander ready for his crib, and ye'll need plenty o' sleep tae, if ye're tae look after this wee laddie.' He traced the curve of a petal-soft cheek with a gentle finger. 'Things will be brighter in the morning, lassie.'

'Aye, maybe they'll seem so,' Sarah nodded, then she smiled wryly. 'Alexander seems such a big name for such a wee bairnie. Perhaps we could call him Alex for a while . . . ?'

'Aye, Alex it is then.' Sandy bent and kissed her cheek in a rare demonstration of his affection for her.

No one would ever know how greatly he had suffered that day, or the fervent prayers he had uttered for her safe delivery. Memories of her mother's death in childbirth had haunted him continually and he had wanted to leave his work at Strathtod and be at Fairlyden; but it was a husband's right to be near his wife at such a time. Yet William had spent the day galloping around the countryside, venting his anger; he had neglected his wife, and rejected his son. For the first time Sandy felt angry and disappointed with his son-in-law. 'But Sarah loves him and I mustna utter a word o' ill against him,' he reminded himself sternly.

Despite her father's optimism, and her husband's belated attentions and regret, nothing could dispel Sarah's anxiety for her son. Mistress Johnstone had insisted she must stay in bed for two whole weeks and the enforced idleness and solitude gave her too much time to brood. She had been shedding a few secret tears over baby Alex when Agnes entered the bedroom unexpectedly. The maid tut-tutted anxiously and busied herself mending the fire. When her mistress had collected herself she came to the bedside and stood looking down at her thoughtfully.

'Just ye wait a twelve month,' she warned cheerfully, 'yon wee fellow will be toddling after oor skirts an' getting intae mischief everywhere. Ye'll wonder why ye worried, Miss Sarah.' Sarah gulped and nodded and remained unconvinced. Agnes sighed and sat down on the edge of the bed, though there was still work to be done in the Fairlyden kitchen.

'Do ye mind o' Bobby Frame?' she demanded briskly. Sarah frowned and shook her head.

'He's the laddie who was hurt at the Mains, when his horse bolted and killed my father; 'twas afore ma brother Nicky was born.'

'Oh yes, I have heard how brave your father was, Agnes, but it was before I was born too. The boy lost a leg, didn't he . . . ?'

'Aye, an' his other leg was mangled 'neath the wheel o' the cart. He was just a boy . . . thirteen years auld, but he was brave, was Bobby. He didna sit doon an' greet. He asked auld Mister Turner if he wad teach him tae make clogs. It wasna easy at first for the laddie could scarce move, or so ma mother said. But he wadna gie in. Well he learned tae be a clogger, a real good clogger tae. He went tae the toon an' he has his ain wee shop noo. An' I'll tell ye something else, Miss Sarah.' Agnes's lip trembled slightly but she went on. 'Bobby reckoned 'twas ma father who saved his life, sae do ye ken what he did? He sent a pair o' clogs for Beth an' me and Nicky every winter, until we could buy oor ain! He still sends mother a pair o' clogs once a year, on the day that father was killed, an' not a penny piece will he tak for them!'

'Bobby Frame must be a very fine man,' Sarah murmured, puzzled by Agnes's sudden revelations.

'Aye, he is a fine man! He overcame his ain troubles, an' he thocht o' other folks tae! So dinna ye fret yersel aboot oor wee master here. Maybe he isna made 'sactly like ither bairns, but he's no' a cripple, whativer folks say. I'm telling ye he'll manage fine, jist like your ain mother did; auld Mr Jardine reckoned she was the brawest woman i' all the parishes aroon' for all she couldna hear a word.' And with that Agnes rose briskly to her feet and whisked an imaginary fleck of dust from Sarah's dressing chest.

Later, as though to remind Sarah of her mother's indomitable courage, Agnes returned with the blue bowl which Mattie Cameron had brought all the way from Nethertannoch. It was filled with an assortment of autumn leaves and berries and the first flowering sprigs of winter jasmine, its little yellow stars glowing brightly amidst the autumn colours.

'Jist tae cheer ye up,' Agnes announced with a faint touch of embarrassment as she set the bowl upon a small table where Sarah would see it whenever she opened her eyes.

Try as she would Sarah could not keep her spirits high. She could hear the sounds of the busy household down below and the hustle of the dairy and she longed to be amidst the cheerful bustle, instead of languishing in her room, alone. She could not rid herself of feelings of guilt; she was convinced that she was entirely to blame for her baby's twisted feet.

After nearly a week of idleness Sarah could stand her own company no longer. She wanted to be where she was needed. Despite Agnes's efforts to remain calm and cheerful Sarah sensed that her hardworking maid must be harassed. She had seemed unusually flustered yesterday, and again this morning.

'It must be all the extra washing babies make, and running up and down stairs,' Sarah muttered to herself. 'And there's my own work to be done too.' Agnes was willing and capable, she thought gratefully, but it was time she relieved the poor girl and took up her own duties again.

That afternoon Sarah slipped quietly out of bed and crept across the room to gaze out of the window at the distant hills. The tide was coming in and she could see the gleam of the Solway Firth shining in the autumn sun. She had only been out of bed five minutes when Agnes came rushing up the stairs.

'Mistress Johnstone said ye werena to put a foot o'er the edge o' the bed for two whole weeks! Is there something ye're needing?'

'It's time I was back in the kitchen again . . .'

'Ye canna come doon yet! Anyway, Miss Beatrice is coming up the track. She'll be expecting tae visit an invalid.'

'I'm not an invalid!' Sarah declared firmly. 'After all cows and pigs have babies and they just go on as usual.'

'Mistress Sarah!' Agnes remonstrated in shocked tones. 'That's different!'

'I dinna see why.' Sarah grinned sheepishly. If she were honest she would have to admit that her legs felt like dandelion puffs and a breath of wind might blow away her wobbly knees. Instead she submitted without protest and climbed back into the big bed she shared with William. 'So I'm "Mistress" Sarah now?' she teased. Agnes blushed.

'Aye . . . weel I keep forgetting. I've kenned ye sae long as Miss Sarah, but noo that ye're a mother . . . an' all. We must all try an' remember . . . I was jist telling Janet the same thing this morn—'

'Aah yes, Janet. How is she? Is she managing to help you with the extra work in the dairy, Agnes . . . ?' Agnes pretended not to hear and avoided answering but Sarah was suddenly alert.

'Janet is helping with the churning, and milking some of my cows, isn't she Agnes? I know she must be busy with four children of her own, but she promised.'

'Och aye.' Agnes frowned and hesitated. 'She's helping as much as she can. 'Tis Louis.'

'Louis?' Sarah echoed sharply. 'What's wrong with Louis?'

'He's bin awfy sick . . .' Agnes's frown deepened. 'He couldna feed the pigs yesterday. Fair doubled up wi' pain he was.'

'Oh dear! Louis is never ill!' Sarah exclaimed in dismay. 'Who fed the pigs?'

'The Master.'

'Oh.' Sarah's tone was flat. William had never liked the smell of the pigs, or their noisy squealing manners.

'Louis seems better this morn, and Janet was oot for the milking, but he's awfy peely-wally still.'

'Was Janet not at the milking at all yesterday?' Sarah asked in dismay.

'No. She didna dare leave Louis. He was terrible sick, Miss Sarah!' Agnes gazed at her round-eyed. 'The Master helped wi' the milking tae . . .'

'Master Fairly helped in the byre!' Sarah echoed incredulously.

'No, no! 'Twas Master Logan . . .' Agnes flushed guiltily. 'I keep forgetting he's no' the Master at Fairlyden anymore. I'm sorry,' she mumbled. Sarah nodded.

'It's time I was back in my own dairy.'

'Oh no! Ye must dae as Mistress Johnstone said. Here's Miss Beatrice coming across the yard now. Carrying a parcel she is tae. Shall I bring her up tae see the wee fellow?' Sarah's eyes clouded momentarily, but she nodded.

She need not have worried. Beatrice seemed to consider her son a beautiful baby and she had sewn him a gown of finest linen and embroidered it with white flowers. Sarah knew the care and love which Beatrice had put into each tiny stitch and her eyes filled with tears. She blinked them away impatiently, but she saw Beatrice's look of surprise. Beatrice knew she had never been one to weep, or to show her deepest feelings.

'I canna think what's come over me!' Sarah muttered shakily. 'Tell me what's going on at the Mill House.'

'Weel, I dae have some news,' Beatrice admitted.

'Good news, I hope?'

'Some good,' Beatrice's eyes were soft, but then she frowned. 'But some bad news tae . . .'

Seven

'I— I've agreed tae marry Dick,' Beatrice announced shyly.

'But that's splendid news, Beattie!' Sarah exclaimed warmly. 'I'm sure you will both be very happy.'

'I do hope sae,' Beattie murmured fervently. 'Of course we must wait until I come out o' mourning. I— I hope I'll no' be a great disappointment as a wife, Sarah . . .' She came and sat beside the bed, looking anxiously into Sarah's face, seeking reassurance, yet unable to confess the dark secret which robbed her of her confidence and joy. Sarah understood a little of her apprehension, thanks to Jeannie Slater's confession. She took Beattie's hands and clasped them tightly.

'Dick is a good man. When he worked for my father, here at Fairlyden, he was always kind and gentle with all the animals, so I know he'll be good to a woman, especially his own wife. I'm sure he loves you, Beattie, and that's the most important thing of all. Dick is sensitive too. I suspect he has just as many doubts about himself as you do, since he's been in prison.'

'Och, I dinna care about that. Anyway it wasna his fault. If he hadna been sae sair provoked . . .'

Sarah nodded, but she changed the direction of the conversation quickly. She had no wish to be reminded of Lord James Fairly and there was no escaping the fact that he had been her husband's half-brother. 'What was your other news?'

Beatrice's face clouded. 'It's no' sae guid. Ye wadna think a man like Mr Sharpe at the Mains wad dae such a thing! He gave us a fine order for seeds and twae sickles and a scythe and a few other things. We thought he was being guid tae us, giving us his trade, but now he says he canna pay.'

'Oh, surely that canna be true, Beattie?'

'It is. I dinna ken what we'll dae. How can we buy more stock for the Store if we dinna get the money frae the customers?'

Sarah stared at her in consternation. 'If things are as bad as that for the Mains then what's to become of the rest of us?'

Beatrice could only shake her head. 'Maybe we shouldna be setting up a Farmers' Store at all if things are so bad.'

Sarah had little comfort to offer. She could scarcely believe that the biggest farm in Muircumwell parish could be in such trouble. Beatrice's news only added to her own conviction that she could not afford to languish in her bedchamber.

As soon as Beatrice had gone, she decided she would resume her work in the kitchen without delay, and she would begin by going downstairs this very afternoon. She had barely made her decision when Agnes burst into the bedroom in a flurry of excitement.

'Mr Bradshaw is here! I told him ye werena tae set foot down the stairs, but he looked ever sae disappointed, and he's brought ye the biggest flowers I ever did see, Mistress Sarah! Shall I gie him a message?'

'I always enjoy Mr Bradshaw's cheerful company, and his guid common sense. I wonder why my father didna mention that he was visiting the Tower House,' Sarah mused. 'I've missed his visits recently. Help me into my clothes please, Agnes. I'll come down.'

'Mercy me, Mistress Sarah! Ye canna dae that!'

'I need to get my strength back, and Mr Bradshaw will cheer me up. Dinna look so shocked,' she added with a laugh as she struggled into her undergarments and petticoats, before pulling on a blue muslin day dress. It was old, but it was clean and comfortable, for she had not yet regained her trim figure. Even dressing, and brushing her long thick hair seemed to exhaust her. Consequently she was less particular than usual and several small curls escaped around her temples and over her smooth white brow.

'Oh,' she groaned softly. 'I thought I was strong as a horse while I was lying abed!'

Agnes was firmly convinced that Sarah would regain her strength instantly, as though by magic, but only when the prescribed two weeks' confinement was up. She frowned her disapproval.

Sarah entered the familiar kitchen on legs which seemed extraordinarily wobbly. She was far more flustered than Agnes had been when she recognised her visitor. She had expected to see Bert Bradshaw, the blunt but kindly Yorkshireman who had bought the Strathtod Estate after Lord James Fairly's death. Instead she was astonished to find it was his son, pacing backwards and forwards across the rag rug in the kitchen. Since her marriage to William she had rarely seen Crispin Bradshaw, but she recalled their first meeting clearly. It had been on her wedding day. She remembered the strange quiver she had experienced when she encountered his penetrating grey eyes. He had such shrewd yet kindly eyes, strangely shadowed as though with sadness, or regret; yet in an instant they were alert, wary; then again they were alight with quiet laughter, like sunshine on a pool of clear water. As she faced him now, across the hearth, Sarah felt those eyes upon her.

Sarah would have been amazed to know how often she had been in his thoughts as the time for the birth of her child drew nearer. Crispin Bradshaw had vowed he would never marry; he would never ask any woman to endure the agonies of childbirth, or suffer grief such as his father, and Sandy Logan, had suffered when birth was so swiftly followed by the death of a beloved woman.

Sarah Fairly was thinner and paler than he remembered; yet she had come through the trauma of birth as admirably as his father had predicted. Indeed Crispin found she disturbed him more than he had believed possible. Her clear skin seemed almost translucent, for it was more finely drawn over her high cheekbones; it made her eyes seem darker and wider than ever and the escaping curls of her brown hair softened her appearance in a way he had never dreamed of. He found himself wondering how it would look when unbraided, streaming down her back in wild profusion, like a young girl's.

The calm, efficient owner of one of the best run woollen mills in Yorkshire brought his thoughts to an abrupt halt as Sarah sank gratefully on to the oak settle beside the fire. A slight flush stained her cheeks and Crispin realised he had been regarding her more closely than was mannerly when she tossed her head and regarded him with a spark of defiance. Her fine dark brows were curved like two question marks, but an uncertain smile hovered around her mouth.

'You are well enough to come downstairs, Mistress Fairly? Your maid—'

'Och, Agnes fusses, but she means well. My muscles will have wasted completely if I dinna move. Besides,' she smiled almost mischievously, 'I'm longing for a bowl o' good porridge and my own wee bowl o' cream. Indeed I believe I could eat a horse!' She blushed faintly but her eyes sparkled. 'I expected to see your father. We speak the same plain language, even if we do have different accents. Perhaps I should choose my words, and thoughts, more carefully for you, Mr Bradshaw . . . ?'

'Indeed no. I am relieved to hear you are recovering your appetite so well. I shall tell my father.'

'I never lost it.' She smiled wryly and added in a conspiratorial voice, 'but Agnes and Mrs Johnstone seem to think I shouldna get hungry if I'm only lying in bed. Agnes said you brought me some flowers. It was kind of you. I miss walking round my garden and . . . Oh!' she breathed with delight as Agnes carried in a large vase containing eight or ten chrysanthemums with huge shaggy bronze heads. 'They're beautiful!'

A faint colour stained her visitor's lean face. The flowers had been grown in the new conservatory which was his father's pride and joy. Bert Bradshaw had hinted strongly that Sarah would appreciate some of his blooms.

'I am glad you like them,' he said simply. 'Now tell me, how is your son? Your father swears he has grown already!'

'My father exaggerates!' Sarah grinned with delight, 'but wee Alex feeds well and he is thriving and content.' Her brown eyes clouded. It was impossible to forget Alex's deformity. Unbelievably Sarah felt her eyes fill with tears. She blinked rapidly and turned away, thoroughly ashamed of such weakness. She sniffed determinedly. 'D-did my father also tell you my son is— is . . .' She could not bring herself to describe her healthy, happy bairn as 'crippled'. William had no such reservations. Neither Sarah nor her visitor had heard him enter the kitchen.

'A cripple!' His voice rang out clearly, startling them both. 'You will have to accept it, my dear Sarah.'

'Mr Logan told me only that his grandson's feet turn inwards. That does not make a child a cripple surely, if he is perfectly normal in every other respect?' Crispin Bradshaw looked severely at William, then his keen gaze moved to Sarah and she saw the light of challenge in his eyes. 'Your father believes he will learn to walk almost as quickly as any other child, and in the direction he wants to go, no matter if his feet do turn east and west!'

'I pray he will!' Sarah murmured fervently.

'He is a cripple. The fact cannot be denied.' William insisted. 'We must face it!' William looked directly at Sarah. Her own guilt made her imagine accusation, even condemnation, in her husband's eyes and her face paled. Yet when she raised her head she met Crispin Bradshaw's level, grey-eyed stare. There was no sympathy in his gaze. Indeed there was a hidden fire, as though he were willing her to deny that her son was a cripple. Her father was right, if she treated Alex as a cripple everyone at Fairlyden would follow her example. She did not want her son to be pampered, and neither did she want him to be regarded as a freak.

'Alex will not always be a babe . . .' she reminded William with a flash of anger. 'He will grow strong in mind, and in body, and perhaps his feet will not be so noticeable as he grows bigger!'

'He will not give in easily if he had his mother's spirit,' Crispin declared with approval.

Once again Sarah had the feeling that strength and confidence were flowing out to her from his steady gaze. She would need both, for Alex's sake. William frowned and turned away. Sarah's heart sank. She loved her husband dearly; she knew how much their son's deformity had distressed him, how he had longed for a fine healthy boy. She knew he was disappointed and frustrated. Pray God she would be able to give him other sons: normal, healthy sons. She was unaware of Crispin Bradshaw watching her closely, or of the disturbing emotions her pensive face aroused in him.

He was almost relieved when she enquired after his sisters. He dragged his thoughts back to his own family.

'Fanny is enjoying her new life as Mistress Smith, and spending a great deal of money furnishing her new house in London.'

'And Freda? She is well, I hope. She has not visited the Tower House recently?'

'No.' Crispin smiled wryly. He was fond of both of his sisters, but Freda was the youngest and she was abominably spoiled. 'She spends much of her time in London with Fanny whenever Eric is away from home. She enjoys the theatres and the parties, but Father misses her lively company. He is planning to hold a party at Strathtod so that Freda might be persuaded to spend some time with him there. And speaking of my father,' he smiled, 'it is high time I returned to the Tower House.'

Sarah nodded. 'Please thank him for sending me some of his precious blooms. They are truly magnificent.' She held out her hand and felt Crispin's firm clasp, before William walked with him to the yard.

A week later Sarah was working in the dairy. Her usual vigour had not returned as rapidly as she had expected. She had always enjoyed churning, but she was dismayed to find the task left her exhausted. She was glad of Agnes's help to carry the clear, cold water from the spring to wash the golden grains of butter, although the cooler weather meant the butter was easier to work and to keep fresh.

The rest of the winter farmwork was falling behind and it troubled her. She had known Louis all her life and she realised now that she had taken his good health and strength, and his willingness, for granted, until the recent bouts of sickness. He was a vital part of the Fairlyden she knew and loved. She remembered how stunned they had all been when Dick was whisked away to prison without warning, but Louis had worked doubly hard to make up for his absence, and again after her father's accident. Although William had helped with the harvest that year, and subsequently taken her father's place as Master of Fairlyden, Sarah knew in her heart that he had neither the strength nor the interest to carry out all the tasks her father had undertaken.

Louis had suffered another alarming spasm that very morning. It had prompted her to insist that Janet should send for Doctor Kerr.

'What did the doctor say?' she asked now as Louis's wife came to the dairy door.

'He didna say much at all,' Janet confessed uneasily. 'He left a white powder for him tae take when the pain is bad.' Janet's brow puckered. She looked white and worried and there were dark circles under her eyes. 'He— he looked awfy grave, Miss Sarah,' she said fearfully.

'Doctor Kerr cares for his patients. You must make sure Louis takes the powder and we'll all pray that it cures him,' Sarah said gently. 'You can tell him that Master Fairly realises how hard he has been working. He agrees we must hire another man. Dick has made up his mind not to return.'

'Ye've asked him tae return tae Fairlyden then, Miss Sarah?'

'Aye,' Sarah flushed. She would not tell Janet that Dick had refused because William was now the Master; he could not bring himself to work for a Fairly. Yet he had known William all his life; he must know her husband bore no resemblance to his half-brother, Lord James Fairly, who had caused Dick and his family so much grief and anguish.

'Dick doesna want to leave the mill,' she told Janet. 'Master Fairly will hire another man, but we shall have to manage until the May hirings.'

'Does that mean we'll hae tae move frae oor wee hoose?' Janet's face turned whiter than ever.

'No! Of course not!'

Relief shone in Janet's eyes. 'I mind when Master Logan built the cottage, specially for Louis and me tae get married,' she murmured reminiscently. 'Aye, we've had oor ups and doons, Miss Sarah. I wad hate tae leave Fairlyden noo, but I ken Master Fairly has nae ither hoose if he hires a man wi' a wife and bairns.'

'Maybe he will hire a single man then.'

'Aye,' Janet summoned a faint smile. 'I'll tell Louis that. Though it isna the hard work that worries him. He enjoys it all when he's well. D'ye mind how you an' me an' Agnes went tae the field tae shaw the neeps last winter, while Louis loaded them intae the carts, Miss Sarah?'

'Yes. It was hard work bending and pulling and cutting off the tops, and it's always so bitterly cold!' Sarah smiled.

'Aye, ye've a better job this year, looking after the wee Master. How is he? He'll no' be sleeping through the nicht yet? Maggie's aye wantin' tae come in tae see him, but I tell her no' tae bother ye. She's that fond o' bairns for all she's the oldest o' oor four.'

'Alex doesna sleep all night yet but he's content. Tell Maggie she can come to see him whenever she likes. She's a good lassie.'

At first it seemed Doctor Kerr's white powder had worked its magic cure on Louis, until William found him doubled up with pain and clinging to the shafts of the cart for support. Everyone at Fairlyden shared Janet's concern.

'That's the Reverend Mackenzie's trap,' Agnes panted one morning a few days later, as she set down the two pails of water she had just carried from the burn. 'Shall I finish the dairy, Miss Sarah?'

'I expect the Minister will call to see Louis at the cottage first,' Sarah murmured anxiously. 'I'm sure Janet will be comforted by his visit. She has known him since she worked at the manse when she was just a girl.'

'Aye,' Agnes agreed soberly. 'Poor Louis will be needin' all oor prayers. I dinna ken what Fairlyden wad dae withoot him. I expect the Minister will want tae see Master Alex as weel though. He's aye been a great man wi' the bairnies, for all he has none o' his ain.'

'Aye, he's a fine man,' Sarah smiled despite her anxiety over Louis Whiteley. She had known the Reverend Mackenzie all her life and he had always managed to bring her comfort when she was most in need, but he was no longer young himself. 'I'll away through to the kitchen and push the swey over the fire, Agnes, and change my apron. No doubt the Minister will be glad of a cup of tea.'

'Aye, he will that, an' a wee bit o' your new baked scone,' Agnes chuckled. 'I'm thinking he was jist waiting 'til ye were at the baking yoursel' again.'

The Reverend Robert Mackenzie cared about all his parishioners and he had been deeply troubled when Doctor Kerr admitted that he was at a loss to know what else to do for Louis. The Minister had offered earnest prayers, but even his faith in the Almighty was shaken at the sight of Louis's pain-ravaged face and the dark shadows beneath Janet's eyes.

Eventually he found himself at Fairlyden and as he walked along the familiar stone-flagged passage which led directly into the kitchen, he was feeling unutterably weary. He was pleased to see Sarah had the kettle boiling ready for a cup of tea. How like her dear mama she had grown of late, he thought. His own strength had failed since the days when he walked, or rode, along the old four-mile track beside the burn to visit his old friend Daniel Munro, and Mattie Cameron, the deaf girl who had become his bride. He sighed and looked at Sarah.

Despite the trauma of childbirth she looked young and fresh, with her welcoming smile and her warm dark eyes. Her smile wavered slightly when he enquired about her baby son, but she lifted Alex from his crib beside the fire and slowly opened his shawl and unpinned his flannel petticoats, apparently unsurprised by his request. Sarah watched as he took each tiny foot in his hands, just as her father had done, gently massaging and manipulating them, but when he looked up his lined face was filled with compassion.

'The right foot is not so twisted as I had feared when William described his son's condition,' he said slowly. 'I have seen the trouble before. Two of the children I recall were much worse than wee Alex here.'

'You know other children who are . . . like this?' Sarah asked incredulously.

'Oh yes.'

'I can scarce believe it. 'I— I thought it must be my fault.'

'Of course it is not your fault, Sarah!'

'I'm sure William thinks it is, and then I feel angry and resentful with him! And yet— and yet in my heart I know I'm to blame . . .' she admitted in a subdued voice.

'William would never think such a thing. How could you possibly cause your child's feet to turn in the wrong direction, Sarah? It is madness to torture yourself with such thoughts.'

'I disobeyed my husband. I went to the mill.' Her face grew pale at the memory of that day. 'When I look at wee Alex, I know he'll suffer for it, then my guilt is a heavy load to bear alone. I know you will keep my confidence.'

'Sarah!' The Minister was dismayed. 'Whatever happened at the mill, I am sure you torture yourself without cause. No one understands why God makes so many apparently perfect children, when he gives others a burden to bear from the cradle to the grave.'

'It wasna God's doing! It was the devil himself – Edward Slater! He trussed me like a fowl for the cooking pot, and he hoisted me to the top of the mill with the pulley!' Sarah's voice broke and she choked back a sob.

'Oh my dear Sarah,' Robert Mackenzie murmured with compassion. 'I am glad you have confided in me. Your guilt is unnecessary. No doubt

Edward Slater hurt you, but I doubt if he hurt your child. No one knows why these things happen. It is God's will.'

Sarah stared at him then a slow smile began to lighten her troubled dark eyes. 'You really believe that?'

'I do, just as I know that God will give Alex many gifts to compensate for his affliction.'

'Thank you, oh, thank you.' Sarah smiled tremulously and her eyes were bright with tears of gratitude. 'I am truly glad you found the strength to visit Fairlyden today.'

The Reverend Mackenzie smiled. Soon he would reach his three score years and ten and he often wondered how much longer God would keep him for His servant. He had seen many troubles in his long life. Today Sarah's sweet smile and shining eyes made even his most difficult tasks seem worthwhile. He could almost forget the aching of his old bones as the pony and trap rattled over the rutted track back to the manse. He hoped fervently that his prayers for Louis Whiteley would be answered.

Beatrice and Dick O'Connor were planning a quiet wedding a year after Jeannie Slater's death. Beatrice alternated between tranquil happiness and near despair, but Dick's gentle manner usually reassured her. He sensed that she was troubled by more than the usual nervousness of becoming a bride and he tried to convince her that few men treated their wives as Slater had treated her own mother. The mention of her father's name made her more tense than ever.

Unfortunately they had other troubles to contend with, as Sarah discovered when Beatrice visited Fairlyden on a cold blustery day at the end of March.

'Mr Sharpe hasna paid the money he owes us yet,' Beatrice confided as soon as she and Sarah were alone together.

'I canna understand why things are in such a state at the Mains,' Sarah frowned. 'The Sharpes dinna even have a rent to find. Mistress Sharpe's father bought the farm for them when they married, or so I believe.'

'It isna just the Sharpes,' Beatrice admitted. 'Last week a man came tae see us. He said he was an agent, collecting debts for one o' the merchants. He was a horrible man. He insisted on looking round the old mill, and even in the hoose! He asked lots o' questions. He wanted tae ken what Dick had done with the grinding stones and the other machinery frae the mill.'

'But I thought everything was too worn to be any use?'

'That's true. Ma— ma father neglected it all,' Beattie muttered bitterly. 'We told the agent but he didna believe us. Dick got indignant. He asked the man who had sent him. We'd never heard o' him, and we've never bought goods frae Liverpool. That's where the merchant is supposed tae be! The man called Dick a liar, aye and a cheat, in front o' twae customers! Now there's rumours spreading around that we canna pay our debts. The agent seemed tae ken Dick has been in prison and he said he wad end up there again . . . Oh, Sarah, I dinna ken what tae dae!'

Sarah gasped indignantly. 'There's nobody more honest than you and Dick!'

'I ken. We dinna owe a farthing tae any o' the merchants. Dick is afraid o' getting intae debt! But we really need more stock tae get customers . . .'

'Surely everything would be all right if Mr Sharpe paid up?'

'Maybe,' Beatrice shrugged helplessly. 'But since the agent's visit Dick thinks he wad only be a burden tae me because people will aye remember he's been in prison.' She gave a hiccupping sob.

Sarah moved across the hearth and knelt beside her, gently stroking her soft fair hair. She didn't know what to say. She could not offer enough money to help. Even with their share of the stallion fees there was little enough left by the time they had paid for the land they rented from Mr Bradshaw, and found the six-monthly wages for Louis and Agnes; then there was food and clothes and the blacksmith to pay, maybe a new pail to buy, or a wheelbarrow, or the other necessary items which always seemed to wear out when they could least afford to replace them. Sarah sighed.

'D'you still love Dick?'

'Of course I dae!' Beatrice's blue eyes flashed.

'Then you must tell him so. And he needs to remind Mr Sharpe about the money! Maybe he's forgotten . . . ?'

'He's been tae the Mains twice, but he hates tae bother Mr Sharpe when his wife is so ill. Ye'll have heard she's dying, Sarah?'

'No! I didna realise she's so bad!'

'They say she is bleeding, and in great pain. It is hard for a man like Dick tae pester at such a time.'

'Aye, I can understand that. Maybe my father would know what to do, if you dinna mind me telling him . . . ? I know he saves some of the money he earns as Mr Bradshaw's factor. Perhaps he could help you.'

'No! I— I mean I dinna mind ye asking Mr Logan's advice. Grandfather Miller aye said he was a wise man, but we canna take his money.'

'I understand,' Sarah nodded. Beatrice was very proud and independent, but if Alexander Logan knew the truth . . . if he really was Beattie's father . . . he would want to help, Sarah was certain of that.

Eight

Sandy Logan was saddened when he heard Sarah's report on Mistress Sharpe's health even though he had little reason to like her. He clearly recalled the year he had laboured at Mains of Muir as a young man; she had been as mean and peevish with him as with her maids. It was true she had mellowed and entertained him as an equal once he had earned respect as a breeder of Clydesdale horses, but in his heart Sandy could not admire her. Nevertheless he was sorry to hear of her pain and suffering. He was also disturbed by the news that Abraham Sharpe was in debt.

'Beatrice and Dick O'Conner will never build up their business if people like the Sharpes refuse to pay their debts,' Sarah declared.

Sandy frowned. 'I canna understand it. Abraham Sharpe isna a man tae take advantage, whatever his faults.'

'If a place like Mains of Muir is in trouble, what hope is there for Fairlyden?' Sarah demanded anxiously.

Sandy shook his head. 'Some o' the smaller tenants on Strathtod Estate are struggling, even though Mr Bradshaw has reduced their rents. Even the bigger ones are refusing tae buy lime, or repair the drains and fences, even though they ken such things are needed if there's tae be a future on the land for them and their bairns.'

'But you said the Sharpes owned their land.'

'Aye,' Sandy mused thoughtfully. 'There's nearly three hundred acres, and all of it good pasture, except for the black, mossy land nearer the Solway Firth. I canna understand how Abraham can be in debt.'

'Well, Agnes says he canna afford to keep all his workers. Her brother, Nicky, is still talking of going to America to find work. It seems the men in Parliament dinna care so long as the industrialists get cheap food for their labourers,' Sarah suggested anxiously. 'William had an argument with Crispin Bradshaw about it.'

'Mmm, but the Bradshaws are different. Most industrialists seem tae want other countries tae dump their grain and beef in Britain so that they can sell their ain iron and steel and machinery abroad.'

'William says there's wonderful opportunities in America and Canada. That's why thousands of Scottish men and women have emigrated.'

Sandy looked sharply at his beloved daughter.

'Does— does William talk o' going back there? Is— is that what's on your mind, Sarah . . .?'

'No, Father!' Sarah sounded shocked at the idea. 'I'll never leave

Fairlyden, no matter how hard we have to work. This will always be my home,' she added softly.

Sandy smiled then and felt himself relax. 'I'm glad, lassie.' His voice was husky, then he added more briskly, 'I think I might ride over tae the Mains tomorrow, after church.'

'Well, if anyone can persuade Mr Sharpe to pay Beattie and Dick, I'm sure you can, Father,' Sarah smiled with relief.

Abraham Sharpe was pleased to see Sandy, and eager to talk. He had no family of his own and despite his wife's ranting and carping Sandy began to realise how badly Sharpe was missing her help and guidance.

'I have cows, and horses and pigs, but I dinna have the money to buy food for them,' he admitted frankly, almost with a touch of bewilderment. 'I have land, but I canna afford labour tae work it, or tae buy lime and seeds anymore . . .' Once the subject was mentioned Sandy found it easy to discuss Dick O'Connor and Beatrice.

'Aah dear me!' Sharpe muttered with genuine regret. 'I didna think o' Dick's reputation.' He pursed his lips and his eyes held a look of pain. 'I havena been able to think o' much else but Florrie recently. I know she aye had a quick tongue, and maybe she was a bit mean wi' the maids, but och, it's terrible tae see her suffer! The funny thing is she never grumbles now.' Sandy waited patiently, for Abraham was talking almost to himself and his feelings for his wife were sincere. At last he added, 'I'm real sorry for the trouble I've caused young Dick, aye and Joseph Miller's granddaughter. She's a fine lassie. I wadna want tae hurt her. But I dinna have the money to pay, you see, Sandy.' He frowned. 'Things have been getting worse at the Mains for some time now.'

'Weel, I suppose it's not surprising if ye're still keeping all the old cows the way you used to do just tae make the farm look prosperous. Ye'll need tae start selecting the ones with most milk. It's no guid feeding twenty if ye can get as much milk frae sixteen better beasts!'

'Weel, ye aye said that, but ye see Sandy, Florrie never milked herself and she liked tae see plenty o' cows i' the fields, and we used tae manage all right . . .'

'Yes, but things are no' sae easy now with the prices falling, and ye're causing troubles for other folk.'

'If ye'll give me a month . . .?' His voice suddenly sounded hoarse. His face had grown strangely pale and there were lines of strain around his eyes and mouth which Sandy had never noticed before. 'Aye,' he sighed heavily, 'a month . . . maybe less . . . I'll pay all my debts then.'

'All? D'ye mean ye've more?'

Abraham nodded miserably.

Sandy sighed. 'Weel, I dinna understand how ye'll get the money then, if ye canna get it now, but if ye're sure . . .?'

'Oh aye,' Sharpe sighed again. 'I'll get the money then, even if I end up in the workhouse . . .' he added almost under his breath.

At first Sandy thought he was making a poor attempt at humour, until he saw a suspicion of tears in the older man's eyes. He stared in consternation at the man who had once employed him for a pittance, but his heart was filled with sympathy.

'I could loan ye enough tae pay the Farmers' Store, but ye must promise tae pay right away, and no' tae tell them where ye got the money. Dick's had a hard enough time, and he's proud, but it wad be a pity tae ruin their wee business afore they've had a chance.'

'Aah, Sandy, ye were always a guid laddie!' Sharpe sighed with relief.

'I'm no' a laddie any longer!' Sandy retorted with a wry grin, adding proudly, 'I'm a grandfather!'

'Ach well, I'll no' forget what ye've done for me this day. And call me Abraham, will ye?' He held out his hand and Sandy took it. He felt strangely sad for the man who had once boasted of owning the best farm in Muircumwell parish.

Just over a fortnight later Sandy attended the funeral of Florrie Sharpe and he knew Abraham had honoured him as a true friend when he offered him one of the cords to lower her coffin into its last resting place.

At the end of April Abraham Sharpe settled his debts in full, all except his debt to Alexander Logan. That became a private arrangement between them. No one knew how he had obtained the money. Many speculated that his wife had left a secret hoard of golden guineas, but Sandy knew Florrie Sharpe had denied herself many of the small comforts which would have eased her last weeks on earth. Sadly it soon became clear that Abraham Sharpe's new wealth was strictly limited when he told Nick Jamieson, his best horseman, he could no longer afford to employ him. He advised Nick to present himself at the May hiring fair to look for other work.

Agnes knew how restless and frustrated Nick had grown; she guessed her brother would try to find a ship to work his passage to America, or Canada. Already he had talked of sending for Sally McKie, his childhood sweetheart, but the mere prospect of journeying to the docks terrified the girl, who had never left her own parish. Betty Jamieson fretted at the thought of never seeing her only son again. They all blamed Abraham Sharpe.

Changes were also imminent at Fairlyden. Sarah suspected she might be unable to carry out all her usual work with the cows and hens by the end of the year. Louis's bouts of sickness seemed to have abated but he was not so robust as he had been and the acute pain in his stomach returned at intervals. Consequently William had had more than he desired of working with the pigs and other daily tasks. He was not content to stay at home and work as Sandy Logan had done.

'I enjoy taking the stallions out, but I am not cut out to be a labourer any more than I was meant to be a minister of the church,' he declared wryly one evening when Sarah was sitting by the fire, busily knitting minute woollen vests for Alex.

'No one expects you to be a labourer, William,' she smiled serenely.

'Maybe not, but there is too much work for Louis. I realise that now. I've been wondering about Jamieson? Agnes has already proved that he comes from a hard-working family. He is young and strong and a good horseman, I believe. There is just one problem. I hear he wants to get married,' William finished gloomily.

'Can you blame him for that then?' Sarah asked with a mischievous grin.

'No, except that it would cost at least sixty-five pounds to build another cottage, even if we built it on to the end of the Whiteleys'. We don't have sixty-five pounds,' he grimaced.

Sandy had been smoking quietly by the fireside. He always supervised the care of his own horses at Fairlyden but otherwise he rarely interfered unless William or Sarah asked for advice. Now he took his pipe out of his mouth and tapped it gently against the palm of his hand.

'Mr Bradshaw offered me the factor's house at Strathtod,' he remarked. 'If ye want to give Nick my room I wad move . . .?'

'Oh no, Father, you canna leave Fairlyden!' Sarah's instant reply warmed Sandy's heart, but he lookd at William, a question in his eyes.

'Jamieson will need more than a room, and Sarah is right, Fairlyden was your home long before it was ours. Anyway,' he grinned ruefully, 'we need your advice as much as the rest of Bert Bradshaw's tenants. Sometimes I think I should change places with Dick O'Connor! Even now his two cows and his pigs are his first concern, yet he has no instinct for driving a bargain. I'm sure there is a great opportunity at the Old Mill.'

'Dick's heart was aye with his animals,' Sandy smiled. 'I'm a bit the same myself and I confess I dinna want tae leave Fairlyden, William. But if ye really want Nicky Jamieson ye wad need to call on him soon. He's a guid man and he has initiative. I could ask Bert Bradshaw if Nick can use the old shepherd's cottage at the head o' the burn. It's a wee bit far away and it's needing some repairs, but I believe Nick wad soon make it weatherproof, and I dinna think he'll mind walking tae Fairlyden every morning – not if it means he can get married anyway. He could cut across the burn most o' the time – except when it's in spate. Nae doubt ye'd give him his midday meal, Sarah?'

'Yes, of course. Agnes would be delighted. So would Mistress Jamieson, if Nick settles down with Sally and forgets about America! I hope Mr Bradshaw will agree to let him use the cottage.'

At the Old Mill Farmers' Store the agent's malicious gossip had damaged Dick's reputation and the trade had suffered. Also there was little demand for cattle cake in spring and summer. Only the pigs required meal purchased from the Store; oats, grass and turnip seeds had all been sown, and few farmers had placed orders for lime. Trade seemed to be at an end until the harvest came round again. Dick was despondent.

Ironically it was William Fairly who came to his aid again. Despite his stubborn refusal to work at Fairlyden, Dick listened to his suggestions and he worked hard, converting two of the old out-houses into a separate store to be used for coal and firewood. When it was ready Dick took the horse and cart to the railway station whenever a coal train was due. Coal extended the trade to customers beyond the farming community, to villagers and widows and cottagers. Dick never considered an order too small and people soon appreciated the advantage of having coal and firewood delivered in quantities they could afford. Although summer was approaching most of the women needed a fire to cook and boil water and customers slowly increased.

Beatrice had listened to William and Dick discussing plans. Now she added a few ideas of her own. Soon the Old Mill Store was supplying almost anything from two-pronged forks to four-pronged ones, from shovels to hoes, and ropes to rakes. In the winter they hoped to regain their trade in animal feed and oatmeal, and maybe in potatoes, but meanwhile their meagre income had been sustained; Dick's confidence had been restored. His dream of making Beatrice his wife became a reality.

It was the beginning of June, 1884, when Beatrice Slater changed her name to O'Connor. She prayed she would be able to cast off the past as well as the name she had grown to hate. The wedding was a simple affair in the Muircumwell Church. Although Beatrice was twenty-six she appeared more nervous than the youngest and most virginal of brides. She had begged Sarah to be her attendant.

Sarah obligingly let out the seams of her best blue dress and adjusted the bustle; after the skilful addition of one or two new bows no one, except her own husband, suspected that her young body was once more swelling with new life, although Alex was not yet nine months old and still suckling. This time William had guessed her secret from its very beginning and the sharing of their hopes and dreams had brought a new understanding and tenderness to their marriage. Such contentment and good health gave Sarah a glow which the London society ladies would have envied.

Sandy had been surprised and touched when Beatrice diffidently asked if he would lead her down the aisle and give her hand in marriage. Beatrice had been shy about making such a request and it had taken all Sarah's powers of persuasion to give her the necessary courage; it was her most earnest wish that Beatrice should be given away by her own father, even though neither of them knew of their relationship.

Ever since Jeannie Slater's death Sarah had tried to forget the secret which had been thrust upon her. She had continued to think of Beatrice as her dearest friend, as indeed she was. Yet as she followed her down the aisle Sarah was struck anew by the knowledge that they were sisters. She wished passionately that she could tell Beatrice. Why, she wondered for the umpteenth time, had Mistress Slater kept Alexander Logan from his own child? What strange events had coloured her past? Why had she allowed someone as gentle, and as sensitive, as Beatrice to believe she was the daughter of a fiend like Slater?

Several times Sarah had been tempted to confide in the Reverend Mackenzie, to seek his advice as she had so often done in the past, but the minister was an old man now with the burdens of so many people weighing on his stooping shoulders. Yet she was irked by the promise she had made to Jeannie Slater. Surely a man had a right to know, and love, his own daughter? Sarah had ample proof that Alexander Logan would never have shirked his duty, indeed he would have been proud of his daughter, especially today. Beatrice looked truly beautiful with her golden curls, and skin as delicate as the prettiest summer rose. If her red lips drooped a little sadly, and if apprehensive shadows darkened her blue eyes, then Sarah chose to ignore them. She prayed fervently that Dick O'Connor would succeed in banishing the unhappy memories of Beatrice's youth.

Sarah could not have guessed at the aching tenderness which filled her father's heart as he led Beatrice towards the altar on that summer's day. In truth Sandy could scarcely understand his own emotions. He simply felt there was some invisible, inexplicable bond between himself and the slender young woman who walked so gracefully at his side, whose haunting blue eyes reminded him of his own mother.

Joey Slater was the only one of Beatrice's brothers to attend her wedding. Now happily married himself, his good wishes for Beatrice and Dick were sincere. He had brought a new fender with a small leather-topped stool on either end, with matching fire irons. He had made them himself for a wedding present. Beatrice blushed painfully when he laughingly declared, 'I've been picturing your bairnies perched on each side o' the Mill House fire, Beattie.' Then his mischievous blue eyes had sobered briefly and he added sadly, 'I hope they'll be better bairns than we were, and that they bring ye happiness, lass. Eddie and me, and the rest o' us lads . . . well we must hae made your life miserable, when we were all at home, eh . . .? Wull especially! He causes trouble wherever he is!'

Earlier Joe had frankly admired Dick's hard work in repairing the old mill buildings to make them secure from wind and rain, and his stoicism in striving to make a living in the face of so many adversities.

'I shall write to Bert and Jamie when I get home. They'll be pleased to know the old place is still here, even though they'll never see it again. I dinna ken where Wull went after oor Eddie and Jock were killed. I ken Bert was glad when he left them in peace.' Joe sighed as he reminisced about his brothers. 'Wull is just like Father. He even stirred up trouble with the Indians, as well as with the white ranchers. I hope he never turns up on my doorstep!'

'I've nae desire to see Wull either!' Beatrice grimaced, 'but I'm pleased ye came today, Joey, and I'm glad the boys are doing well in America. Please give them our best regards . . .' she looked shyly up at Dick as he came to take her arm again.

Sarah caught her father's eye and smiled. It was good to see Beatrice and Dick so happy together. She could only pray that their future at the Farmers' Store would be prosperous enough to keep them fed and clothed, and in good health; few people in Muircumwell expected more, and even in the little country parish, there were those who struggled to survive on less. In the dirty, overcrowded towns, many succumbed to the unequal battle despite the prosperity of the iron masters and factory owners. Sarah had heard Crispin Bradshaw criticising the conditions under which men, women and children existed. She knew it was his ambition to improve the lot of his own workers.

Sarah and William's second child, William Jonathan Fairly, was born at the beginning of December. Sarah had kept in good health throughout the months of waiting. Nicky Jamieson was now married to Sally, his childhood sweetheart and he seemed content to work at Fairlyden, despite the three-mile walk to his cottage at each end of the day. Although William had hired him as a ploughman and general worker he had understood the importance of healthy cattle and pigs since boyhood, and he had learned to milk at his mother's knee. He was proud of the pair of horses which had been entrusted to his care, and he preferred working in the fields, but he was willing, and able, to turn his hand to most of the tasks around Fairlyden. Consequently Sarah's life was less fraught during William's frequent absences, although she never missed the milking until the morning her baby was born.

The falling prices of eggs and butter remained her greatest anxiety. Sometimes butter had to be brought back from the market, or sold to the merchants, who waited like vultures to buy it up and cart it off to the cities to sell at an excessive profit. Sarah knew that her only weapon was to produce the best quality possible and get it to the markets early. It was imperative that the eggs and butter should provide for the household's requirements, from oil and candles, to food, clothes, boots and coal. If anything remained it was put into a wooden box ready for the winter slump, and to help pay the cash wages at the end of May and November. The money from the pigs and from their small flock of sheep was needed to buy turnips, oats and grass seeds, and when any remained Louis was dispatched with the horse and cart to bring lime.

It troubled Sarah when her father used the money he earned from his horses to pay Mr Bradshaw for Fairlyden's rented acres.

'Ach lassie,' Sandy smiled fondly, 'Fairlyden is still my hame. The rent is my payment for the trouble I gie ye. I'm better off now than I've been all my life!'

'You know very well you're no trouble!' Sarah smiled. 'But you still work hard and you might need your own money some day, Father.'

'Och I save most o' the money frae my work as Mr Bradshaw's factor so dinna worry, lassie. I'm pleased tae keep my horses here at Fairlyden and tae bide wi' ye.'

Ray Jardine, at the Muircumwell General Store was less willing to purchase the Fairlyden butter than his father had been. He was not averse to stocking a poorer quality if he could get a cheaper product. Also Sarah suspected he had guessed William was responsible for encouraging Beatrice and Dick to open up the old mill as a Farmers' Store and he resented any threat of competition.

Sarah tried not to allow the niggles of everyday life to intrude on her brief respite when Billy was born. Alex was still only fourteen months old but he appointed himself as a small devoted guardian almost from the hour of his brother's birth. He made valiant attempts to walk unaided. It made Sarah's heart ache to see his small feet tripping one over the other as she lay watching him making his progress around her firelit bedroom. Alex never gave up. When he fell, he picked himself up cheerfully, or dragged, pulled and crawled his way towards his chosen goal, usually his mother's bedside, or the wooden crib in which his infant brother slept so soundly, for Billy was a happy and contented baby.

This time Sarah enjoyed her confinement as the grey clouds scudded across the December sky, and the flames shot up the bedroom chimney. She knew she had much to be thankful for now that she had leisure to watch Alex's antics, to listen to his childish chirruping, and marvel at the words he had learned without any apparent effort, or help from anyone. His dark eyes would regard her gravely, then his rosebud lips would attempt to frame each word she uttered. If she laughed aloud, he chortled merrily as well. When her attention was taken with feeding Billy, Alex would lie on his back on the rag rug in front of the bedroom fire and intently examine his toes; sometimes he sprawled on his stomach and tried to pull out the brightest pieces of the rug which Sarah and Agnes had made with such painstaking care on winter evenings.

When Alex was tired after his day's childish ploys he would curl up on the big bed until Billy's feeding session was over. He never displayed the slightest sign of jealousy or resentment. Best of all Sarah liked the early evenings when William came to sit with her and bring her the day's news, after his evening meal. Alex would lie in his big wooden cot in the corner, all bathed and clean, calling to the shadows flickering and dancing up the wall, until his baby eyelids grew heavy and he fell asleep to the soothing murmur of his father's voice. In the small wooden crib Billy also slept contentedly and William would stand looking down at him, his dark eyes filled with pride.

Sarah knew there would always be an extra special place in her own heart for Alex, her firstborn, crippled son, just as she had learned to accept that a small part of William's heart would always be denied him, however unconsciously. Billy, on the other hand, had their full approval and Sarah knew she would never forget the happy unity and contentment of those shared evenings during the first weeks of her son's life. Perhaps this period of happiness set a stamp on Billy's nature; certainly he was the happiest and most contented of children. Agnes often referred to him as 'Fairlyden's ain ray o' sunshine,' throughout his early childhood.

At the Mill House Beatrice heard the news of the birth of Sarah's second son with a pang, whether of envy or anxiety she scarcely knew. She had been married six months but there was no sign of a child for her and Dick. This would not have troubled her had she not been plagued by the past. Since the night she had become Dick's wife she had known he was the gentlest and kindest of men, totally different in every way from the brutal sadist who had been her father. But the memory of him coloured her relationship with Dick, no matter how hard she tried to forget the past. She simply could not respond to her husband's tender loving.

Nine

As time passed Alex learned to walk with a swinging motion which sent his skirts swirling, and by the time he was three years old he followed Sarah eagerly to the pigs, the byre and the dairy. His dark eyes were always alight with interest and his questions rarely ceased. He seemed to sense his father's reserve from an early age, but he was never in doubt about the love of his Grandfather Logan. As soon as he could climb he clung precariously to the gate at the head of the track from Strathtod to await Sandy's return each evening. He was assured of a ride in the saddle for the last few yards to the water trough and into the stable. It delighted Sandy that his small namesake never showed the slightest fear of horses. A warm rapport developed between grandfather and grandson.

Billy spent his time wheedling sweetmeats out of Agnes in the kitchen. She could not resist his bright eyes and wide, gap-toothed grin. Then in no time at all he was investigating the outside world, running after his adored Alex. The two small boys were often in trouble as a result of their mischievous ploys.

At the end of September, 1886, Sarah presented them with a baby sister. After the initial excitement, however, they displayed little interest in this new addition to the family; they were a self-sufficient pair. It was left to thirteen-year-old Maggie Whiteley to adore the latest dark-eyed young Fairly. Maggie was the eldest of Louis and Janet's four children; she was kind and patient with the two boys, and Janet had trained her already in many household duties. She knew all about scrubbing the stone-flagged floors in Fairlyden's long passage, kitchen and scullery, she could black-lead the range almost as well as Agnes, and she was not averse to working in the dairy or learning to milk the cows. It suited Sarah well to have an extra pair of willing hands, however small, and also a pair of sharp young eyes to observe the antics of her erring sons. Both Louis and Janet were relieved that their eldest child had found work, especially work so close to her home, for Maggie loved her family dearly, especially her father; leaving Fairlyden to find employment had been her secret dread. Louis's bouts of sickness still recurred at intervals and his thirteen-year-old daughter worried secretly.

Agnes treated the girl with her usual kindliness. She made a space for her in the large room above the Fairlyden kitchen, and she helped Maggie carry her small parcel of clothes up the wooden steps and indicated the oak chest which would be hers during her years at Fairlyden. Maggie already knew that Agnes would not stand for laziness or untidiness but she was a willing, pleasant child and Sarah was anxious to maintain the happy atmosphere in her home. William rarely interfered in domestic matters. Privately he often congratulated himself on having a wife who was not only pretty and loving, but also an excellent manager of her household. If Sarah was disappointed that her husband was not as keen to farm Fairlyden as she had once hoped, she did not criticise and William continued to enjoy his dealings with the horses and cattle.

When Ellen Fairly was six weeks old Sarah wondered why Beatrice had not yet called to see her; she had volunteered to sew another of her exquisite lawn dresses and Beattie never forgot a promise.

'Maybe Beatrice is ill. Could you call at the Mill House on your way back from the market, William?' she asked anxiously.

William duly reported that Beatrice was well. 'Though she's unusually pale and tense,' he added thoughtfully.

'Then I shall visit her myself,' Sarah decided.

The boys were not pleased to be left behind, for they were now familiar with Aunt Beattie's kindness and they were afraid their small sister might devour any sweetmeats or butter toffee which might be waiting for them at the Mill House.

'Treats must be earned, not expected,' Sarah chided her sons sternly. 'But do not fret, Ellen is too small to eat anything yet,' she added with a gentle laugh, which reassured Alex and Billy. Mama was not often cross with them, but when she was, then even Alex managed to run with remarkable speed. They would not forget the time they had chased all the hens out of their small wooden house so that they could play undisturbed one wet afternoon. The result had been some very bedraggled hens and no eggs, plus two small boys in great disgrace.

The autumn day was fine and remarkably mild for the middle of November so Sarah was surprised to find the door at the Mill House firmly closed when she drove into the yard. A delicious smell of new baked bread drifted into the air so she knew Beatrice must be at home.

'Hello Beatrice!' she called cheerily, lifting the latch with one hand, as she cradled Ellen in her arm; the door was securely barred. Surely Beatrice could not be bathing in the early afternoon! Yet what other reason could she have for barring her door? The door at Fairlyden was never locked, even when there was no one in.

She rapped loudly and Ellen whimpered in protest, gazing up from the cocoon of Sarah's shawl with wide dark eyes. Sarah heard footsteps and then Beatrice's voice.

'Who is it?' There was no trace of welcome.

'It's me, Sarah!'

'Sarah!' The exclamation was almost a sob as Beatrice instantly pulled open the door. 'Och, I'm pleased tae see ye!' There was more than welcome in Beatrice's voice now. She sounded close to tears and there was inexpressible relief on her strained face. William was right, she was pale. Sarah frowned.

'Why did you bar the door, Beattie? What's—?'

'Aah, ye've brought your baby!' Beatrice interrupted, swiftly deflecting Sarah's questions. But Sarah was not deceived; she was patient and would bide her time. Something was wrong; Beatrice was definitely not herself.

'May I hold her?' Beatrice held out her arms and Sarah put Ellen into them, aware of the wistful yearning in Beatrice's blue eyes.

'Still no sign of a bairn for you and Dick?' she asked gently. Beatrice shook her head and turned away, beckoning Sarah towards the hearth, but not before Sarah had seen the sheen of unshed tears.

'You've plenty of time, Beattie,' Sarah comforted softly. 'You'll probably have far too many babies once you start! Real rascals they'll be too, if they're like my boys . . .'

'Ye havena brought Alex and wee Billy then?' Beatrice made a visible effort to swallow the knot of tears.

'They were not pleased to be left at home! You spoil them, Beattie, and they know already.'

Beatrice smiled, but her eyes were shadowed. 'They're too young tae spoil.' Her voice cracked, despite the effort she made to control it.

'Aah, Beattie,' Sarah crossed the hearth and laid a comforting arm around her shoulders. 'I'm sure you'll have children soon. Remember how long Janet had to wait before Maggie was born, then the others just followed one after the other. I remember . . .' Sarah shuddered; the memory was not a pleasant one and it wakened others. 'I— I remember how Maureeen O'Leary taunted her.'

Beatrice stifled a sob.

'What is it, Beattie?' Sarah asked in dismay. 'Surely Dick disna blame you . . .?'

'Oh no! D-Dick's wonderful.' Beattie gulped. 'I— I'm not worthy o' him . . .'

'Of course you are! And I know Dick would agree!' Sarah protested. She remembered the barred door. She looked down at Beattie's bowed head as she rocked Ellen in her arms.

'I'll put the kettle on,' Sarah said slowly. 'I can smell your newly made bread and it makes me hungry. Is it still a success in the shop?'

'Aye, it's a great success. I can scarcely bake enough.' Beattie managed a wobbly smile. 'Lots o' folks come tae buy my "English bread". Mr Sharpe probably did me a favour when he asked if I could make him some bread wi' yeast instead o' his housekeeper's soda scones. He really misses his Florrie ye ken, for all she was such a mean, crabbit woman.'

The kettle began to sing and Sarah warmed the big brown teapot, then spooned in the tea leaves from the caddy on the high mantelshelf. The very fact that Beattie allowed her to do this without protest troubled her. She glanced over her shoulder and caught Beatrice unawares staring absently at the shiny black range; there was a whole world of pain and anxiety in her blue eyes and her face looked white and pinched.

Even when Sarah held out a cup of tea Beatrice remained lost in her own troubled world. Sarah set the cup down on a corner of the table and gently lifted her baby from Beatrice's lap, tucking her expertly into the crook of her arm.

'Drink your tea, Beattie,' she instructed quietly but firmly. Beatrice lifted the cup almost automatically and Sarah drew up a chair and reached for her own tea. She sipped in silence, waiting for her old friend to confide in her, but the silence remained unbroken except for a moving coal behind the black ribs of the grate. At length Sarah set down her empty cup and sighed.

'What's troubling you, Beattie?'

'Nothing.'

'Of course there is. Haven't we always shared our troubles?' She looked down at her sleeping baby. 'As well as our joys.' Sarah waited again. At length she decided she had no right to press Beatrice; clearly she didn't want to share her troubles. She drew her feet together ready to rise from the high-backed wooden chair.

'Wull's back.'

Sarah blinked at the sound of Beatrice's flat, brittle voice.

'Wull . . .? Wull Slater? Your . . . brother!'

'Aye.'

'From America? Is— is he staying here?' Sarah asked incredulously.

'No!'

'Where is he? What does Dick say . . .?'

'Dick disna ken!' Beatrice lifted her head and stared at Sarah, her blue eyes filled with fear.

'What does Wull want? Why are—?'

'Money!'

'You didna give him any?'

Beatrice nodded and Sarah's heart sank. She waited in silence for Beatrice to go on. Eventually she did. Once started the words poured forth in a torrent of anxiety and bitterness.

'He threatened tae tell Dick all kinds o' vile things . . . .' She shuddered, 'I told him Dick l-loves m-me, that he wadna believe his filthy tales . . . He laughed – horribly! Then— then he said, "I sent yon agent. He came tae spy out the way o' things between you an' O'Connor." He . . .'

'The agent!' Sarah interrupted sharply. 'The one who was supposed to have come from a Liverpool merchant? To collect money from Dick?'

'Aye. Wull sent him here, tae see if there was any money and if Dick had finished the repairs!' Beatrice gritted her teeth. 'But it isna just a wee bit of money he wants, Sarah. He wants an easy life without any work! He was always idle! Aye, and sly! He says he'll see Dick back in prison – "one way or another, I'll rouse his temper!" he jeered. He's just like Slater!'

'Dick would never listen to Wull!' Sarah comforted, but Beattie's face was white.

He— he might,' she whispered hoarsely. 'Wull . . . kens things a-and . . .' She suddenly hid her face in her hands.

'Oh Beattie, my dear!' Sarah touched her bowed head in concern.

'He— he called me a bastard. He said Slater wasna my father . . .'

'How could Wull know such a thing?' Sarah asked tensely.

'Slater told him when he was drunk once, Wull said. B— but Joey and the rest dinna ken . . .'

'Did he say who your father was, Beattie?' Sarah asked breathlessly.

'No, an' I dinna care who he was. I'm glad Slater wasna my father! Glad!' She stared at Sarah, her blue eyes bright with challenge and anger and bitterness.

'I'm glad too,' Sarah said softly. 'I know you always hated Slater when we were at school.'

'Aye, and I've hated him more since!' Beattie muttered, clenching her teeth; her blue eyes glittered like slits of ice.

Sarah shivered. 'Oh Beattie . . . dinna let Wull upset you. He aye caused trouble for you, even when he was a boy . . .'

'That bit o' news pleased me!' She laughed harshly. 'I told Wull I was thankful tae hear it. He was like a— a blown-up pig's bladder after it's pricked wi' a pin! He expected me tae get hysterical, I think. Deep down I always thought Slater couldna be ma father, Sarah. Once, when I was young, I heard him arguing wi' Grandfather Miller. It was when Mother nearly died, after she lost her last baby. Slater swore at Grandfather and said she wasna innocent when he took her. I didna understand such things then . . .'

'So, if you welcomed Wull's news, Beattie, why are you so frightened of him coming back?' Sarah asked carefully. 'Dick would understand. He never liked Slater either. He'll be glad to know he's not your father.'

Beattie's blue eyes glazed with renewed fear.

'Wull said Dick wadna look at me when he'd finished talking tae him.' Beattie gave a half-choked sob. 'He's just as vicious as Slater used tae be! He threatened tae tell Dick that I— that Slater . . .' She broke off shuddering. 'I didna want tae dae such things, Sarah! Slater – he forced me!' She began to sob quietly.

'Ssh, Beattie,' Sarah soothed helplessly. 'You can forget about Slater and the past now. He's dead, and Dick loves you . . .'

'Wull said he wad claim the Store if I didna give him money tae keep silent . . .'

'He canna claim the Store!' Sarah gasped indignantly. 'Can he?'

'I— I dinna ken. He's the eldest son since Eddie died . . .'

'I thought the mill belonged to your grandfather? Anyway the buildings would have fallen down if Dick hadna been here.'

'Grandfather had given half o' the mill tae Slater, when he married Mama.'

'But Slater died before your grandfather.'

'Aye, and the house was still his. He said it would be mine when he was gone . . . and the pigs,' her voice cracked, she had loved her grandfather dearly, '. . . and his mare. But he didna write it on a paper, and he died before Mama. Wull and that man who called himself an agent, they've been finding out such things!' Beatrice muttered bitterly. 'He says everything belonged tae Mama on the day she died, and now the house and the mill are his.'

'But that's so unfair! He knows how hard you had to work, with the house to keep and nursing your mama. He must know how hard Dick has worked to repair everything.' Sarah looked around her at the clean, cosy kitchen. The black patches of damp which had stained most of the ceiling had almost gone now, and the lime-washed walls were clean and fresh, the door had been mended and even the window frames could be shut.

'Wull's been waiting until Dick put the place tae rights,' Beatrice whispered dully.

'Surely he canna claim the Store and . . . and everything? It isna just! You must tell Dick, Beattie!' Sarah said urgently. 'He has a right to know of Wull's threats.'

Beatrice's face was deathly white. 'Dick mustna ken Wull has been here! He mustna hear his evil tales! I— I couldna look into his face, sae kind, sae patient he is wi' me . . .' Again she choked back a sob. 'Wull always told such lies!'

'Dick would know Wull was exaggerating.'

'Aye, and that wad be worse! Dick wad strike Wull tae the ground for the evil things he says. A saint would be driven tae hit Wull Slater! I would have hit him myself, if I'd been a man!' Beattie declared vehemently. Then her voice sank. 'But if I'd been a man he couldna have said such things. Wull wants tae rouse Dick's anger. He wants tae have him back in prison. He said so.'

Sarah stared down at Beatrice's pale, distraught face in dismay.

'Where is Wull now?'

'I dinna ken,' Beatrice shrugged. 'He— he said he wad be back . . . but Sarah, I havena any more money. We've little enough as it is, and Dick working all the hours the guid Lord sends!'

'Well, you canna give him money if you havena got it,' Sarah frowned.

'That's what I said, and Wull laughed.' Beatrice shivered at the memory. 'He said that wad suit him fine because he wad just move into the hoose. Here! along wi' Dick and me, and— and . . .' Beatrice began to shake uncontrollably. 'He's just like Slater! I thought I'd seen a ghost when he came in at that door! Even his eyes are the same . . .' She could not bring herself to tell Sarah that Wull had called Dick an old bull who would never sire a calf. 'I canna deny that the Mill House was Wull's home as much as mine. We shared the same mother! Yet he did nothing tae keep one stone standing upon another! I'm ashamed tae be kin tae him. Dick only kens Joe and he likes him well enough. But Wull . . .' She shuddered again. If Dick ever discovered what a lying scoundrel Wull Slater was he might be tempted to kill him, for all he is so mild and kind. The thought of Dick being hung for murder terrified her even more than Wull Slater's threats.

'So you bar the door because you're afraid Wull might return . . .?' Sarah murmured her own thoughts aloud.

'Only when Dick's away frae the yard,' Beatrice insisted defensively. 'He's delivering coal today.' She sighed. 'He works so hard, but he'll never enjoy being a storekeeper! Ye ken how much he loves the land and animals, Sarah.' Her face softened. 'He spends all his spare time on oor few wee pigs, and the two cows.' She looked up and Sarah knew she was making an effort to regain her usual cheerful composure. Beatrice had never been the type to get hysterical over trifles. Wull must have really frightened her.

In the weeks before Christmas Sarah saw Beatrice twice. The first time was when she visited the Farmers' Store to stock up with oatmeal and flour in case the winter weather should come suddenly and cut Fairlyden off from the village. Sarah sensed that Beatrice did not wish to discuss their last meeting; she was more on edge than ever. Even Dick seemed unnaturally subdued as he loaded her purchases into the trap.

Sarah's second encounter with Beatrice was on a bitterly cold December morning. Beatrice had walked the four miles to Fairlyden, supposedly to bring small gifts for the children for Christmas.

'Wull came again!' she whispered anxiously, the moment Agnes left them alone together in the cosy warmth of the Fairlyden kitchen.

Sarah looked at her strained face with concern. 'You're making yourself ill with worry, Beattie.' Her voice expressed her anxiety.

'I'm all right!' she said wearily, 'but what can I dae, Sarah? Wull is threatening to move in wi' Dick an' me. I gave him all the money I had. Sometimes I think we should just let him have the place!' she added desperately, and Sarah looked at her in dismay.

'You would not leave the Mill House, Beattie? Your own home?'

'I'd rather sleep in a ditch than share it wi' Wull Slater! Aye I wad! He brings back more bad memories than good ones for me!' Beatrice retorted with a bitterness which surprised Sarah. This was a Beattie she had never known.

'You must tell Dick!' Sarah repeated urgently. 'He will protect you and—'

'Oh aye, he wad! But who wad protect him afterwards? That's what frightens me! It's not just the hoose, or the mill that Wull Slater wants. He could never bear tae see anybody happy, even when he was a wean. He aye made trouble, and he never cared who suffered, or got a beating. He enjoyed it! I tell ye, Sarah, he's just like Slater!' Beatrice shuddered violently, recalling her childhood punishments at the hands of the sadistic man who had given her his name. 'D'ye remember how quickly Constable Ross suspected Dick after Slater's accident? He wad arrest him for sure if there was more trouble. And there will be trouble if

Wull moves in wi' us. Dick is sae honest. Wull's a cheat and a liar—' She broke off as Agnes returned carrying Ellen, all smiles and chortles.

Beatrice left soon afterwards. She had eaten nothing, and only sipped half-heartedly at her cup of tea.

Sarah could not get her out of her mind despite the excitement of preparing for Christmas. Louis had had two bouts of sickness again recently, but he had recovered in time to help pluck and clean the geese and ducks ready for the market; there was butter to churn as usual, and pies to be baked. There were stockings to fill, each with an apple, an orange, a penny and some nuts, as well as the tiny gloves and socks which Agnes had knitted, and the two wooden horses which Louis had carved so painstakingly for Alex and Billy.

The greatest excitement of all was the party which Bert Bradshaw was to hold at the Tower House on Boxing Day. William, Sarah and the boys were invited to go with Sandy to have luncheon with the Bradshaws, but the real party, at least as far as the children were concerned, was to be held in the afternoon. All the children on the estate were invited, as well as all the men and maid servants who could be spared from their duties. Bert Bradshaw had hired a *Punch and Judy Show* to entertain them in the large hall. Afterwards there would be lemonade and tea and sugary buns, as well as an apple for each of the children to take home.

Even Sarah caught the feeling of excitement. Fanny and Freda Bradshaw were to be at the Tower House for Christmas, along with Fanny's husband and Crispin Bradshaw. Sarah's smooth brow creased when she thought of Bert Bradshaw's only son. She had a great respect for him, and for the things he did to help the workers in the Bradshaw woollen mills and in the temperance society, but she was never quite at ease when she was with him. The fault was hers, Sarah decided. It was all very confusing, and very irritating; she was a self-possessed, respectably married woman, she told herself sternly.

Nevertheless the more she thought about Crispin Bradshaw, the more she realised he was the very man who might give her advice to help Beattie. Sarah knew instinctively that he would respect her confidence, and he had met Beatrice. Surely he would know whether Wull Slater had any right to live at the Mill House, even if the laws of inheritance were different from those in his native Yorkshire. He would know what could be done to stop Wull frightening Beatrice.

Fanny and Freda had seen the Fairlyden trap arriving and both were at the door to welcome them with laughter and cheery greetings and exclamations. Behind them came Bert Bradshaw, as eager as a boy himself as he swung first Alex, and then Billy, high into the air.

'Eeh by gum, but yer fine lads, y'are an all! Soon be bigger than me! Yer will!' Alex and Billy giggled; they were always entertained by Bert Bradshaw's broad Yorkshire accent, and his funny, unfamiliar teasing. 'And Sarah!' He drew her forward into the large hall, and to her astonishment he kissed her cheek, his blue eyes twinkling as he glanced upwards to where Freda had tied a bunch of mistletoe. 'Your turn now, Crispin!'

Freda chortled. 'It's all right for you to kiss Sarah under the mistletoe. She's a safely married young woman, so you needn't be frightened of losing your precious freedom.'

Sarah's cheeks flamed with embarrassment but everyone seemed too busy and excited with their own greetings to notice her confusion, everyone except Crispin. His expression was as grave as usual, his grey eyes as penetrating too, and yet Sarah could have sworn she saw laughter lurking in their depths as he bent his head. His was no fleeting kiss on her cheek as his father's had been. He placed his lips firmly on the dimple at the corner of her mouth.

'Mmm, I have wanted to kiss that intriguing dimple since the first time I saw it!'

Sarah's eyes widened and her pink colour flared again. Surely Crispin Bradshaw could not be . . . flirting with her? Everyone knew he was a serious and confirmed bachelor. Yet in her confusion Sarah felt as breathless as though she had run all the way from Fairlyden. She glanced round to see whether William had noticed the kiss, for her husband was a possessive man. William was too engaged in conversation with Bert Bradshaw, however, and before she could move towards him Crispin took her arm and drew her towards a large room in which a huge log fire sent showers of sparks up the cavernous chimney.

'You are looking exceedingly pretty, almost like a lady Santa Claus. Red suits you, Sarah.'

'I— I . . .' she stammered in confusion. Compliments were so out of character for Crispin Bradshaw, or at least the Crispin she thought she knew. She shot him a startled glance. He was teasing her! She could see the laughter quite plainly in his grey eyes now; it made little flecks of light like sunbeams dancing on the water, she thought. In fact Crispin Bradshaw seemed altogether different with that little smile lifting his serious mouth and his expression and manner so relaxed. Yes, that was it, Crispin was less stern, more human today than she had ever seen him. She looked up and found herself feeling as shy as a young girl as she met his intent regard.

'It— it was kind of your father to ask us all to luncheon.'

'He said you would brighten up his dull old Tower House and make us all appreciate it more. And of course he was right, you decorate the place beautifully.'

'I didn't know you possessed such a silken tongue, Master Bradshaw!' she said, blushing like a schoolgirl and chiding herself for her stupidity.

'And I had thought you would be so used to adulation that you would have forgotten how to blush long ago! Does William not pay you compliments any more?'

'He is my husband!'

'Is there a rule then, which says when a man is married he cannot tell his wife how pretty she looks?'

'N-no, of course not.' A small frown creased Sarah's smooth brow. It was a long time since William had bothered to tell her she looked pretty. Then she raised glowing dark eyes to Crispin's face and smiled gaily.

She did not hear his indrawn breath and was unaware of the effect her smile had had on Crispin Bradshaw's usually quiet heart as she murmured softly, 'There is a matter I would discuss with you, if we could be— undisturbed for a short time perhaps?'

'Is that wise, Mistress Fairly?' His voice was tense, cool even.

Sarah turned back to him in surpise; he never addressed her as Mistress Fairly, except in the presence of servants. Her concern for Beatrice overrode her preoccupation with Crispin's change of mood, however.

'Perhaps it is not wise to interfere, but Beatrice is my— my dearest friend. She needs my help.'

Crispin Bradshaw blinked rapidly. Sarah wondered at the changing expressions flashing over his lean face – disappointment? Relief? She was not sure.

'Come through to the conservatory then. I will show you my father's plants as we talk. We shall not be disturbed for a few minutes.'

Sarah explained the situation at the old mill as clearly as she could but she was disappointed in Crispin's wary comments.

'If Wull Slater is the eldest surviving son I think he can claim the heritable property. Your friend should consult a lawyer without delay.'

'But the mill was almost derelict. There was no real trade left. Besides Wull Slater has done nothing, not even for his own parents, since he was thirteen!' Sarah protested. 'How can he return now, to claim the results of Dick and Beatrice's hard labours? It isn't fair!'

'Life is seldom fair,' Crispin agreed with a sigh. 'It may be that a lawyer would advocate payment be made to the O'Connors for the work and money they have spent on restoring, or maintaining the property, but I would advise Mistress O'Connor to reach an amicable agreement with her brother in the circumstances, although of course I am no lawyer, least of all a Scottish lawyer.' Crispin sighed again as he saw Sarah's deep disappointment, and yet she had come to him for advice, and the thought pleased him. He wondered why she had not consulted her husband. Thinking of William he decided it was time they rejoined the others. He smiled down at her and took her arm.

'Come, forget all your problems for today. Luncheon must not be delayed. There is the entertainment to enjoy. And Sarah,' his grey eyes twinkled, 'remember to tell my father how much you like his plants . . .' Again there was the hidden laughter. 'Even though you have not looked at a single leaf!'

Mrs Bunnerby obviously enjoyed cooking, and with the help of her young assistant and her two kitchen maids, she had indeed made a luncheon 'fit for the queen' as young Alex described it, puffing out his small stomach to show how full it was, long before all the courses had been served. They had eaten rabbit soup followed by fried eels, fowl scollops, roast goose and vegetables and a golden yellow sauce, the recipe for which Mrs Bunnerby had inherited from her own Yorkshire grandmother, as well as bacon cheeks garnished with brussels sprouts. Then there was a whole host of delicacies for Master Bradshaw's sweet tooth; mince pies and plum pudding, whipped cream, custard in glasses and a compote of apricots. Sarah was embarrassed when her sons pleaded to be excused from the meal before it was half finished, but Bert Bradshaw had insisted the children should join them at table.

'I keep tellin' our Fanny, I reckon nowt uv these fancy nurseries,' he declared. 'I like to see t' littl'uns eatin' up an' enjoying 'emselves. Come on Fanny, let young Robert down from t' table then these two little fellers can play an' all.'

At the end of the meal Sarah wondered how she would ever stay awake to watch the afternoon's entertainment. She didn't want to contemplate the drive home in the trap before the December darkness blotted out the wintery afternoon completely, but she knew there would be the cows to milk and pigs and calves to feed. Agnes had volunteered to stay at Fairlyden to look after baby Ellen. Sarah knew she would gather the eggs from the nesting boxes and feed the hens. The foxes were on the prowl early since the weather had turned cold and the days were so short; it was vital to have the little trapdoors firmly closed and the hens shut in before nightfall.

'Come along lass,' Bert Bradshaw boomed beside her. 'Find a gud seat for t'entertainment and forget about t'work. Are any uv yer workers comin'?'

'Louis and Janet and their four children will be on their way now,' Sarah smiled. 'You're very generous to us all, Mr Bradshaw.'

'It's a pleasure, lass, specially t'see all t' littl'uns enjoying 'emselves. There's refreshments for all uv 'em after. I want all t' kiddies to 'ave a Christmas t' remember, even if they do all go back 'ome t' porridge and owld clothes,' he declared with his big smile.

Ten

At the Farmers' Store trade had been better the day before Christmas than it had been since Dick and Beatrice married. Everyone seemed to need stocks of coal or cattle cake, bags of flour and oatmeal. Even the poorest labourers tried to enjoy some festive cheer. Added to the usual items was an assortment of brightly coloured baubles, knitted socks and gloves made by Beatrice and several wooden toys which Dick had made during the winter evenings by the fire. Every one of these had been sold.

Both Beatrice and Dick were greatly relieved, though for very different reasons. Beatrice had been troubled about finding money to provide something extra for their own Christmas since she had given everything she had saved to Wull Slater. As far as Dick was concerned merchanting was simply not his line, but he was willing to do anything to earn food and clothes and keep the roof over the head of his beloved wife. He never troubled Beatrice with his problems, but he was constantly aware of sly remarks, men who tried to involve him in cheating a neighbour, or wary dealings from those who knew he had served his time in prison, and in such a small community such news travelled speedily and was often exaggerated. Added to the problems with his work was his anxiety concerning the change in Beatrice.

So as the busy day drew to its close Dick heaved a sigh of relief. He was looking forward to a day spent in his wife's company, without the constant demands of customers. He had seen Beatrice slipping across the darkened mill yard towards the village and he guessed she had gone to Mr Jardine's store to make a few last-minute purchases. He knew she had boiled a piece of ham from the pig he had cured in the autumn, and she had killed one of the hens; he hoped she had made one of her rich fruit puddings. He would, of course, pretend to be surprised when she presented him with a special meal on Christmas Day.

Dick had a surprise of his own. He had made a little wooden crib and he had kept it hidden in the Store; surely it could not be long now before Beatrice presented him with their first child? Dick sighed. Beatrice loved Sarah's children. He was sure she wanted a child of her own, and he longed for a little girl to dangle on his knee, or a son to take with him to see the piglets. He had also bought a silk purse with beads like the one Mistress Sharpe had carried when she went to church. He knew it was an extravagance but he had wanted to give Beatrice something special. He sighed again. If only he could make her forget the unhappy memories which seemed to haunt her; if he could persuade her to relax when he took her in his arms; if only she would let him love her as he wanted to love her.

In the darkness Beatrice did not see the shadowy figure beside the wall of the old mill as she scurried back to the house with her few provisions. She had just reached the kitchen in time to hang the pan of mutton broth on the swey when Dick came in. She turned to him breathlessly, her cheeks pink from hurrying.

'Come ye tae the fire, Dick. It has been a long day, and I'm sure ye must be hungry . . .'

'Aye, lassie, I am, and the mutton smells good. Ach, Beatrice . . .' He moved eagerly across the hearth and put his arm around her thin shoulders as she straightened up. 'I'm glad tae see ye looking so excited, and with your ain cheery smile again. I think I'm the luckiest man alive!'

'Oh Dick,' Beatrice murmured tremulously, but her blue eyes glowed with pleasure. To Dick's delight she turned into the circle of his arms and hugged him fiercely. 'Oh, but I'm glad ye'll be at home tomorrow, jist the twae o' us together! I'd never dae anything tae hurt ye, Dick. Ye're guid and patient wi' me,' she exclaimed fervently. Then, as though embarrassed by the sudden relaxation of her own private barriers, she straightened and her voice became brisk. 'But ye'll no' be patient for long I'm thinking if I dinna get ye something to eat.'

Dick was pleased. Beattie looked happier than she had looked for weeks.

'Ach, I'd wait all nicht if I aye got a greetin' like yon!' he teased and watched the colour rise in her cheeks. 'I'm looking forward to a wee bit o' peace myself, lassie. Maybe we could walk tae the woods o'er by Strathtod if the day is fine.'

They had just eaten the small piece of mutton and Dick was mopping up the remains of the soup with a chunk of bread when a loud thump at the door startled them both.

'Are— are ye expecting a— a customer . . .?'

When Dick shook his head Beatrice's face paled, yet she had no reason to suppose Wull Slater would return, especially so soon; he knew she had nothing more to give him.

As Dick flung open the door the sound of the familiar nasal tones seemed to freeze the blood in her veins. She could not move from her seat at the table, but she gasped as she listened to Wull Slater's brazen words.

'Ye must be Master O'Connor! I'm Wull Slater. Aah, but it's good to see my ain hame agin after all this time! I've been looking forward tae seeing ma sister Beatrice; an' tae think I've jist managed tae get here in time for Christmas . . .'

Dick had been gaping at the stranger in surprise. Now he stepped back, unsuspectingly, taking the other man's hand in greeting, drawing him into the cosy kitchen with warmth in his voice and a welcome on his lips. He had never known any of Beatrice's brothers in their youth, and only Joe had managed to come for his parents' funeral, and for Beatrice's wedding. He had liked Joe and he knew Beatrice had been pleased to renew their relationship. Typically unselfish, Dick swallowed his hopes of spending a day in the company of his beloved wife. The arrival of a long-lost brother would add to her joy this Christmas. She rarely mentioned any of her family. No doubt they had all been glad to make their escape from such a father as Edward Slater.

'Beatrice, see what a surpise for ye!' He drew Wull forward. 'Have ye come frae America, er . . . Wull?'

'I hae been tae America, aye . . .' He looked around the Mill House kitchen feigning surprise at the changes. 'Aah, but there's nae place like hame.'

He turned to Beatrice. She could not bring herself to rise from the table. She was sure her legs would not support her.

'Come on lassie, are ye no' going tae welcome your brother!' Dick cast an apologetic glance at the man standing beside him. 'Your arrival must hae given Beattie a shock.'

Wull moved forward so that Dick O'Connor could not see the mocking smile on his thick lips. 'Are ye no' going tae welcome your ain brother, m'dear?'

Beatrice saw the malevolent gleam in his small piggy eyes; in that moment she loathed him as much as the man who had sired him. Pride, and the need to dissemble for Dick's sake, brought her stiffly to her feet and round the corner of the table. She held out her hand, but she could not bring herself to utter a single word of welcome, even in pretence.

Wull Slater smirked and, avoiding her outstretched hand, he pulled her to him in an embrace which took Beatrice by surprise. There was nothing brotherly in the stumpy fingers which ran warningly down her spine, while he kissed her cheek. Almost instantly Bearice pushed herself away from him, her breath coming in a startled, angry gasp. Fortunately Dick had turned to the fire, to reheat the remaining broth for Wull Slater's supper. He did not see the wild glance of desperation which flashed briefly in his wife's blue eyes. He straightened and turned to Wull.

'I'm afraid there's no meat left in the pot, but the broth is good, and there's fresh bread. Beatrice is a fine cook, as ye'll see if ye're staying for Christmas.'

'Oh aye, I shall look forward tae sampling whatever Beattie has tae offer.'

Beattie caught the sly smile on Slater's square, swarthy face and her lips curled in contempt, but Dick was kind and hospitable. He would share his last crust. And Wull Slater would take it! He was the image of his father. She moved past him reluctantly and took a plate from the kitchen rack.

Dick watched her anxiously. Her pale face worried him and she did not seem at all happy to see her brother. He frowned. Or was she ashamed of him, her husband? He looked keenly at Wull Slater.

Wull sensed his scrutiny and reacted like the actor he was. He sipped delicately at the broth and broke a piece of bread from the chunk on the board which Beatrice had set upon the table. She remembered how he used to grab and gobble.

'Mmm, this is delicious!'

Beatrice gasped. Wull Slater had never shown appreciation for anything in his life. She sank on to her chair and rested her chin on her hands, staring at him in disbelief, knowing full well he was acting a part for Dick's benefit. His eyes took on a yearning expression and Beatrice held her breath wondering what he was planning next. She had not long to wait.

'I knew I'd find a welcome i' ma auld hame! Man, Dick, ye dinna ken what it's like tae wander in foreign lands, an' on the high seas, awa' frae all that's dear tae ye.'

Beatrice gritted her teeth. It took all her control not to scream at him, hypocrite that he was. Instead she listened as he continued to claim Dick's attention.

'Mind ye, I wadna like tae be a trouble tae ye, but I see ye hae nae bairns yet, an' I expect the auld room'll be empty and waitin' tae welcome me . . .?' He gave a theatrical sigh. 'Och, but it's grand tae be back i' dear auld Scotia, wi' my ain family . . . ma dear sister that I havena seen since I was a wee bit laddie! An' I expect I was a great trouble tae ye, Beatrice m'dear . . .' He heaved another of his sighs. 'I tell ye it's grand tae be back.'

'Of course, I'm sure it is,' Dick replied huskily, remembering the two grim years he had spent in prison, away from his own family. His mother and father had died while he was away too; how he had longed to see them again, just once more. 'Ye're welcome tae stay a while. We havena much, for the mill trade is finished i' the likes o' Muircumwell. Big power mills hae sprung up in all the ports; they take the grain an' the oil seeds as soon as they come off the big new steam ships. We're struggling tae get a Farmers' Store going wi' anything that'll turn an honest penny. Master Fairly frae Fairlyden has been very good at helping us.'

'Master Fairly?' Wull echoed sharply and his eyes narrowed.

'Aye, but it's hard work selling when naebody has much money tae spend,' Dick declared with feeling.

'I suppose it must be.' Wull skimmed lightly over Dick's problems, just as he had always avoided work, or anything that required thought or effort, Beatrice remembered bitterly. 'But I kenned fine I wad be all richt, once I'd reached the auld mill. After a' it is my hame as weel as Beatrice's.'

Dick frowned uncertainly, but he made no reply. Beatrice could not meet his eyes. She wondered if he had heard the note of steel in Wull's whining voice. She bit hard on her clenched knuckles in an effort to remain silent; she must not provoke Wull in front of Dick. Her husband was far too honest himself to see through a sly, twisting wretch like Wull Slater.

She was scarcely aware that she was staring at him until her gaze was held by the middle button on his coat. It had been stitched on with thread a shade lighter than the other two. Even as she stared in growing disbelief he leaned back in his chair, replete; the fronts of his jacket fell apart. Subconsciously she realised she had noticed that it was too tight for his stocky frame when he came in, now she saw clearly; the sleeves were long, the black material was frayed a little at the cuffs. It was Joe's coat! Wull was wearing Joe's clothes!

Beatrice sat up, her heart hammering. She had always considered Joe to be the best of her brothers. She had been pleased when he came to her mother's funeral; she had been delighted when he had returned again for her wedding. She had believed him when he said neither he nor the rest of his brothers wanted anything from their old home. He had said she deserved the little that remained. She frowned trying to remember what Joe had said about Wull.

'Just like father. He even stirred up trouble with the Indians. I hope he never turns up on my doorstep . . .' Yes, that was it! But Wull must have found Joe, and Joe must have sent Wull to the Mill House! He must have bribed him with the clothes off his own back. Beatrice's heart cried out in protest. She had trusted Joe.

She stared at the gold watch chain stretched across Wull's bulging stomach. There was a small fob. She would have recognised it anywhere. Sometimes it glowed a brownish red, sometimes a greenish brown, depending on the light. Grandfather Miller had given it to Joe, his own namesake, the only one of his grandsons who bore any resemblance to himself. Yet Joe had given away his gift. He must have used it to get Wull out of the house. Beatrice felt sick at heart, let down, utterly defeated. Why, oh why had she not confided in Dick when Wull first returned? Why had she not trusted him to believe her version of the past? Why . . .? Because Dick would be angered by Wull's lies and taunts; Wull would provoke a saint beyond endurance.

Christmas Day was a subdued affair at the Mill House. Dick was at a loss to understand his wife's cool attitude towards a member of her own family. He had chided her for her lack of warmth as soon as they were alone in their chamber the previous evening. Beatrice had been upset because Dick thought ill of her. She had turned her back on him so that he would not see her tears. Dick had tried to take her in his arms, but she could not respond; she was painfully conscious of Wull Slater's presence in the bed on the other side of the wall, his sniggering and sneering. For the the first time Dick and Beatrice had come close to quarrelling. Already Wull Slater was stirring up trouble between them and Beatrice did not know how to put it right. She could not welcome the man she loathed and despised, aye and feared.

Even Wull could not keep up his act of earnest gratitude and gentility indefinitely. Beatrice saw Dick's surprised glance when he fell into his old ways and grabbed a large portion of the chicken and crammed it into his cavernous mouth before Dick had even said grace. Wull was unaware of Dick's raised eyebrows as he reached for more, expelling wind as he did so in order to devour the rest, like the glutton he was.

'Perhaps it is a long time since he tasted good cooking like yours, Beattie,' Dick excused him quietly when Wull made a hurried dash down the garden to the closet.

'He was always greedy. He eats like the pigs!' Beatrice retorted bitterly. 'I tell ye, Dick, Wull has always caused trouble, since the day he was born!'

'Eh, lassie,' Dick chided tolerantly. 'Ye havena seen him for years. He was only a laddie then. He canna cause trouble for ye now, and he is your brother, your ain flesh and blood.'

Beatrice bit back the words which sprang to her lips when she saw her husband's wistful expression. Dick had loved his family dearly. They had been very close. She knew he would harbour bitter regrets to the end of his days because he had been in prison when his parents died. Life had not been easy for any of the O'Connors once they were known to have a brother who was branded a felon. Dick had not blamed his brothers for leaving the district, but he missed them.

Darkness was falling when a timid girl of about eleven came to the door of the Mill House and asked to speak to Dick.

'What is it, Milly?' Dick asked patiently. 'Has your mother run out o' oatmeal again?'

'Oh no, not this time Mr O'Connor,' she said hurriedly, ''Tis Grandmother. She wanted us tae gang for Christmas Day, so we did. We've just come hame. She had bought a chicken for oor dinner, for a treat ye ken.' Dick nodded and waited. 'It was fair grand.' Milly's eyes glowed and Beattie guessed the girl's family were very poor. 'We had tatties tae, an' a wee bowl o' custard after. It was lovely.' The girl sighed with ecstasy at the mere memory.

'So what can I dae for ye, Milly?' Dick prompted gently.

'Och aye. Weel, ye see we didna ken Grandmother hadna any more peat for her fire until we were comin' hame. She'd spent the money on the chicken see. Now Mother says, please could ye tak her a wee bag o' coal, an' maybe a wee bitty wood? Tomorrow . . .? Please, Mr O'Connor?' Milly looked up at Dick anxiously. 'Father says he'll pay, soon as he can.'

Dick nodded resignedly. 'It's too cold tae be without a fire, lassie. I'll see your grandmother first thing tomorrow morning. Bentira village, isn't it?'

'Aye. Oh thank ye, Mr O'Connor!' The girl's eyes glowed with gratitude and on impulse Beattie handed her a mince pie from the plate she had been carrying to the table for their own Christmas tea. Milly's pleasure was out of all proportion to so small a gift and Beatrice guessed the family enjoyed few luxuries, yet they cared for their grandmother.

'Poor Dick,' she sympathised as he closed the door. 'It's a long way to Bentira village . . .'

'Aye, ye're too soft wi' such folk!' Wull Slater's whining voice interrupted before Dick could reply. 'There's nae wonder ye're no' making money frae the Store.'

Dick was surprised at Wull's interference and criticism.

'Nae man wad see an auld body freeze in this weather! And Beattie and I have enough for our needs,' Dick said quietly, but Beattie recognised the note of anger beneath his level tones. Wull had always been totally insensitive.

'I'll show ye how tae run things now I'm back,' Wull persisted. 'I shall mak more money out o' this place than ye ever dreamed o', O'Connor! Come tae think on't, I dinna ken why Father didna dae mair than grind corn.'

Dick's eyes widened in surprise.

'Ye canna mean tae stay here!' Beatrice gasped.

'Why not? It's ma hame, and it seems Dick needs somebody like me tae push him along a bit. Ye're too easy wi' folks like yon cotter family, man.'

'It is my Christian duty tae help an auld woman!' Dick protested cooly.

'All richt, all richt, if ye say so, but jist this once, mind. I shall be needing a share o' things frae now on, sae ye'll need tae be mair particular about making money.'

'Ye'll need tae work for your share then,' Beatrice began heatedly.

'Whisht, lassie,' Dick intervened firmly, though his eyes narrowed speculatively as though seeing Wull Slater for the first time. 'We'll talk about this tomorrow, when I return. I'll set out early for Bentira in case the weather changes. If ye dae mean tae stay a while wi' us though, Wull, maybe ye'll feed the pigs and clean out the sties. That wad be a great help.'

Beatrice held her breath, waiting for Wull's objections; he had never liked work. Only this morning he had lain in bed while she milked their two cows and fed the hens and ducks. Dick had been busy with his own chores. Only hunger and the fine smell of the Christmas dinner cooking had brought Wull from his chamber.

Wull made no reply, but when Beattie glanced at him in surprise she saw his beady eyes fixed on her, and there was a calculating gleam in them that sent shivers down her spine. She remembered then; the young Wull had never argued openly, or told tales in their presence; yet how often he had watched and gloated while she or Joe or Jamie had endured a beating from their father. Even their poor mama had suffered as a result of Wull's spite and laziness.

'Dick!' Beatrice realised her voice sounded unnaturally sharp and high. She made an effort to smile. 'Maybe . . . er, d'ye think I might come with ye tomorrow? To Bentira? To the auld woman? I could milk the cows early, and . . .' For a moment she saw Dick's face lighten with pleasure and she knew he would have enjoyed her company, but then he frowned and his gaze moved briefly over Wull. Dick had serious doubts about the fellow's reliability, for all his fine talk, but he would not voice his doubts about his brother-in-law to Beatrice.

'Better not. It's a long way and it will be a cold day tomorrow, Beattie, if I'm not mistaken. Besides there might be a few customers needing things frae the Store.' He saw his wife's face cloud with disappointment, but her swiftly lowered lashes hid the fear in her blue eyes. His expression softened. 'Maybe we'll be able tae take a few drives together in the summer, if Wull is still here tae mind the Store. Ye could come to the market at Annan, or even Dumfries; ye could help me choose some new items tae tempt the local women.'

'Aye,' Beattie nodded, 'aye, I'll dae that, Dick,' but her voice was flat.

Wull had not risen from his bed by the time Dick had fed and groomed the mare and eaten his own breakfast. Beatrice had finished milking her two cows.

'You go, Dick, I'll feed the pigs and stirks if Wull doesna rise soon. Please hurry back,' she added anxiously.

Dick grimaced. He was sure Beatrice loved him when he looked into her worried blue eyes. Yet she had turned away from his embrace again last night. He knew she had lain awake for a long time. Her body had been rigid beside his own and he could not understand the tension in her. He had hoped the arrival of her brother might have made her happy and relaxed, but she seemed more tense than ever.

As usual the pigs squealed, shoved and squabbled in their eagerness to guzzle the swill which Beatrice had just mixed for them. It was impossible to avoid getting splashes and slops on the hems of her skirts, but at least the pigs were thriving, Beatrice thought proudly as she stood back to view the youngest litter lined up at the trough. The sows had reared larger litters since Dick took over and the man in charge of the bacon curing at Annan had declared them the best quality pigs to pass through his premises. Modestly Dick had given the credit to the strain of pigs her grandfather had bred over the years, and although Beatrice knew this was true in part, she also knew that it was Dick's care which had resulted in the sows producing so many live pigs, and rearing them all. Pigs were strange creatures and not all sows were happy to rear their offspring. Many young pigs had been smothered by a clumsy mother, or even eaten by a disturbed one. Dick seemed to sense these dangers and prevent them. Beatrice sighed heavily. If only they had enough land for Dick to be a proper farmer.

Beatrice had mucked out the byre, bedded and watered the stirks and cows and prepared the turnips and hay for the evening feed, but still there was no sign of Wull. Eventually she returned to the house with an armful of wood she had gathered for the fire. She blackleaded the grate and tidied the kitchen. Once the dirty tasks were finished she went to her chamber to wash and change as she always did, in case any customers should come to the Store. Although Ray Jardine stocked such items as oil and candles he always grumbled if customers disturbed him after he had shut up his shop for the night. Consequently many of the local customers had begun to call at the Farmers' Store instead. If they happened to smell the bread which Beatrice now baked twice a week for Mr Sharpe at the Mains, they often bought a loaf as well, if they could afford it. So Beatrice liked to appear clean and fresh at all times of the day. Today it was necessary to change her skirt and flannel petticoat to rid herself of the pungent odour of pigs.

She poured cold water into the basin on the marble-topped wash stand in her bedchamber and stripped off her clothes, down to her white frilly drawers. The December morning was bitterly cold and the Mill House did not have the luxury of bedroom fires unless someone was very ill. Beatrice wasted no time on her ablutions. Even so she was shivering as she dried her face and arms on the linen towel. So intent was she on her task that she did not hear the faint squeal as the door of her chamber opened.

Beatrice was glad to lay aside the towel. She turned to reach for the clean petticoat and blue woollen gown she had set out on the bed in readiness. As she turned she jumped violently. Wull Slater's narrowed eyes were moving over her in an insulting scrutiny.

'Wull Slater! Get out o' my chamber!' Beatrice knew she had been foolish to let him see her fear that first day when he had appeared so unexpectedly. He had always liked to taunt and tease. He had inherited his father's streak of cruelty, his desire for power over anyone, or anything, weaker than himself; like the time he had deliberately broken the wing of a young fledgling. It had fallen from the nest and Joe had been trying to help it to fly. Wull was cruel and selfish, and totally unpredictable.

'Get out of my bedchamber!' Beatrice tried to control the hysteria in her voice.

'Och, that's no way tae speak tae yer long-lost brother, m'dear.' Wull's own voice was slow and mocking; his eyes continued to travel insolently over her shaking limbs.

Beatrice snatched up her petticoat and held it in front of her. She was shivering, but it was not just the cold December air which chilled her now.

'Ye needna pretend tae be sae modest. I ken how ye encouraged ma father . . . I wonder what the braw Dick'll say about that when he hears . . .?' The drawling words halted as he watched the colour drain from Beatrice's face. His words had unlocked a floodgate of memories which Beatrice had tried desperately to forget. Wull Slater was the image of their father – his face, his short, square body, even the sound of his whining voice, and his calculating eyes . . .

Suddenly Beatrice was twelve years old again, bathing in front of the fire in the tin bath; her mother was putting the boys to bed. It was Saturday night. Their father had gone to the Crown and Thistle; at least he had pretended to go . . .

'He was vile!' she muttered vehemently, scarcely aware that she was speaking her tormented thoughts aloud. 'He was an animal!'

Wull watched her unnervingly. The goose pimples stood out on her arms and she trembled. Why should she stand like a craven coward in her own home? In her own bedchamber! Her eyes flashed defiantly and she thrust the petticoat over her head, but she did not wait to fasten it as she grabbed her dress and put it on quickly. She felt better, warmer, less naked.

'I have work tae do,' she moved towards the door, still buttoning up her dress. Wull Slater was blocking her path. He did not move. 'I said I have work to do, and so have you, if you intend to say here.' Subconsciously Beatrice had dropped the broad slang of their childhood. She was speaking clearly, as Sarah had taught her to speak when they were children, so that her dear mama could understand their words, even though she could not hear them.

'There's nae need tae put on airs like a lady wi' me!' Wull snapped irritably.

Beatrice grimaced. 'It would be difficult to pretend to be a lady with pigs to feed and byres to clean, while you lie in your bed.'

A dull flush of anger crept over Wull's sallow skin. 'There's nae need tae sharpen yer tongue, just because I've come back tae claim the mill.'

'Ye didna come back to claim your share o' the trouble, or the work!' Beatrice snapped angrily. 'The place would have fallen about our ears if we had depended on you!'

'Ach, ye're as bad as Joe!'

'Joe . . .?' Beatrice's blue eyes flashed but before she could say any more Wull laughed derisively.

'Aye, Joe. He told me Grandfather Miller intended tae leave ye the Mill Hoose, and his half o' the mill. He was aye a silly auld fool!' Wull sneered. 'Joe thought I wad keep awa' frae ye if he gave me a suit o' clothes and his gold watch! Feels sorry for ye, does Joe, just because ye looked after oor mad mother!'

'Joe tried tae bribe ye with his ain suit? He— he gave ye Grandfather's gold watch tae— tae keep ye away frae here?'

'Aye.' Wull laughed mirthlessly. 'Joe's a fool tae. He should hae kept what was his, like I mean tae dae. You an' Joe were aye the old man's favourites!' he added spitefully. 'But I'm the oldest son now, and that's what counts. Ye'll have tae work for me.'

'You make me sick!' Beatrice almost spat with contempt, but inside she felt a small glow of gratitude to Joe. At least he had tried to protect her from Wull's greed. 'Move out of my way . . .'

'Not sae fast, my fine lady!' Wull growled and grabbed her arm, spinning her roughly away from the bedroom door. 'Remember your braw convict's no' here tae protect ye now . . . It's about time we sorted out a few things now there's just you an' me . . . I've some things I want tae sell in that Store. That husband o' yours had better agree or I shall spread word around that he stole 'em . . .'

'Ye want Dick tae sell stolen goods?' Beatrice's face paled. 'Ye must be mad! Dick wad never dae that!'

'He will – if ye persuade him, and ye'd better, if ye value his freedom!' The small round eyes glittered menacingly.

Eleven

At the Tower House Bert Bradshaw ushered men, women and children into the great hall as eagerly as a child at his first party. He knew that some of his larger tenants despised him because he had not been born a 'gentleman'; they resented his refusal to join their shooting and hunting parties – parties which he now knew many of them could not afford to attend either. Bert Bradshaw spoke with a broad accent, and an English one at that, and he made no pretence at being a gentleman. He did not excuse late rent payments from any of his tenants, large or small, but he was always fair and reasonable and the smaller tenants had learned to respect him.

There were those who disliked him employing a factor who had been no more than a small working farmer, however knowledgeable he might be, and they were jealous that the owner of Strathtod should extend the hand of friendship to Alexander Logan and his family. Nevertheless Bert was determined that none of the children on the estate should suffer on account of their parents' bigotry. They were all invited, tenant or labourer. It made him happy to give a little happiness to others, especially at such a festive time and he was sorry that some of the workers had been forbidden to attend the Boxing Day entertainment. This did not prevent a good attendance or spoil the enjoyment of the rest.

Sarah was seated beside one of the long windows with Fanny and Freda. Fanny's small son was crouched at their feet together with Alex and Billy. Like the rest of the children the little boys were agog with excitement the moment the Punch and Judy Show began. Many of the parents were as enthralled as their children. Louis and Janet and the four young Whiteleys had arrived in good time and were well placed on the opposite side of the hall.

Sarah did not notice Louis creep out almost as soon as the show had begun. Janet frowned and pursed her lips. Louis had been sick again that morning and he had been reluctant to set out on the long walk across the fields to the Tower House, but none of his children had ever seen a professional entertainer before and even Janet had looked forward eagerly to visiting the Tower House. She was soon engrossed in the antics of Mr Punch and his dog, Toby, so she was barely aware of the time passing.

Sandy, too, had seen Louis leaving, and he was concerned when he had not returned by the end of the show; indeed Louis's continuing bouts of sickness worried him. They reminded him too much of his mother's illness, though hers had been so brief.

While the children were forming into a long line to receive their apples and thank Mr Bradshaw, Sandy strolled outside.

He found Louis clinging to the wall of the ash pit behind the Tower House kitchens. His face was grey, his skin damp with perspiration, yet he was shivering like a man with an ague. Sandy limped towards him as fast as he could.

'Man, Louis, ye're in an awful state!' he exclaimed in consternation. 'We must get ye hame at once!' Louis made no reply. He was incapable of moving from the wall which supported him. His eyes were sunken in his lean face. 'I'll bring the pony and trap tae the back door and help ye in, for ye're in no state to walk.'

'Janet . . .?' Louis gasped weakly.

'Aye, I'll get Janet and she'll come i' the trap tae. Dinna worry, we'll soon have ye in your bed.' Sandy grasped his stick and hurried to the stables. He found William overseeing the harnessing of the pony and his own horse.

'Louis is sick. He's bad.'

William turned. 'I'll bring the trap to the back, shall I? We'll take him home in it?'

Sandy nodded briefly.

Sarah received the news of Louis's latest sickness with some dismay but she needed all her own self-control to calm Janet, who had burst into tears and was upsetting Maggie and the younger children.

'He didna want tae come,' Janet sniffed remorsefully. 'He wasna weel this morn!'

'Never mind that now, Janet,' Sarah spoke briskly. 'You will go home in the trap with Louis and my father. But it would help if you could take Alex and Billy. I'll walk back.' She glanced ruefully at her fine leather boots. They were not meant for rough walking over fields and burns on a winter's day. 'Ask Father to tell Agnes what has happened and I'll be home for the milking as soon as I can.'

'Oh Mistress Sarah, I'd forgotten . . .'

'Never mind the work, Janet. The cows will have to wait for once. Nothing matters so long as Louis gets home quickly and safely into bed.'

'I will take you home in the carriage, Mistress Fairly, and the children, if you can wait a little while,' Crispin Bradshaw said quietly, appearing at her elbow. 'Mistress Whiteley, the trap is waiting for you. Your husband will feel better when he is lying in a warm bed. Master Fairly has ridden ahead. I think he intends to summon the doctor.'

'The doctor! Again?' Janet gasped in dismay.

'He may be able to help your husband.' He ushered Janet gently but firmly to the waiting trap, carrying her youngest child, but at the door she turned.

'Ye'll hurry hame right now, across the fields, Maggie,' she bid her tearful daughter. 'And mind the other twae. Oh, and put an oven shelf i' the bed tae warm it, if ye're hame before us, lassie. It will tak a wee while for the pony and trap to get back tae Fairlyden by the road! Louis will . . .'

'My father will have wrapped him well in the rug. Now do hurry, Janet,' Sarah urged anxiously. 'I shall be home as soon as I can.'

It took a little while for the crowd to disperse. Alex and Billy were hopping up and down with excitement at the prospect of riding in a closed carriage, but within minutes of piling on to the well-sprung seats the excitement of the day became too much for them and they curled up on either side of Sarah and laid their heads in her lap. Crispin Bradshaw watched almost enviously as Sarah's hand gently smoothed the dark curls on each little head until two pairs of eyelids closed sleepily. Then she stared out at the grey December day. It would be dark soon. Her stomach churned as she thought of Louis. He had looked so desperately ill. She knew her father was very anxious about him. Maggie too; the girl adored her father. The thirteen-year-old was little more than a child herself, but she was very reliable.

'Don't look so anxious, Sarah,' Crispin's deep voice drew her attention from the passing grey landscape. 'Louis may not be as bad as we feared once he gets home.'

'But he has had so many bad turns on and off these past few years . . .'

'Yet he always recovers.'

'I was thinking of Agnes, too. There is a lot of work to be done before night, and neither Janet nor Louis will be there, nor William if he has ridden for the doctor.'

'Perhaps I could help?' Crispin offered.

Amusement lit Sarah's dark eyes for a moment as she glanced at his long-skirted coat and smart dark trousers. She had never noticed before what long legs he had. She looked up and caught him watching her and she blushed as furiously as any gauche young girl.

'I dinna suppose you would be much good at milking cows and feeding pigs?'

'I have turned my hand to many things though not, I confess, to milking cows.'

'And what about chopping turnips for the bullocks, or pushing hay down from the loft for the cows?'

'I could try. Maybe you have some suitable clothes I could borrow?'

Sarah saw he really meant what he said. She shook her head. 'William hates such tasks. I wouldna ask you to help. Indeed you've done more than enough already.'

'Would you believe me if I said it is a pleasure to help you, Sarah?' His voice was level, but his grey eyes held Sarah's and she was disconcerted by the expression in them.

'I— I . . .' Her voice trailed away in a breathless halt when Crispin leaned forward and took one of her hands in both of his. His grey eyes were fixed intently on her face.

'I mean it, Sarah. It is a pleasure to help you. I hope you will come to me if ever you are in need?'

'I . . . yes, I suppose so.' Sarah murmured uncertainly.

Deep, deep within Crispin's cool grey eyes there was a glimmer of fire, of a passion which was chained by his iron control, yet there was a yearning too. 'Promise me, Sarah?'

'Yes, I promise,' Sarah whispered huskily, but in her heart she knew her need would have to be great indeed before she would risk involving Crispin Bradshaw more closely in her life. He was kind and strong, and yet she was afraid . . . not of Crispin, but of herself, she realised with a start, and in the same moment she was conscious of her gloved hand still clasped in his. She withdrew it sharply. The sudden movement disturbed Alex. He sat up and rubbed his sleepy dark eyes.

'Are we nearly home?' he mumbled, and his voice wakened Billy also. Sarah was almost relieved to give her attention to her small sons for the short journey which remained.

'Beatrice!' Sarah exclaimed in astonishment when she entered the kitchen at Fairlyden to find her old friend pacing backwards and forwards across the hearth, clutching a fretful Ellen.

Despite her own anxiety over Louis and her preoccupation with the many tasks needing urgent attention, Sarah was instantly aware of Beatrice's agitation. Before she could frame the questions which sprang to her lips Beatrice rushed into nervous speech.

'Wull's back! I— I had tae get awa frae him, Sarah! I didna ken where else tae run . . .'

'Are you all right? Did he harm you?' Sarah asked quickly.

'I'm f-fine n-now.' Beatrice took a deep breath striving for control. 'Your husband brought news o' Louis's sickness. Agnes wanted tae go tae the cottage tae prepare a warm bed. I said I wad look after Ellen but she's inconsolable . . .'

'I expect she's hungry . . .'

'I will bring her tae your chamber!' Beatrice suggested instantly. Sarah recognised the desperation in her blue eyes. Their silent message was clear, I need to talk to you alone.

Behind her Crispin Bradshaw had seen it too. The strain on Beatrice O'Connor's pale face and the purple bruise darkening her jaw told him clearly that she was in some kind of trouble. She was shivering, despite the blazing fire behind her and the woollen shawl pinned so tightly across her chest. She was too preoccupied even to acknowledge him, yet Crispin knew she recognised him. He had called at the Mill House once or twice to buy some of the English bread she sometimes sold instead of the more usual soda scones which the local people preferred. Beatrice O'Connor had always greeted him pleasantly, and her smile changed everything about her fine serious features.

'Aunt Beattie!' It was young Alex who broke the moment of tension. Both he and Billy released their grip on Sarah's skirts, forgetting their tiredness in their eagerness to tell Beattie of their visit to the Tower House.

'Not just now, boys!' Sarah spoke quietly but firmly. 'There is much to do and I need Aunt Beattie to help me. As soon as I have fed Ellen I must go to milk the cows. Louis is ill and Janet must stay with him, maybe Maggie too. I want you to be very good and come to the byre with me, when we have all changed our clothes.' Billy's response was a huge yawn and a tired rub at his eyes. Alex made no protest but his eyes were shadowed with fatigue.

'I will keep an eye on these two fine fellows,' Crispin offered.

'I canna ask you to do that!' Sarah protested. But Crispin shook his head and smiled at the two little boys. Ellen gave an impatient wail.

'Oh dear!' Sarah felt harassed. If only William or her father would come.

'If Alex and Billy can get into their nightshirts I shall search all my pockets until I find two new farthings.' Alex and Billy immediately began to oblige.

'That is bribery,' Sarah declared. 'And I couldna possibly allow you—' Ellen gave a deafening and prolonged wail. Crispin smiled at Sarah's despairing grimace.

'Your daughter knows I am right. She needs you, and so does Mistress O'Connor. Your sons will be safe with me. Tonight is an emergency,' Crispin reminded her.

'Mr Bradshaw is right,' Beatrice spoke in a strained voice. 'If he will mind the boys, I will help ye with the milking and the pigs, Sarah. But first ye must attend to Ellen. May I come with ye?'

Sarah nodded and turned towards the stairs while Crispin Bradshaw, in his well-cut clothes, made himself perfectly at home in the modest surroundings of Fairlyden's kitchen, and two weary and bemused small boys appeared more than willing to do his bidding.

Once they were upstairs in Sarah's bedchamber, Beatrice seemed reluctant to mention the reason for her unexpected presence so late on a bitingly cold winter's afternoon. She held Ellen in the crook of her arm and moved the small objects on Sarah's washstand restlessly from one place to another and back again.

'Your dress is beautiful, Sarah,' she remarked without a trace of envy.

Sarah's colour increased slightly. 'My father brought me the material for Christmas.' She had no idea that Sandy had asked Bert Bradshaw to bring it specially from the Yorkshire mills, or that his son had chosen the dark crimson wool himself. 'I sent away for one of those paper patterns. But Beatrice, please tell me what's troubling you. Has Wull been asking for money again?'

Beatrice made no reply. Sarah crossed the room to stand beside her.

'Now that I have changed my dress I will take my noisy daughter. Come and sit beside me . . .?' she suggested gently. 'Would you like to borrow another shawl?' she asked with concern when Beatrice shivered.

'I— I'll be fine, Sarah, if I can just stay here. I— I think Dick'll ask at Jardine's store when he sees I'm not at hame. I t-told Ray Jardine I had tae c-come tae Fairlyden urgently.'

'Why, Beatrice?'

'If— if ye c-could lend me one of your d-dresses, Sarah, and a coarse apron, I'll help ye with the milking.'

Sarah bit her lip. It was plain that Beatrice was upset; she seemed desperately afraid too, but Sarah knew her well enough to realise she would only confide in her when she was ready.

'There's a dress in my chest, but it will be too big for you. Maybe you'll be able to pull it in with the apron strings . . .?'

Beatrice nodded wanly and unpinned her shawl. It was then Sarah saw the torn bodice of her own dress and the scratches and congealed blood which marred her white skin.

'Oh, Beattie!' she whispered in horror.

Beatrice's face was a stiff mask but she made no effort to hide the ugly bruises which circled her neck and darkened the soft white flesh of her upper arms. She let her own dress fall to the floor and pinned together the torn bodice of her flannel petticoat before pulling Sarah's dress over her head. When she looked up Sarah saw that her eyes were bright with unshed tears but her mouth was hard and angry.

'Wull came tae stay on Christmas Eve. He lost his temper because I wadna dae as he asked!' she said tightly. 'He didna escape unscathed though! I fought him . . . aye I scratched him like a cat!' Beatrice almost spat the words and her blue eyes glittered. 'He'll carry the marks for many a day.' Then her face crumpled. 'But I darena return hame . . .' she whispered fearfully.

'Where is Dick?' Sarah asked sharply.

Slowly Beatrice began to talk, recounting Wull Slater's arrival, his play acting, his demands . . .

'Dick should hae been back frae delivering the coal by now!' she finished anxiously. 'I canna gang back alone!'

'Of course you canna,' Sarah soothed. She changed her guzzling infant to her other breast, modestly hidden by the folds of her shawl. 'Dick is sure to come when Ray Jardine tells him where to find you.'

'What if he sees Wull first? Supposing they had a fight!' Beattie whispered hoarsely. It's what Wull Slater wants – tae get Dick back in prison. He doesna care how! He thinks he can take over the Farmers' Store, aye an' everything in it! He thinks I'll be his slave while he acts the gentleman,' she added bitterly. 'He thinks I'll have nae place tae bide if Dick is sent tae prison again . . .' Suddenly she slumped down on to the bed and hid her head in her hands, sobbing uncontrollably.

'Beattie! Oh, my dear!'

'It's Dick I'm worried about!' Beattie sobbed. 'I dinna ken what we're going tae dae. Wull Slater called me a whore! He— he's going tae – taunt Dick wi' his vile stories, and . . .' she shuddered. 'I dinna want tae talk about it, Sarah!'

'I know, Beattie, I know!' Sarah said gently. 'Come, see Ellen has finished feeding for now and she will sleep in the crib downstairs while I'm at the byre. I will make a cup of tea. It will calm you and warm you a little. Then I'd be truly glad of your help with the milking.' Sarah knew she had to keep Beatrice occupied until Dick came to Fairlyden, and she and Agnes would be glad of the help too.

'I— I'm sorry for bringing my troubles here,' Beattie said softly now.

'I'm very glad you came to me,' Sarah declared firmly. 'Try not to worry. We'll decide what to do while we're at the milking. It is a good place to think, against the warm flank of a cow, with the milk strumming into the pail. By the time we're finished Dick will be here.'

'I do hope sae!' Beatrice whispered fervently. 'I shall never forgive myself if he's in trouble on account o' Wull Slater! I dinna care about anything else, except Dick, but I canna bide at the Mill House if Wull Slater stays! I'd sooner bide in the guttter!'

Both Sarah and Beatrice had forgotten Crispin Bradshaw's presence until Sarah went to put Ellen in the wooden crib beside the fire and saw him still sitting there, nearly hidden from view by the high back of the oak settle. Billy and Alex were perched one on either knee, their dark heads and rosy cheeks cradled against his broad chest. Yet Crispin looked happy and content. He gave no sign that he had overheard their conversation, despite Beatrice's flaming cheeks. He smiled up at Sarah.

'Your sons have had a busy day,' he said softly. 'If you show me their room I will carry them to bed.'

'I canna ask you to do any more!' Sarah was shocked.

'You're not asking. I am offering. Anyway it would be cruel to waken them to climb the stairs.'

Sarah led the way and in no time the boys were safely tucked up together in the large cot which they now shared. Sarah was surprised at the fleeting expression of sadness on Crispin's face as he looked down on their angelic faces, but when he straightened Sarah thought she must have imagined it.

'I couldn't help overhearing Mistress O'Connor,' he said in a low voice as he followed Sarah back down the stairs. 'I guessed she was in some kind of trouble. Let me know if I can help.'

'Thank you,' Sarah said slowly. 'Beattie is my dearest friend. She is— is like a sister!'

'She is fortunate. I believe you are a very loyal friend.' He sighed. 'Now I will call at the cottage to enquire after Louis Whiteley. I fear he is a very sick man. Goodnight, Sarah.'

'Goodnight, and thank you. You've done a lot for all of us today.'

Crispin smiled down into her face and Sarah felt her colour rise once more. Beatrice had gone through the scullery into the dairy beyond; they could hear the murmur of voices and Sarah guessed Agnes had returned to start the milking. Sarah lowered her gaze from Crispin Bradshaw's compelling grey one.

'Goodnight,' she said softly. 'I wish you a safe journey back to Yorkshire tomorrow.'

When he had left she went to join Agnes and Beattie in the dairy.

'Mistress O'Connor says she is staying tae help with the milking,' Agnes declared with a sigh of relief. 'I've given her Janet's stool an' piggin. Is that all richt, Mistress Sarah?'

'Yes. I expect the cows will be fidgeting and wondering why we're late.'

'Aye,' Agnes nodded. 'Nicky came o'er the burn with Janet's bairns. He said he wad gie us a han' wi' the milking if we were no' finished when he's chopped the turnips for the bullocks and the wee stirks. He's bringing in the fodder an' water for the kie tae . . . as soon as he has seen tae the horses. He was wondering aboot the pigs, Mistress Sarah . . . an' there'll be Louis's pig tae. I doot Janet'll be sae worrit she'll never mind tae feed it.'

'I think young Thomas will attend to it,' Sarah murmured as she settled herself on her three-legged stool. 'He's a good laddie although he is only twelve, and small for his age. Louis has trained him to help.'

'I wonder what's keepin' Master Fairly,' Agnes muttered anxiously, echoing Sarah's own thoughts. 'Surely Doctor Kerr should hae been here by now . . .? I've never seen Louis as bad as this before.'

William had ridden to Muircumwell as fast as he dared. He knew Louis Whiteley was gravely ill, but as the daylight faded the road had become treacherous in places; the mud had frozen in rough humps and ruts, making it all too easy for his horse to stumble. It was dark by the time he reached the doctor's house, and to make matters worse there was only a young maid to answer his knock. Nervously she informed him that Doctor Kerr had been called to a patient and she had no idea where he might be or how long before he returned.

'Your mistress then? Tell her . . .'

'She's awa oot tae, Sir.' The girl sounded nervous. 'She had tae go tae Mistress Bryson's . . .'

'Then please tell the doctor we need him at Fairlyden as soon as he returns.'

'Aye, Sir. Ye want him tae gang tae . . .? What was the name, Sir?'

'Fairlyden!' William repeated sharply, then more patiently, 'Please give me a paper and a quill. I will write a message for the doctor.'

William frowned as he untethered his horse a few minutes later. The young maid was little more than a child. The doctor's housekeeper must be ill, or away. He felt uneasy. Would the girl remember to give the doctor his note?

Twelve

Dick O'Connor had taken longer than he anticipated to deliver the coal and firewood to the old woman in Bentira village, but he was glad he had kept his promise. He had found Mistress Little in urgent need of warmth and a hot drink by the time he arrived at her isolated cottage. Dick had kindled the fire himself and filled up the old woman's water bucket from the well, then he had waited for the kettle to boil. The woman had been pathetically grateful, despite her fine spirit of independence. They had shared a pot of tea and the oatcakes and cheese which Beatrice had packed for him.

On the way home his mare had cast her shoe and he had had to return a mile and a half to the Bentira forge. The blacksmith was an elderly man and it had taken him some time to blow up his forge and shoe the mare. Consequently Dick was cold and hungry by the time he returned to the Mill House and the winter's afternoon was already darkening.

There was no sign of Beatrice while Dick busied himself grooming and feeding the mare.

She'll be making a tasty meal, nae doubt, Dick thought to himself. An expectant smile erased the lines from his tired face as he pushed open the Mill House door. He was bitterly disappointed to find the kitchen cold and empty, the fire burned to grey ash. There was no sign of his wife, or her brother. Frowning, Dick made his way to the little byre; he looked in the adjoining bullock shed, the pig sties, the hen house. He called Beatrice's name but there was no reply.

He went back to the house and up to the bed chamber he shared with Beatrice. He stared at the mud-splashed gown and petticoat lying on the floor, the dirty water still in the basin on the marble-topped washstand. Beatrice was always neat and tidy. His frown deepened and his heart filled with foreboding, yet he had no real reason to be concerned. Where was Wull Slater? There was something about him Dick could not trust, despite his initial sympathy for a man returning to his family after a long absence. He glanced into the room where Wull Slater had slept. The bed was unmade; a bundle of tangled blankets and the feather quilt were heaped in the middle. Dick clattered down the narrow wooden stairs and out into the yard again. It was almost dark now and he could hear the animals moving restlessly in their sheds. It was almost feeding time. Dick's own stomach churned emptily.

He crossed the yard to the mill. At first he thought it was empty for the door was firmly shut. He pushed it open and took the lantern from its hook by the door and lit it. On the ground floor he kept the food for the cattle and pigs, sacks of ground corn meal, bran and the slabs of linseed cake, as well as bags of potatoes, carefully wrapped against the penetrating frost. He searched every corner. He mounted the stairs to the floor where they kept the tools and small bags of grass and turnip seeds, and packets of garden seeds, when these were in season. He looked around at the pile of twine, the forks and hoes, a scythe and a couple of sickles, the pails and scuttles, curry combs, whetstones, awls, hedging hooks. He sighed. Everything seemed just as he had left it, late on Christmas Eve; Beattie could not have had many customers in today. Even the black lead and wooden clothes' pegs, the nails and hammers and a selection of tin trays were neat and undisturbed. He and Beattie tried to think of everything their customers might require. Beattie had even scrubbed out the little building which had been the kiln so that she could have a clean and separate building to store oatmeal and flour and the jams and jellies she had made during the summer.

Dick was about to retrace his steps and go down to the old kiln shed when he heard a rumble on the floor above. They had no stock to keep on the top floor yet, so Dick was puzzled by the noise.

'Beattie!' he called. 'Are ye up there, lassie?' But it was Wull Slater's face which appeared at the top of the wooden ladder. In the dim light he looked like his father's ghost. Dick felt a chill run down his spine. He was standing almost on the spot where Edward Slater's twisted body had lain.

'What are ye doing up there?' he asked sharply. 'Where's Beattie?'

'I dinna ken!' Wull snapped sullenly, and his tone plainly implied that he did not care either.

'What are ye doing up there?'

'I'm taking a guid look at ma ain property, O'Connor.' His voice held a sneer. He climbed down the wooden ladder.

'What do you mean?' Dick asked with a frown, as he walked ahead and down the stairs to the ground floor. He hung the lantern on its hook and turned to face his brother-in-law. Wull had dropped his obsequious act. He glared belligerently at Dick.

'Ye're just like your father!' Dick exclaimed involuntarily.

'Aye, well at least I'm his ain flesh an' blood, an' what was his is mine now! Ye'll be working for me frae now on. The Mill House is mine! All this is mine!' Wull swept an arm around the contents of the mill, causing Dick to step back or take a slap in the face.

'I dinna ken what ye're talking about. Where's Beattie? The house is empty. The fire's out. Did she no' say where she was going?' Dick was hungry and angry and his anxiety about Beatrice was increasing with every syllable of Wull Slater's ranting.

'Why should I care where she's gone?' he drawled sullenly. 'She never had any right tae be here, and neither hae ye. I've had a guid look, an' I ken what's here, so . . .'

'What did ye say!' Dick gripped Wull Slater by the shoulders. 'Have ye been frightening Beattie? Is that why she's gone? Where is she? Where . . .?' His fear for Beattie made him shake Wull. Dick was a tall man, and a strong one; hard work had seen to that.

'That bitch!' Wull snarled through chattering teeth. 'She went out as soon as ye'd gone, whoring, I shouldna wonder!' He glared malevolently at Dick's white face.

'Why you— you!' Dick's grasp tightened and Wull Slater struggled to free himself.

''Tis true!' he growled furiously. 'She is a whore! She admitted it! She slept wi' my ain father. You ask her!' he taunted slyly. 'Or are ye afraid o' the truth?'

'Ye're a liar!' Dick almost howled with rage. He thrust Wull Slater backwards through the open door, out into the mill yard. 'I'll droon ye like the rat ye are if ye utter such lies again!'

'It's the truth. Ma father told me himself!'

Dick felt rage boiling in him. He had known since his wedding night that Beatrice was troubled and afraid. Now he knew why. He also realised she would never have given herself willingly, least of all to her own father. He pounced at Wull and seized him by the collar.

'Ye wad slander your ain sister? Your ain father? You—'

'Let me go, or ye'll swing for this!' Wull gasped furiously. 'She's a bastard . . .' He struggled, powerless to free himself as Dick's iron grip tightened. They were moving nearer to the water; he could hear it rushing. 'I tell't the bitch ye'd be back in jail afore long!' he gasped. 'Ye should hae swung when ye attacked the Earl!'

'Where is Beattie? What have ye . . .?' Dick's voice trailed away and he drew Wull Slater close, staring down into his broad, sullen face. A faint beam of light streamed from the lantern, swaying in the open door of the mill. Scratches showed plainly on Wull's sallow skin. Dear God, Beattie, what has he done tae ye, my lassie? he cried silently. Aloud his words came through gritted teeth.

'Ye fought wi' her! Why? What have ye done tae her?' But it was the rage glittering in Dick's eyes which made Wull Slater quiver with fear, like the craven coward he was beneath his sneering bravado. He had taunted a mild-mannered mouse and found the raging lion in Dick O'Connor.

'I was only haeing a wee bit of fun,' he whined. 'She panicked.'

'Beatrice wouldna have scratched ye like that without reason!' Dick wondered how he could have been so blind. Wull Slater was the image of his father and Edward Slater had been a liar and a cheat, and worse! Dick recalled the terror in Beattie's eyes on their wedding night. He had never quite succeeded in banishing the horrors of her past, and now he understood why. His grip on Wull Slater tightened involuntarily. 'Tae think we made ye welcome in oor ain hame! Ye'd better get awa frae here richt now! Ye're not worth swinging for, but I'll dae it if ye ever come near Beattie and me again!' He gave Wull a heave which sent his stocky figure sprawling onto the frozen earth. Dick's only thought now was to find Beatrice. He turned towards the house.

'O'Connor!' Wull Slater bellowed furiously. 'This is my place now, I tell ye! Ye'll *take* the orders, aye ye and that prim bitch ye call your wife!'

'Ye're mad! Mr Miller aye said everything he had wad be Beatrice's. As for the mill, it wad hae fallen doon long since if it had waited for ye coming back!'

Dick turned away again. He did not wait to see Wull scramble to his feet and grab the iron bar standing just inside the door of the Old Mill Store.

Some sixth sense made him glance over his shoulder just in time to see Wull creep up behind him. Dick lunged instinctively. Wull was taken by surprise. The iron bar clattered to the ground. He bent to retrieve it but Dick kicked it out of reach and sent him sprawling across the yard with the force of his clenched fist. Wull howled with anger. He rolled to his feet and came at Dick like a butting stag. Dick felt the breath leave his body and his knees buckle as he fell to the ground clutching his stomach. Wull seized his advantage and kicked him in the face, sending him reeling backwards. Wull had taken him by surprise but he would not do so again. Dick was fit, and light on his feet; he sprang aside as Wull lunged at him; then they were wrestling together, fighting furiously, rolling ever nearer to the mill pond which had driven the great wooden wheel not so long ago.

William Fairly walked his horse away from Doctor Kerr's with a feeling of dissatisfaction. He was certain the young maid would forget about his note. Sarah would never forgive him if anything happened to Louis because he had failed to bring the doctor. Indeed William would never forgive himself. He had learned to respect the stoical Louis, who tackled so many tasks at Fairlyden with unfailing cheerfulness. Despite his own education and travels William realised that the quiet countryman knew far more about nature and the lore of the countryside than he would ever know. Sarah's father had taught Louis to plough, but it was his own skill and determination which had won him so many trophies at the local ploughing matches.

William made up his mind. He would not ride back to Fairlyden without speaking to the doctor first. He would ride round to the Mill House. Beatrice would make him a cup of tea perhaps. But no, Beatrice was at Fairlyden! He had been too preoccupied with thoughts of Louis's illness to pay much attention to her presence when he had stopped briefly at Fairlyden earlier. He frowned now, and for the first time he wondered why Beatrice O'Connor was so far from home so late on the day after Christmas. There had been a bruise darkening her jaw, he recalled. He mounted his horse almost automatically and rode towards the mill. He would call on Dick O'Connor and find out what was amiss.

Even before he saw the shapes rolling on the ground in the semi-darkness William heard the grunts and scuffling, a groan and a clatter. He flicked the reins and his horse quickened its pace obediently.

A narrow beam of light streamed out from the door of the Mill Store. It was enough for William to recognise one of the men.

'For God's sake, O'Connor! Have you not caused enough trouble with your fighting!' William shouted angrily.

Dick did not answer. He was breathing hard. Wull Slater was neither fit nor tall, but he was thickset and heavy and he fought in the meanest possible way.

William slid from his horse and raised his whip, bringing it down across them both.

'Stand up! Both of you! What's the meaning of this? Is this the reason Beatrice is seeking refuge at Fairlyden with bruises on her face?'

'Ye've seen Beattie?' Dick spun towards William and his heart surged with relief. He scarcely knew what his beloved wife might have suffered at Wull Slater's hands, but at least she was safe!

'You did not know?'

'I've been awa' most o' the day, delivering coal. When I returned the hoose was empty. Beattie ran away frae him!' Dick almost spat in his contempt. 'Her ain brother, Wull Slater!'

Neither of them noticed Slater roll silently towards the iron bar he had dropped earlier.

'He says the house and the mill are his! He's been checking the stock in't tae!'

William whistled and moved his head to look at Slater's recumbent figure. Only Wull was no longer recumbent. He raised the bar hastily intending to fell Dick from behind.

'Look out!' William reacted instinctively, bringing his whip down heavily across both of Slater's wrists as Dick spun around to defend himself. Wull gave a screech of pain and the bar clattered to the ground. William moved to pick it up and then faced them squarely.

'Now tell me the whole story,' he commanded. He had learned to mix and deal with men from every walk of life during his weeks on board ship, and during the first months he had spent in America; twice he had come near to starving; he had survived honestly by his own wits, yet William Fairly, youngest son of the late Lord Gordon Fairly, had retained the influence of his early upbringing. Neither Dick nor Wull questioned his inbred air of authority.

'I ken Joseph Miller intended Beattie tae have everything that belonged tae him, though it was little enough by the end, the way his trade and buildings had deteriorated. He told me often enough in the little time I had with him,' Dick answered, and despite his anger there was a note of sadness and regret for the fine old miller.

'Ye've no proof o' that. Who wad believe the word o' a convict!' Wull Slater crowed triumphantly. 'I've been keeping an eye on things! Oh aye, I watched the auld place being repaired,' he jeered malevolently.

Dick gasped. 'Why you . . .'

'That's enough, Dick!' William commanded. 'So you think the Mill House should be yours?' He turned to Wull Slater with a look of contempt.

'There's nae doot! It is mine, the mill tae, or maybe I should say, "The Farmers' Store",' he amended mockingly. 'As I told Beatrice, everything belonged tae my mother on the day she died, because ma grandfather died afore her!' His yellow teeth gleamed triumphantly in the flickering light of the lantern. 'I've made enquiries. It's all mine. I'm the oldest surviving son.'

'Well, Dick?' William queried with a frown.

'It's nothing tae dae wi' him!' Slater gibed. 'His bitch o' a wife was on'y ma mother's bastard! Ma ain father told me that once when he was in his cups. She's nae claim tae anything!'

This time it was William who gasped. He looked sharply at Dick and saw his lean jaw clench in the faint gleam from the lantern but it was impossible to see his eyes.

'Could this be true, Dick?' William asked with a note of disbelief.

'I dinna ken! But I reckon Beattie wad be pleased tae ken she wasna spawned by a devil like Slater. As for the rest . . . surely he canna take everything? Why Beattie and me, we've worked for months tae build up the hoose and the auld buildings for the Store. He must hae been skulking around watching! The lazy . . .' Dick's fists clenched when he thought of the way Beatrice had worked until her knuckles bled and her knees were raw.

'Keep calm, Dick!' William warned sharply. 'And you needn't smirk, Master Slater. If you want the buildings you will have to pay Dick and his wife for their labours in carrying out the repairs . . .'

'What! I'll pay for naethin'! They're mine I tell ye. Everything's mine that's in these buildings.'

'And as for the stock,' William went on coldly and with the same air of authority, 'I have an interest in that myself.' Dick stifled a gasp, but William threw him a quelling glance.

'Y-you?' For the first time Wull Slater lost some of his bragging confidence.

'When you have the money to pay for the stock, and for the repairs, you can come to see me,' William announced firmly. 'Or of course we can put the matter in the hands of the lawyers and they will sort it out. There might not be much left to claim of course by the time you pay their fees . . .' William finished mildly.

'Why you— you . . .' Wull Slater blustered and spluttered.

'Of course if you don't have enough money to take over the stock yourself you could let the buildings for a small rent.'

'Rent?'

'Yes. Dick and his wife could keep their business and pay you a rent for the buildings . . . when they have proof they belong to you of course.'

'Rent it tae them! Never!' Wull Slater uttered a stream of oaths which made Dick wince. William's dark eyes narrowed in contempt.

'Then you must wait until the stock is sold before you take over the property.'

Wull Slater opened and shut his mouth several times before he shouted, 'I'll set fire tae the lot afore I'll leave that bitch livin' here in comfort! And as for—'

William cut him short and his tone was grim. 'I am a witness to your threat to set fire to the mill! Also you cannot deny that you assaulted a woman in her own home. Mistress O' Connor has bruises to prove it. Doctor Kerr is going to Fairlyden now.'

'The doctor . . .?' Dick gasped with dismay, but William silenced him with a frown and an imperceptible shake of his head.

'Doctor Kerr will be able to bear witness against you if necessary, Slater. I cannot imagine what the judge would make of your conduct. I believe Mistress O'Connor cared for you most diligently when you were a child, did she not?'

'Judge!' Wull echoed, his sullen voice rising with alarm. He had had enough trouble with the law one way and another. It was the reason he had sent the agent before he came slinking back to the mill in the first place, intending to lie low for a while after a bit of sharp dealing at the port.

'If you come near the mill, or bother the O'Connors in the next three months, this whole affair will be set before a magistrate, and I shall offer myself as a witness against you.'

William spoke with far more confidence than he felt. He had scant knowledge of the law, but he guessed Wull Slater had less, even though he was such a shifty character. He was irritated that the fellow would not agree to accept a rent for the premises, especially when he had done nothing to deserve it, either before, or since the death of his parents. William was certain the Farmers' Store could grow into a thriving business with the right man to make the decisions. He had had vague plans at the back of his mind that he might become a partner in it himself one day if he won the confidence of the O'Connors.

Dick guessed Slater had no money to buy the stock, or anything else. He had probably expected to move into the Mill House and share its comforts and its profits, without any effort of his own. Either way Beatrice and he would soon be homeless, Dick thought with a sinking heart.

'I'll be back!' Wull muttered. 'It'll gie me pleasure tae turn ye oot, aye an' your bitch o' a wife!'

Dick clenched his fists but he stood tensely and watched Wull slink away; then he turned to William Fairly.

'Why is Doctor Kerr visiting Beatrice at Fairlyden? Is she hurt? Did—?'

'Your wife is at Fairlyden. She seemed well enough except for a bruise on her face. I came to Muircumwell to get the doctor for Louis. He has been taken ill again. I fear it is serious. Doctor Kerr was visiting another patient. I shall return now to make sure he gets my message.'

'I'm sorry tae hear about Louis!' Dick said with genuine concern. 'I hope ye get the doctor this time. Wad ye tell Beattie I'll be up at Fairlyden as soon as I can, tae bring her hame, but I'll need tae milk the two cows, and feed the pigs an' hens before I set out.'

'I'll tell her, Dick.'

'Aye, and Mr Fairly . . . I— I thank ye for your help this night. I'm glad ye came when ye did.'

William grimaced in the darkness. He knew how much pride it cost for Dick O'Connor to thank a Fairly.

'I'm glad too, Dick.' He sighed. 'But I doubt if we Fairlys can ever make amends for the way you and your family suffered at the hands of my half-brother.' Even William was a little surprised at his own humility.

'Ye've done enough tonight, Master William,' Dick said warmly. 'The very thought o' yon prison makes me shudder, but I was sore provoked . . .'

'Slater is an objectionable wretch, but I don't know whether I have helped you much, Dick. You and your wife need proper advice.'

'Why did ye tell Slater the stock belonged to ye?' Dick asked curiously.

'I merely said I had an interest in the stock,' William corrected. 'It is true, though not as Slater assumed. I guessed he would be easier to — persuade, if he thought I was involved. He might have insisted on staying with you, or taking over everything without paying, if he thought it all belonged to you and your wife!'

'Aye, ye're right there!' Dick sighed. 'And Wull Slater could never bide under the same roof as Beattie and me. I dinna ken what she'll think o' this nicht's work. I only ken her grandfather intended her tae have the mill, and everything that belonged to him, but I never heard o' him writing it doon.'

In his own heart Dick blamed himself. He didn't care about the Farmers' Store, but the Mill House had been Beattie's home all her life, and he had nothing to offer her in its place. He had nothing to offer her at all except his labours – and his reputation as an ex-prisoner, he thought despondently.

Thirteen

Back at Fairlyden Sarah had only just started milking her second cow when the byre door opened and her father scanned the row of shadowy stalls. He looked white and strained, almost gaunt in the flickering light of the oil lantern. His gaze fell on her and she raised her dark eyebrows in a silent question.

'It's Louis, he's getting worse, lassie. The pain's something terrible! He's rolling all o'er the bed with it, and ye ken Louis isna one tae complain.'

'No, I know,' Sarah murmured anxiously. 'What did the doctor say?'

'William has only just returned, but the doctor wasna hame. He left a message. Could ye . . . do ye think ye could come an' talk tae Janet . . .? I'll help Agnes wi' the milking if ye'll comfort her an' young Maggie . . .'

'Of course I will, but you canna milk, Father. You canna bend your knee.'

'Ach, I think I could manage the cows on the right side if I stretch ma leg in the grip.'

'Well, maybe one or two,' Sarah conceded reluctantly. 'We dinna want you having another broken leg, and Beattie is here. She's helping us.'

Sandy's eyes widened in surprise but he saw the warning look in Sarah's eyes and he asked no questions.

When Sarah reached Janet's cottage she was surprised to find Louis lying quietly in the box bed in the kitchen. After her father's report she had expected him to be thrashing around the bed in pain.

'It seems tae hae eased at last,' Janet whispered huskily and her eyes reflected her relief.

Maggie's eyes were red-rimmed from weeping.

'I think it would be best if you went to the milking, Maggie,' Sarah said gently, knowing it was better for the girl to be occupied when there was so little she could do to help her father.

Maggie looked questioningly at her mother, who nodded. 'Maybe he'll sleep a wee while. Try not tae worry, lassie.' She gave her daughter a quick hug in a rare gesture of affection, but the tears sprang once more to Maggie's eyes as she left the cottage. Her young heart was sorely troubled for the father she adored, but she went obediently.

'You're exhausted, Janet,' Sarah said sympathetically. 'Sit down and I'll brew you a cup o' tea.'

Janet obeyed like a bewildered child, but her eyes rarely left the box bed where her husband lay so still. Sarah made the tea and poured a cup for Janet, then she moved closer to the bed and looked down at Louis. He seemed to have aged ten years in the past few hours. His face was grey and drawn. He opened his eyes, sensing her presence. He seemed pleased to see her beside him but Sarah was shocked to see his eyes so sunken in their sockets. Her heart felt cold with fear; she looked anxiously across the little kitchen at Janet's bowed head.

Louis moved his hand weakly on the covers and his eyes searched Sarah's face. She took his hand in hers and felt the faint pressure in response.

'The pain, is it a little easier, Louis?' she asked softly.

''S gone,' he whispered faintly, so faintly that it was no more than a thread of sound.

Sarah was dismayed but she said calmly, 'You need to rest now then, eh? Get your strength back.' She struggled to summon a smile. 'It'll be spring again before we know. You'll—'

'No.' Louis's voice was very low, but it was firmer. His eyes pleaded with her to listen and Sarah bent lower.

'It's the end o' the furrow, Miss Sarah . . .'

Sarah shook her head but she did not interrupt. It was clear Louis had something on his mind and she could see the unutterable weariness in every line of his pain-ravaged face. An icy chill swept through her veins. She had seen that look once before . . . when she was a child . . . in her mother's bedroom . . . She covered Louis's fingers with her other hand, willing him to take strength from her.

'Ye'll watch o'er Maggie for me . . .?'

'Of course. Maggie is a good girl.'

'Aye . . .' The sunken eyes brightened briefly, then his gaze moved past Sarah to his wife, rocking gently in her chair, her head still bowed, the cup of tea untouched at her side. 'Ye'll gie her time, Miss Sarah . . .? Tae look aroond?' Sarah drew in her breath. She had never considered the full implications of Louis's illness before, but it was clear that he had. 'We hae . . . a wee bit . . . put by . . . but ye'll no' let Master Fairly . . . put her ontae the . . . road?' His voice grew wavery and for a moment he closed his eyes as though the effort of lifting the blue-veined lids was too great. Then he was looking at Sarah again and she saw his anxiety.

'Dinna worry, Louis, please. You know I would never let your family starve.' Sarah was rewarded by the faint lift of his lips, the merest flicker of a smile, before the door opened. Doctor Kerr came in, followed by Dick O'Connor. Sarah gave Louis's hand a final, reassuring squeeze before she stepped back to make way for the doctor and Janet.

'I got a lift up wi' the doctor in his trap,' Dick said quietly. 'Is there anything I can do tae help, think ye?' His eyes looked towards Janet, standing beside her husband's bed, listening to the doctor's calm voice issuing instructions. Sarah shook her head.

'Not here, Dick. I will return later myself, when the doctor has gone.' Sarah moved towards the cottage door and Dick followed. 'Beatrice is helping Agnes with the milking.'

'Is she— is she all right then?'

'Wull Slater frightened her, but she is all right.'

Dick expelled a long breath of relief. 'Thank God! Master Fairly dealt with Wull Slater, at least for the time being, but it seems we'll have tae sell off the stock and look for another place.'

'Oh Dick! Are you sure Mr Miller didna make a will? You must see a lawyer.'

'So long as Beatrice is all right, I dinna care about anything else. I'm no' cut out tae be a shopkeeper anyway, or a merchant, as Mr Fairly calls it, but the Mill House is Beattie's hame. She'll take it badly if we hae tae leave it.'

'Maybe not so badly as you think!' Sarah said quickly, recalling Beatrice's own words. 'Her happiness depends on you, Dick, not on the mill or where she lives.'

'It's kind o' ye tae say so, Miss Sarah, but . . .'

'It's true. She told me so herself.'

'We'll find a way then,' Dick sighed and glanced back at Louis's cottage, 'jist sae long as God grants us our health an' strength.'

There was nothing Doctor Kerr could do for Louis. He knew the sickness and pain was caused by an inflammation inside the lower abdomen but he could do nothing to relieve it. He had seen the condition before. This time the easing of Louis's pain did not reassure him as it had reassured Janet. He guessed that the offending part had burst and brought relief, but in bursting it would spread its poison through the blood and Doctor Kerr wished passionately that he could do something to prevent it.

Louis Whiteley died the following evening, just after Maggie had finished helping with the milking. She was distraught in her youthful grief and Janet could offer her daughter little comfort. Her own grief was intensified by her anxiety. She had four children. She knew better than anyone how hard Louis had worked at Fairlyden; she knew how badly Fairlyden would need another man to plough and sow, to reap and mow as the seasons came and went. Master Fairly would need the cottage to provide a home for a new labourer, the cottage where she and Louis had made their home since the day they married, the place where each of their children had been born. It was the first time the sturdy little house had known death.

Sandy was equally troubled. He understood William's predicament as Master of Fairlyden, but he had known Louis since he was a boy of thirteen. All his life he had been a willing worker, utterly loyal and without any complaint.

Sarah could not remember a time when Louis had not been a part of her life at Fairlyden. Janet too had shared so many of her own sorrows, and more recently her joys; the barriers of maid and mistress had rarely been in evidence through the years they had worked together, and learned together.

William remained silent, understanding Janet's anxiety, and Sarah's concern for her and her family. He had no easy solution to offer.

So the dawn of the new year of 1887 was overshadowed with sadness and the threat of change. The life of each and every person at Fairlyden, from the youngest infant to the oldest man, was interwoven, one with the other, each a link within the human chain which formed the daily life and seasonal toil at Fairlyden.

It was five months before the May term, the time when men and maids usually changed their employers. Before then there was load upon load of manure to dig from the cattle sheds and cart and spread over the fields, there would be ploughing and harrowing, corn and turnips to sow. William knew Nick Jamieson would welcome such responsibilities for he had sensed a restlessness in him of late. If Nick and his wife moved to Fairlyden he would have more time and energy for such tasks too, and he would be close at hand to watch over the cows and sows. Yet William found himself reluctant to ask Janet to move out of her home.

Eventually William decided to call at the Mill House to ask Dick O'Connor if he could lend a hand with the most urgent of the spring work. His own attitude to Dick O'Connor had mellowed now that he felt his happiness with Sarah was assured, and he had sensed that Dick's attitude to himself had also improved since the night of his fight with Wull Slater.

William was surprised to find Dick in excellent spirits considering the precarious state of his future and before he could voice his proposition of work at Fairlyden Dick forestalled him.

'Beattie and me . . . we've decided to rent a wee place of our own, Master Fairly. We were going tae come tae Fairlyden next Sunday tae tell Mistress Fairly.'

William could barely conceal his surprise. 'A wee place . . .?'

'A farm.'

'I see . . .' William was puzzled. He knew Sarah had already discussed the O'Connors' situation with her father in case there was anything for Dick at Strathtod. Sandy had been unable to help. Most of the tenants had accepted their new laird and, whether or not they approved of Bert Bradshaw, they had all elected to renew their leases. 'Are you sure about this, Dick?'

'Aye. It's in ma blood tae tend the animals, and Beattie agrees. I ken it'll be a struggle, but it's what we want.'

'But where will you get a farm to rent? And the money for stock . . .'

'Mr Bradshaw, young Mr Bradshaw that is, he came into the Store on his last visit. He came for some o' Beattie's bread, but he knew how things were at the Store. He said he could help us. He kens o' twae wee farms in Yorkshire. He says they're nearly in ruins and we wad need tae work hard. I wadna mind that, so long as Beattie is willing tae gang wi' me. We've bin saving everything we can frae the Store because we're no' buying any new stock. Wull Slater will hae tae make his ain business, if he can!'

'I doubt if he will have much success!' William declared cynically. 'He has neither brain nor brawn.'

'Well, that'll be his ain affair now, thank God,' Dick muttered fervently. 'Anyway we hae the twae cows and the mare, an' the pigs. Mr Bradshaw says we can take them on the train. I'm tae gang masel first to see both the farms. Mr Bradshaw is going tae meet me at Leeds station. He thinks I'll be able tae bargain for a year free o' rent, if I promise tae improve the farm. He says a lot o' landlords are doing that. Things are real bad down there on account o' all the imported wheat and such like.'

'Then how can you hope to succeed when so many have failed?' William asked dubiously.

'Beattie an' me – we dinna mind hard work. We wadna grow corn. We shall make a living the same way as Mistress Fairly, with cows. If we've milk and butter and eggs we wadna starve and we'd keep some pigs tae pay the rent maybe, and just grow enough corn tae feed them.'

Dick's eyes glowed with anticipation and William had no heart to dampen his enthusiasm further. He hoped Crispin Bradshaw knew what he was about.

'Well, Dick, it seems every man has his own dreams.' William sighed and looked around the mill yard. 'I could have made a good merchant's business here. I suppose Wull Slater will let it go to ruin again if he is as idle as his father.'

'Aye, nae doubt he will. Er . . . I'm no meanin' tae interfere, but have ye heard that Ray Jardine is looking for a guid housekeeper? When he heard Beattie an' me were giving up this place he asked if I kenned anybody that could bake bread like Beattie does.' Dick grinned suddenly. 'He doesna like any competition. He's been a wee bit more friendly recently!'

'Why should I be interested in Jardine's problems?' William asked, puzzled.

Dick scuffed the toe of his boot uneasily. 'Weel Beattie an' me, we thought Janet wad need tae move out o' the cottage, come the term . . . Louis's widow wad make a guid housekeeper and Beattie wad soon show her how tae use the yeast tae bake loaves o' bread, instead o' soda scones . . .'

William blinked. 'I will tell Mistress Fairly, and maybe she could mention it to Janet. Thank you, Dick.' He decided his journey to Muircumwell might not have been entirely wasted after all. Then he frowned. 'Sarah will miss your wife if you take her away to Yorkshire.'

'Aye, they've aye been friends. Mistress Sarah has been guid tae us, but Beattie will be glad tae get away frae Slater.'

* * *

Janet was immensely grateful when Sarah tentatively mentioned that Ray Jardine was on the lookout for a live-in housekeeper.

'I ken ye wadna put us out without a roof o'er our heads, but I wad feel settled in ma mind if I just kenned I had a place and work tae dae,' Janet explained anxiously. 'Ye'll be needing Nick Jamieson near at hand tae help when the cows calve, and the sows are farrowing.'

'Well Ray Jardine is not the most generous of men, but he has a big enough house above the store. I hear he wants someone to look after his father, as well as a woman who can bake bread to sell in his shop. So be warned Janet, dinna let him beat you down,' Sarah's jaw jutted with determination. 'You're not so desperate as to plead with him for every farthing, remember. Did Maggie tell you she wants to stay here, at Fairlyden?'

'Aye, she did, and I'm grateful, Miss Sarah. It makes one mouth less tae feed. But there's just one thing; I canna make bread. I always bake soda scones on the girdle – just as Mistress Simons taught me tae dae when I worked at the manse.'

'I'll ask Beatrice to teach you before . . .' Sarah's brown eyes clouded, 'before she moves to Yorkshire.'

'Ye'll miss her, eh Miss Sarah?' Janet said softly. 'Och noo jist listen tae me! Calling ye Miss Sarah as though ye were a bairn still. Mind ye I've felt like an auld woman these past weeks.'

'But you're only thirty-nine, Janet. It's the worry and trouble that has made you feel older. I hope things will be better soon for you.'

Janet dressed with care in her black skirt and her best black shawl before she set out for the Jardine store. She had lost weight since Louis's death, and despite the birth of four children her figure was still neat and trim; she had good features too and even her mourning garb could not dim her clear skin. Janet was unaware of all these things. There was a quiet desperation in the set of her mouth and anxiety in her eyes. She needed a place where she could work and have her children with her; Anna, her youngest, was barely six years old.

The interview went well at first. Ray Jardine knew Janet had worked at the manse when she was a girl, and she had had plenty of experience at Fairlyden since then. She looked neat and clean. She would not disgrace him if he needed her to help in the shop from time to time. She was alert enough.

'And— and there's accommodation? I mean rooms, above the st-store, for me and ma three bairns?' Janet asked finally, her nervousness very evident despite Sarah's advice.

'Three! Three bairns did ye say?' Ray Jardine exclaimed. His face stiffened. 'I canna feed three bairns as weel as yourself! Anyway I only hae one room tae spare.'

Janet's eyes widened in consternation. 'Surely ye have a wee loft, for Thomas?' she pleaded. 'The twae lassies wad share my room. They willna eat much. Thomas wad run messages for ye . . .?' she added pleadingly, but it was no use. Ray Jardine shook his head. He had heard the workers at Fairlyden were well fed. He had seen the Whiteley boy from time to time. He was small for his age, but he would eat plenty.

'Your laddie wadna be much use for lifting sacks o' flour and potatoes and sic like. No, there's no place for ye here if ye've a boy tagging along wi' ye!'

Sarah knew at once that things had gone badly when she saw the dejected droop to Janet's shoulders as she toiled up the track back to her cottage. During the milking Janet told her all that had transpired. Sarah's mouth tightened.

'Ray Jardine is a mean man!' she exclaimed furiously. 'He has plenty of room above the shop, as well as his own rooms at the back. Thomas would have earned his keep!'

Later Sarah related Janet's experience with Ray Jardine to William and her father when Agnes took Alex and Billy off to bed. She had promised to tell the children a bedtime story to take their minds off Maggie, who had been given leave to run home to the cottage to hear her mother's news.

A timid knock on the door leading from the stone-flagged passage halted Sarah in mid-sentence.

'Why Thomas!' she exclaimed as she opened the door, but her welcoming smile changed to a frown as she noticed the boy's white young face. She was almost convinced he had been crying, yet she had known Thomas all his life and he was a tough little fellow.

'Come on in, laddie. You've just missed Maggie. She's gone to see your mama.'

'I ken. I waited 'til she'd gone hame. It's Master F-Fairly I wanted tae see . . .?' He stammered nervously and stared anxiously up at Sarah. 'D'ye think he wad gie me a job, as weel as Maggie, Mistress Fairly?' he whispered in a choked voice. 'If it wasna for me, ma mother could gang tae Mr Jardine's. I— I'm jist a burden tae her.'

'Oh Thomas that's not true!' Sarah almost hugged the lad's thin shoulders, but she stopped herself in time. Thomas was the man of the Whiteley household now and he had been proud to tell her so only a few days earlier. 'Your mother told me how much you help her, Thomas. But come in and speak to Master Fairly.' She led the way into the kitchen where her father and husband were enjoying a pipe of tobacco on either side of the fire.

'Here's a young man wanting to work for his living!' she announced in a cheerful tone, but her eyes sought William's urgently, silently beseeching him to be gentle with the boy.

'I thought ye were still at school, Thomas?' Sandy remarked.

'Aye, but I'm twelve an' some o' the boys leave afore they're thirteen, Mr Logan, if— if they're needed at hame.' He turned to William anxiously. 'Mr Jardine willna consider mother because o' me. If I had a job . . . if I could work for ye, Mr Fairly, she wadna need tae bother about me. Mr Jardine wad take her in then, wi' jist ma twae wee sisters. I could sleep in the hay loft above the horses. I wad work hard. I can feed the pigs and I wad dae the hens and the geese and I can milk, can't I, Mistress Fairly?' He stopped for breath and looked pleadingly at Sarah.

'Aye, I'd forgotten that, Thomas. Your mother taught you to milk when your father was ill last summer, didn't she?'

'Aye, I wad dae anything, anything at a' Master Fairly, if ye'll keep me here. I wadna eat much!'

'Well now, Thomas,' William blinked. 'You will need to give me time to think. This is a surprise you see, and I really think you ought to stay at school a while yet. It is the law now for boys and girls to go to school.'

'I ken my three Rs, Master Fairly, an' the dominie says if we can read an' write and count oor pennies, we can dae 'maist anything. I wad work really hard, honest I wad. If only I didna need tae be a burden tae Mother . . .'

'You're not very big yet . . .' William said doubtfully.

'I mind his father wasna very big either when he first came tae Fairlyden,' Sandy said comfortably between puffs at his pipe. 'Louis wad be about thirteen when the Reverend Mackenzie brought him frae Bentira village. He shot up like a weed, and he broadened out well enough in the end . . .' Sandy's blue eyes met and held William's dark ones.

'Well, I've been thinking that we need another man besides Nick, but I'd thought of a strong man to help with the heavy work. I did think I might make a bothy in the little store next to the dairy though, for a single man. I dare say Nick Jamieson and his wife would let Thomas stay with them until it's ready . . .' William said slowly.

'Aye, I'm sure they would!' Sarah exclaimed eagerly. 'And Thomas could eat with us. He and Maggie would be a comfort to each other, if Janet moves down to Muircumwell. The lassie's missing her father something terrible.'

'Well, young Thomas, it seems everybody at Fairlyden wants you to stay, but you will not earn much money, at least not until you can do a man's work.'

'Ye mean I can stay, Master Fairly?' Thomas asked incredulously.

'Yes, you can stay, for a year anyway, until we see what sort of man you're going to make.'

'Oh thank ye, Master Fairly! Thank ye,' Thomas breathed. His eyes glistened. 'I'll work hard, I promise ye I will! Oh whew, I maun tell ma mother!' He turned and sped along the passage and out of the door before Sarah could say a word. She looked at William and her own eyes were also bright.

'You're a good man, William Fairly, and somehow I dinna think you'll regret giving young Thomas a trial.'

'If he's as loyal and willing as his father, ye'll have a guid man some day,' Sandy agreed, and Sarah knew her father was pleased by William's decision too.

'Well, it will be a relief if Nick Jamieson moves to the cottage. He will be close at hand when I'm away at the markets, or with the stallion.' William grinned suddenly. 'So maybe it was not just young Thomas I was considering after all. I wouldn't like you to think I'm a saint when I'm not, my dear Sarah.'

Gradually the changes at Fairlyden fell into place. Janet and her two young daughters moved to Mr Jardine's store; Nick and Sally Jamieson moved into the Fairlyden cottage. William made plans to turn the little store room into a bothy. Sarah accepted each change as it came, but she refused to dwell on Beatrice's forthcoming move to Yorkshire. Neither she nor Beatrice had ever been further away from Muircumwell than Annan or Dumfries. Yorkshire seemed like another world.

Another problem nagged at Sarah's mind as Beatrice's departure drew nearer. Could she, indeed should she, keep her promise to Beatrice's mother? Surely Beatrice ought to know that her father was Alexander Logan? Suppose they never saw her again? The thought made Sarah quiver all over, and she pushed it away. After all, the Bradshaws had travelled quite safely many times, and Crispin's sisters, Fanny and Freda travelled all the way from London at least once a year. Of course they had enough money to travel in comfort. Sarah knew that neither she nor Beatrice would ever have money, or time, to spend travelling in railway trains and carriages.

The end of March arrived, and still Sarah had kept Jeannie Slater's secret. Then it was the morning of departure. Sarah had promised to be at the Mill House early, along with her father and her husband. They were to help Dick and Beatrice walk the cows to the station. Crispin Bradshaw had advised them to lay claim to the animals as payment for Dick's labours in repairing the mill property. Wull Slater had not reappeared and they had no idea where he could be found, even if they had wanted to contact him. On the other hand he had caused no further trouble.

'I canna believe he'll not suddenly waylay us at the eleventh hour and stir up some unexpected trouble,' Beatrice confided nervously to Sarah. 'He played so many horrible tricks when we were young.'

As it happened Slater had deemed it wiser to keep out of the way. He had not anticipated such a spirited resistance to his own devious plans, either from Beatrice or her husband; even less had he expected Dick O'Connor to have the support and help of a Fairly. He had a whole selection of ill-gotten goods which he needed to dispose of quietly and his accomplice at the Liverpool port had become increasingly impatient, even issuing one or two threats.

'Slater will find it difficult to get the animals back from Yorkshire,' William grinned, a little maliciously, 'and he owes you these at least, Dick.' Two of the sows had been loaded into the cart, not without a great many protesting squeals; there they were restrained by a large woven net. It was a heavy load for the mare. William had brought one of the Fairlyden carts to take Beatrice's household equipment, clothes and bedding. Sarah and Beattie walked behind the little procession; now that the final parting had come there was still so much to say and yet they could not speak. They would start together, stop, cough nervously and swallow hard. In no time at all they had covered the two miles to the station. There were plenty of willing hands to guide the cattle into the trucks, then the mare and her cart was driven up the ramp into another, before being unyoked for the journey. William's cartload of boxes and packing cases were stowed on board. Sarah hugged Beatrice fiercely, but she could not restrain a few tears despite her determination to be cheerful. Beatrice was weeping openly. She looked pale and tired, but she smiled sweetly at Dick as he handed her into the third-class compartment, shut the door securely and leaned out of the window to wave a last goodbye.

'You'll write me a letter, Beattie!' Sarah called. 'T-tell me everything . . . about your new house, the dairy . . . the byre . . .'

'I w-will.' Beatrice could say no more for the tears gathering in her throat, but Dick seemed happy to be embarking on his new life, casting off the shackles and the shadows of the old, as the train belched out smoke and puffed out its plumes of steam as it gathered speed.

'I do hope they will be happy!' Sarah whispered fervently.

'Aye, lassie, so do I, so do I,' Sandy muttered, and wondered why he felt so melancholy.

Fourteen

Sarah immersed herself in the spring work, cleaning the house from top to bottom, liming the dairy and byre, planting her garden. She appreciated the company of Agnes and young Maggie, and of Nicky Jamieson and his wife, Sally, but she still missed Louis's cheery whistle coming from the stable each morning, she missed Janet's prattle and even her caustic comments when William brought home extra cows to milk. Most of all she missed Beatrice. They had shared so many of their joys and sorrows since they were small children.

Young Thomas Whiteley changed his school days for the life of a working lad without a grumble.

'He is neat and quick, observant too,' Sarah remarked one evening when she was enjoying a rare moment of peace with her father and husband. 'He shows great promise as a milker, and that is a task the men at Fairlyden avoid whenever possible!' she added dryly. Maggie was pleased to have at least one member of her family close at hand and they both visited their mother and younger sisters each Sunday.

'Mother says tae tell ye she's settling doon at the Jardines',' Maggie reported. 'She likes the days when she has tae help in the shop while Mr Jardine delivers his orders, and now that she's getting used tae the big Carron range he put in, she's baking lots o' loaves o' bread wi' yeast, just as Mistress O'Connor showed her.'

'Old Mr Jardine likes having Mother there tae. He told me sae,' Thomas added proudly. 'He says she makes him warm and sees tae his comforts. He doesna mind me and Maggie going tae visit either. He says he misses the shop and hearing a' the news, and we're very welcome tae visit him.'

'I'm glad about that, Thomas,' Sarah smiled kindly, for she knew the boy had been worried about his mother moving to a new home.

Naturally Sarah turned to William for her own comfort. He understood her needs. He cradled her in his arms in the darkness of the night, loving her gently in the big feather bed, smoothing away an occasional tear. Unfortunately the season for travelling with the stallions had come round once more.

'I'm afraid I shall have to stay away again for a week at least, Sarah my dearest,' William murmured one night.

'I know,' Sarah sighed. She had posted the notices to the local papers herself, stating the farms or inns where their latest young stallion,

Logan's Bobby, could be located at certain dates and times. She knew William could not renege on such arrangements.

It pleased William to know that Sarah loved and needed him, despite the demands of her busy life and the calm face she presented to the rest of world. He was proud of her shrewd judgement. He admired the way she reared their children, calmly accepting Alex's imperfection, loving him just the same, instilling good sense into his more mischievous brother, comforting Ellen when the troublesome teeth kept her from sleeping. Sometimes he almost envied her efficiency in looking after the cows, churning, marketing her eggs and butter, cooking and washing and keeping his home; several times he had had reason to appreciate her cool, clear-sighted mind when decisions had to be taken, or in times of crisis – and yet this paragon of a woman needed him in a way no other woman had ever needed him. She loved him. When he returned after their enforced partings she greeted him with a passion which had been absent in the earlier days of their marriage when she had been a shy young bride.

William accepted that the contentment and happiness he had found in his marriage to Sarah more than compensated for the lack of challenge in his present work, but he missed the tenuous involvement he had had with the Farmers' Store now that Wull Slater had taken over.

On one occasion, when he had been away all week with the stallion, Sarah walked to meet him when she saw him returning up the Fairlyden track. They strolled companiably, side by side, as he told her of the people he had met and the places he had been.

'Father is delighted with the demand for Logan's Bobby,' Sarah remarked with a smile, 'though I doubt if he'll ever believe another horse can be as good as Logan's Lucifer.'

'Oh, I don't know about that. He has high hopes of a mare by Logan's Lucifer and she is just coming to the foaling. We both hope she will breed Fairlyden's future stallion – and make both our fortunes!' he added with a wry chuckle. 'Your father was pleased when Lucian and Baron were selected to travel in Lanarkshire and Wigtownshire too.'

'Aye, he was. I know he likes some of the work as Mr Bradshaw's factor, but his real interest in life will always be his horses. I received a letter frae Beatrice this morning. Dick wishes the Fairlyden stallions were a bit nearer to his own mare.'

'Mmm, Yorkshire is too far away for me to travel,' William murmured and his dark eyes gleamed wickedly. 'I couldn't stay away from you for so long!' Then he sobered. 'You know how much I miss you even when I'm away for two weeks, don't you, Sarah?' he asked gruffly.

'I hope you do, for I miss you terribly!' Sarah responded and William was delighted with her rosy blushes and sparkling eyes.

'Maybe when Billy grows up he will take the Logan stallions further afield; the railways are spreading everywhere; it will be different then.'

'Aye, maybe,' Sarah said slowly, biting her lip. William never mentioned Alex, or considered what he might do with his future, yet already he showed a keen interest in the horses, and indeed in all the animals. It was almost as though his own father had forgotten he was their eldest son. William did not notice the sudden clouding of her brown eyes. His attention was too taken up with the stallion who had recognised his own stable and was eager now to reach it.

'Did Beatrice and Dick have a satisfactory journey? Are they settling into the farm?'

'I think so, but the farm sounds very dilapidated. Beatrice says it will be several years before Dick has everything to his satisfaction.' Sarah frowned, thinking of Beattie's letter.

'There was a hole in the roof of the bedroom,' she had written. 'Several holes in fact. Fortunately our first night was dry. We lay in bed and looked up at the stars, but we were much too tired to look at them for long.'

Beatrice O'Connor could not tell anyone, even Sarah, just how happy Dick had made her that first night in their ramshackle new home. Everything had seemed so bleak and alien when they arrived. She had clung to him like a home-sick child. It was the first time she had allowed him to touch her since Wull Slater's return had resurrected all her old unhappy memories.

Everything had seemed so much worse than they had expected, cheerless and derelict. The feel of each other's arms was the only thing that was warm and familiar. Dick had been so gentle, yet Beattie had sensed his deep anxiety, his need of comfort. In her efforts to reassure him they would be happy together and that she did not mind the dreadful house, or the muddy yard and tumbledown sheds, Beatrice had forgotten her own fears. Incredibly Dick had found himself arousing a response in her such as he had craved since the day they were married; Beatrice had given herself to him completely, and at a time when he so badly needed her loving.

Amidst the grinding toil, the strangeness, the dirt and grime and chill of those first days at Highvale Farm, Dick and Beatrice had shared a tenderness that was beautiful and precious, a love they both knew they would cherish and share for the rest of their lives. Beatrice could mention none of this in her letter, but a little of her new hope and happiness shone through the lines, despite the mundane details.

> Dick has patched the roof now and we think it is secure against the wind and rain. I have scrubbed until my knuckles are raw, but I have whitened the walls and the main part of the house is clean. I have edged all the stone flags with yellow stone as seems to be the fashion here.
>
> Tomorrow I start on the dairy. It is very strange really, right next to the kitchen, but down three steps! Yet the door from the dairy is level with the farmyard and the byre is straight across the yard. I must remember, Sarah, the folks here do not call it a byre. It

is a cowshed. An old man visited us today and he called it 'a mistle'. Indeed the local people have many strange words. I fear I shall never understand them all.

Our byre is very small – just three rickety wooden stalls in a stone shed with the heavy loft up above and a stone staircase running up the outside wall above the door. I do believe the stalls might fall down when Dick cleans out the manure! It is so high I can scarcely get in the door. Dick has promised to clean it out before our two cows calve. They have settled down in their fresh pastures and I am looking forward to having calves and being able to milk them again. Dick is going to market next week to see if he can buy two more. He is so full of plans. There are two little sheds on either side of the byre. One day he hopes to put stalls in them too. One day!

There are so many other things to do first. There is a young girl in a house near here. She would like to work for me, but I have no money to pay her until we get some milk and eggs to sell, and she does not want to live with us and work for her food because her mother is crippled. She makes me feel I am very fortunate, even if I am a little sad when I think about dear familiar faces.

Dick thinks the land will produce good crops when he has had time to plough it and sow new grass seeds. He says we must save all the money we can to buy lime. Of course you understand such matters, better than I do, so I must not bore you. There are great holes in most of the hedges and they are all growing higher than Dick! There is a small village less than a mile away, and a few miles further there is a much newer, larger village. The men there work in the coal mines. They look very pale and sickly. I wonder if they will buy my milk, when I have some to sell? The hens we brought have stopped laying completely. Dick says it is the shock of moving. I hope they start to lay again soon. Jenny and Pug, our two sows, have settled down nicely. There is a nice little orchard at the back of the house and they like to root under the trees.

Please write soon, dear Sarah, and give me all your news. I miss you all so very much. Please give the boys and Ellen a hug from me.

Sarah had read the letter three times. Despite the hard work and strange surroundings she sensed Beatrice was happier and more relaxed than she had been since Wull Slater reappeared in he life. Sarah was relieved. She often felt guilty for not sharing Jeannie Slater's secret. She longed to tell Beattie they were more than friends: they were sisters. It was not part of Sarah's nature to be deceitful; for the thousandth time she asked herself what possible reason Jeannie Slater could have had for withholding the truth from both Beatrice and her father. Surely neither her battered pride, not her shame, could be reason enough to deprive two fine people of the truth. Sarah had pondered the situation many times and wondered how her father could have placed himself in such a situation. She had known Jeannie Slater only as a pale shadow of a woman, a half-demented, soulless creature. Sarah could not visualise the pretty, vain and coquettish girl who had been Joseph Miller's only child, his pride and joy, a little spoiled, a little wayward even – before her spirit had been so cruelly broken. Whatever Jeannie Miller had been, Sarah knew her father would never have shirked the responsibility of caring for his own child. She shuddered.

How bitter, how angry he would be if he ever discovered that a child of his had suffered so cruelly at Edward Slater's hands, Sarah thought. Was that the reason Jeannie Slater had continued to hide the truth from him? Yet Edward Slater was dead now, and so was his wife. Sarah felt renewed anger that she would be burdened by her promise to the dead woman.

Sarah wrote regularly to Beatrice, and each time the same anger and doubts entered her mind, yet she could not bring herself to break the promise she had made to Mistress Slater during the last conscious minutes of her time on earth.

June 1887

My Dear Beatrice,

We all look forward to your letters. My father reads them with special interest. Dick's toils and problems, and indeed your own, bring back memories of his first years here, at Fairlyden. He still recalls your grandfather's help with gratitude.

William has been busy travelling around the area with Logan's Bobby. Most stallion owners send a groom, but William says he enjoys accompanying the stallion himself. I miss him when he has to stay away. The season has ended now though, so he is at home every night. It is almost haytime and every pair of hands will be needed, as you know only too well. We must pray for fine weather.

Maggie helped me to clean out the small room at the end of the passage. It is the room where mother slept on her first night at Fairlyden. It was very damp but I have aired it well. Agnes whitened the walls and ceiling. We have put in two iron beds with fresh straw mattresses and two wooden presses to hold clothes and personal possessions. Father insisted we should use this room instead of the one next to the dairy, because it has a fireplace. He has never forgotten his own experience of bothy life at the hands of Mistress Sharpe.

William hired a young man named Peter Elliot at the Annan Fair. He is nineteen, and very strong. He seems pleasant, though a little slow, especially in the mornings. William chastised him for his impatience with Boyo, our young gelding, on his first day and he was rather sulky. Thomas Whiteley has moved into the bothy also and considers himself a real man now! Indeed I swear he has grown already.

You say the minister of your church is called a vicar? How very strange. I am sorry you find him so stern, and also that you must take new vows before he can accept you into his flock. There can be few men as well loved as our own Reverend Mackenzie. He is a good man and a true servant of the Almighty. I passed on your good wishes, dear Beatrice, and he seemed very pleased you had remembered him, amidst your many toils. I fear for him sometimes. He looks so tired and frail. Except for your dear self, I consider him the most valued of my friends. It grieves me to know that the day is fast approaching when his final call from God must come. He sends you a message and says you are not to worry if the church you must join is a little different from our own. He is convinced that all paths will lead to one God, for those who are true Christians. He seems to think that our own churches must join together again in peace and unity, if our religion is to survive, but there are still many, especially in Strathtod, who are bitterly opposed to the Free Church.

Already Wull Slater has been in trouble for his sly dealing. He sold oats – which he claimed were the best quality seed bought from Aberdeen – to Mr Clark at Burnside farm. Scarcely any of them have germinated, although he charged a very high price. He has scarcely any other stock, and no garden seeds or potatoes. He does not keep a cow or a pig, or even a horse, so there are no coal deliveries either.

I am glad your cows are milking well and that Dick has managed to make extra stalls and a channel to keep them clean. Do you find it a great advantage to live on the edge of a large village, Beatrice? It must surely be better to sell your milk fresh to the women who come to your door, than to make it into butter and carry it to market, though I do not think I would care to have the heaps of coal dust you describe blotting the beautiful horizon. Prices are still low. Sometimes I almost despair when I must bring butter home again after taking so much care. Sometimes I sell it for a pittance.

Did you enjoy Crispin Bradshaw's visit? We have not seen him at Fairlyden for some time. I believe he is planning to join his sister Fanny and her husband in London for some days in mid June for the Golden Jubilee celebrations. What a long time our good Queen has reigned.

Well, dear Beattie, I have enjoyed this little 'paper conversation' with you, though I would prefer to have you here beside me. I have been glad to sit quietly and write for a while though. I have been so tired recently. I cannot think what can be the cause.

Sarah paused and rested her chin on her hand, staring dreamily into space. She had a shrewd idea what was wrong with her. Her cheeks burned, and her mouth lifted in a tender smile. What a wicked woman I must be, she thought unrepentantly, to allow William to turn my very bones to water and set my blood afire whenever he looks at me with that certain expression in those dark eyes . . .

'Mama! Mama! Come quick. 'Tis Alex . . .'

'Alex? What's he done?' Sarah jumped to her feet, startled out of her reverie, her heart thumping as she ran after Billy's small figure, already disappearing through the door again.

'Nothing! He canna! Come quick!'

'But where is he?' she called in panic.

'Doon the garden! He's fallen intae the closet!'

Sarah gasped and ran down the path to the little stone house. Inside she found Alex hanging stoically on to the edge of the long scrubbed wooden seat, his rounded chin almost resting on his knees, the rest of him suspended through the large hole in the centre.

'Oh Alex!' Sarah exclaimed in a mixture of relief and exasperation. She allowed him to wait a moment or two longer while she removed a smaller wooden lid at the far end of the closet seat. Then she grasped her erring four year old firmly under the armpits and hauled him from his uncomfortable throne.

'There!' She sat him, none too gently, over the smaller hole. 'You know Grandfather Logan made this one specially for you two boys,' she admonished. 'You gave me a terrible fright!' Alex was safe now and he grinned up at her unrepentantly, his dark eyes melting her irritation as they always did.

'Billy dared me tae try that yin, cos I said I wad soon be as big as Papa, an' he still only has a wee. . .he's only a bairn yet!' Sarah stifled a grin.

'Well dinna let me catch you trying it again, or I might just leave you hanging there until you really are as big as Papa!'

Fifteen

As the months went by the reason for Sarah's tiredness gradually became apparent to everyone at Fairlyden, but bearing children was accepted – even expected – as a natural consequence of marriage.

Even so as 1887 drew to its close Sarah was finding it increasingly difficult to cope even with her normal daily tasks. Her unborn child drained away her strength, but only her father seemed to notice her unusual lack of energy. Sandy viewed her rapidly increasing bulk with secret dismay.

'Sarah, lassie, ye've been tiring yourself too much, making Christmas pies and plucking geese . . .'

Sarah opened her eyes with an effort and looked up from her seat on the wooden settle beside the fire in Fairlyden's cosy kitchen. It was a dark night and bitterly cold, with the wind whistling and whining at every crack. Sarah had her mending basket beside her, filled with an assortment of socks, all waiting to be darned. Her wooden mushroom was clasped in her hands but the temptation to rest her head and close her eyes had been too much.

'I'm all right,' she murmured wearily. She summoned a smile, 'It's just the thought of all Billy's wee socks needing to be darned that overwhelms me!'

'No, lassie, it's more than that. I've watched ye for weeks now, trailing one foot after the other. I ken it's no a man's business, but surely the babe canna be much longer now?'

Sarah flushed. 'About the beginning of February.'

'Another month!' Sandy's exclamation, and the anxiety behind it drew William's attention from the book he was studying.

'Your father is right, Sarah. Surely Agnes and Sally could manage the milking, especially now that you have instructed Maggie so well. I will send young Thomas to help also. He is keen to look after the cows, and the boy would do anything for you.'

'But I like to be at the milking myself!' Sarah protested. 'I need to keep an eye on things. Anyway it's almost a rest to sit down and rest my head against the flank of a cow,' she added with a faint smile. 'Even so,' she stifled a yawn with an effort, 'I think I'll leave the mending for tonight and go to bed or I'll be falling asleep beside the fire.'

She went through to the scullery to check that everything was in order for morning. The byre lamps stood on the stone table where they were trimmed and filled each day. She paused to wipe a sooty glass shade, then she lifted her own candle from the few still waiting to be claimed, and returned to the kitchen to bid her father good night. She paused in the shadowy doorway as she caught the end of his conversation.

'I never thought o' ma ain wife carrying twae bairns! Mattie never complained either, but I kenned she was tired near the end . . .'

Sarah caught her breath. Her father's voice was ragged as he broke off; his mind would always be tortured by the thought of her mother's suffering, alone, in her silent world.

'I dinna mean tae interfere, William, but I'd never forgive mysel' for keeping quiet, if anything happened tae Sarah.'

His weathered face was illuminated by the light of the flickering flames and Sarah saw the deep lines of anxiety.

Silently she withdrew into the scullery again, her heart beating fast. She had been just a child when her mother died. Her attention had been taken up by the arrival of her new baby brother, then the death of her beloved Mama. It had never occurred to her to question the reason for her mother's death; who would have answered her questions anyway? The horrid O'Leary who had come as Danny's wet nurse? She shuddered at the thought. Only now did she understand. Her father's strained voice echoed in her head. She looked down at her bulging pinafore; involuntarily she pressed her hand dazedly over her swollen body. She hitched her skirts a few inches and stretched out first one leg and then the other, gazing at her puffy ankles. A tremor of fear shivered through her. Alex! she thought, Who would care for ma wee crippled laddie, if I die? And Ellen, and Billy . . .? Take a hold o' yourself Mistress Fairly. Tell them you're not going to die! Cows have twins and they dinna die! Why, pigs have a dozen or more!

But you're neither a pig, nor a cow, came the insidious voice of fear. Sarah frowned and straightened her shoulders, deliberately clattering the candlestick on the stone table as a reminder of her presence before she entered the kitchen, her back straight. The candle flame flickered in the draught but the hand which held it was steady.

'Good night,' she said cheerfully.

'I'll be up in a minute, Sarah,' William replied and she sensed a new tension in him.

Minutes later he joined her in the privacy of their chamber. 'Maybe you should heed your father's advice, Sarah. He is wiser and older than we are, and he is concerned about you.'

'Because he thinks I might have two babes instead of one,' Sarah stated flatly.

'You heard?'

'Aye, I heard. I didna know Mama died having a second baby, until tonight, but even Father canna be sure there'll be two.'

'Your grandmother had twins also . . .' William said slowly. 'Did you know that?'

'No . . .' Sarah's face went a little paler, then she squared her shoulders and pursed her lips. 'She didna die! And neither shall I.' William came to her and held her close against his heart.

'Dear Sarah, I could not live without you; Fairlyden could not manage without you either. I pray with all my heart you will have just one baby, and even that is burden enough, my own sweet, brave wife.'

Sarah clung to him for a moment, her heart pounding with a fear that would not be denied, but then she pushed herself gently away from him and looked into his face.

'I willna stay away frae the milking, but I'll take care. I couldna bear to leave you, William, or our bairns . . .'

'When the time comes, I shall do as your father wishes and ask young Doctor Kerr to attend you, Sarah, from the first sign.'

'No!' Sarah's face flamed. 'This is women's work! I have never had a doctor! I willna have a doctor.'

William pulled her close once more.

'Don't get upset, my love.' He held her until she was calm again. He knew how modest she was despite the love they shared. He did not argue, neither did he mention the matter again.

Sarah looked at her puffed-up fingers and the plain gold band, almost hidden from sight, and alarmingly tight. She was glad she had not told Beatrice of her suspicion that she was expecting twins when she received a happy letter giving her the joyous news that Beatrice and Dick were to be parents at last. She guessed that Beattie was already a little worried because she would soon be thirty years old.

Less than a week later Sarah wakened William in the night.

'Would you rouse Agnes to kindle the fire, and set the kettle on the swey,' she gasped as a spasm of pain caught her breath.

'Is it the babe?' William asked in consternation, already leaping into his breeches.

'Aye . . .Will you bring Mistress Johnstone . . .? She promised to attend, though she says she's getting too old. My babe's to be . . .' she gasped as another spasm caught her unawares, '. . .the last.'

William needed no urging to hurry but before he left the room Sarah stifled a moan and in a flash he was back at her bedside, staring down into her damp, pale face by the light of the candle.

'William . . .' she whispered hoarsely a few seconds later, 'would you stay . . . with me? I— I'm feart, now the time has come.'

'Aah Sarah, my love!' William fell to his knees beside the bed, clutching her hand in both of his. 'Just give me a minute or two to waken Agnes. I will send Peter with the trap to bring Mistress Johnstone.' He paused as Sarah's face creased in pain. 'I shall return at once,' he promised as soon as the spasm had passed.

William did not tell Sarah that he intended sticking to his intention to send for Doctor Kerr as well. As soon as he had wakened Agnes and Peter he sat down at the table and penned a brief note to the doctor, sealing it with wax melted in the candle flame just as Agnes clattered down the wooden stairs into the kitchen.

'I'll just take this out to Peter, then I'll wait with Mistress Fairly. You— you'll know what to do, Agnes?'

'Aye . . . leastways until the midwife comes.' She looked at William's white strained face and tousled hair. Once she had dreaded him coming to live at Fairlyden because he was the son of an Earl, but he was a man like any other, and he was worried about Miss Sarah. Agnes gave him a kindly smile.

'I'll bring ye both a cup o' tea when the fire has burned up enough tae boil the kettle. It'll likely be a while afore the babe comes intae the world, for all he's making himsel' known i' the wee sma' hoors.'

Agnes was certainly correct in her prediction, William thought several hours later. He had felt exhausted long before Mistress Johnstone ushered him out of the chamber so that she might attend to her business with his wife, and that had been two hours ago. He had fumed and fretted because there was still no sign of Doctor Kerr. Agnes had been to the byre and helped Sally and Maggie and Thomas finish the milking. William watched her ladling the bowls of porridge and setting out the little bowls of cream, but he refused to eat any himself. He had never worried as much as this when his other children were born, but he knew it was different this time. Sarah had not had such good health. He could not sit still and watch the others eat their breakfast. He paced restlessly and in the end Agnes ushered him outside.

'Awa' and hae a bit o' fresh air in yer lungs Master Fairly! Ye're giving me indigestion walking the floor like that!'

William obeyed as meekly as a child.

'There'll be no more babes,' he muttered in a harsh whisper when Sandy appeared at his elbow.

Sandy did not reply. He rested his elbows on the garden wall and bowed his head in silence. His face was pale and drawn, and William wondered if he was praying. He looked at Sandy's thick hair with surprise. Sarah's father had no more silver amongst his red-brown curls than he had himself – maybe even less. Alexander Fairly was a very fit man for his age, except for his lame leg. William prayed that Sarah had inherited her father's stamina.

Young Doctor Kerr joined them a little while later.

'Have you seen Sarah? Is she all right?' William demanded urgently, while Sandy watched the doctor in anxious silence.

'Yes . . . for the time being. I am just going to eat the porridge your maid has set out for me, and I would advise you two gentlemen to do the same. It would scarcely do if you faint with hunger while Mistress Fairly is doing all the work.'

William scowled. 'Shouldn't you be with your patient?' he asked abruptly, then, 'Did. . .did Sarah put you out . . .?'

'No, Mr Fairly.' The doctor grimaced wryly. 'I dare say your wife would have tried, had she been in a position to do so.' In fact Sarah had been extremely relieved to see the doctor and she was glad William had had the good sense to disregard her wishes. Doctor Kerr had been calm and reassuring. He had insisted that Mistress Johnstone must scald everything again under his vigilant eye and instructed her to scrub her hands thoroughly with carbolic soap before she touched his patient.

'I didna want you to come!' Sarah gasped. 'But I'm glad to know you're here,' she added with her usual candour. 'There . . . there's more than one babe, isn't there?' Doctor Kerr hesitated. 'Dinna pretend with me, Doctor!' Sarah commanded with asperity.

He smiled then and some of his inner nervousness left him. He had discussed the case with his father as soon as William had first informed him of his wife's condition. He knew that Sarah's mother had died giving birth to twins. His father had told him it had been the breach presentation of the second babe, the time lag and the consequent loss of blood which had killed Mistress Logan. His father had assured him that Mistress Sarah Fairly possessed both courage and stamina, and her husband had acted wisely, no doubt spurred on by Alexander Logan.

Even so Doctor Kerr felt hot, sticky and quite exhausted by the time Sarah's first child at last entered the world and he marvelled at his patient's courage and strength.

'You have a fine baby daughter, Mistress Fairly,' he assured her as he handed the wailing infant to the midwife. 'Now you must rest a little while, ready for our next wee battle. As soon as I have washed my hands I will go downstairs and ask your maid to bring you a cup of tea. I could certainly do with one myself!'

Sarah did not reply.

Sixteen

'Dinna go away, Doctor,' Sarah pleaded weakly as Doctor Kerr dried his hands with habitual thoroughness. He turned to look at her. Some of her hair had escaped from its thick pleat and was curling in damp curls over her brow and around her ears. Her eyes were shadowed with fatigue, perspiration shone on her face and trickled in tiny rivulets down her neck, yet she was still a beautiful woman. Doctor Kerr eyed her with concern. The puffiness of her hands and ankles had disturbed him, but she had told him the birth was early. Once it was over he hoped her good health would be restored. Even so, maybe he ought to talk to her husband, warn of the possible danger to her life if she had any more children, at least within the next couple of years. Mr Fairly seemed to be a man of good sense so perhaps he would take heed, unlike the husbands of many of his patients.

'Would you like Mistress Johnstone to bathe your face and hands now that she has finished the baby?' he suggested kindly.

'No!' Sarah bit off the word in a sharp gasp. 'The baby! It's coming . . .'

Doctor Philip Kerr could scarcely believe it. The first birth had been extremely prolonged and exhausting. Mistress Fairly had had no time to gather her strength to embark on the birth of a second. He groaned inwardly for he longed to straighten his tall frame to its full height, an impossibility in the bedroom with its sloping ceiling; he had hoped for a five minute breath of the fresh February air, and time to savour a cup of strong sweet tea before the next stage of Sarah's ordeal began.

It seemed no time at all before the second child was safely in his hands, another girl – smaller, shorter than the first, but perfectly formed. After the first loud wail the babe opened a pair of dark wondering eyes which exactly matched the fuzz of hair which covered her tiny head. Despite the waxiness of new birth Doctor Kerr found himself looking at the child with as much pride as if he had produced her single-handedly. He was still a bachelor and he had had every intention of remaining so until this brief moment of wonder, yet the child was by no means the first he had delivered.

'Is— is it all right . . .?' Sarah asked wearily.

'You have another pretty daughter, Mistress Fairly!' he announced jubilantly. 'You are one of the best patients I have encountered in my career to date. Now I shall leave you in the care of Mistress Johnstone while I tell your husband and your father the good news. They have been very concerned for you.'

'Thank you, Doctor,' Sarah murmured huskily.

'I will send your maid up with some tea in a little while. Then I prescribe a good sleep followed by two weeks' bed rest. I confess I am exhausted too.'

Sarah smiled back at him, tears of relief and gratitude in her dark eyes. 'And I confess I was rather frightened,' she admitted with a flash of her old humour. 'Now I think I could sleep for a whole week!'

The twins differed from each other in almost every possible way from the moment they were born. Sadie, the one who had taken such an interminable time to enter the world, was a demanding infant from the beginning, eating much, sleeping little while her smaller sister, Katherine, was content and good natured.

Sarah was delighted when the Reverend Mackenzie agreed to christen them the week before Easter. She knew it was an honour for the Minister was becoming increasingly frail. He had recently accepted temporary help from a young minister in training. It made Sarah's heart sad to see his white hair and trembling hands; even his wonderfully resonant voice had grown weaker of late, though his parishioners still flocked to hear his sermons every Sunday.

William collected him in the Fairlyden trap and, except for Sadie's loud wailing as the Minister made the sign of the cross upon her brow, the christening went smoothly. Even Alex and Billy were on their best behaviour, with shining faces and looking like real boys in their first trousers and new Eton collars. Janet had also come especially for the christening. She looked older and Sarah was dismayed to notice so much grey in her brown hair, and yet there was a new acceptance, almost serenity in her eyes.

Afterwards they all gathered around the table in the Fairlyden kitchen for the christening tea while young Maggie bustled importantly, eager to demonstrate to her mother how well she managed Ellen and the boys, while her Mistress settled the twins in their crib, and Agnes poured the tea.

'You'll have a piece of my ginger cake?' Sarah offered when the Reverend Mackenzie sat back in his chair.

'No thank you, Sarah, not today, my dear. I do not seem to require so much sustenance as I did when I came to Fairlyden as a young man.'

Sarah looked into his lined and tired face with deep affection.

'Aye, ye've shared many a happy hour, and a few sad ones tae, round this very fireside, Reverend Mackenzie,' Sandy declared with a reminiscent smile. 'I'm very glad ye managed tae come again today.'

'We are very grateful to you,' Sarah murmured with a gentle smile. She knew her father shared her own regret when it was time for William to take the Minister back to the manse.

'I get tired so quickly,' he apologised, 'and I do so want to make a good job of preparing my Easter message. I have a feeling it may be my last.'

Sarah and her father recalled his words with deep sadness when the young minister came riding up the track from Muircumwell early in the evening on Good Friday. Sarah knew at once that he had brought sad tidings when she saw his grave expression.

'Mistress Simmons went up to waken the Minister when he did not appear for breakfast at his usual time,' he informed them sadly. 'The old doctor came himself, immediately. He assured us that the Reverend Mackenzie had died very peacefully in his sleep.'

'He was a good man . . .' Sarah murmured brokenly. Many pictures flitted through her mind of her childhood and teenage years when the Minister had visited at Fairlyden, and the many times he had helped and advised her.

'He'll be badly missed. He was friend tae many, and he had a special place in the hearts o' all o' us here at Fairlyden,' Sandy told the young minister sadly.

Sarah was astonished when the lawyer asked her to be present at the manse after the Reverend Mackenzie's funeral, since she was named as a beneficiary in his will. She knew the Minister had once had a small income from his family in addition to his stipend, and he had inherited a bequest from a bachelor uncle, but his family had never been exceptionally wealthy and Sarah guessed the Reverend Mackenzie had helped many of his parishioners. One man he had helped considerably had been Daniel Munro, his closest friend – the man whom she had regarded as her father for so many years.

'It was the Reverend Robert Mackenzie's wish that you should receive some pieces of furniture from the manse,' the lawyer intoned in his dry voice. 'These include a piano and the large mahogany bookcase, and its contents.'

Sarah's lips trembled and her face was pale. The bookcase contained the Reverend Mackenzie's own collection of leather-bound books. He had loaned many of them to her mama, and brought pleasure to her silent world . . . The lawyer was droning on and Sarah tried to swallow the lump in her throat and pay attention.

'It was the Reverend Mackenzie's intention to restore this to the wife of Daniel Munro, a man he evidently regarded as his closest friend, according to one of his letters.' He sniffed and lifted a small, scuffed leather case from the table in the front of him. He sprang the catch. Sarah gasped. Pinned to the faded blue velvet pad was the most beautiful brooch she had ever seen.

'The letter was found beneath the pad. It relates to a cash transaction and the purchase of some cattle,' the lawyer announced flatly. 'I understand the brooch was originally purchased by the late Lord Johnathan Fairly for his mistress, Sarah Munro.' Sarah heard the disapproval in the lawyer's voice. 'Apparently Daniel Munro asked the

Reverend Mackenzie to sell it because he needed money. Clearly the Minister felt the brooch was a family heirloom which ought to have been treasured. He purchased it himself, intending to restore it to Mistress Mattie Munro. However, since Mistress Munro. . .er that is Mistress Logan . . .Ahem! Since your mother is now deceased, Mistress Fairly, this also falls into your possession.'

Sarah stared at the wizened face of the lawyer in astonishment. Her mouth formed a silent 'O'. She gulped.

'Th-thank you . . .' she whispered hoarsely at last, totally overcome by the Minister's thoughtfulness, and his selfless generosity. Her eyes were bright with tears.

William was delighted that his wife should possess such a beautiful piece of jewellery, and especially one which had been chosen by his own grandfather. He did not seem to mind that Lord Johnathan Fairly had bought it for his mistress, rather than his own grandmother.

Beatrice also seemed pleased to hear of Sarah's good fortune.

Highvale Farm
June 1888

Dearest Sarah,

I was so sorry to hear your news of the Reverend Mackenzie's death. He was a good friend to my family, especially Grandfather Miller. I am glad he did not suffer.

You always enjoyed reading, I remember, so you will appreciate his gifts to you, if your large household allows time for leisure. Maybe one day you will also have time, and a special occasion, when you can enjoy wearing your beautiful brooch.

Already I seem to spend so long between the milkings, just cooking and washing. We have made great quantities of rhubarb jam, also strawberry. I think I told you Milly moved in to live with us after her mother died? This will be very convenient when the baby arrives in a few more weeks! I can scarcely believe it. I am in excellent health now and just eager to have my baby in my arms.

Dick works terribly hard. He has made fifteen stalls in the byre now and already it is full since our last two new heifers calved. He has hired a young man, Walter Wright, to help and he also lives in the house with us; no bothies in this area! He is a good worker and we are very glad to have him.

I was not surprised to hear that Wull Slater had got into debt, and it is typical of him to run away and leave decent people in the lurch. Do you really believe he has gone to Australia? I do hope so. Certainly Dick and I have no wish to see him again. I hope the sale of the mill and the Mill House will pay all that he owes. Perhaps William will buy the mill? He told Dick he would like to become a merchant. Perhaps he would stop dealing in cattle at the markets then, though he was fortunate to make so much profit on his Irish stirks. Dick has bought six at five pounds, three shillings and sixpence each and he hopes to sell them at a profit in the autumn. I cannot envy you, Sarah, suddenly finding extra cows to milk, even if they do make a profit when William sells them a week later.'

'Mmm,' Sarah muttered to herself, 'but they dinna always make a profit! The last two had milk sae thick it was like rice pudding, and some o' our own cows have the trouble now.' Maybe Beatrice was right. Perhaps William would be more content as a merchant but they could never afford to buy the Mill House. She went on to read the rest of Beatrice's letter.

You say that your twin daughters are not at all alike. Who does Sadie resemble with her grey eyes and mouse brown hair? I am sure William will learn to love her in time, after all he is her father. It is a pity she is not a contented baby, but Katherine seems to make up for her, and at least she resembles both you and William if she has brown eyes and dark curly hair. It is strange that twins can be so different – Katie so small and chubby, Sadie so long and thin. I suppose your busy household is responsible for your tiredness and no doubt it makes you a little out of patience with Sadie's constant demands for milk?

The next time I write I hope I shall be sending news of my own baby. I feel so very, very excited!

Crispin Bradshaw called in two weeks ago. He had really enjoyed the Golden Jubilee celebrations in London and he remarked how wonderful it was that our little queen has shown herself once more to her people. He said the joy and gladness in the atmosphere was tremendous and that he felt proud to be a part of an empire which stretches to all corners of the earth. I expect he will be telling you all about it. He is looking forward to visiting Strathtod later in the summer.

I must end now, dear Sarah, but do take care of your health and give my kindest regards to your father and your husband, and my love to the children.

Ever your affectionate friend,

Beatrice

It was not by letter that Sarah received news of Beatrice's child, but from Bert Bradshaw. He rode over to Fairlyden especially to tell Sarah himself.

'Nearly died, she did, t'poor lass. It were that long! Dick was that worrit. Poor feller, 'e still 'asn't gotten ower it. Doctor reckons it'll be weeks afore Beatrice gets right again. Fever 'as made it worse for 'er!'

'Fever!' Sarah stared at Bert Bradshaw in horror. 'Beatrice has a fever? Is she going to be all right? Wh-what about her baby? Is. . .is it . . .?'

'T' babe's all right now. Least ways I think she is,' the kindly

Yorkshireman added with a worried frown. 'T'doctor an' t'midwife had a real job t'get 'er t'cry though; nearly gave 'er up for dead! So Dick said.'

'Oh no!' Sarah gasped in horror. 'Poor Beattie.'

'Dick says she's all right now though, lass. A real good little thing, 'e says. Never cries, even in t'night.' He peered at Sarah uncertainly. 'I don't reckon it's natural, mind you wi' a new babby like that, 'ardly cryin' at all . . .?'

'No-o . . .' Sarah agreed slowly, 'but if Beattie's so ill, she'll be glad the baby is contented. Perhaps it's nature's way o' compensating. Is Beattie still very ill with the fever?'

'There's no wunder t'lass 'ad a fever. Y'should 'ave seen't mucky black fingernails on that woman, an' 'er callin 'erself a midwife. Filthy beesom! Good job Dick sent for t'doctor in t'end.'

Sarah's face paled with concern. Supposing anything happened to Beatrice and she did not even know they were sisters!

'Sit down lass!' Bert Bradshaw exclaimed in concern. 'I didn't mean t'worry yer like that! Mistress O'Connor is going t'be all right y'know. She'll not die any road.'

'Oh dear!' Sarah was glad to slump down on to a kitchen chair. She had never fainted in her life, but she felt sick with worry for Beatrice, and remorse . . . Why, oh why, had Mistress Slater made her promise not to tell her secret?

'Mama! Mama, Sadie's crying again!' Billy skidded to a halt as he saw Mr Bradshaw.

''Mornin' Master Billy, 'ow are yer? When are yer goin' ter school now?'

'Guid morning, Mr Bradshaw.' Billy grinned widely, showing a wide gap where he had lost a top front tooth. He edged a little nearer to the jovial-faced Yorkshire man and Bert put his hand deep inside his coat pocket and pulled out two packets of sherbet powder.

'I expect this'll keep yer quiet while I finish 'avin' a little talk t'yer mother, eh? Save one for Alex now!'

'Thank ye, Mr Bradshaw!' Billy beamed widely, his dark eyes sparkling. He almost collided with Ellen, who always followed him like a small shadow whenever she got the chance, especially since Alex had started school.

'Aah! 'ere's me favourite sweet'eart!' Bert pulled out a packet of jelly sweets and offered one to Ellen. She stood quietly at his knee, smiling angelically as she accepted the small sweets one by one, while Bert Bradshaw went on talking.

'Dick specially wanted me t'tell yer that 'is wife'll not be fit t'write for a bit. She's that weak. 'E wundered if you'd write to 'er, just t'cheer 'er up like. 'E says she fair looks for'ard t'gettin' yer letters, an' all t'news. They both do, if you ask me, but Mistress O'Connor's a bit down in't spirits after 'er bein' s'badly.'

'I shall write at once,' Sarah promised. 'I just wish I could see her!'

she added longingly, 'but it's so far away and . . .' A loud wail came from Sadie. Sarah grimaced. 'And the twins demand all my time and attention just now, especially Sadie. I couldna possibly go to Yorkshire. I must send Beatrice the clothes I have made for her baby though . . .'

'I'll take 'em for yer, lass. I like t' call at t' farm, specially when Beatrice 'as bin bakin'!' His blue eyes twinkled and he rubbed his rotund figure. Bert Bradshaw had developed a sweet tooth in his later years. 'Maybe Crispin'll think uv somethin' t' cheer 'er up an' all. 'E keeps an' eye on 'em. 'E feels a bit responsible y'see, for 'em moving down t' Yorkshire. Life's not bin easy for 'em!' Bert Bradshaw paused and frowned. 'By the way lass, did Sandy tell you that old Mr MacNaught is givin' up West'ill?'

'No . . .I don't think my father mentioned it . . .'

'It's bin neglected a long time. Poor man's not fit y' see, an' it's a bit steep i' places, but 'e tried 'ard. Any road West'ill land joins Fairlyden fields at t'north end so I wundered if you an' Mr William would like t'rent it. Yer father once said Fairlyden would be a grand farm if it 'ad a bit uv rough 'ill land for running sheep. The way things are at present I'm not spending any more money improvin' a place like yon.' He sighed. 'You see what yer 'usband says lass. 'E could 'ave it for ten an' six an acre. Sandy says it needs lime, an' some uv it ought t' be drained. 'E reckons there's fifty acres that could be real good land on't opposite side o' t'brook. . .er t'burn I mean, an' there's a nice little wood . . .'

'Thank you for offering it to us, Mr Bradshaw.' Sarah frowned uncertainly. She knew her father would never have missed such a chance to increase and improve Fairlyden. The addition of Westhill would give them almost two hundred acres rented as well as well as the fifty acres they owned. 'I dinna know what William will say. His heart isna really in farming. We'll let you know . . .'

'Aye you do that, lass. Remember you've two lads growin' up an' times'll not allus be this bad.'

On that more cheerful note Bert Bradshaw took his departure, leaving Sarah with a lot to think about. The first thing was to make a parcel of baby clothes, and to write Beatrice a very cheerful letter.

Sarah was always pleased to have a visit from Mr Bradshaw, and especially when he brought news of Beatrice, but the visit had delayed her morning tasks. Sadie was even more fretful than usual, and the butter had refused to come, despite the wonderful new churn. To make matters worse Sarah was constantly tired. Her sleep was broken by the twins and their insatiable demands for milk. When she entered the scullery towards the end of the day her temper was shorter than it might otherwise have been. Agnes was in the adjoining dairy, getting ready for the afternoon milking and Sarah jumped at the sound of a nerve-shattering clatter as Maggie rushed into the dairy with unusual haste and clumsiness. Sarah saw a shadow dash past the window, but her attention was distracted by the sound of the girl's gasp; it was almost a sob, and Ellen was whimpering too.

'Mercy me, lassie!' Agnes exclaimed, with a note of exasperation, 'whatever's got intae ye? Near knocked me ower, ye did!'

'I'm s-sorry.' Maggie gasped. 'I— I . . .'

'An' I've telt ye afore, Maggie, ye mustna run when ye're carryin' any o' the bairns. Ye might hae fallen, or dropped Ellen.'

Maggie sniffed and stifled a sob.

'I had tae run, or he wad hae caught me! I— I hate him, Agnes! I— I think I'll leave Fairlyden!'

'What!' Agnes was startled. 'Och whisht lassie, dinna greet! Surely it wasna that Peter after ye again? I told Nicky tae gie him a talking tae. Frightening innocent lassies, an' ye nae mair than a bairn! Wait 'till I see him.'

'No! Please, Agnes, dinna say anything tae him!'

'And why not indeed?' Agnes had put down her pails and now she stood, hands on hips, puffing out her chest as Sarah moved to the adjoining door, pushing back her hair with a weary hand. She halted in surprise at Maggie's next words.

'He said he wad break ma arm for sure the next time, if I dared tell the Mistress he'd taken some o' her eggs.'

'Taken the eggs!' Agnes gaped open-mouthed. 'B-but I thocht— I thocht he was stealin' a kiss or twae!'

'Why wad he want a kiss?' Maggie frowned in genuine bewilderment.

'But I thocht . . .Och weel! I've bin wrang altogither! Nae wunner Peter jist laughed i' Nicky's face when he told 'im off for pesterin' innocent lassies! Is that what he'd bin aboot the last time he frightened ye then, Maggie?'

'No. He— he wanted me tae tak twae butter pats frae the dairy. He was goin' tae sell 'em tae some auld packman he kens. He said if the Mistress found they'd gone he wad say the collie dog had stolen them. I told him I wadna dae sic a thing, so he twisted my arm richt up ma back, an' he said— he said he'd make Thomas suffer if I didna help 'im next time.' Maggie bit back another sob and Ellen, who had been resting her head on her shoulder and sleepily sucking her thumb, stirred restlessly.

'Want doon, Maggie. Doon . . .' She wriggled in Maggie's arms. 'Mama,' she called happily, 'Mama!' as she caught sight of Sarah in the doorway. Sarah found herself moving into the dairy feeling as guilty as if she had committed a crime herself. Then she saw the colour drain from Maggie's young face, and her eyes widened with fear.

'Maggie!' She caught her hand, then slipped an arm around the girl's shoulders as she swayed. 'Dinna faint, lassie. You've nothing to fear frae me! Surely you know that?'

'He – Peter Elliot said if— if ye found out he'd say Thomas an' me had stolen the things. He said he wad tell the Master he had seen us takin' them tae Mother tae sell frae Mr Jardine's shop. He said we'd all end up in prison!' Maggie's voice ended in a wail.

'Och Maggie!' Sarah's voice reflected both exasperation and pity. 'I've known you far too long to believe such a tale! Peter Elliot was trying to frighten you into helping him to steal. I shall have to speak to him!'

Maggie gazed up at Sarah fearfully. 'B-but Thomas . . .?' she whispered anxiously.

'Aye,' Agnes frowned. 'Thomas'll be i' the bothy on his ain wi' Peter. Whae can tell what he might dae tae the laddie . . .?'

Sarah's mouth tightened and she frowned impatiently. 'Where did Peter put the eggs he has stolen, Maggie?'

'He— he hid them, 'neath an empty sack . . .' she gulped tearfully, 'in the meal kist, the wee yin in the stable.'

Sarah nodded. 'Well, you take Ellen to the kitchen, and keep an eye on the twins. And Maggie, dinna leave the house again today, not until I've spoken to Master Fairly about this.'

'V-very w-weel, Mistress Fairly.'

'Och lassie, dinna be feart,' Agnes chivvied, looking at Maggie's frightened face with compassion. 'The Mistress'll soon deal wi' that scoundrel, jist ye wait an' see!'

Sarah frowned and bit her lip. Normally she would leave William to deal with such matters, after all he was the Master, and he had hired Peter. But William is never there when I need him, she thought irritably.

'I'll go now and see where he's hidden the eggs anyway,' she declared aloud. 'He willna get off lightly when the Master hears! You and Sally start the milking, Agnes. I'll join you soon.'

Sarah found six eggs just as Maggie had described, but beneath the meal on which they lay her fingers encountered something else. She pushed the meal aside to find some brown paper. She unfolded it curiously and saw four of her best wax candles, and a pair of woollen socks. She guessed the socks belonged to Maggie's brother, Thomas. She pursed her lips in anger and shut the lid of the chest carefully. She would show them to William as soon as he returned.

Usually Sarah was in the byre, her head tucked against a cow, and her eyes on the milk filling her pail at this time of the afternoon. Certainly Peter Elliot did not expect her to walk round the end of the stable just when he was taking out his ill temper on a young mare. Sarah stared in horror when she came upon him muttering furious oaths and kicking at the mare's belly with his heavy clog. The poor animal was trapped between the shafts of a cart, which was already backed firmly against the barn wall; she could not escape the blows. In terror she began to rear on her hind legs, endangering the cart and bursting the leather traces. Elliot yanked furiously on her bridle and Sarah saw the blood spurt from the corner of the animal's mouth where the metal bit had cut cruelly.

'Stop it! Stop it at once you. . .you young fiend!' Sarah shouted furiously.

Peter Elliot spun round at the sound of her voice. His eyes popped and his mouth gaped, but only for a moment.

'She wadna back the cart,' he muttered sullenly. He was still holding on to the bridle and the mare was shivering and sweating nervously, rolling the whites of her eyes in fear.

'The cart is as far back as it will go,' Sarah spoke through gritted teeth. 'Unless you expect the mare to shove it through a stone wall two feet thick!' Fury was boiling inside Sarah but she controlled it as she moved closer to the frightened horse.

'There my girl . . .' she spoke soothingly, 'you're all right now . . .' She patted the silky chestnut neck gently and felt the stickiness of the mare's sweating body.

'She needs tae ken who's boss!' Peter Elliot muttered sulkily.

'And so do you!' Sarah stepped back from the mare, her fists clenched as she strove to keep her temper. Peter Elliot blinked as he saw the anger and contempt in her flashing dark eyes. In contrast Sarah's voice was low and icy.

'You'll not stay at Fairlyden one minute longer than term day.'

Peter Elliot gaped at her. 'Ye canna tell me tae leave!' he burst out indignantly.

'We value our animals too much to keep the likes of you!'

'Master Fairly hired me.'

'And no doubt Master Fairly will tell you to leave,' Sarah answered coldly. 'He doesn't tolerate ill treatment o' the horses.' Sarah spoke with a great deal more confidence than she felt. She was responsible for the maids, but she never interfered with the men.

'We'll see about that!' Peter Elliot retorted angrily.

Sarah knew his type now. He would lose no time in spreading malicious gossip, or in making out that William was ruled by his wife. Many farm labourers relished such talk, and Sarah had no wish to be known as another Mistress Sharpe, especially when such talk was neither true nor just. She could tell Elliot that she knew of his dishonesty, of course, but she had no wish to make young Thomas, or Maggie, suffer his malice; his treatment of the mare had given her good reason to avoid involving them.

The atmosphere in the Fairlyden kitchen was strained as they gathered round the table for the evening meal after the milking was finished. Alex and Billy exchanged glances and got on with their soup. Ellen was always good at meal times, especially when Agnes helped her spoon in her porridge. William had not yet returned from some business in Muircumwell and Sandy often ate his evening meal at the Tower House if Bert Bradshaw was staying there. It gave them an opportunity to discuss the affairs of the estate and Bert enjoyed the company.

Sarah was tired and her tension was increasing. She badly needed the support of her husband, especially over the issue of Peter Elliot. He had glowered at everyone at the table, but gobbled his soup with his usual appetite. Maggie could scarcely raise her eyes from her plate;

she looked pale and utterly miserable. Sarah had not had an opportunity to tell her she had not mentioned her name, or the theft of the eggs, in her confrontation with Peter Elliot. Only Thomas ate with his usual gusto, apparently oblivious to the tension in the air. Long before Sarah had finished her own meal, Sadie was making her usual high-pitched wail in a bid for attention.

Sarah rose with a sigh and plucked both the twins from the crib.

'Come upstairs and help me put them to bed as soon as you've finished, Maggie,' she instructed wearily.

'I'll come right awa'!' Maggie said with relief.

'Finish your soup!' Sarah said more sharply than she had intended and saw Maggie's eyes fill with tears. 'I need to feed them both first,' she added more gently. 'Just come when you're finished.'

Out of the corner of her eye Sarah saw Peter Elliot giving Maggie a compelling stare before he pushed back his chair and strolled outside. Sarah knew he wanted Maggie to follow him but Maggie was not so foolish as to be led astray by him. Janet and Louis had brought their family up to be honest and hardworking.

'Why can't you be as content as your sister?' she murmured as she looked down into Sadie's angry little face. Sadie's tiny mouth seemed thin and mean even when she pouted. Katherine was such a contrast with her rosy, smiling face and laughing dark eyes. Already she was a great favourite with William. He had more patience with her than he had ever had with any of his other children, even Billy.

As soon as she heard William's horse cantering into the yard Sarah thrust Katherine into Maggie's willing arms.

'Finish undressing her and put her to bed, Maggie, please.'

She ran down the stairs, feeling the tension mounting in her chest like a hard ball, but she was determined to speak to William before he saw Peter Elliot. There was so little opportunity to hold a private conversation, except when they retired to bed, and that might be too late.

Seventeen

William had just led his mount, Demon, into his stall and he was humming a merry tune as he began to brush the horse's glossy coat.

'William! I . . .'

'Hello, my dear. I'm sorry I'm late. Were you getting anxious? I have already eaten – with Sir Simon Guillyman, as a matter of fact.'

Sarah was too preoccupied with the trouble over Peter Elliot to detect William's suppressed excitement, but he realised at once that something was bothering her.

'What is wrong, Sarah . . .? Is it Katie? Or Billy . . .?' he asked sharply.

'All the children are fine!' Sarah only just managed to stop herself from snapping when her husband showed such obvious preference for his two favourite children. 'Sadie has been girning all day, but she's well enough!'

'She resembles her Uncle James already!' William replied incautiously.

Sarah stared at him. William never mentioned his half-brother's name, Sarah knew he felt only anger and contempt towards the late Earl. William looked faintly uncomfortable. The moment he had first seen Sadie she had reminded him incredibly of James, and perhaps a little of his father, but it was not an opinion he had ever expressed aloud, even to Sarah. Tonight though he had drunk freely of Sir Simon's wine.

Sarah's face paled. For a moment she forgot her apprehension over Peter Elliot's dismissal. 'You canna mean that, William? James was only your half-brother! You said he inherited his faults frae his mother's side.'

'Don't distress yourself so, Sarah dear!' William set his dandy brush aside and left his horse to lay a comforting arm around his wife's shoulders. She was very thin, he thought with a frown. 'No man, or woman, could ever be as bad as James, and he did take after the Griers. It was just a careless remark.'

'But you must have thought there was some resemblance . . .?'

'Well, Sadie does seem different to the others, but she's just a babe! She'll grow into a fine young woman, of course she will!'

He laughed too heartily, Sarah thought uneasily.

'I hope you're right!' she muttered fervently.

'So! Why were you in such a hurry to see me that you could not wait until I came to the house?'

'I— I wanted to talk with you alone. William, I know I shouldna have lost my temper, but I was so angry and . . .'

'Hey! Steady now, Sarah! What exactly have you done?'

'I found Peter Elliot kicking one of the young mares in the belly, really vicious he was. I said we didna want men like him at Fairlyden. I— I told him he would have to leave at the term . . .'

William looked at her blankly. 'Did he argue? Did he upset you?'

Sarah stared up at William. Suddenly she burst into tears.

'Sarah! Oh my love! If Peter Elliot harmed you I will . . .'

'N-no, he didna! I— I've just been worried because. . .well because I thought you would think I was taking over y-your authority a-and . . .'

'Aah Sarah!' William's arm tightened around her shoulders and he pulled her close. 'You know better than anyone what is best for Fairlyden . . .' He frowned. 'But perhaps I have been leaving you with too great a burden . . .? Certainly Peter Elliot must go at the term. I suspect he is a thief, as well as cruel with the animals. I have warned him already, but there are still three months before the term and I'm reluctant to put him on to the road without a character. I shall speak to him again, more sternly this time.'

'Oh William,' Sarah turned into the circle of his arms and hugged him tightly. 'You've such a fine air of authority. I'm sure he'll behave himself until November, if you deal with him.'

'I'm glad you approve, Mistress Fairly!' William's dark eyes twinkled. 'I have some news for you, but we shall discuss it later, in the comfort of our bedchamber. Right now I must attend to Demon.'

'And I must see that Ellen and the boys are in bed,' Sarah murmured, giving him a wobbly smile.

William gently tilted her chin and turned her face up to his. 'You're very pale, Sarah,' he said anxiously. 'Are you well enough?'

'Yes, I'm fine, just tired. I expect it is with feeding the twins. Bert Bradshaw came over today. Beatrice and Dick O'Connor have had a baby daughter. Poor Beattie has been very ill with fever. She is still recovering. So I consider myself fortunate. I never had the fever and we have five strong healthy children.'

'Are you trying to banish my fears after the good doctor's warning?' William asked with a tender smile. He bent his head close to her ear. 'Remember I love you very much, Mistress Fairly, but you must not tempt me. There must be no more young Fairlys for some considerable time.' His dark eyes sparkled and the colour flooded Sarah's pale cheeks for an instant.

'You always knew how to cheer me up, William,' she smiled, her anger and apprehension dispelled. 'Now I shall go and listen to your sons saying their prayers. But I am impatient to hear your news remember.'

Sandy had returned from Strathtod by the time William came into the kitchen. The two men settled themselves beside the dying fire and lit their pipes for a smoke before retiring. Agnes and Maggie had already gone to bed.

'Did ye tell William about Mr Bradshaw's proposition, Sarah?' Sandy asked as soon as she joined them.

'About Westhill? No, we havena had time to talk yet. Indeed I had almost forgotten . . .' She sighed. 'It seems so long since this morning!'

'Forgotten!' Sandy echoed incredulously. 'Why, it's a great opportunity! The addition of Westhill land would make Fairlyden a fine farm for both cattle and sheep; it wad be one o' the biggest on the estate . . .'

'But Father, things are so uncertain! Some weeks I can scarcely sell the butter we have now, and the eggs are almost as bad in the summer.' She sighed. 'If only I knew how to make some of the hens lay their eggs in winter!'

'That's all the more reason tae keep more sheep then, and maybe grow a few acres more corn tae feed the Irish cattle William buys at the market. Ye might even grow a few potatoes to sell wi' your eggs, Sarah,' Sandy argued persuasively.

'Even in the east the weather has been terrible for growing corn this year; it's even wetter here in the west.'

'Maybe ye'd have more interest in Fairlyden if ye could grow more corn, William?' Sandy never criticised Sarah's husband but he was disappointed that his interest in the daily running of Fairlyden had waned instead of increased. William did not answer. 'The time tae take on extra land is when nobody else wants it,' Sandy persisted. 'Even if things are no' sae good in the market place, ye dinna owe anybody for anything, do ye? Alex and Billy will need land tae farm some day. There's folks i' the toons beggin' for food, despite all the big cargoes comin' frae other countries, accordin' tae Crispin Bradshaw.'

Sarah looked anxiously at William, wondering why he was so quiet. For once she felt a little vexed by her father's enthusiasm, when she had not had time to discuss Mr Bradshaw's offer with William. His heart was not in farming, as her father's was, and since the birth of the twins her own life was too full, and her energy too little, to cope with any more burdens.

'We'll talk about Westhill later . . .' William promised, puffing on his pipe.

'Och, I wish I was young again!' Sandy exclaimed frustratedly. 'Or even if I hadna been lame . . .There's such opportunities!'

'Mmm, and such low prices, Father . . .' Sarah reminded him with a wry smile. She knew he missed farming himself, even though he was grateful to have his work as factor for Mr Bradshaw.

Later, in the privacy of their own bedchamber, William declared, 'I'm afraid your father must be very disappointed, Sarah, but you know I shall never make an ordinary working farmer. Anyway, I have other plans.' He looked at her, his dark eyes pleading with her to understand.

Sarah's heart sank. Did he still yearn to go back to America? Was that his news?

In the candlelight William saw the anxiety in her dark eyes. 'Don't look so worried, my dear. I realise now that Fairlyden has been too great a burden for you to bear alone, and I'm sorry. I intend to change that!'

'No! Please William, d-don't change anything! I— I'm all right!'

'You're strong and brave, and you work too hard, but you're my wife, Sarah. I don't want you to be an old woman before you ought to be.' He glanced towards the crib where the twins were sleeping. 'I know the twins sap your strength . . .'

'But they'll soon grow! Already Katie enjoys her gruel. Sadie will grow more content when she learns to accept it too . . .' Suddenly the exhaustion and irritations she had felt earlier seemed nothing in comparison to the prospect of leaving Fairlyden, of travelling thousands of miles across the ocean to a foreign land . . .'I dinna want to leave Fairlyden!' she muttered in a hoarse whisper.

'I'm not asking you to leave Fairlyden, my dear, at least not yet.'

'Then. . .then why are you looking at me so strangely, as though. . .as though you know I shallna like your news . . .?' Sarah asked.

'Aah Sarah!' William laughed ruefully, 'you are far too shrewd.'

Sarah eyed him thoughtfully, aware now of the suppressed excitement she had been too preoccupied to notice earlier.

'What is it, William?'

'I want you to hear everything before you make a decision. I shall not blame you, Sarah, if you refuse my request.'

Sarah stifled a yawn with an effort. She felt deadly tired, yet she knew she would never sleep until she knew what was on William's mind.

'Tell me,' she said quietly.

'Sir Simon Guillyman invited me to Avary Hall. I told you I dined with him. He had heard that I was interested in the Farmers' Store when the O'Connors were at the Mill House and he wondered if I would like to run such a store myself – as his partner. The mill buildings are on his land and the house and the mill are to be sold to pay off Wull Slater's creditors. Sir Simon intends to buy them back. Apparently they belonged to the Guillymans many generations ago. Anyway we had a long discussion . . .'

'But William, that's wonderful!' Sarah exclaimed in genuine delight, and relief. 'Beatrice said you had some grand ideas for her and Dick, but they hadna enough money to put them into practice . . .' She stopped. 'What is it you want me to do that I shallna like . . .?' she asked, suddenly fearful. 'Fairlyden! Is—?'

'Sir Simon and I have rather different plans to the O'Connors' little enterprise. If we can come to an agreement . . .' His gaze fell as he encountered Sarah's watchful dark eyes. 'The Farmers' Store would be renamed "Fairly and Guillyman's Agricultural Merchants". We would aim to sell, or at least to trade in, everything farmers might require. Not just scythes and ordinary tools, but the latest mowing machines. We may even sell the new self-binding machines; they do more than cut the corn, they roll it up a canvas elevator and even tie it into sheaves, and drop them in rows all ready for stooking.' His dark eyes shone with enthusiasm in the candlelight. 'We shall supply turnip seed and grass seed – only the best quality of course; we may even sell some of the new phosphate fertilisers.'

William fell silent for a moment. Sarah knew from the faraway look in his eyes that he was seeing a vision of the future which she would never understand, dreaming of the machines he had seen working in America, machines which were already used on some of the grain farms in the south and east. William was convinced there was a place for them in the west too. As she watched him his eyes slowly returned to her face.

'There is a problem of course . . .'

'Life is full of problems,' Sarah said tensely.

'As Sir Simon Guillyman's partner,' William said carefully, 'I need more than just knowledge and ideas and contacts with the merchants. I do not want to be just a storekeeper. I must provide some of the money to buy the initial stock. When it is sold we shall use our profits to buy more. I am sure the business will be a success, Sarah!'

'I'm sure it will,' Sarah could not stifle her yawn, 'but dinna waken the twins!' She grimaced. 'Though Sadie will be up soon enough!'

'You are tired, my dear. I will tell you the rest tomorrow . . .'

'The rest? What— what was the request you thought I might refuse . . .?' she asked, suddenly alert again.

'I need your help. You know I spent all the money I brought back from America to pay off your father's loan, so that Fairlyden would be secure . . .?'

Sarah's face paled and her heart began to race. 'I remember,' she whispered hoarsely. 'Now you want to s-sell F-Fairlyden?' She shivered, but not with cold.

'Not Fairlyden, Sarah . . .' William flushed. 'I want to sell the diamond brooch, the one my grandfather bought for his mistress . . .'

'The brooch the Reverend Mackenzie left to me . . .?' Sarah said slowly. 'Would a brooch be worth so much?' she asked incredulously. Whatever the brooch was worth in money the thought of selling a gift made her feel cold and mercenary. The brooch had been preserved with care, and no doubt with some sacrifice by her old friend, the Minister. Sarah felt disloyal, ungrateful.

'I thought you were pleased the brooch had been returned to me – to your own family . . .?'

'I am. I was. . .but I need money and it is better to sell a piece of jewellery you will never wear, than to sell Fairlyden, surely?'

'Anything is better than selling Fairlyden,' Sarah agreed, and she was thankful William's plans did not include journeying to America, either for him, or his family. In her heart Sarah was sure the Reverend Mackenzie would expect her to do whatever was best for her family, and for Fairlyden . . .Surely he would have considered William's happiness important too?

'Well . . .?' William prompted warily.

'You're right, William. Of course you must sell the brooch . . .' In the candlelight Sarah saw the relief in his dark eyes.

'Thank you, Sarah,' he whispered huskily. He pulled her gently into his arms and held her close, his lean cheek resting against her hair. 'I will ask Crispin Bradshaw to have it valued in London. I know I can trust him and it will bring a better price in the capital city. When Fairly and Guillyman's becomes a success I shall make it up to you. I shall buy you as many trinkets as your heart desires.'

'Oh William, it isna trinkets I desire, so long as we have each other and our bairnies . . .'

'And Fairlyden!' William added wryly. 'I'm afraid your father will be disappointed when we do not agree to rent Westhill.'

'He'll understand when he hears about your plans, and it wadna do if every man wanted the same thing frae life,' Sarah smiled tiredly.

'You are a good wife, Sarah, and an understanding one.' William kissed her gently before he blew out the candle.

It was the end of August before Crispin Bradshaw travelled to Scotland, and even then his visit was a brief one. He lost no time in calling at Fairlyden with news of the O'Connors. Sarah greeted him eagerly. She had received no letters from Yorkshire although Beatrice's baby daughter was now almost a month old.

'Mistress O'Connor is still very weak and easily tired, though her baby is extremely content and a pretty little thing with pale gold hair and blue eyes,' Crispin assured her.

'But Beattie . . .? She hasna written, not even a few lines?'

'No.' Crispin frowned. 'Dick says his wife has been low in spirits. He blames the ordeal of the prolonged birth, and then the fever. It is my own belief that Mistress O'Connor has some secret anxiety, or perhaps she is homesick.'

'Homesick?' Sarah echoed in dismay. 'But she seemed so happy with Dick, and the farm, and being so busy and everything . . .'

'Yes, she was, while she was in good health, though I suspect she must have pined in silence many times. I know she longs for your letters. She even welcomes my visits,' Crispin smiled ruefully, 'especially when I have been at Strathtod and can take her news of you and Alex and Billy.'

He looked shrewdly at Sarah and she blushed beneath his grey-eyed scrutiny. 'You are not looking so well yourself, Sarah. Do you find the twins draining your strength?' Incredibly Sarah found the tears springing to her eyes at the unexpected gentleness in his deep voice and the concern in his eyes.

'I'm fine,' she muttered gruffly and turned away abruptly so that he would not see her weakness. But Crispin had already seen and he was dismayed. Sarah Fairly was not a tearful woman. She was strong and tough, both mentally and physically, but he had noticed at once that she had lost weight and her beautiful dark eyes were shadowed and strained. He sighed heavily.

'It would have helped your friend, Beatrice, to see a familiar face, a dear friend; but obviously you cannot leave such a busy household as this.'

Sarah turned to him is surprise. 'You mean me . . .? Travel to Yorkshire to see Beattie?' Then the light died out of her face and she slumped into the chair opposite Crispin. 'No, of course I couldna possibly go and leave the twins and Ellen,' she sighed, 'especially now, with the harvest coming on and the weather likely to continue as bad as ever. William is busy getting the old mill ready to open again as a store . . .' She stopped short. She had no wish to be disloyal to her husband. She knew William loved her, but he was so engrossed in the affairs of Fairly and Guillyman's Store.

'I do long to hear from Beattie. I wish there was something I could do to cheer her up. What about poor Dick? How is he?'

'Dick works too hard. I fear his fellow farmers think Scotsmen must be a little mad, but they are also a little envious now that his efforts are bearing fruit, when many of them can scarcely support their families. Of course Dick is missing Beatrice's help, especially with the milking and the dairy. He is so busy and she is so often alone. I believe she finds it difficult to converse with her neighbours, especially when her spirits are low.' He smiled wryly. 'She always seems pleased to see me, but even I speak with the same "queer Yorkshire tongue".'

'Oh no, you're quite easy to understand, Crispin, much easier than your father, but then you've travelled in many parts of the country.'

'Maybe, but I cannot give Beatrice news of her old friends. It is a great pity she has no family to cheer her at such a time.'

No family! Sarah's face paled.

'Are you all right? Sarah . . .?' Crispin was on his feet in an instant, bending over her, his grey eyes anxious.

'I— I'm fine . . .' she looked up at him, her dark eyes wide and troubled. 'Crispin. . .do you truly believe it would help Beatrice to see someone belonging to her . . .? I— I mean someone frae home . . .?'

'Anyone, except Wull Slater! It is only my opinion of course, but I thought a friendly face and a familiar tongue would be a better tonic than rest, or the medicine, which the doctor insists on prescribing, and charging for!' he added grimly.

'My father has known Beatrice all her life. He is very fond of her . . .' Sarah said slowly.

'Sandy Logan?'

'Beatrice's grandfather was his great friend,' Sarah said hastily, her cheeks flushing slightly. 'He could give her all the local news . . .He could tell her about Alex and Billy . . .'

'Maybe you're right . . .Perhaps he could even take young Alex with him . . .?' Crispin agreed with more enthusiasm. 'It might be of benefit to Alex too. I hear he has had a difficult time since he started school. I expect the other children tease him about his feet . . .'

'Aye. He has had a black eye and several bruises and torn clothes, though he never complains or gives a reason for his injuries.'

'But it is not difficult to guess. Children can be very cruel. A visit to Yorkshire on the train might serve to boost his morale as well as Beatrice's! Not many of the village children travel so far from home on a railway train, and a sight of his smiling face would certainly gladden Beatrice's heart, I'm sure.'

'But my father's work, he . . .'

'No doubt my father will agree to his factor's absence for a week, or even two,' Crispin smiled. 'He has grown very fond of Beatrice. He says she reminds him of you in many ways. It must be. . .Sarah! Are you sure you are all right?'

'Y-yes. I think I need a little air . . .' She pushed herself to her feet. 'Crispin, will you walk with me, in the orchard perhaps . . .? Where we can be alone. Undisturbed.'

'Is that wise, Sarah?'

She was very close and Crispin's grey eyes were wide with surprise; a faint colour stained his prominent cheekbones, but Sarah seemed unaware of his discomfiture. He realised with a pang that she was totally unaware of him as a man, yet he could smell the lavender scent of her hair and clothes and it disturbed him. He stepped back a pace. Something was clearly troubling Mistress Sarah Fairly and he knew he ought to feel pleased that she regarded him as a friend in need.

'The twins are having their afternoon rest. The boys and Ellen are helping Agnes search for hens' nests, but they may return any time.'

She turned and walked out of the door, along the passage and into the yard. Crispin followed and at length she halted beneath the trees where she had sought refuge as a child. She faced him.

'Crispin, I made a promise once, to someone who was dying. I promised to keep her secret, and I have. Until now . . .' she added huskily and raised her troubled eyes to Crispin's face. 'Sometimes it is a burden. You see it— it concerns people who are dear to me . . .'

'Does your husband know?' Crispin interrupted uncomfortably.

Sarah just shook her head. 'Will you promise never to breathe a word to a living soul, unless . . .'

'William should share your secrets, Sarah!'

'No, he— he enjoys a glass of good wine, on occasion . . .He would not betray my secret intentionally, I know that, but the wine might . . .' She looked up then, her dark eyes meeting his grey ones. She smiled faintly. 'You dinna indulge in such things, do you Crispin? You're still in favour o' the temperance movement?'

'I have other. . .weaknesses, Sarah,' he looked down at her intently, then sighed softly, 'but I do not indulge in alcohol. I shall do my best to ease any burden you may wish to share with me, at any time,' Crispin declared gravely.

Slowly Sarah began to tell him of her last conversation with Beatrice's mother, Mistress Jeannie Slater. It was a relief to talk about it and Crispin did not interrupt until she had finished speaking.

'So, Sandy Logan is your natural father, Sarah? My father had heard rumours that he was not just your step-father,' Crispin mused. 'If Mistress Slater was telling the truth that would mean Beatrice is your half-sister!' He whistled as the full implications began to dawn on him.

'Yes, Alexander Logan is my own father,' Sarah declared firmly, almost defiantly. 'He has been wonderful to me. Always. I know he would have cared for Beatrice too, if she is his daughter.'

'So! Was Mistress Slater telling you the truth? Or do you think it was all a figment of the poor woman's imagination – a result of her deranged mind?'

'I don't know,' Sarah answered quietly. 'I have asked myself often! Mistress Slater seemed, she seemed so certain, and yet. . .I know my father isna a man to deny his own flesh and blood without a reason! Certainly he wadna have left Beattie in Slater's care if he had known she was his daughter!' Sarah shivered at the memory of Edward Slater. 'She hated him! So, why didn't Mistress Slater tell her?'

'Because she was too ashamed perhaps? Because she was afraid Beatrice would reject her, maybe even leave her? Certainly Beatrice would have wanted to know who her real father was . . .'

'Aye, but surely she had a right to know!' Sarah declared vehemently.

'Maybe not. Perhaps there had once been doubt in Mistress Slater's own mind? Perhaps she was afraid Alexander Logan would deny such a possibility? Perhaps Mistress Slater preferred not to bring any more unhappiness into other lives? Your father, your mother? You? Maybe when she was dying, she realised she wanted someone to know the truth. Someone who cared deeply for her daughter?'

'Yes. I keep asking myself, supposing I tell Beatrice, and then my father refuted such a possibility! She would feel more alone and rejected than ever. Surely Mistress Slater should have told him? Didn't he have a right to know?'

'Put yourself in her position, Sarah! If you loved someone, if you gave them everything you had to give – your body, your soul, without reservation – and found yourself utterly rejected . . .?' Crispin shuddered and Sarah stared at him in surprise. He squared his shoulders. 'No doubt Mistress Slater's pride was hurt by Sandy's earlier rejection, however unintentional. As time passed I suppose it became more impossible for her to tell him. Who can be sure what is in another person's mind?' His grey eyes met Sarah's brown ones, and it was Sarah who looked away. 'I can understand that Mistress Slater would be afraid of Sandy's rejection in the circumstances.' Crispin sighed. 'I'm afraid I cannot be much help to you, Sarah.'

'You have helped, just by listening.' Sarah smiled wanly.

'Mmm, but I think we must not risk upsetting Beatrice when her spirits are low already. Perhaps it is better that she should know nothing yet. Maybe Mistress Slater has helped in another way. You would never have suggested asking your father to visit Beatrice if her mother had not confided in you, and I'm sure Beatrice will be pleased to see him. I know Dick would enjoy discussing his farm, and showing him around. Would you permit young Alex to travel with us?'

'If William is agreeable, and I think he will be.'

Sarah could not bring herself to admit to a man like Crispin Bradshaw that William paid little attention to his first-born son.

Eighteen

Highvale Farm
30th September, 1888

Dear Sarah,

I can scarcely believe how different I feel since your father's visit with Alex, and I am improving every day. I cannot tell you how pleased I was to see them, although no doubt they told you I could do nothing but weep when Alex threw his chubby arms around my neck and hugged me so lovingly. You have a fine son, Sarah, so merry, so bright and yet so full of affection, and he regarded our wee Meg with such tenderness. He told me all the news of Fairlyden, and even a little of his trials at school. That was on his last night here, when I was saying good night. How cruel children can be!

Your father gave Dick and me all the news of Strathtod, Muircumwell. . .everywhere. It was wonderful to hear a guid Scots tongue again! He reminisced about his first days at the mill with my grandfather, and about the fine meals my grandmother used to cook for him. Once when I was reading a story to Alex, your father said I reminded him of his own mother.

He went round all the fields with Dick and admired our pigs. He says his leg is not so painful as it was and he looks very fit and well: Dick could not believe he is almost fifty-two years old. I confess I shed more tears when the visit was over.

I expect Alex told you all about travelling over the moors and the train puffing out black smoke up the hills. He was thrilled to see the other trains at Leeds station. Crispin took him for a ride in a horse-drawn tramcar when they arrived in Leeds and he was so thrilled. It is such a pity Crispin Bradshaw does not find a nice wife and have children of his own. He is so very kind and patient.

Thank you so much, dear Sarah, for the lovely little dresses and petticoats you sent. Also we were very grateful for the joints of ham and lamb, and the roasted chicken and huge plum cake. I hope I shall soon be back to cooking again and I have planted the herbs you sent. I have written a short note to Janet. It was kind of her to send the pink woollen clothes. I had to dress Meg in the tiny boots and gloves to convince Alex they were big enough.

Meg is almost too good! Sometimes I worry because she sleeps so much, but Dick says she takes after his youngest brother, Rory. Apparently he was a very contented baby and rarely cried.

We had to take her to church to be christened. She is named Margaret after Dick's mother, and Alexandra, because that is one of my names and I like it, but as you see we call her Meg.

Everyone is complaining about the bad harvest weather, and the prices – wheat only fetching thirty-one shillings and eleven pence a quarter, but I just feel so happy to be regaining my health and to be able to help Dick again.

I am glad the twins are sleeping better at nights now, Sarah, and I do so look forward to having your letters.

Ever your ever affectionate friend,

Beatrice.

It was a long harvest and a poor one at Fairlyden and everyone was relieved when the last sheaf of corn was safely in the stack. William had helped as much as he could but much of his attention had been taken with alterations to the premises for his new venture. 'Fairly and Guillyman – Muircumwell Agricultural Merchants' opened on the first of November. Many of the farmers looked in out of curiosity and several ordered their spring oats, barley and bean seeds.

William had spent much of the autumn travelling to those farmers in the Lothians who had good quality seeds to sell and he brought back samples for the customers to inspect so that they could be reassured they would suffer no more of Wull Slater's tricks. William had also ordered a quantity of Canadian clover and ryegrass seed, and a new kind of turnip seed from Holland. He already had contacts from his cattle dealing at the markets and his travels with the stallions.

Twice each week William dined at Avary Hall with Sir Simon and Lady Guillyman, so that they could discuss their new venture.

'Sir Simon insists that our premises and the stock must be insured,' William told Sarah one evening as they sat around the fire after supper. 'It might be a good idea to insure our own house, and the buildings too.'

'What, here at Fairlyden?' Sarah asked in surprise.

'Yes, of course. It would be a wise precaution. After all people have been insuring their property in London since the Great Fire of 1666.'

'London is a different matter!' Sarah declared robustly. 'Who would set fire to Fairlyden? It's a waste to pay good money and never get any benefit.'

'We should certainly reap a great benefit if we had to rebuild the house!' William argued.

'Mr Bradshaw believes in insurance,' Sandy said slowly, puffing thoughtfully at his pipe. 'But he says it's essential tae ken exactly what the insurance company intend tae cover in return for the money.'

'There you are then, Sarah. I shall ask Mr Blakely, the agent, to insure the house at least.'

Sarah bit her lip but she made no further protest. She had to budget very carefully to make the money from the eggs and butter cover all her household necessities and this winter Billy would be going to school, as well as Alex. They would both need warm trousers and jackets and she had already bought a large quantity of wool to knit vests and socks. They would also need new clogs. On Agnes's recommendation she had taken Alex to Dumfries to see Bobby Frame. The clogger had examined and measured his feet with great care and promised to make a pair of specially shaped clogs.

'I canna cure the wee fellow's trouble, Mistress Fairly, but I reckon I can help him walk a wee bit better.'

'You are not listening, Sarah!' William complained. 'I said Sir Simon Guillyman has some useful contacts with a shipping company,' he went on enthusiastically. 'They will be useful if our business expands as we expect. It is four years since Mr McCormack's string binder was awarded a gold medal at the Royal Show at Derby, yet how many have we seen around here?' He rubbed his hands together. 'I'm sure Fairly and Guillyman's will be a success. I have ordered a horse rake and a turnip drill, a Ransome plough and a set of harrows already. It is a good job Crispin Bradshaw negotiated such an excellent price for my grandfather's diamond brooch.'

Sarah was silent. She wanted William to be a success, and she did not begrudge him the money from the brooch, but he had so little interest in Fairlyden's affairs and the responsibility weighed heavily on her. Peter Elliot was sly and he was becoming more difficult to manage again now the term day was drawing near.

'I shall buy you lots of fine gowns and trinkets when I get the business established, Sarah,' William declared jovially, noticing her sudden silence.

Sarah could not stifle an exasperated sigh. It isn't fine gowns and trinkets I crave! she thought wearily, it's support frae my own husband I need! To manage our own living at Fairlyden, to guide our bairns . . .

Sarah was relieved when the end of November arrived at last. William insisted that Nick should accompany him to the hiring fair this time. Nick was proud that he was to be given extra responsibility but the thought of helping to select a fellow worker made him nervous.

'You will work with him, and be responsible for him,' William declared brusquely. 'You will find it is not so easy to judge a man's character, or his ability, on a single meeting. Mistress Fairly will look after the milking and the women, as she has always done, but the crops and the care of the animals will be in your hands. I shall be away from home during the week, so you will be responsible for young Thomas Whiteley, as well as the new fellow.'

Nick was jubilant when he told Sally of his new responsibilities.

'Many's the time I wad hae told Peter Elliot I'd report him tae the Master for bein' sae cruel wi' the horses. He's ruined the young geldin' the way he pulled on yon bridle . . .'

'Weel, sae long as ye're happy, Nicky . . .' Sally murmured in her quiet voice. She adored Nick; to her he was the most wonderful man in the world so it seemed only reasonable that the Master should appreciate his abilities and his hard work.

'I've anither bit of news tae, Sally,' Nick grinned. 'I'm tae get an extra five pounds a term, that'll be twenty-eight pounds in cash! Just think on't! Why Sal, ye'll be able tae buy as much tea as ye can drink!' Sally smiled at him. He knew how much she loved a cup of tea, but she had always been thrifty. It was the way her grandmother had brought her up – had been forced to bring her up.

'I'm real proud o' ye, Nicky, ye ken that, tea or no tea.' She sighed heavily. 'If only I could gie ye a bairn. How prood it wad be, havin' ye for a father . . .'

For a moment Nick's own eyes clouded, then he forced a smile. 'There's time yet, lassie.'

'I'm gettin' old, Nick! I shall be twenty-five next month, an' ne'er a sign! Agnes was remindin' me that ye're thirty-one tae. I ken she wad like a wee nephew or a niece.'

'Och, dinna heed Agnes, Sally! She's all heart! She jist wants bairns tae spoil.'

'Mmm . . .' Sally sighed again, 'but I still wish we had one.'

'Weel we'll jist hae tae abide by the Lord's wishes, lassie,' Nick comforted her. 'At least we hae each other.' He pulled her to him and held her close against his hard chest. She could hear the steady beat of his heart. 'I thank Him many a time for that!' he whispered huskily, and Sally could feel the swift passion rising in him. She smiled up at him. Nick could always comfort her, but today there was no time for more than a hug and a kiss or two. She wished him well as he donned a clean collar and his second best tweed jacket, ready to accompany the Master. She had polished his Sunday boots with extra care.

As it happened Nick recognised one of the young men lined up along the side of the street.

'That's Ewan Donnelly!' he exclaimed involuntarily.

William looked at the tall, fresh-faced young man. He was clean and tidy, and he held his head high.

'You know him?' William's eyes narrowed. He would make his own decision in the end, but it always helped to know a little of a man's background, his character, and his family's too if possible.

'His father rented a wee farm neighbouring Main's o'Muir,' Nicky informed him now. 'He died suddenly, one winter morning. . .oh, about six years ago. Everybody kenned he was a fine horseman. Some folks reckoned his grandfather came o'er frae Ireland during the famine. His widow gave up the farm an' moved tae the toon tae keep hoose for a cloth merchant. I never saw Ewan again. Some o' the men at the Mains reckoned he was hairt sair when his mother wadna keep the farm. He wad be about twelve then. His mother married the merchant eventually. I heard tell he wanted Ewan tae join him in the woollen trade but Ewan went tae stay wi' yin o' his sisters who had married a farmer. His other sister lives in the toon. Agnes sees her sometimes at the market. She's married tae a shopkeeper.'

'So he comes from an honest, hard-working family?' William asked.

'Ah aye,' Nick answered without hesitation.

'Then I shall speak to him. If he has inherited his father's skill with horses he would be a good man to have at Fairlyden . . .' Extremely good, William thought to himself, I shall have little time to travel with the stallions now. But William knew the income from Alexander Logan's horses had kept Fairlyden afloat when other farms had gone bankrupt, and it would be a few years before Fairly and Guillyman's was well enough established for his share to support his wife and family and a decent home, and he had other ideas too . . .Besides it would be unthinkable to neglect the Logan horses. The progeny from Logan's Lucifer was doing well in various parts of Scotland and already Logan's Bobby had made his mark. Neither Sarah nor her father would forgive him if he allowed the Clydesdale trade to sink into oblivion.

Ewan Donnelly settled down to life at Fairlyden as though he had been born to it. He was cheerful and willing and there was no doubting his love for the horses, Sarah thought as she watched him setting out with a perfectly groomed stallion the following spring. It was a beautiful morning, she had a letter from Beatrice in her apron pocket and as soon as she had finished washing down the dairy she would open it. It always cheered her to receive a letter from Beatrice.

Highvale Farm
April 1889

My dearest Sarah,

Dick and I are sorry indeed to hear trade at Fairly and Guillyman's has not been good. I am sure things will improve now that spring is here.

I am fortunate indeed that Dick works so hard. We always do the milking together. I suppose I am fortunate that Meg is still so contented. She is eight months old now but she still lies in her bed and sleeps most of the time. Many of the farms in this area depend almost entirely on corn and bullocks, with only a single cow for the household and no milk or butter to sell; some have sheep. Many can no longer pay their rents. The landlords cannot let the farms. How can our British government be so blind? So many of the farm labourers have gone to look for work in the factories, or in coal mines. Sir George Emly, our own laird, offered Dick fifty-five acres of extra land. Dick did not take it. He has too much to do already and he is suspicious of machines, although I am sure the horse-drawn hay rake will save a lot of time and toil.

It was good to hear of Logan's Bobby's success with the Glasgow Agricultural Society. It is a great honour and I'm sure your father will be proud – also Alex. Already he admires his Grandfather

Logan. He told us that he wants to breed horses one day. Violet sounds a lovely young mare. I shall look forward to hearing news of her foal. How fortunate that Ewan Donnelly is so eager to look after the horses. I think I remember his father coming to the Muircumwell mill for oatmeal and bran. He was a gentle, quiet man. If Ewan is the same I can quite imagine him setting Maggie's young heart fluttering!

The twins will need all her attention now that they are walking, but Ellen sounds a kind, sensible little girl for her age. I can just imagine Billy being a mischief at school. It will be pleasant for Alex to have company on the long walk to Muircumwell – and also at school! No wonder the other boys have decided they prefer to have your sons as friends rather than enemies!

Sally Jamieson has my sympathy if she longs for a child. She always seemed so calm and quiet. I liked her very much and I can understand that she finds it hard to talk about her childless state. It is a pity Agnes considers her reserved.

We get a shilling a gallon for our milk just now but we have only eight pence left after we pay to send it on the train to Leeds. We sell as much as we can to the women from the village but they come at the strangest times. It is very tiring with such interruptions.

Beatrice's letter was long and chatty and Sarah enjoyed it though the news of Meg made her uneasy. Beattie's baby seemed almost too good. It seemed unnatural to be so contented and still need so much sleep.

Fortunately Beattie's forecast about Fairly and Guillyman's was coming true. William had sold a Ransome plough and some harrows as well as filling all his orders for oats and turnip seeds. He had also reached an agreement with a quarry owner a few miles away and now he was taking orders for lime which the local farmers were to collect with their own horses and carts. This promised to be quite profitable and William had decided to buy the boys a pony to ride to school.

'I can walk very well, thank you, Sir!' Alex had declared proudly. He was fiercely independent and determined to do whatever other boys do, especially his younger brother, Billy.

'Whisht!' Billy muttered, digging his elder brother in the ribs. 'I've bin pleadin' wi' father tae buy us a pony. I told him ye couldna keep up.'

'Course I can keep up wi' ye!' Alex declared indignantly. 'I dinna need a pony, I tell ye!'

The two boys chased each other out of the kitchen and into the yard, in a friendly squabble.

'Alex is an ungrateful wretch!' William declared irritably.

Sarah's heart sank. It was becoming more evident that William had little time or patience for his eldest son. Alex preferred his grandfather as his confidant and helper and he always accompanied him on his

Sunday strolls with Nick Jamieson around Fairlyden's crops and meadows.

'Alex asks questions about every field, crop and animal,' Sandy remarked one Sunday afternoon when they had just returned. 'He remembers when the seeds were sown, and when his favourite cows had their calves. Ye'd think he had an eye for a guid horse already. There's nae doubt he'll be a farmer one day, even though he canna follow the plough himself.'

'I'm glad to hear that!' Sarah said with relief. 'He never thinks of anything else.'

'He's a cripple and the sooner he realises it the better!' William declared with some annoyance. 'It is no use encouraging him. He must read his books and learn his lessons at school.'

Sarah did not reply. Alex had no difficulty with his lessons and it troubled her that William seemed to resent his six-year-old son knowing as much, and sometimes more, about the working of Fairlyden than he did himself. Sandy was also troubled by his attitude, and by William's obvious preference for Billy. It was to Billy's credit that he never tried to take advantage. He and Alex were the closest of companions.

It was early the following summer that Crispin Bradshaw delivered a letter from Beatrice in person.

'You will be pleased to hear that Beatrice is keeping much better now, Sarah,' he said, handing it to her with a smile.

'Better? Has Beattie been ill then?' Sarah's face lost some of its colour. Beatrice was expecting her second child.

'No, not ill exactly, but the news of my sister's death upset her badly. It reminds us all too clearly the great risks women face at such times.'

'Yes. It was distressing news indeed. Freda was so young, and pretty. To lose a daughter and a grandchild must be a terrible blow for your father. How is he?' Sarah had grown fond of the blunt-spoken Yorkshireman whose success had not changed his views on life at all.

'He cannot accept that Freda is dead, I'm afraid,' Crispin answered sadly. 'She was the youngest, and although I know she was abominably spoiled as a child, we loved her just the same.'

'Yes, I know you did. I really am very sorry, Crispin,' Sarah said gently.

'Beatrice did not know either of my sisters very well, but she is sensitive, and her own condition makes her extra anxious. If anything should go wrong I think she is concerned for little Meg. I thought you might be able to reassure her.'

Sarah nodded and tore open Beatrice's letter. It was shorter than usual and after the preliminary greetings Beatrice's concern for Meg became evident.

I feel so fit and well. I am sure nothing can go wrong this time, Sarah. In any case I am not afraid to die if that is God's will, except that I love Dick so very much, and I am afraid for my little Meg. What would be her fate in this unkind world of ours? Dick is already forty-five and it is hard for a man alone with any young child. I could never trust any of Slater's sons to care for her, even Joe, and although we share the same mother. I have no other kin and Dick has had no contact with his own family since the death of his parents. He still blames himself for their deaths and he feels he brought shame upon all his family.

In my heart I know Meg is not like other children. She looks so small and delicate, almost like a fairy with her golden curls and blue eyes. Now that she has at last left the cradle behind she does not walk – she runs everywhere, as light on her tiny feet as a butterfly. She chatters constantly, yet neither Dick nor I can understand a word. Her favourite companion is our collie dog. He alone seems to understand her needs and he is her most loyal guard, even sleeping beside her cot each night. So you see, Sarah, I need your prayers for my safe delivery, for Meg's sake. I am in good health. The baby is not due until mid-September but Dick insisted that I should arrange to have a different midwife. I have been to see her. She is a very clean and respectable woman.'

Sarah looked up from the letter. 'She is afraid there would be nobody to care for Meg if anything happened to her. I will write and reassure her, though I pray to God Beattie will be all right.'

'How will you reassure her?'

'I shall tell Beattie I would look after her child as though she were my own, if such a thing was needed.'

'Would your husband permit that, Sarah? And would Beatrice not wonder why you should make such a promise, when you have five children of your own?'

'Of course William would agree. He may be a little distant with some of his own bairns,' she said defensively, 'but he would understand . . .'

Crispin nodded. 'Like you, I shall pray for Beatrice's safe delivery, but she really was a very sick woman after Meg's birth and she is no longer young.'

'It's very good of you to care, Crispin.'

'I feel responsible in a way, at least for the O'Connors being so far away.'

'Dick will always be grateful to you. I know that. He was never happy at the Store, even without Wull Slater's interference. He is meant to be a farmer.' She hesitated and looked up at him.

'Are you thinking I should tell Beattie her mother's secret . . .? Is that it, Crispin?'

'I think it would reassure her to know she does have kin of her own. I fear Meg will be a problem child, and in her heart Beatrice knows it too. I suspect she also wonders if she is in some way to blame – perhaps through the man who was her father.'

Sarah nodded slowly. Her brown eyes were troubled. 'Aye, she must often wonder what blood runs in her veins. I couldna write such things in a letter though . . .I couldna go to Yorkshire either; it's such a long way.'

Crispin looked at her gravely. 'Would you like me to tell Beatrice exactly what you told me?' he asked quietly.

Sarah raised her head sharply. Crispin's steady grey eyes were fixed upon her face and she saw the kindness in his expression, the sensitive curve of his mouth.

'You really care about people,' she whispered, almost to herself. 'I— I would be very grateful, Crispin, if— if you would tell Beatrice, as clearly, and as gently as you can . . .Beatrice knew her own mother better than anyone. Perhaps she can judge whether she was telling me the truth. I canna, I darena presume to ask my father if— if . . .'

Crispin nodded. He understood Sarah's reticence. How would any respectful daughter ask her own father how many women he had bedded and whether he thought he might have sired a child here or there? And what good could it do now? Beatrice's childhood was over and Alexander Logan would be filled with remorse, even anger.

'I will do as you ask, Sarah,' Crispin said quietly. 'I know it will bring Beatrice O'Connor great reassurance.'

Nineteen

Beatrice did not mention Crispin Bradshaw's revelations in her letters to Fairlyden but Sarah was sure she sensed a new confidence and a certain contentment.

In August the Bradshaws were once more in residence at the Tower House and Crispin rode over to Fairlyden soon after his arrival. He brought Sarah some welcome news. Beatrice had given birth to a son early the previous day, the twenty-eighth of August, 1890.

'He was a little early, but he seems perfectly healthy and Dick said Beatrice was very well this time.'

'Oh, I am relieved!' Sarah exclaimed fervently, clasping her hands almost as though offering a prayer of thankfulness there and then. Crispin's expression sobered and he lowered his voice although they were standing in the middle of the farm yard.

'Beatrice is grateful to you, Sarah. Quietly jubilant in fact. She asked me to give you a message. She said, "I do not believe Mother would tell a lie, especially when she knew she would soon be facing her Maker. I think pride, and her own secret shame, could have been the only reason why she withheld the truth from a man as honourable as Mr Logan. I am proud and relieved to think such a man may be my father. I have worried about the qualities which I might pass to my own children. Now I am happy." Then she smiled and added, "Tell Sarah I have always regarded her with all the affection of a dearly loved sister, but no word of this will pass my lips, since it was my mother's dying wish".'

'I'm glad she knows at last, and that she doesna blame my father,' Sarah whispered huskily. She half turned to look into Crispin's clear grey eyes. 'Th-thank you,' she found herself stammering as nervously as a young girl. 'Thank you for helping us,' she repeated more firmly.

'You know I will always help you if you need me.' Crispin put a hand on her shoulder. 'I think—'

'Aah, so you've returned for another visit, Crispin?' William's voice startled them both. 'It doesn't seem long since you were last here.' There was a brittleness in his tone which Crispin did not miss, but his own voice was level, his gaze steady as he returned the greeting.

'William!' Sarah's colour came and went almost guiltily and William's already watchful eyes narrowed even more.

'You seem surprised to see me, Sarah.'

'You're much earlier than usual.'

'Yes, I am.' He offered no explanation. 'So, Crispin Bradshaw, you once told me Strathtod didn't mean anything to you, yet you seem to like it well enough these days?'

'I have always liked to *visit* Strathtod Estate,' his gaze flickered briefly over Sarah's face, 'and its people.'

'Yet you once described the estate as an "indulgence" if I remember correctly?'

'Strathtod is my father's only indulgence; it is proof of his own achievement, more than fulfilment of his boyhood dreams. It means a great deal to him because he earned it through his own sweat and toil. It can never be that for me; I have done nothing to earn it. I have other dreams. That does not mean I do not enjoy Strathtod's clean fresh air, the peace, the beauty . . .' Crispin sketched a wide arc with his arm. 'Maybe I appreciate it all better than those who see it every day?' His grey eyes held William's briefly. 'I certainly appreciate it more than some of my father's tenants who find one grumble after another while they sit astride their horses and go chasing after foxes, or shooting game.' There was anger and contempt in his voice now.

'You disapprove of your father spending money on the estate?' William asked coolly.

'It is my father's land and he earned the money. I would never spoil his pleasure, but if you are asking whether I would spend money to help those who are perfectly able to help themselves, my answer is no. I would always consider the small tenants, the labourers, the children – if I understood their problems. But it seems to me that even they have many advantages over the people in our factories, people who live in cramped, damp little hovels, in smoke-laden air. I know children who have never tasted fresh milk, who have never seen butter, much less a cow or a green field. They are the ones I aim to help – some day. Even now they are grateful, very grateful, because we keep on providing them with work.'

It was the first time Sarah had heard Crispin Bradshaw speak at such length, or with such intensity, and she had never seen him so near to anger. She knew it was William's mocking tone which had provoked his outburst.

'Crispin came to bring me news of Beatrice,' she intervened swiftly, anxious to ease the tension which had sprung up so suddenly, and so unexpectedly, between the two men. 'She had a baby son – in the wee small hours – yesterday.'

'Aah, so that is the reason for your call?' William seemed to relax. 'I wondered what could bring you to Fairlyden so urgently. I saw the Strathtod coach was at the station to meet you. Is Mistress O'Connor well? And the child?'

'I understand they are very well this time,' Crispin replied easily. He smiled at Sarah, almost as if promising to preserve the peace. 'Dick says his son entered the world with the minimum of trouble. His name is to be Richard Joseph, but little Meg's version is Ricka. Dick is so relieved to hear her trying to speak that I believe almost any interpretation would suffice.'

'Mmm,' William nodded. 'Dick's brother, Rory O'Connor, was never a clear speaker, and he never attended school, but he knew almost everything that went on around Strathtod, isn't that so, Sarah?'

'Aye! He even saved my life once. But I hope Meg isna like Rory, for Beattie's sake. He was fond of animals, and already Meg prefers Dick's collie dog to other children, and the farm cats instead of the rag doll Beattie made specially for her.'

'There's nothing wrong in that. Our own children like animals, all except Sadie anyway,' William declared. 'And speaking of animals, I have a surprise for Katie. Where is she?'

'Just for Katie?' Sarah always tried to treat the twins exactly the same. Already Sadie displayed jealous traits although she was only two and a half. Katie always responded with such innocent generosity that it endeared her to everyone. She would offer her own spoon, her own piece of apple, even her own boots to her twin, whenever she saw Sadie's bottom lip begin to droop.

'I have brought her a puppy. You must have noticed how eagerly she toddles after the collies. This one is a little black terrier. Sir Simon's wife breeds them. The puppy is the smallest from a recent litter.'

'But Katie's still so young!' Sarah protested.

William smiled and shook his head.

'You'll see. Where is she?'

'Here she comes now. Sally took both the twins down to the burn while she was washing a blanket.'

William returned to the stable to retrieve a covered basket. He opened the lid and lifted out a small bundle of black fur.

'Papa, Papa!' Katie ran towards him excitedly and he caught her in his arms and swung her high in the air.

'How's my favourite little lady today then? Look what I've brought for my Katie!'

'Me swing, Papa! I want up!' Sadie cried, waddling after her sister. William lifted Sadie in his arms and gave her a quick peck on the cheek.

'See the little dog I've brought.'

'No like dogs!' Sadie screamed and fastened her arms round William's neck like a limpet.

'For goodness sake, Sadie!' William exclaimed irritably, 'it's only a puppy. It can't hurt you.'

'No! No! Take it awa'!'

'Here, you take her, Sarah.' He thrust Sadie impatiently at Sarah and crouched down to where Katie was already petting the little dog ecstatically. 'You must give him a name, Katie.'

'Oh William, she's over young . . .'

'Box. Furry box. . .dog.' Katie chortled, hugging the little dog while it licked her face with the tip of its tiny red tongue. William sighed.

'I suppose you're right. . .but see how she loves him already.'

'She's a bright child though!' Crispin marvelled. 'He does look like a black fur box on four miniature legs, except for his little pointed ears, and his stumpy tail . . .'

'We can't call him Box!' William frowned.

'What about Samson?' Sarah suggested laughingly.

'He's not an Alsatian! I know he's small, but . . .'

'Sam, Sam, Sam!' Katie carolled. She began to run as fast her little legs would go. The puppy set off after her. 'Sam, Sam, Sam!' she squeaked happily. 'Can Sam sleep in my cot tonight, Mama?'

'No!' Sadie wailed. Sarah often thought Sadie was not quite as sharp-witted as Katie, for all she looked a good six months older, but she evidently understood well enough when it suited her.

'Sam can sleep in the kitchen. I will find him a bed of his own.'

Katie looked disappointed but she was a happy little girl and she rarely protested.

Alex, Billy and Ellen loved Sam on sight and the little dog seemed to return their affection for he settled down at Fairlyden with barely a whimper from the very first night, but it was to Katie that he attached himself most constantly, much to Sadie's displeasure.

Trade at Fairly and Guillyman's Agricultural Merchants did not increase as fast as William had hoped and as one year passed into another he had a tendency to become disgruntled and short-tempered. Sarah was sympathetic. He had put all his energy and all the money they could spare into the venture.

'It isna that people dinna want to trade with you,' she consoled, 'but how can farmers buy your new machines when they get so little money for their own produce?'

'The machines would make them more efficient!' William argued stubbornly.

'Not if they couldna sell what they produce,' Sarah insisted patiently.

'The farmers should stick together. If they stood firm the merchants would have to pay them all the same price instead of playing one against another and browbeating them down and down.'

'But the price o' meat has fallen so badly that they are pleased to take any price. Now some women willna buy milk for their bairns because the newsheets tell them they'll get tuberculosis, and . . .'

'That's foolish!' William exclaimed.

'Maybe, but people believe things if they're printed in the newspapers, even when they're exaggerated. There was a warning about typhoid coming frae milk a few weeks ago. Soon people will be feart to eat and drink at all!'

'They eat shiploads of meat from Argentina, just because it suits the merchants to exchange it for their industrial goods. It must be months old! The latest craze is a fruit called pineapple, sold in sealed tins!'

'Oh aye! Janet tasted some. Ray Jardine got a tin for her to taste before he sells any in his shop. She says it's delicious.'

'Well we don't want anything from a tin, Sarah!' William declared emphatically. 'We may all be poisoned.'

'Och William! You're getting narrow in your opinions!' Sarah teased. 'You must be getting old!'

'I'm only forty-six! Your father's fifty-eight! Mind you, I'll swear he's getting younger since his horses have been in such demand.'

'I know,' Sarah hugged his arm and looked up at him, her brown eyes sparkling with mischief.

'Why you minx . . .' William relaxed and grinned. 'I do believe you're just wanting me to prove I'm still young enough to be your husband!'

'Mmm. . .maybe. When the boys are in bed,' she gave him a provocative smile, then her expression sobered. 'Your business has had other benefits, William. Father says you've made a lot of contacts and brought extra trade for the stallions. We had twenty-five mares here this spring, apart frae the ones Ewan visited with the young stallion.'

'Well I need to make some contribution,' William frowned. 'Your father shares the profit from the horses with us and we need that money to pay the rent for the rest of the Fairlyden land. Things wouldn't be so good for us without the horses.'

'Ewan is very good with them. He has tremendous patience, and he's very observant. Do you miss travelling with the stallion, William? Is that why you're a— a wee bit discontented recently?'

'I'm not discontented! We-ell . . .' He looked down at his wife with a startled frown. 'Sarah Fairly, you are far too observant! Can a man have no secrets?'

Sarah smiled. 'I dinna like to see you unhappy, William.'

'Well, things have improved since we got Fred Clark to look after the Store. I can get around the markets again, both to sell the seeds, and to buy one or two cattle when I see a bargain.'

'Yes, you made a good profit with the store cattle.'

'That was because they had a drought in England and we had plenty of grass. The prices are just as bad as ever again,' William muttered gloomily. 'Wheat is down to twenty-two shillings and ten pence a quarter.'

No wonder people canna afford to buy new string binders! Sarah thought. Aloud she asked anxiously, 'Does Sir Simon know you deal in cattle while you're selling Fairly and Guillyman seeds and machines at the markets, William?'

'I don't suppose he does. I never thought about it. I've had some good orders for seeds though, on account of the cattle I've bought. Sir Simon agrees that it's essential to go to the markets and talk to the customers. But . . .'

'What . . .?' Sarah prompted, seeing the worried frown creasing her husband's brow.

'Och it's nothing.'

'There's something troubling you, William,' Sarah said softly.

'You're too shrewd, my dear! I confess I am a bit worried. Sir Simon has not been himself lately. He has grown thin. . .and he complains of pains in his head and back.'

'I see . . . He's not an old man, is he? Janet says his wife is only about thirty. She says she's very comely . . .?'

'Er yes, yes she is . . .' To Sarah's surprise William flushed. 'I – er. Sometimes, recently, she has confided in me . . .She has no family of her own you see, except for a distant cousin in America. I think it distresses her because they have no children. Sir Simon wants a son to carry on at Avary Hall, and now that he is unwell . . .'

'But William!' Sarah was shocked. 'You dinna think . . .? I mean Sir Simon Guillyman isna *so* ill, is he? He— he's not going to die . . .?'

'I certainly hope not, for his own sake, as well as Fairly and Guillyman's. . .but sometimes he loses his balance and he can't remember what I have told him only a moment before. At other times he is very sharp-witted . . .He insisted we should increase the insurance on the premises and the machines we store. He doesn't take any chances . . .'

'Och, insurance!' Sarah muttered irritably. 'I still canna see any reason to waste our own hard-earned pennies on insurance premiums.'

'Simon has even insured his own life.'

'His own life? Can he do that? Why does he want to do that?'

'He says if he dies he wants his wife to have enough money to live in comfort for the rest of her life. He tried to persuade me to insure my life too.'

'You dinna feel ill. . .do you, William?' Sarah clutched his arm anxiously.

'No, of course not. The doctor once told me that the cholera might have affected my heart, but I've hardly even sneezed since I got such a good wife!' His eyes twinkled down at Sarah, then he sobered. 'But maybe I should consider Sir Simon's advice when we have five children to bring up. I would like them all to have a fine schooling, Sarah . . .'

'Aye, so would I! Even if we had to sell Fairlyden to pay, we must get the bairns their education.'

'Sir Simon says land is not worth a pittance just now. That's why he wants Elsa. . .er, Lady Guillyman to have money from an insurance if he should die . . .'

'Dinna talk of death,' Sarah pleaded huskily. 'I saw a picture in a magazine yesterday, advertising soap. It was a little boy blowing bubbles. The artist was a man named Sir John Everett Millais; the bairn in the picture is his grandson, but he reminded me so terribly of Danny . . .'

'Aah Sarah, my dearest!' William put his arms around her and held her close. She never mentioned the little brother she had loved so dearly, but he knew there would always be a small corner in her heart for him as long as she lived. 'It's a lovely evening,' he said gently. 'We should not be melancholy. Shall we take a stroll and see where Katie has gone with Sam? I do declare that dog is her constant shadow. I can scarcely believe it will soon be four years since I brought him home for her.'

'Aye, he hasna grown much either! She smuggles him up to her bedroom and hides him under the bed, if Sadie doesna see her. She thinks I don't know. I dinna tell her I used to try the same thing. . .but Buff's first loyalty was always to my mother . . .' Sarah smiled reminiscently. The picture of the little boy and his bubbles had made her remember many of the happy aspects of her own childhood as well as the sad ones.

Unfortunately relations between William and Sarah were not always sweet and calm. The following spring William suddenly took it into his head to order Nick to rear a certain roan calf for use as a future Fairlyden stock bull. He had shown no interest in Fairlyden's affairs since he became Sir Simon Guillyman's partner and Nick Jamieson was surprised and confused by his instructions.

'Mistress Fairly has already chosen the next young bull. He's a calf out o' Queenie, the auld red and white cow . . .' Nick said uncertainly.

'This roan calf is far sturdier. He will make the best bull,' William declared impatiently. 'Just look at him, man! He's far bigger and stronger already than the red and white.'

'But Mistress Fairly says Queenie gives the most milk, and the creamiest . . .She thinks Queenie's calf wad pass on some o' her qualities tae oor other kie . . .'

'Nonsense!' William snapped irritably and strode away to the house, leaving Nick in a quandary. He and Thomas were castrating all the bull calves that morning. It was one of the few tasks he detested.

'The roan calf wad make a fine bullock!' he muttered to Thomas Whiteley. 'An' the Mistress usually kens best aboot the cows – even though she is a woman . . .'

'Aye!' Thomas agreed, chewing thoughtfully on a piece of straw. 'We could leave baith o' the calves for noo . . .Let the Master an' Mistress Fairly sort it oot between 'em . . .'

Nick agreed but he had to explain to Sarah. She would not criticise her husband in front of Nick or anyone else, but her dark eyes sparkled dangerously and Nick was thankful he would not be present at the confrontation.

Sarah rarely lost her temper, and never with her husband, but she was outraged by William's unexpected interference.

'You never even see the cows these days, William!' Her brown eyes sparked with anger and there were twin flags of indignant colour on her high cheekbones.

'You're an attractive woman when you're angry, Sarah . . .' William murmured with a tolerant smile. 'But you are only a woman, remember my dear. How can you know which animal to keep for a stock bull? The roan calf is by far the healthiest and strongest.'

Sarah was incensed. 'Dinna try to flatter me with fancy words!' she fumed. 'I may be a woman but I've known which of the cows give most milk since I was a bairn! I milk them every day, twice a day in fact!'

'My dear Sarah,' William exclaimed mildly, 'I know how hard you work. When Fairly and Guillyman's really gets going though, there will be no need for you to milk at all, or perform any of the other menial tasks you do at Fairlyden. You will have maids enough for the milking. I shall buy you pretty gowns. Maybe we shall visit America. That is the place to see how farming should progress. We could see the very latest harvesting machines . . .'

'I dinna want to go to America!' Sarah's face paled. 'I dinna need fancy gowns!' Her eyes were bright with unshed tears now. 'I thought you wanted to keep Fairlyden because it once belonged to your Grandfather Fairly . . . But you dinna care any more!'

'Sarah, Sarah . . .' William chided softly as though she were a petulant child. He would have put his arms around her but for once Sarah resisted. William's dark eyes hardened. Sarah saw, but she was too incensed by her husband's sudden, unwarranted interference to heed the signs.

'I know as well as any man which cows milk best and which calves we ought to keep. The roan calf's mother has hardly any milk to give and she dries up after a month or two. What good would that be if all the cows went dry so soon?'

'The roan calf is strong and healthy and that is the one we shall keep as a bull!' William declared coldly. 'It is not a woman's place to argue or to decide on such matters. That is my final word on the subject!' He strode out of the house, leaving Sarah bitterly aware of her weak position as a woman. Everything belonged to her husband, yet he rarely looked at the animals, and he never had time to look at the fields these days. But 'tis Fairlyden keeps us all in food and clothes and with a roof over our head, Sarah seethed inwardly. She would not ask her father's opinion on this matter. She could not involve him in any dispute with her husband. Instead she tidied her hair and put on a clean white cap, then she went in search of Nicky Jamieson.

'We shall rear both the roan and the red calves as bulls, Nicky,' she informed him firmly.

Nicky looked at the twin flags of colour on her cheeks, her bright eyes and the proud tilt of her head.

'Aye, Mistress Fairly,' he acknowledged without expression, but he watched her slim straight figure thoughtfully as Sarah stepped briskly towards the dairy to check the creaming pans.

'Mistress Fairly's a fine-looking old woman!' Thomas Whiteley observed admiringly. 'Do ye no' agree, Nick?'

Nick Jamieson choked.

'Old did ye say? Mistress Fairly's twae years younger than I am, an' I dinna feel auld yet, young Thomas! But ye're right, she is a fine lookin' woman. I dinna ken why Master Fairly spends sae much o' his time doon at yon Store, or hawkin' wee bags o' seeds aroon' the markets . . .'

'Ma mother say's it's the Fairly nature, tae gamble,' Thomas declared knowledgeably. 'She reckons buyin' and sellin' at the markets is a kind o' gambling . . .'

'Aye, I suppose it is, in a way . . .' Nick agreed slowly. 'I dinna suppose he aye maks a profit on all the beasts he brings hame tae Fairlyden anyway. I wadna be bothered with some o' them ill-thriven wee stirks.'

'Mother says it used tae mak her real mad when he brought hame heifers. She says some o' them wad dae nothing but kick, but Mistress Sarah never grumbled.'

'No, she wadna. Master Fairly's a lucky man!' Nicky agreed.

'Mmm . . .' Thomas frowned and lowered his voice. 'But Mother says the Master spends an awfy time up at Avary Hall, and sometimes Lady Guillyman comes doon tae the Store . . .'

'Och, that'll jist be tae discuss business while Sir Simon's no' weel!' Nicky exclaimed. 'Aah, here's Ewan, coming frae the smiddy already, wi' the twae mares shod an' ready tae work! We'd better hurry young Tom, and no mair gossip aboot the Master mind!'

Twenty

Fairlyden
June 1895

Dearest Beatrice,

How glad I am to write of summer days after such a terrible winter. There has been so little time for writing, but at last the spring cultivations are past, the new corn crops sown, the turnips drilled – and today an unexpected hour of peace! Ellen is helping Ewan to feed a wreckling pig with milk from one of those newfangled bottles. She is a born nurse for there is nothing she likes better than looking after sick animals. Alex has gone to mend a hole in one of the hedges with Nick. Sadie and Katie are spending the day with William and Billy.

In February the twins spent their seventh birthday helping to chop turnips for all the animals. William promised them a treat to compensate, so today he has taken them to Annan to visit one of his customers who lives on the edge of the Solway Firth. They were very excited. I do believe Katie has smuggled Sam into the pony and trap beneath her skirt for he is nowhere to be seen. She loves her little dog, and Sadie gets so jealous. I do not know what William will say when they reach the railway station and he finds there is an extra passenger! No doubt he will forgive Katie for he adores her. I love all my children, Beattie, but Katie is such a happy little girl and so kind and generous that I find it difficult to chastise her myself sometimes. Poor Sadie! She is so different. It is almost as though they are two halves of a whole; one half has inherited all the happiness and laughter, the other all the misery and spite. I'm sure the good Lord must have intended them to be more equally mixed. Perhaps even He makes mistakes sometimes? I am afraid the Reverend Mace would criticise me roundly. He is such a staid man, and so pompous! I find it hard to like him. Alex and Billy often receive his glares of disapproval when they fidget during his long sermons. We lost a true friend when God took away the Reverend Mackenzie.

Such blethers you will think I write, dearest Beattie! In truth it is wonderful to sit down on such a fine afternoon and write as though you were sitting at the other side of the kitchen table at Fairlyden.

I thought the winter would never end. The burn was a solid block of ice for several days in February. It was a terrible struggle to get water for the animals, and we had extra bullocks which William had bought cheaply at Dumfries market from a man who was already running short of winter fodder. Even our turnips got a little frozen despite Nick and Thomas's efforts to wrap the pit with layers of straw and earth. Some of our Scottish rivers were frozen and Mr Bradshaw said there were great lumps of ice in the River Thames too. I feel so sorry for him. He has never quite recovered from Freda's death. Even Strathtod brings him little solace these days. Do you not find that his blithe spirit seems almost to have deserted him, despite the valiant battles he has fought in the past?

Even Father says he has been rather melancholy, especially since the government introduced death duties on agricultural land in last year's budget. The gales at the end of March caused a great deal of damage to some of the Strathtod farms but Mr Bradshaw says he cannot spend any more money this year as it has taken so much for repairs already.

Sir Simon Guillyman died in April. Doctor Kerr had warned Lady Guillyman that he had an illness which affected his brain, as well as other parts. Apparently he acted very peculiarly for many months before he died, flying into terrible rages, or weeping like a babe, and even shouting wild accusations at his wife – whom I believe he loved dearly, although she had not given him a child.

William is relieved that Lady Guillyman has consented not to claim her husband's share of the Fairly and Guillyman's stock – at least until William can raise sufficient funds to buy it all and be entirely independent. Of course he must now pay a rent for the use of the old mill premises which Sir Simon Guillyman bought when Wull Slater disappeared. William had intended going to Holland to see a new variety of turnip, but he has had to postpone it. He often returns home very late in the evenings, but he insists he enjoys the challenge now that the business is entirely his own. Unfortunately he rarely sees anything of Fairlyden except when . . .

Sarah stopped and stroked the end of her quill thoughtfully. She could not tell Beatrice of her anger and indignation over her husband's unwarranted interference with the bull calf. Yet she had not forgotten the incident, despite William's coaxing and tender loving. She dipped her quill in the ink and continued.

. . . he buys cattle at the markets in the hope of selling them at a profit. Such transactions never make a fortune for all the extra trouble and work they give. Also I am always a little afraid in case they bring some illness to our own healthy cattle. Alex incurred his father's wrath recently when he dared to criticise four young heifers which William has accepted from a customer in payment of his account to Fairly and Guillyman. Two of the heifers have given birth before their time, so they have no milk, and of course their calves were dead. Now we shall have to keep them for another nine months or more. They are so scraggy they would not make even the poorest meat.

I am fortunate to have Father's advice always at hand, and Nick Jamieson is very conscientious, especially with the field work and cultivations. Ewan and Thomas are good workers too, and very loyal. Alex spends every spare minute with them, or with his grandfather, although I fear his poor twisted feet must tax his strength at times. He never gives in, or complains. He has a keen eye for all the animals and already he seems to sense sickness almost before it has begun.

I am afraid William gets quite irritated because Alex shows no interest in the business of Fairly and Guillyman although the dominie says he is very good at his lessons and would soon learn to help with accounts and ordering. On the other hand Billy rushes to see a new plough, or the latest hay rake or harrows as soon as they are delivered to the Store. He is eager to accompany William whenever he can and he seems to understand the qualities of the various seeds. Yet in spite of their different interests Billy and Alex remain the closest of companions.

Dick will be so proud he has a son. I suppose Richard will start school in the autumn? Perhaps you should not worry too much about little Meg and her lessons. She sounds such a happy child. I would love to see her, Beattie, and you too of course . . .

While Sarah was writing her long newsy letter to Beatrice, William, Billy and the twins were seated in a railway carriage bound for Annan. Sitting opposite to Sadie was a tall, slender young woman dressed in black from head to toe. Her face behind the black lace veil was pale, and while she could not be described as pretty, her regular features and darkly fringed grey eyes made her decidedly striking.

'I am not sure I should have accompanied you today, William,' she murmured in a low voice when she saw Billy eyeing her curiously. 'It is not yet three months since Simon died . . .' Her words were belied by her expression of eager anticipation as her gaze moved to the soot-specked window of the carriage, and to the flying fields and trees.

'Nonsense,' William declared firmly. 'You are respectably attired in your widow's weeds. This is a matter of business.' William looked down into Billy's bright brown eyes. 'I intend to visit a customer today, as well as bringing you and your sisters on a pleasure trip, young man. This is Lady Guillyman, who is kindly retaining an interest in the firm of Fairly and Guillyman.'

'Pleased to meet ye, Lady Guillyman . . .' Billy murmured in his most polite voice.

'And I am pleased to meet you too, Master Fairly. What a charming son you have, William,' Elsa Guillyman smiled wistfully through her filmy black veil. Billy's young heart was immediately captured. 'Indeed all your children are delightful.' She glanced across at Sadie, but her grey eyes widened as she saw one booted foot hastily withdrawing from a vicious kick at her sister's bulging skirts. Katie shifted hastily. There was a half-smothered yelping sound.

'Whatever was that?' William frowned.

Katie was immensely relieved to see the lady passenger begin to smile. She was confident that she could placate her dear papa, but she had not expected they would have the company of a lady in the railway carriage. She had been forced to keep Sam hidden longer than she had anticipated.

'I suspect your daughter has a rather precious bundle hidden below her voluminous skirts . . .' Lady Guillyman smiled.

'Katie?' William looked stern.

Guiltily Katie wriggled from her seat and stood in the middle of the swaying carriage. Immediately Sam's small black head popped out from beneath her skirts. The little dog's eyes were as bright and dark as Billy's and Katie's and he cocked his head on one side and viewed his surroundings with canine curiosity.

'What is the meaning of this, Katie?' William demanded.

'Oh please dinna be angry, Papa!' Katie looked at him appealingly. Katie always reminded William of the way Sarah had looked the first time they met; she had been just a child too. He felt his anger melting, despite his need to exercise his authority in the presence of his companion. 'I— I didna ken we would . . . that is I didna want Sam tae miss the treat ye promised us . . . but I didna ken we wad hae a . . . lady in oor carriage . . .' Katie finished in awed tones. 'He'll be good your Ladyship!' She turned her wide brown eyes pleadingly to Lady Guillyman's face.

'I'm sure he will,' Elsa smiled. She bent and patted Sam's little black head. 'Sam's mother lives with me, did you know that? Perhaps you would like to come to visit her, and Sam too of course. Indeed we shall soon have some puppies for you to see . . .'

'Oh, that wad be wonderful!' Katie breathed, her eyes shining ecstatically.

'Are you sure you don't mind?' William asked doubtfully. 'Katie seems to take Sam everywhere, except to school, and even then he seems to know the time school finishes and he runs to meet her . . .'

'Of course I don't mind. I am pleased to know that one of my dogs has found such a devoted little girl to love him. I am sure he will be as good as gold.'

'He's never guid!' Sadie muttered under her breath and earned herself a quelling frown from her father.

At the station William hired a trap to take them to the farm beside the shore, but he stopped at a little shop on a corner owned by a rosy-cheeked old lady who seemed to know him well. He bought three gingerbread men and a stone bottle of ginger beer which the old lady had made herself.

'Now you three children can have a picnic on the sand while Lady Guillyman and I discuss our business with Mr Johnstone,' William told them with a smile, then his expression sobered. 'Billy, you will take care of your sisters. The Solway can be very dangerous, even to grown men, though I think it should be safe enough near the farm.'

'Oh, we'll be good, Papa!' Billy and Katie chorused merrily.

'I want to collect some shells,' Sadie announced unexpectedly.

'And you will see Sam behaves himself, Katie?' William asked sternly. 'Don't let him chase the hens. Mr Johnstone is a very important customer. I am hoping he will place an order for one of the new self-binding machines. And don't allow Sam to disappear after rabbits either. If he gets lost you'll have to leave him behind. Trains don't wait, you know.'

'He'll be guid, won't ye Sam?' Katie bent down and hugged the little black bundle affectionately.

She did not see the yearning tenderness on Lady Guillyman's face, but William did. Sir Simon Guillyman had once confided his longing for a son. William realised Elsa Guillyman had shared her husband's great desire for children. Now it was too late. She was already a widow. She must continue to lavish her abundant affection on her dogs.

William introduced Mr Johnstone to his companion, while the children waited politely a few feet behind him.

'I'm pleased to meet you, your Ladyship, sure I am, and sorry I was to hear of your troubles, ma'am.'

'Thank you, Mr Johnstone.' Elsa gave him a sweet smile. 'As you know I am still in mourning but Mr Fairly asked me to accompany him today to assure you that the business will remain unchanged. I understand that you are one of Fairly and Guillyman's best customers.'

'Aah,' Mr Johnstone flushed with pleasure at the inferred compliment. 'Ye must come away intae the house, Lady Guillyman.'

William congratulated himself on persuading Elsa to accompany him as they followed their host round the side of the garden to the front door of the long, low, whitewashed farmhouse.

'Polly,' Mr Johnstone called to his wife, 'Polly, come and meet Mr Fairly and Lady Guillyman . . . and . . . and the children.'

Mrs Johnstone bustled into view looking a little flustered. 'Come away into the front parlour, your Ladyship. I'll bring a tray o' tea. And what about you, my dears? Would you like a cup o' buttermilk?'

Before they could answer William intervened. 'These are my children, Mrs Johnstone. I promised them a little treat but they will not trouble you. They have their own refreshments if you would be kind enough to direct them to the shore? They would like to play for a while on the sand and collect shells to take home.'

'Aah, then just follow me to the kitchen and I'll show ye the way to the creek . . . Just down through the vegetable garden and along the little path. Ye'll be there in no time. The tide is just coming in.' She was a motherly woman despite her husband's success and she smiled reminiscently. 'Many's the time I used tae run down tae the creek and take off my boots and stockings on a hot day. I lived in a wee hoose further along the shore and I used tae like making wee footprints in the sand.' She gave them a conspiratorial wink and lowered her voice. 'Maybe your papa will wait until the tide goes out again. That's when ye'll find the best o' the shells. Enjoy yourselves, m'dears. . . .'

'What's a creek?' Katie asked as she set Sam down on the path to trot along on his own short legs.

'Aah, aah, she doesna ken what the creek is!' A voice mocked from the branch of an old apple tree as they passed beneath.

'Oh! Ye made me jump!' Katie looked up at the face peering through the leaves and began to giggle. 'Who are you?'

'I'm called Gordon, after the General ye ken,' the boy added proudly. 'The yin that was killed in India. This is Hamish, ma wee brother.' Another tousled head appeared amidst the branches.

'Are ye going tae the watter? Can we come along wi' ye?'

'Aye,' Billy answered eagerly, pleased to have company besides his sisters.

'Your trousers are awfy funny,' Sadie remarked with cruel candour as Gordon lowered himself carefully from the tree and turned to help his brother. 'An' they're patched everywhere!' The two boys looked down at their bare brown legs and feet and flushed.

'That doesna matter. They're very neat patches,' Katie said kindly, 'and Mrs Johnstone said we could take off our boots too and make footprints in the sand. We've never been tae the shore before.'

'What, never?'

'No. Oh look Sadie! Look Billy! All that water!'

'Aye, ye can gang for miles and miles across the sand when the tide's oot,' Gordon informed them. 'Nearly tae England!'

'Is it deep, the water I mean?' Billy asked.

'Only if ye get in a channel, or when the tide comes in. Sometimes there's currents though.' Gordon frowned and hoped they wouldn't ask about the currents for he didn't understand them very well himself, except that they were dangerous. He began to run to the edge of the water, happily dodging the lapping waves. His younger brother followed and in a moment all the children were running joyfully with Sam doing his best to keep up with them, stopping every now and then to utter a joyful bark.

'What's his name?' Gordon asked. 'Shall I throw him a stick? Can he bring it back?'

'He canna dae anything except bark!' Sadie said scornfully. 'He belongs tae ma sister.'

'Are you twae sisters?' Hamish asked.

'They're twins,' Billy announced.
'They dinna look like twins,' Gordon said sceptically.
'We are!' Sadie snapped.
'We're both seven,' Katie offered.
'Ye must be tweens then I s'pose, but ye're littler than she is, and prettier.' Sadie scowled at him but Hamish didn't seem to notice. 'I'm nearly ten and Gordon's twelve. Mother says he's the man o' the hoose noo that oor father's deid. . . .'
'Oh . . .' Katie regarded him solemnly. 'Here, wad ye like the legs off my gingerbread boy? Papa bought one for each o' us, for a treat.'
Hamish gobbled up the gingerbread boy with relish, while Gordon threw a piece of driftwood for an ecstatic Sam and pretended not to notice as Sadie crammed hers into her small mean mouth all at once. He knew that was so she needn't offer him any.
'Have half o' mine,' Billy offered, giving Sadie a look of disgust.
'Thank ye!' Gordon accepted instantly. 'I'll show ye oor secret cave, shall I?' he asked, eager to repay one good turn with another and having nothing else to offer.
'Aye I'd like that,' Billy grinned, his dark eyes shining expectantly, 'but what aboot the lassies. I'm s'posed tae keep an eye on them.'
'Weel, it's no' a proper cave. It's jist a wee hidey hole, an' we'll no' be far awa'.'
'I want tae gather shells!' Sadie declared sullenly.
'Here Katie, you throw this for your dog and then he willna follow us. He kens how tae bring it back, noo. See how he likes that, eh?' Gordon threw the piece of driftwood along the empty stretch of sand and Sam ran after it.
'Come on, Billy, we'll disappear afore he turns roond and chases after us!' Gordon whooped happily, pleased to have a new friend in his humdrum young life. 'Ye'll find the best shells where the sand's wet!' he called to Sadie, 'but ye'd best tak off yer boots!' The boys ran off and disappeared around some large sandy knolls partly covered in shaggy green grass.
'Help me collect some shells, Katie, or I willna let ye help me mak a necklace.'
'I'd like tae mak a wee box covered with shells, like the one Agnes has on her wooden chest,' Katie said as she bent to poke two fine cockle shells out of the sand. 'I could mak it ever sae pretty and gie it tae Mama at Christmas. Och, here comes Sam. He loves this new game . . .' She threw the piece of driftwood along the edge of the water. The tide was coming in quickly now and Katie squatted on the sand and struggled with her boot laces. At last she pulled off her woollen stockings and put them neatly together beside her little pile of shells.
'Ooh, it's lovely tae feel the sand on ma bare toes, Sadie.' She picked up the driftwood Sam had just laid at her feet and threw it joyfully. 'You try it, Sadie. I'm gonna dance wi' the waves at the edge o' the

water.' She shivered deliciously as the ice cold water rippled over her small bare feet.

'All right, wait till I get ma boots off. I've found some lovely shells. They're nicer than yours, Katie Fairly!'

'No they're not! Oh do hurry up, Sadie! It's lovely and cold.' She skipped with delight, hoisting her skirts higher as a larger wave lapped almost to her frilly drawers. 'Och, Sam's back already! You throw the wood for him this time, Sadie. You can throw further than me.'

Sadie could not resist teasing the little dog who claimed so much of her own twin's affection. She pretended to throw the wood then hid it behind her back. Sam set off, skidded to a halt in a flurry of sand, and turned back to Sadie with a puzzled look on his pointed little face. Slyly Sadie drew the stick from behind her back. Sam saw it and bounced towards her in a frenzy of excitement, jumping as high as his short legs allowed.

'Sam! Oh! You horrid, horrid dog!' Sadie shrieked angrily as the bewildered little dog landed amongst her shells, scattering them in the loose sand and breaking one particularly fine pink specimen. 'I hate you!' she shouted and hurled the piece of driftwood furiously into the water. 'It's gone now!' she muttered spitefully. That'll teach ye a lesson!' But Sam had seen the piece of wood flying through the air this time and he darted after it with an excited bark. He had no fear of the water, but in no time at all the rushing tide had swept him off his short little legs and he couldn't see the stick, or anything else except a great expanse of grey waves. Instinctively he turned back to the shore only to be bowled sideways by an incoming wave, which swept him down the sandy beach, momentarily hiding him from sight.

Katie had heard her sister's angry shriek and turned to see what had caused it. The brief tableau flashed before her eyes. They widened in horror. She could no longer see her beloved pet. She began to run back along the sand towards Sadie, holding up her impeding skirts.

'What did ye dae tae Sam? I canna see him!' she gasped, long before she reached her twin.

'He's all right!' Sadie retorted sullenly. 'Look! There he is! Awa' doon yonder! He's no' sae far frae the sand. Look ye!' She pointed to Sam's small black body riding the crest of a wave some twenty or thirty yards further along the sands, before he disappeared once more. 'He'll be all right. Dogs can swim, can't they! Anyway it's only shallow. Look ye can see the sand!'

'But I canna see Sam!' Katie almost sobbed. 'Sam! Sam!'

'There he is! Another wave jist washed over him,' Sadie called almost gleefully.

'It's taking him awa'! He's going tae droon! He's too wee . . .' Katie picked up her skirts and began to run through the shallow water diagonally towards her beloved pet, but she couldn't see Sam any more for the rising, curling waves.

About thirty yards away Sam scrambled on to damp sand, shook his bedraggled fur and began to trot towards Sadie. Suddenly he paused and turned to face the roar of the incoming tide. He barked sharply, wagging his short tail furiously. He barked again but Katie could not hear for the noise of the waves. Sam whined and ran towards the shallow water. Katie saw him then and turned towards him, smiling widely in her relief. She was unprepared for the giant wave rolling up behind her, gathering her small figure in its great curve. Katie lost her balance completely. She screamed.

'Sadie! There's no floor.' She tried desperately to regain her balance. Suddenly she felt Sam's warm wet tongue on her cold cheek. She reached out for him instinctively, just as another wave washed over them, sucking at her skirts, surging and heaving.

'Sadie!' she screamed. 'Sadie! I'm stuck! Help me! Sam, oh Sam . . .'

Sadie stared in horror as the relentless waves seemed to gallop towards the shore.

'Katie! Come back, Katie! I'll gie ye some o' my shells . . . Oh . . . Katieeee . . .' Her high-pitched wail reached Billy and his two new companions, who were exploring the dunes and grassy mounds on their way back to join the search for shells. They began to run.

'Oh Gawd!' Gordon gasped. 'It's your sister, Billy! The wee yin!'

'Where? I canna see her!' Billy struggled to hide his fear.

'In the watter . . .' Gordon was already pushing his braces off his skinny shoulders and tearing at his flimsy shirt as he ran. He tossed them on the sand as they reached Sadie. 'Look after ma claes. They're all I hae. Mother'll kill me if I lose 'em.'

'I canna see Katie now!' Sadie sobbed.

'There she is! Wi' the wee dog! Doon the way! Ooh . . .' Gordon's face paled. 'Ham! Bring Mr Johnstone! Run, Hammy!'

'Dinna gang in, Gordy! Mother said . . .'

'Run! Fetch help!' Gordon plunged into the lapping waves. They looked harmless, clear and shallow.

'I'm comin' tae!' Billy began to tug at his shirt.

'No! Dinna! It's gettin' deeper! The tide's comin' in but I can swim. Maybe she's caught i' the mud. Watch the watter! Tell Mr Johnstone when he comes . . .'

Billy glued his eyes on Gordon Conway but in no time his blond curly head had become no more than a sleek dark speck tossing in the waves as they sucked and seethed. Sadie began to scream again. Billy's attention was distracted.

'Stop bawling will ye!' He had only turned his eyes from the water for a second but when he looked again he could no longer find Gordon's head. There was just a great grey expanse of water and the tips of the waves catching the afternoon sun and hurting his eyes. He began to run, moving parallel with the shoreline, straining his eyes to catch a glimpse of Gordon's bobbing dark head.

'Bring his claes wi' ye!' he croaked at Sadie; his throat was dry with fear.

Twenty-one

They did not find Katie's little body that day, or Gordon Conway's. Neither was there any trace of Sam. William refused to leave the shore, even when the tide had gone out and the great expanse of sand was smooth and distressingly bare. Still William refused to move. He stood there gazing at the receding waters, silent and grim-faced. Sadie had been hysterical. Mrs Johnstone put her to bed with a calming drink. Hamish and Billy sat on the dusty steps like two miserable stone statues, waiting . . . just waiting . . .

It was Lady Guillyman who did her best to comfort Gordon Conway's distraught mother and in the end it was on her instructions that Mr Johnstone spoke bluntly to William.

'I ken ye're near sick with grief, Mr Fairly,' he began awkwardly, then his voice strengthened. 'But ye have a wife and other bairns tae think of. Ye must go tae them . . .'

'No!' William answered bleakly. 'I will not leave Katie . . .'

'Ye must! Look man, think o' other folk will ye!' Mr Johnstone said in desperation. 'Mistress Conway is a widow. Gordon was a fine laddie, nearly ready tae work . . . How do ye think she feels? The longer ye stay here the worse it is for her. Her laddie's dead because o' your bairn! Ye must leave now . . . We'll send ye news when . . .'

'You don't know they're dead!' William spoke harshly.

Mr Johnstone opened his mouth and shut it again. He looked helplessly at Lady Guillyman.

'We'll send ye news,' he muttered hoarsely.

Eventually William allowed himself to be led to the pony and trap and it was Lady Guillyman herself who took up the reins and drove them to the station, who ushered him and his weary, white-faced children into the railway carriage.

They sat in silence until it was time to climb from the carriage.

'I will drive,' William said stiffly.

'No, you go straight back to Fairlyden. I will ask the station master to hire a carriage to take me to the Hall,' Lady Guillyman suggested. William looked up then. 'It is better this way,' she said gently. 'You must break the news to your wife, William, without delay . . .'

'Aah Sarah . . .' he whispered hoarsely. 'How can I tell her? Why did it have to be Katie . . .'

She saw the agony in his eyes. She wondered if God had extinguished

Katie's merry little spirit because William had loved her too well, if ever such a sweet and innocent child could be loved too much . . .

Sarah had guessed that something was amiss when William was so late returning from the day's outing with the children, but nothing had prepared her for the full horror of the day's tragedy. She had had no premonition when she had kissed Katie's petal-soft cheek and looked into her merry brown eyes as she bid them all goodbye earlier that day.

'No!' she whispered. 'No! I dinna believe it!' She sank down on the nearest chair. She could not bring herself to ask the questions — the how and where and when — the why . . .? Why my sweet little Katie, her heart cried silently.

Each day William returned to the shore, sometimes riding all the way on his big black horse, Demon; sometimes travelling by train, silent, and sunk in his own dark thoughts. It was two weeks before Katie's bloated little body was washed ashore further down the coast. And nearly four weeks before Gordon Conroy's wasted corpse was found in a remote inlet many miles away. The waiting was an enormous strain, and all the more so because William was so withdrawn. Sarah felt too numb with grief to ask the questions which hammered relentlessly in her brain, waking and sleeping. She had overheard Sadie and Billy talking in troubled tones and realised that William had been accompanied by Lady Guillyman, as well as the children. It was a time when they needed each other desperately, and yet neither could bridge the chasm of silence which had suddenly opened between them.

Business at Fairly and Guillyman's deteriorated; accounts were neglected, orders went unattended, customers were dissatisfied. Eventually the storeman, Fred Clark, approached Lady Guillyman.

'I dinna ken what tae dae, yer Ladyship. I canna talk tae Master Fairly no more. He doesna listen, he doesna eat. He sits at his desk in the Mill Hoose . . . but he jist stares intae space. It isna guid for him, and it isna guid for me or the business! Customers are going back tae the auld suppliers in the toon. Trade's going tae ruin . . .' He looked at Lady Guillyman's troubled face. 'Maybe I shouldna hae come . . .' he faltered.

'Oh yes, Fred, I am glad you did. It is better that I should know how— how things are. After all I still have some interest in Fairly and Guillyman's.'

Elsa had deliberately kept away from the Store, and from William. She was afraid her presence would remind him too painfully of their tragic day together, but she had wondered how he was accepting his loss and she had longed to comfort him. He had been a pillar of strength to her during the last months of her husband's illness and she would have helped him in his own loss, but William had a wife, and other children, while she had no one, except her cousin in America.

* * *

At Fairlyden Sandy was sitting on the large flat stone outside the back door, overlooking the neat farmyard. He watched Sarah walking slowly from the direction of the small paddock behind the stable. He knew she had been shutting in the hens for the night. The children were already in bed and the world was quiet and peaceful, yet Sandy sighed heavily. The sight of Sarah's drooping shoulders and bowed head troubled him greatly. There was no joyful spring in her step these days. He watched her pass the stable, the little loose box, the byre. She walked up the slight incline towards him, glancing in the dairy, making sure the door was firmly closed against marauding cats. She joined him on the stone seat, but there was no mischievous greeting on her lips, no sparkle in her brown eyes . . .

'William is even later than usual tonight,' he remarked.

'Aye . . .' Sarah's eyes moved to the distant track beyond the buildings. 'He works too hard . . .' She sighed. 'He's tired, yet I know he doesna sleep soundly . . .' She turned to Sandy. 'I'm worried about him, Father . . . He has never mentioned Katie's name . . . He does not speak of her, or of what happened on that dreadful day.' Her voice shook. 'I canna help thinking of the boy too; he was just a bairn . . .'

'A bairn with great courage.'

'His poor mother,' Sarah whispered hoarsely. 'I— I . . .'

'Have ye asked William about it, Sarah?'

'How can I, if he doesna wish to talk . . .?'

'Billy blamed himself. Did ye ken that? Alex told me and I talked tae Billy. It seems William instructed him to look after his sisters so he felt he was at fault.'

'Oh poor Billy! I had no idea . . .'

'I think I have reassured him.' Sandy's tone hardened slightly, 'but neither you nor William seem tae remember ye have four other bairns . . .'

'Father!'

'I'm sorry, lassie.' He reached out and took her hand. 'I ken I'm a fine one tae talk, after the way I treated you and Danny, but that's why I'm asking ye tae try and accept what's happened, and then put it behind ye. We all loved little Katie. We all miss her. Sometimes – well sometimes, I think maybe she was too good for this world . . . Anyway it was God's will and life must go on. Though I've wondered how the laddie's mother is facing up tae such a loss tae. She's a widow.'

'I know so little,' Sarah murmured, her brown eyes troubled. She had thought of the unknown woman often in the dark hours of her own sleepless nights. She would like to meet her, yet what could she say . . .?

'Ye must talk tae William, Sarah. Maybe he thinks ye blame him for Katie's death.'

Sarah was silent for some time.

'Lady Guillyman was with him that day . . .' Her voice was low, but Sandy heard; he detected her hurt and uncertainty too.

'Aye.' He puffed at his pipe, but his blue eyes were regarding Sarah keenly. 'So Billy said.'

'Surely it isna usual for a lady to go calling on people like that, especially while she is in mourning for her husband?'

'Aah Sarah, lassie . . .' Sandy sighed. 'I'm sure William only persuaded her tae go because he wanted tae impress Mr Johnstone, so that he wad order one o' the new string binders. I told William myself that Johnstone fancies himself as a gentleman, even though he kens he's neither born nor educated to be one . . .'

'You knew William was taking Lady Guillyman?' Sarah asked incredulously.

'Weel, not exactly . . .' Sandy admitted honestly. 'Listen to me, Sarah.' He turned to face her. 'William loves ye. He loves the bairns tae, maybe not all o' them as much as he should, but I reckon that's part o' the Fairly character. I ken he doesna spend much time at Fairlyden, but William kens in his heart that ye manage it better than he ever would himself. He needs ye. Ye must talk tae him about Katie, instead o' torturing yourself. William needs tae ken ye understand. Billy shared his worries with Alex. Sadie misses Katie more than anybody. Young as she is, Ellen understands that. She shares her bed wi' Sadie tae comfort her.'

Sarah's eyes softened. 'Ellen is a sensible, kind little girl. She says she wants to be a nurse like Florence Nightingale when she grows up . . .'

'Aye, she'll be a good nurse. She's just like your ain mama, Sarah . . . kind and patient . . . always caring . . .' He stared away into the distance towards the purple mountains with their rims of gold already merging away into the shadows of the encroaching night. Sandy did not see the mountains though. His thoughts were filled with the woman he had loved beyond all others. Sarah rose and went quietly indoors, leaving him to his contemplations and his memories of the past.

She resolved to act upon her father's advice for he was a wise counsellor and she hated the constraint between her and William. She longed for their old familiar loving, the teasing, the understanding. Even arguments were better than the strained polite conversation they had nowadays, she decided ruefully. She felt bone weary at the end of each long day, yet so often her sleep was haunted by terrible dreams and she awakened unrefreshed.

'Tonight I must stay awake until William returns,' she muttered as she climbed into bed. She rubbed her eyes and stifled a yawn as she reached for the little bible which had belonged to Grandfather Cameron.

The Mill House had been used as an office for Fairly and Guillyman's ever since William took over, but some of the larger pieces of furniture still remained, pieces which had been too heavy for Beatrice and Dick to transport to Yorkshire, and which Wull Slater could not dispose of easily. William had added a heavy oak desk and it was at this that Elsa

Guillyman found him seated when she entered the Mill House on that summer evening at the beginning of August. His head was in his hands and he seemed unaware of the creaking hinges as she pushed open the door and closed it gently behind her. For a moment she stood looking down at his bowed head, still well-covered with a thatch of thick hair, though Elsa thought there was more silver in the unruly curls than when she had last seen William at the beginning of June. She moved forward until she was standing beside his chair.

'Isn't it time you went home, Fred?' he asked wearily.

'Fred went home some time ago!' Elsa said softly.

'Elsa!' The name slipped out unconsciously and for a fleeting moment a warm welcome glowed in Williams's dark eyes, before they were hidden by his heavy lids. He pushed himself up from his chair.

'Lady Guillyman . . .' he murmured and held out a hand politely. 'What brings you here, at this time of day too? Will you have a seat?'

'I think you know me well enough to use my God-given name, William, at least when we are alone.'

William nodded but he did not speak as he drew forward a chair and waited for her to be seated before resuming his own seat. He looked tired and there were dark shadows beneath his eyes; eyes which no longer gleamed with humour or softened with kindness. He was dull and lifeless, and unutterably weary.

'Did you want to see me about the business?'

'You did not bring last month's accounts, so I thought perhaps I should call on you here . . .' To her consternation William buried his head in his hands once more and groaned aloud.

'I am a failure!' he muttered. 'In every way I am a failure.'

'William!' Elsa was dismayed. She had hoped to rouse him from his apathy. She had half expected his anger or indignation, for she was not a working partner as her husband had been. She had not expected such utter despondency. She stood up and moved around the desk, touching his shoulder lightly. 'You are not a failure, William. Please do not speak such nonsense in my presence. When did you last eat?' William shrugged and made no answer. Elsa crossed to the neglected black range which had once been the centre of life in the Mill House kitchen. She poked the fire into life and swung the swey over the fire. 'I don't suppose you keep anything to eat here, but I will make you a cup of tea. Come, sit over here and rest a while. You look exhausted.' She pointed to the large horsehair sofa which almost covered the wall adjacent to the fire. William obeyed her as obediently as a child who needed guidance from a loving parent and Elsa's heart ached with pity.

She poured two cups of strong tea and added sugar from a tin on the mantelshelf, then she sat beside him and they sipped in silence for a minute or two.

'I'm sorry about the rent,' William said at length. 'I— I'm afraid I've been neglecting everything . . . recently.'

'I understand, William,' Elsa murmured softly, 'and you know I am not concerned about the money. It is you I am worried about. I— I know you will never forget Katie . . . but you must try to accept, to put the past behind you. You must care for your other children, and for your wife . . .'

'Sarah blames me! I know she blames me for Katie's death!'

'Oh no! Surely you are mistaken, William?'

He shook his head, then he drained his cup and leaned forward to set it on the fender stool before clasping his head in his hands once more. He sat there, just staring down at the floor.

'William . . ' Elsa touched his shoulder gently. 'Look at me. Please . . .?'

Slowly he lifted his ravaged face to hers.

'I am sure your wife cannot . . . cannot accuse you of causing the death of your own child. You loved Katie too!'

'Sarah doesn't accuse me! She doesn't utter a word of reproach even! She is just so quiet. She has never asked how— how it happened . . .' His deep voice cracked for a moment. 'If only she would weep so that I could comfort her, if she would rage, or scream . . . But she just looks at me with her eyes so dark and sad . . . I cannot bear it! I know it was my fault Katie died but . . .'

'No William, oh no. You cannot take all the blame on yourself. Do you think I have not blamed myself a little too?'

'You?' William looked startled.

'I persuaded you to give Katie a dog of her own, and it was Sam who . . . who lead her to her death . . .' Elsa's voice broke as she pictured again the little rosy-cheeked girl with her bright brown eyes and her merry smile, her chubby arms locked around the little dog.

'Oh my dear Elsa!' William was shaken out of his own misery. 'I had no idea! Is that why you have stayed away so long? I thought perhaps you also considered me a thoughtless, useless father without—'

'No, William! Do not torture yourself, my dear! I cannot bear it!' Elsa cried. She stroked his pale cheek with gentle fingers. 'No wonder you have grown so thin and haggard . . .' When William lowered his head and laid his cheek against her bosom, like a child seeking comfort, her arms closed around him instinctively and they sat there on the hard, dusty seat while she rocked him gently to and fro. Gradually Elsa became aware of the warmth and weight of his head against her breast. Her breath became uneven – but she did not move away, or push William from her. Slowly William became conscious of the softness of his pillow, the sweet scent of Elsa's perfume, the warmth and firmness of her arms around him. He turned and looked up into her face and saw her eyes so troubled, yet so full of kindness and tender understanding . . .

'Oh God, I need your comfort, Elsa. Katie was my child; my favourite child, though may God forgive me for saying it . . . I need someone who understands . . .'

Twenty-two

Neither Elsa nor William intended their embrace to be anything more than a gesture of comfort. But William had not made love to Sarah with natural virile abandon since the birth of the twins, and not at all since Katie's death. A chasm had developed between them and he could not bridge it. Each night Sarah lay at his side in the big feather bed they had shared since their wedding, but she was so still, so contained within herself. William felt they, too, were separated by the cold expanse of the surging Solway. He could not rid himself of the feeling that he had failed Sarah as well as little Katie; he had allowed their own beloved child to die.

In the arms of Elsa Guillyman he felt no such guilt, nor did he feel a raging desire for her body. He felt only the warmth and comfort that a child might crave, yet William Fairly was not a child and Elsa's arms were not those of a mother, but those of a desirable woman who had herself been deprived of a loving husband for many months even before Sir Simon's death. She too knew the loneliness of long nights, the emptiness of the future which stretched before her.

She saw the faint question in William's eyes as he turned to her and gently drew her down on to the long hard sofa. She neither rejected nor assisted him when he slowly opened the buttons of her bodice, but as he laid his cheek against the naked warmth of her breasts, desire stirred in her and she slid beneath the weight of his body willingly and without hesitation. Later she might regret this interlude, but now she needed William Fairly as much as he needed her.

After several weeks of need and denial, William came swiftly to arousal, but he did not move away. Instead he lay in Elsa's arms as quiescent as a child, and she held him there, his head cradled on her breast until he slept. There were tears in her grey eyes and one or two trickled down her cheek and on to William's thick hair. Elsa had loved her husband dearly, but in the nine years of their married life she had never experienced the total fulfilment she craved. As she held William in her arms she knew in her heart that she had hoped, just once, to reach some new pinnacle in her life.

Perhaps I am not as other women, she thought. Maybe I expect too much. She had yearned desperately for a child. As she lay quietly, her eyes closed, half dreaming, she remembered Simon as he had been, young, handsome and full of life. In the last weeks of his life he had changed; he had become a stranger, possessive, jealous, angry, and finally – childish. Doctor Kerr had explained that he was not responsible for the changes in his personality; it was the 'thing' growing in his brain. He was no longer the man she had married.

As she lay in her dreamy, half-sleeping state she remembered her husband with all her old love, all the old aching longing he had aroused in her. The memories of the man he had become in the last few weeks of his life could now be put aside. In her mind she confused him vaguely with the man now sleeping in her arms. Perhaps she dozed a little herself, for when she opened her eyes the shadows of the summer evening had lengthened, the little room in the Mill House was growing dimmer for the window was small. Elsa stirred. Her limbs were cramped and it was time to waken William. He must return to his wife. This evening must never be repeated. She would see to it that they did not meet alone again. Elsa was not a wicked woman and she had no wish to hurt Sarah Fairly, or her children. They had suffered enough already.

William opened his eyes and stared up at her in a bemused fashion. Gradually memory came flooding back. His dark eyes widened and a dull flush stained his cheeks.

'Oh God!' he muttered. 'Can you forgive me, can you ever forgive me, Elsa . . .?'

'There is nothing to forgive . . .' She smiled at him, a singularly sweet, sad smile. 'You needed comfort, and I gave it to you in the only way I knew. It must never happen again, William. I loved Simon, as I know you love your own wife. Perhaps it is fortunate that I cannot bear a child though . . .' She tried to smile and managed a wobbly grimace which did nothing to hide her secret misery. 'I hope no harm has been done to anyone.'

William edged on to his side on the narrow sofa and looked down into her face with grave concern.

'I think perhaps there has . . .' he said slowly and with one finger he gently traced a tear stain beneath her eye and down the side of her temple. 'I needed you, Elsa, but I should not have used you so . . .'

Elsa saw the tender concern in his dark eyes, his troubled expression. 'Perhaps— perhaps I used you too, William,' she admitted softly. 'The last memories of my husband were . . .' she shuddered. 'It was not— not pleasant . . .' She looked up into William's face pleading for understanding. 'He was not himself. It was not Simon Guillyman, the man I married, but some— some fiend within him. It was a memory I could not banish . . .' her voice sank to a whisper. 'Now I think I shall . . .'

'Oh Elsa, my dear!' William gathered her into his arms then, holding her gently against his broad chest. 'I had no idea . . . Yet I knew how changed Simon had become in those last few weeks. I did not guess you had suffered in such a fashion.'

'Today you have helped me to remember the real Simon a little . . .' Elsa tried hard to sound bright, even brisk, but it was impossible when she was cradled in William's arms and her voice shook. William remembered his swift arousal.

'I was utterly selfish. In my own torment I took you, but I gave nothing in return.' He looked down into her face and Elsa trembled at the look in his eyes. 'This time the pleasure will be yours, I promise you, Elsa!'

'William! N-no. We cannot . . . We must not . . .'

'For this fleeting moment – a moment in time – this small shabby mill kitchen is the whole world – our world, with only the ticking of the clock on the wall, Elsa . . . And the fire, burning low in the grate, and the purple shadows of evening stealing through the window . . .'

As he talked in that deep, gentle voice his hands were moving over Elsa's body, arousing exquisite sensations she had never known before, finding places she barely knew existed, places which throbbed with life . . . and expectancy . . . and a raging, undeniable desire. William's hands possessed a sensitivity she had never thought possible in any man; they moved as though playing a rare and delicate instrument – and that instrument was her own body . . . Slowly, with infinite patience, he brought her to the final crescendo, a rousing climax, a triumphant song; but the only voice was Elsa's own in a long low moan of pure joy, of utter and complete fulfilment.

It was indeed a single, beautiful never to be repeated moment. Neither wanted to spoil it with mundane words. Neither spoke as they dressed without haste. When she was ready to leave Elsa took William's hand and held it briefly against her cheek. Grey eyes met brown.

'Thank you,' she whispered. Then she was gone; a slim, erect figure walking gracefully through the shadows of a summer evening.

Sarah had been far too tired to stay awake. When she awoke it was to the sound of the birds heralding the dawn. Beside her William was still sleeping and his face looked younger and more relaxed in the clear light of the early summer morning. Sarah crept away to the milking. Tonight I must stay awake. I will not retire to bed without him, she vowed silently.

William had already set out for the Store by the time Sarah returned to the house after the morning milking, but she was surprised when he returned to Fairlyden in time for the simple midday meal of broth with cheese and bannock. He had brought some account books with him.

'I thought I would do these here, in your kitchen, Sarah.' He smiled up at her and her heart gave a little jolt. 'I have neglected you too much of late, my dear.'

'You're not going back to the Store today? Oh William, I'm glad!' Sarah's brown eyes echoed her pleasure. She thought her husband looked less tired and there seemed to be a new firmness in his step, and fewer shadows haunting his dark eyes. Sarah wondered if her father had spoken to him too. However slight the change, and whatever the reason for it, she felt a glow of thankfulness.

That evening Sarah took particular care with their meal, making William's favourite baked ham and roasted potatoes, with boiled onions and parsnips. She had also made a custard of eggs and milk with caramel sauce for a special treat. She noticed the glow in the children's eyes, and how Agnes and Thomas and Ewan cleaned up their plates with even more relish than usual, how her father and her husband seemed to eat with real enjoyment again. Yes, she decided, we must not mourn for little Katie and waste the precious gift of joy she brought to all of us, however sore our hearts might be.

Afterwards Sarah always wondered why it had taken so long to bridge those few inches of feather mattress which had stretched like a mile-wide gulf between herself and William.

'Tell me about Katie, William,' she whispered softly, taking his hand and holding it against her heart. 'I want to know . . . I need to know how she . . . died . . . everything about that day . . . Father says Billy blamed himself, poor laddie, but it was the will of God . . . not the fault of any human being.'

William had not talked of that dreadful day to anyone. He had tried to block it from his mind, yet the memory of Katie's rosy, laughing face, her merry brown eyes and wind-blown curls had haunted him and filled him with constant remorse.

If only he had not tried so hard to persuade Johnstone to order the binder, if he had not lingered so long over the tea, if he had not taken Elsa Guillyman . . . if . . . if . . .

Once he had begun to talk the words flowed from him in an unstoppable flood. Sarah drew closer, her arms clasping him tightly; once she felt his tears mingling with her own in the darkness. At last his voice trailed away to a halt and he shuddered.

'And what of the boy's mother, Mrs Conroy?' Sarah asked in a broken whisper. 'Is she . . . is there anything . . . I know nothing can ease her grief at the loss of her son, but is there anything at all we can do for her, William?'

'I don't know . . .' William murmured on a note of wonder. 'Dear God, Sarah, how sunk I have been in my own sorrow! The woman is desperately poor, though she works for Johnstone. I paid for the laddie's funeral of course, but that cannot help her – or her other bairn . . . Hamish was his name, I think . . .'

'Could we visit her, William?' Sarah asked diffidently. 'Perhaps take a warm jumper and a pair of Billy's outgrown trousers, a basket of food maybe . . .?'

'Yes! Yes, we will do that, Sarah. Why did I not think of such things! Could you go tomorrow? I would like to know that the boy and his mother are well . . .'

'Yes, William, we will go together, tomorrow,' Sarah promised. She leaned closer and kissed his whiskery cheek, and despite her grief for Katie a small wave of thankfulness filled her heart. As they turned into each other's arms their loving was almost reverent; a gentle, soothing unity in their shared grief. They had each other.

It was October before William managed to make his visit to Holland to see some varieties of turnips with a view to importing seeds.

'I cannot take the word of the importers. I must see the conditions in which the crops are grown, and whether they are diseased, and what kind of soil is used.'

'I understand, William.' Sarah smiled at him. She knew how much he wanted to make his business a success, but she also knew he had inherited a restlessness, a craving for new sights and experiences; if a journey across the English Channel could keep him content then she would be happy too. She had never forgotten that William had given up his plans to return to America for her.

William had not seen Lady Elsa Guillyman alone since the evening at the Mill House. She always made sure her personal maid was around when he was expected at the Hall to pay the rent or discuss the progress of the business. On this particular occasion she had driven down to the Mill House but she had chosen the middle of the day when she knew Fred Clark would be there. When they had discussed his proposed trip to Holland, William walked with her across the empty mill yard to the rail where she had tethered the pony.

'You seem troubled, Elsa,' William said with a frown. 'Are you worried about the money I owe for Sir Simon's share in the business?'

'Oh, I am not worried about that!' Elsa assured him. 'Indeed I am not worried at all,' she added quickly.

'No . . .?' William was unconvinced. 'Then why are you looking at me so keenly? I shall be quite safe you know and I shall be back within the month. Then I have other plans for Fairly and Guillyman's if you can leave the money for Simon's share a little longer? There is a new contraption which is causing some talk. It lifts small ricks of hay on to a sort of low sledge so that they can be moved more easily and more quickly into the barns. It would be a big advantage in our wet Scottish weather . . .'

'I have every confidence in your judgement, William,' Elsa interrupted quickly. 'I shall always know Fairly and Guillyman's is in good hands while you are at the helm. Please remember that.'

She looked at him intently, almost as though she was committing each and every feature to her memory. William blinked.

'I shall be back before your know it,' he smiled. 'Meanwhile it is good to know you have such faith in me. Take care of yourself while I am away, Elsa.' He rarely used her Christian name now for they were never alone. He lifted her hand and kissed it.

'Goodbye, dear William,' she murmured huskily. William's face was puzzled as he watched her drive away. There was something about Lady

Elsa Guillyman which he did not understand. He was sure something was troubling her, but she had chosen not to confide in him.

William's trip to Holland was a great success but it took longer than he had expected and it was the first week of December before he returned to Fairlyden. He was tired and eager to be home.

'Father! Father! Ye're back!' Billy came running towards him, his brown eyes alight with pleasure. William was amused. Billy was eleven now. He just managed to restrain himself from bestowing an unmanly hug.

'It's grand to be back, Billy! My, I'll swear you must have grown half a foot in the weeks I've been gone!' he teased, standing back a pace to view Billy's erect young figure, before they turned and walked together to the house.

'Mother and Agnes and Meg cleaned the hoose frae top tae bottom ready for ye coming hame, and there's roast lamb and . . .' Billy clapped a hand to his mouth in boyish fashion, his dark eyes wide. 'I forgot! I'm supposed tae keep that as a surprise!' William smiled.

'So your mama has been cooking a special meal for my return, eh? I'll not tell her I know already, but I hope she's made one of her clootie dumplings, well filled with fruit. I've missed her good cooking.'

He fell silent. He had missed Sarah badly while he was away. He realised how well she attended to his every comfort and cooked his favourite dishes, and she always listened to his ideas and offered sensible advice. He sighed. He was thankful they had healed the awkward breach after Katie's death.

'Was it a successful trip, Father?' Billy asked eagerly.

'Yes. I made several new contacts and I have some ideas for expanding the seed and machinery business.' He frowned. He wished Alex would show the same interest as Billy. He was twelve now and a bright, observant lad, but he had no interest in the new machines. A hay rake and a horse was a great deal faster than a man with a fork, and the mowers could cut as much as ten men with scythes. Maybe farmers didn't have money to buy them yet, but good men were getting scarce, many of them attracted to the towns, dreaming of streets paved with gold. It was the same in Europe. Trade in machines was bound to increase and he would convince Alex somehow. Anyway the boy would never make a farmer with those twisted feet of his. He should be pleased there was a place for him at Fairly and Guillyman's.

First I must discuss my ideas with Lady Guillyman though, he reminded himself, although she had said she would not withdraw Sir Simon's money, or interfere with his plans. William smiled faintly. He had almost forgotten the brief interlude with Elsa as a woman. He was grateful that she had not added any complications to his life. He loved Sarah and he had never intended to hurt her. Elsa had helped him at a crucial time, and he hoped he had also helped her to overcome her own secret horrors.

Everything, including Elsa Guillyman, was dismissed from William's thoughts by the warmth and excitement of his welcome.

'Did ye bring any presents, Papa?' Sadie demanded as soon as everyone had greeted him.

'One or two. I brought your mama a Dutch bowl so that she can throw out that old blue bowl she keeps in the front parlour.' He grinned at Sarah over their daughter's head, and stooped to lift a brown paper parcel carefully from one of his bags.

'Thank you, William,' Sarah smiled warmly, but in her heart she knew she would never throw out the blue bowl which her mother had brought from Nethertannoch. Maybe it did look old but it had travelled all the way from China. As a child Sarah had often gazed at it and wished it could talk and tell her of all the places and sights it had seen. It had been a wedding gift to her great grandmother from the lady of the house where she had worked before her marriage. Sarah remembered how her mother had treasured it. It will always remind me of my childhood and my own dear mama, she thought. I'll put it away in a cupboard and set William's gift in its place.

The meal that evening was a happy affair.

'Father hoped ye'd made a clootie dumpling, Mother!' Billy chuckled, 'but I didna tell him, did I Father?' William's dark eyes twinkled almost as merrily as his son's as he solemnly shook his head.

'No, it was a very pleasant surprise. I missed your delicious cooking Sarah.' He watched his wife flush with pleasure at the compliment. As his eyes met hers, Sarah saw the smouldering fire in their dark depths and she knew that William had missed more than her cooking. Her heart beat an excited tattoo.

Sarah Fairly, you're thirty-six and far too old for such girlish passions; she admonished herself silently, but the blood sang in her veins as she held her husband's gaze.

After the children were in bed Sandy plied William with questions about his trip. He had always been interested in the latest developments in farming. They talked together for some time and Sarah listened almost as avidly as her father.

'So if Lady Guillyman agrees to leave her husband's share of the money in the business a little longer, I plan to expand the stock at the Store. I shall need Alex to help of course . . .' He broke off, seeing the dismay on their faces.

'Alex wants tae be a farmer!' Sandy said gruffly. 'His heart's set on it.' He had always known his eldest grandson would be a farmer; it was all the boy talked about; all he dreamed about.

'Alex is a cripple! He can never . . .'

'Dinna say that!' Sarah gasped and her face paled. 'Alex is not a cripple, William.'

William saw the hurt in her dark eyes. 'Well . . . maybe he's not a cripple exactly, but he'll never be fit to plough and do the work of an ordinary farmer.' He grimaced with unusual bitterness. 'He may be the eldest Fairly son, but you both know I can't afford to buy Strathtod estate and bring him up as a gentleman. He'll have to make do with Fairly and Guillyman's.'

'Weel the laddie still has another year at school,' Sandy said placatingly. 'Maybe Lady Guillyman will change her mind and come back frae America by then, so ye'll be able tae discuss your plans with her first.'

'America!' William stared at Sandy. 'Lady Guillyman has gone to America? Surely you must be mistaken?'

'No-o,' Sandy frowned and threw Sarah a puzzled look. 'She did say it was America she was bound for, didn't she Sarah?'

'Aye. She came to Fairlyden to bid the children goodbye and— and to assure herself they were all well, and as happy as they could be after . . . well, after Katie.'

'I can't believe it!' William exclaimed.

'She was charming!' Sarah said, 'Not at all haughty or condescending, as I feared. Indeed I liked her. She seemed concerned for all of us.'

'When did she leave? When will she be back? Did she say why . . .?'

'We thought ye wad ken,' Sandy said with a frown. 'She left about three weeks after ye'd gone tae Holland. She said she was going tae visit her cousin in America.'

'I see.' William shrugged. 'I suppose any changes which might affect her can wait for her return.'

'But she doesna mean to return! At least not if she likes it over there . . .' Sarah exclaimed. 'Did she not mention her plans before you left, William?'

'No,' William frowned. 'I knew nothing, but I shall see Fred Clark in the morning, maybe he will know more . . .' He stifled a yawn. 'I must say I am pleased to be back . . .' His eyes rested on Sarah and she felt herself blushing. Her heart sang. She had liked Lady Guillyman but she had been well aware that she was an extremely attractive woman, a wealthy widow, and a well-born lady – far more suited to William Fairly, the youngest son of the late Earl of Strathtod, than Sarah would ever be . . . Yet the message in William's dark eyes was for her, and only her. She was his wife. A rush of relief and happiness washed over her.

William was more concerned about Elsa Guillyman's sudden departure than he cared to admit however. As Sir Simon's widow she had every right to withdraw her money from Fairly and Guillyman's, but he knew he could not carry on the business without her support, even less expand. He had an uneasy feeling that Elsa's flight concerned him. Had the evening they spent together influenced her decision? It had meant no more that a pair of comforting arms to him, and he had believed Elsa had felt the same. He remembered the long look she had given him before she left. Why had she visited Fairlyden? She had never expressed a wish to meet Sarah before, and he was sure it was Sarah she had wanted to see, for she had encountered all his children at the old mill on various occasions.

He left early for the Store the following morning. Fred Clark could give him no more information than he had received from Sarah, but there was a thick white envelope awaiting him and it was sealed with wax in two places. William took it into the little room which had once been the front parlour of the Mill House. Swiftly he scanned the neat copperplate writing. He read it twice, then threw it aside in exasperation. It told him almost nothing. He was to contact the Guillyman lawyer, who would forward any letters. She had made it clear to him that her husband's share of the money was to remain in Fairly and Guillyman's for as long as he needed it.

'. . . for I trust you implicitly, William. Do not be alarmed by Mr Bogle's grim manner, or his comments if you should meet with him,' she had written.

How can she trust me implicitly? William asked himself angrily, when she leaves me no address, no indication of her plans, no reason for such a sudden departure! He strode out of the office.

'I'll ride to the station, Fred,' he announced briskly. 'I should be in time to catch the train for Dumfries. I intend to call upon Lady Guillyman's lawyer.' Fred Clark looked anxious. 'Don't worry, Fred. Fairly and Guillyman Agricultural Merchants will continue as before. Your job is quite safe, indeed I intend to expand. My eldest son will be coming to join you soon. He is a bright boy. You will find him a great help when he can take over the accounts and leave you to attend to your stock.'

'Young Alex? But he always says he wants to be a farmer, and breed horses like his Grandfather Logan . . .?'

'That's just boy's talk,' William replied through tight lips. 'I shall be back this afternoon.'

The journey was a wasted one. Lady Guillyman's lawyer refused to divulge anything of his client's destination, or her future plans. Avary Hall was to be maintained, but all the rooms had been closed except for the servants' quarters. These were occupied by a middle-aged couple who had worked for Sir Simon Guillyman's father.

'So Lady Guillyman does intend to return to the Hall eventually?' William seized the information.

'Not necessarily,' the lawyer replied coolly. 'The Hall is hers for her lifetime, if she requires it, but it must remain in the Guillyman family.'

'But Sir Simon had no family.'

'He had a distant cousin. Lady Guillyman insists that the estate and the Hall must be maintained in good order. If she finds she has no desire to return after two years or so, then it will pass to the relatives of her late husband. Now good day to you, Mr Fairly.' Mr Bogle was brusque to the point of rudeness and William had no option but to leave his offices as disgruntled and frustrated as when he had entered.

Twenty-three

Alex had always been a happy boy despite his handicap. He rarely allowed it to hold him back from joining Billy and their school friends in their boisterous games. Yet he was sensitive and keenly observant; he cared deeply if any of the animals were sick. He and Ellen spent hours tending a sick lamb or a wreckling pig which would have died but for their patient care. The first time Alex heard his father discussing his plans for expanding the business of Fairly and Guillyman's he paid little attention, until he heard his own name mentioned as an assistant to Fred Clark.

'I dinna want tae work with seeds and bits o' iron, Father! I want tae grow crops. I want tae have Clydesdale horses like Grandfather's.' His dark eyes glowed with boyish dreams, but William's face darkened.

'There is no place for you at Fairlyden. It needs men who can work hard, men who can walk behind a plough all day, with their feet in the furrow, men who can drill the corn and harrow, spread the manure or trudge through snow looking after ewes which insist on hiding themselves in the furthest glen. You could never do such things with your twisted limbs, Alex. Consider yourself fortunate that I am building a business where you can earn your daily bread respectably.'

It was the longest speech William had ever made to his eldest son and Alex stared at him, white-faced and silent. Then he rushed out of the house, refusing Billy's company.

As soon as they were alone, Sarah tried to reason with William but he was adamant.

'I have told you before, I cannot afford to keep Alex as a gentleman, and Fairlyden is not big enough to support a farmer who is unable to perform all manner of work himself.'

'B-but you dinna work at Fairlyden, William,' Sarah gasped. 'We employ Nick and Thomas and Ewan to do the heavy manual work.'

'I earn my living elsewhere, as Alex must do. It has always been my intention to buy you a bigger and better house, Sarah, with servants to do all the work. I don't want my wife milking cows for ever.'

'But it's the cows and hens that provide our daily bread!' Sarah exclaimed in dismay, 'and I love Fairlyden, and the cows. I dinna want a big house in the town . . .'

'You have no ambition for yourself or our sons then, Sarah? Anyway, Alex would have to work under Nick Jamieson, and even if I agreed to that there is no place for him here unless you ask Ewan or Thomas to leave at the term. Would you do that?'

'Oh no! We couldna! Besides we need Ewan to travel the stallion!'

'Of course we do,' William agreed more gently. 'Alex could never do that either.'

'But—'

'Don't argue with me on this, Sarah. I know you have never accepted that Alex is a cripple. Anyway my son should surely prefer to work for me, rather than for a common labourer.'

'But Nick is a good farmer now. He would always be fair with Alex, and they get along splendidly,' Sarah protested. 'Even my father says Fairlyden has never looked better. Nick works terribly hard . . .' Sarah saw her husband's drawn brows, but she was not easily daunted and her heart ached for Alex. It was not his fault he had been born with his tiny feet twisted. 'He would have to work under Fred Clark at the Store . . .' she persisted stubbornly.

'Only until he understands the way things are run in business. I intend to stock some medicines for sick animals – black drenches, red drenches, Stockholm tar, that sort of thing. He would be able to advise the customers which to use. I am doing this especially to give Alex an extra interest . . .'

'It would not be the same as working with his own animals,' Sarah protested, but for the first time William refused to be influenced by her opinions. He had great ambitions for Fairly and Guillyman's. He planned to expand a lot further than one store at Muircumwell, but he could not afford to employ another man who would need wages, maybe enough to support a family.

Alex grew moody and withdrawn as the weeks passed. Sarah knew that it was the knowledge that his father considered him a cripple and the prospect of working at the Store which were responsible for the change in him. It saddened her to see her own son so unhappy. Whenever William talked about Fairly and Guillyman's, or mentioned a new product, or an order for some new machine, Alex walked out of the room if he could; if he could not escape he sat in silence, taking no part in the conversation. Sarah began to dread these occasions when she saw William's face darkening with displeasure. Afterwards he invariably blamed her for not facing the facts when Alex was born, and for allowing him to dream impossible dreams beyond his ability. The matter was causing a rift between them.

'I have never tried to influence him,' Sarah protested on more than one occasion. 'Alex has always been keen to help. Sadie is the only one who thinks she should have been born a lady!'

William refused to listen. He knew Alex had an excellent memory, he was good at figures and he was reliable. The merchanting business held the key to the future. William's anger with his elder son grew as the months passed. Alex remained stubbornly silent, unhappily aware that he was the cause of a widening breach between his parents, yet unable to comply willingly with his father's wishes.

* * *

It was the beginning of May 1896 when Bert Bradshaw called at Fairlyden. Sarah was delighted to see him. He had not been to Strathtod since Christmas. She thought he seemed more cheerful than he had been since Freda's death. Although he was Fairlyden's landlord, in part at least, and owner of the rest of the Strathtod estate, he still preferred to sit in the kitchen rather than the front parlour.

'It's warm and cheery in 'ere, and by gum! I do like t'smell uv your bakin', lass!' he chuckled boyishly.

Sarah returned his smile. She knew he was as eager to sample her cakes as he had been on his very first visit to Fairlyden. He was especially fond of her gingerbread.

'Mr Bradshaw, surely you could stay at Strathtod for a while? Crispin says our pure Scottish air is good for you . . .'

'Oh aye, I'll bet 'e does!' His eyes twinkled. ' 'E grumbled plenty when I bowt t' estate, but I've noticed he's grown fond uv t'Tower 'ouse 'imself; or is it me favourite little Scotch lass 'e likes t'visit, I wonder?' He laughed when he saw the blush in Sarah's cheeks, then he sobered and a fleeting sadness passed over his round face. 'I wish 'e'd found 'imself a nice little wife like you, lass, an' settled down. I'd like to 'ave seen 'im wi' some children. 'E were allus good with t'little'uns, were our Crispin . . .' He shook his balding head sadly, 'But 'e's left it a bit late now. 'E thowt t'world uv 'is mam when 'e were a little lad. I reckon that's 'ad a lot t'do with it. 'E blamed me a bit, for 'er dyin' like that, y'know.'

'I'm sure you're wrong, Mr Bradshaw! Crispin thinks the world of you too, I know he does.'

'Aye, mebbe. We've grown a lot closer these last few years, even though I bowt Strathtod instead uv building another new factory. 'E didn't fancy t'idea uv being a landowner in't beginnin'. It's 'elped 'im, knowin' you, Sarah lass. 'E thinks a lot of you y'know . . .'

Sarah knew she was blusing again and she felt annoyed with herself. Crispin Bradshaw was a man she could trust and rely on, she valued his friendship, but it was a completely innocent friendship, and she knew Bert Bradshaw, of all people, would not want it any other way. So why did she blush so readily when he paid her a simple compliment? she asked herself irritably. Yet she could not deny that there was an awareness between herself and Crispin, though neither would ever admit it. Crispin was an honourable man and her own loyalties were to William.

'I'm sure I have done nothing to influence . . .'

'Oh aye, you 'ave, lass. You've 'elped our Crispin ter see women can be tougher than they look. Your friend Mrs O'Connor . . . 'e likes her an' all.' He shook his head again. 'It's a real shame about 'er little lass though. Nowt but butterflies in 'er 'ead y'know, an' such a pretty little thing she is, aye pretty as a picture.'

'I'm sure she is,' Sarah smiled. 'Can I get you some more tea, Mr Bradshaw, or a piece of fruit cake . . .?'

'Aye, I'd like that. Ta, lass. Yer a real grand wife t' William Fairly.'

Sarah was aware of his keen scrutiny as he accepted a large slice of cake. It was easy to forget what a shrewd man Bert Bradshaw was, she thought, with his cherubic face and genial manner.

'Sandy tells me yer 'aving a bit trouble wi' Master Alex and his dad. Pity that. Still I 'spect it'll work out in't end. It's like me an' our Crispin were over buyin' Strathtod.'

'You mean Alex will agree with his father eventually?' Sarah asked, and wondered why she felt disappointed in the man she regarded as her friend as well as her landlord.

'Aw, I don't know about that, lass. It might be t'other way round in t'end. I've 'ad t'admit our Crispin 'as been right many a time y'know.'

'I see,' Sarah frowned. 'The trouble is William is right. We havena a place here at Fairlyden for Alex unless we ask Thomas to leave, and I couldna do that. Anyway Alex couldna manage all the ploughing and heavy work, even if his feet were normal. He is still a boy.' She sighed. 'But I know he will hate working in the Store!'

'Aye, t'lad's like 'is Grandfather Logan, a born farmer. Between you an' me, lass, I don't think Sandy would've stuck at the factor's job if 'e hadn't 'ad 'is 'osses an' you t'come 'ome to every night, and Fairlyden to walk around on a Sunday afternoon wi' your Nick Jamieson.'

'Aye,' Sarah murmured thoughtfully. 'You're probably right, Mr Bradshaw. My father has always loved horses, but he is grateful to you and he always says how well you treat him at Strathtod.'

'Earned every penny as my factor, 'e 'as, lass. Saved me pounds, I'm telling you! I treat 'im as me friend 'cause that's what 'e is.' Bert Bradshaw shrugged his broad shoulders. 'But I wouldn't stand in 'is way, and that's really what I came t'say, lass. You talk to 'im! Tell 'im t'seize 'is chance.'

'Chance . . .?' Sarah frowned. 'What chance would that be, Mr Bradshaw?'

'Aah,' Bert Bradshaw wagged a stubby finger and winked conspiratorially. 'You ask 'im lass, ask 'im about that Mr Sharpe that 'e used t'work for when 'e first came t' these parts. It might be t'best solution for young Alex an' all. Not that I want Sandy to leave Strathtod, mind you, by gum no! But I shan't be spendin' much more money on improvements now, not at my time o' life, not with t'government making all sorts uv new taxes t' pay afore a man can think uv dying in peace, any road. Sandy's brought Strathtod back t' life, as best 'e can anyway with some uv t' tenants we 'ave. An ordinary factor could manage now if need be. So you be sure an' tell y'father lass, aye, tell 'im t'grab 'is chance. 'E thinks 'e's getting too old t'change, but 'e's a lot fitter now than 'e was when 'e injured 'is leg. You tell 'im that!'

'Aye, I will,' Sarah murmured, baffled by Mr Bradshaw's riddles.

Sarah was consumed with curiosity after Bert Bradshaw's visit. When the evening meal was over and peace descended on the Fairlyden kitchen for a little while she mentioned the subject which had been puzzling her.

'Mr Bradshaw was here today, Father.'

'Oh aye?' Sandy drew on his pipe but his eyes had narrowed warily. 'William not hame yet?'

'No, he is delivering some grass seeds. Don't change the subject, Father!' she admonished with a teasing smile. 'Mr Bradshaw roused my curiosity.'

'He told me he'd been telling tales!' Sandy replied dryly.

'So what has Mr Sharpe to do with it?'

Sandy frowned. He was silent for a while.

'I wadna even think o' takin' up Mr Sharpe's proposition just for maself, not at my age . . . It was Bert Bradshaw who thought o' including Alex. He's a shrewd man, that! But I wadna want tae interfere between William an' his family.'

'What exactly does Mr Sharpe want you to do?'

'Do ye remember when he caused Dick and Beatrice all that trouble because he couldna pay his debts?'

'Indeed I do!'

'Ye see, lassie, the Mains was like a lot o' other farms, it hadna been paying. After Mistress Sharpe died Abraham sold the Mains tae Captain Fothergill.'

Sarah gasped. 'He had to sell the Mains! To pay his debts?'

'Aye, and the doctor's bills, and an extra maid to look after his wife when she was sae ill, and such like things. He wadna sell while Mistress Sharpe was alive. He didna want tae upset her. He's still ashamed that it came tae that anyway. Part o' the trouble wad be his wife's fault though. She was never at the milking; she didna ken which were guid cows and which werena, and Sharpe himself aye attended tae the field work and the horses. He left the dairy tae the women and they kept more and more animals for less and less milk. They all needed feeding, but there was nae more money coming in.'

'Aye, I can understand that!' Sarah agreed, remembering her argument with William over which bull calf to rear as a future stock bull.

'Mr Sharpe sold the Mains tae Captain Fothergill and he pays a rent like most other farmers now. The Captain has a reputation for being a fair landlord, and Mr Sharpe has a good lease, but he's getting old and he misses his wife. He's not fit tae look after the land. The hedges are all neglected. Some o' the fields have never been ploughed, but he doesna want tae leave the Mains. It's been his home for fifty years, ever since he got married. Some o' his neighbours have been complaining bitterly tae Captain Fothergill so he's told Mr Sharpe if he doesna improve, he'll hae tae give up and move out . . .'

'It seems so sad,' Sarah said sympathetically, 'but what does he want you to do about it, Father?'

Sandy sighed. 'He needed Mistress Sharpe tae manage his affairs, for all she was such a dragon! He has nae family, naebody o' his ain. He has naewhere else tae go. So . . . Sarah, he wants me tae join him.

I had a bit money saved frae my job as factor, and from the horses and I loaned it tae him when he owed Beatrice and Dick O'Connor. He couldna pay it back by the time he'd paid everybody else, even after selling the land. So he reckons about half the stock's mine anyway. I hadna thought he'd let things get as bad as that.'

'But surely you would not move frae Strathtod to the Mains, Father?' Sarah asked in consternation.

'Mr Bradshaw advised me tae speak wi' Captain Fothergill myself, tae make sure he wad let me carry on the tenancy if I went tae the Mains as Abraham Sharpe's partner. I rode down there today.'

'What did the Captain say?'

'Och!' Sandy's eyes sparkled with humour, but he puffed on his pipe with infuriating slowness. 'Mr Bradshaw had already written him a letter o' recommendation! He told the Captain aboot the things we hae done at Strathtod.

'Captain Fothergill already knew about Fairlyden and the Clydesdales I've bred. He has twae mares by a Fairlyden stallion. We talked sae long aboot the horses I almost forgot the real reason for my visit! But he hadna forgotten. He said I wasna sae young tae be takin' on a farm the size o' the Mains, but he'd heard I'd a couple o' grandsons.'

'How did he know that?' Sarah asked in surprise.

'Nae doubt Mr Bradshaw took it on himself tae inform him!' Sandy remarked dryly. 'I'm glad Bert Bradshaw is my friend and no' my enemy!'

'I think he wishes you well, Father. He doesna think you're too old to start a new challenge.'

'I'll soon be sixty.' He sighed, but not unhappily. 'I've just another ten years tae ma allotted span, if the guid Lord allows me tae live that long anyway. But the Captain knew all about Alex. He wad like tae see the laddie, if William can be persuaded that is. He says he wad consider the lad as a tenant for the Mains when Sharpe and me are finished, but only if he proves he can farm it as weel as any other man wad dae, wi' all his limbs in guid order . . .'

'Oh Father,' Sarah's face paled. 'You know how lame he is. He could never do as much work as other men.'

'He wadna need tae dae everything himself at the Mains. It's a big farm, lassie, and it needs a man who can use his head as well as skill wi' the plough and such like. It needs somebody tae see that the other men dae things right, and at the right time! Alex misses naething! He kens what should be done already at Fairlyden, and when and why. I'm not sayin' it wad be easy for him, mind! He wad have tae rise afore five every morn, the same as the rest, and he wad need tae learn tae plough, and drill, and harvest the corn sae that he wad be able tae tell other men how tae dae the work. I ken ye've taught him tae milk, and he kens plenty about the pigs and calves. I told the Captain that, aye and what the dominie said about the laddie.'

'That William should send him to the Academy at Dumfries?'

'Aye. Well he wanted tae ken how Alex could leave the school tae work wi' me at the Mains and him not yet fourteen. I told him Alex had reached Standard V by Easter, so he is allowed tae leave the school now. He seemed quite impressed. He said, "The Lord is merciful. He usually compensates man's weaknesses with unexpected strengths." I jist hope I'll have a guid few years tae guide the laddie though.' Sandy's eyes were shining and Sarah knew he wanted to take up this new challenge at the Mains both for his own sake and for Alex's. But could William be persuaded?

As Sarah had feared, William adamantly refused to give his permission for Alex to work anywhere except at Fairly and Guillyman's Agricultural Merchants Store.

'I need him there. The Store holds the future for all of us. I have negotiated a tenancy for premises in Dumfries, by the River Nith. The cattle are all sold there and the farmers would pass right by the door. I shall send Fred Clark there as soon as Alex can manage the Muircumwell Store.'

'But Alex is only thirteen!' Sarah protested.

'You were barely thirteen when you took over the running of the Fairlyden household, my dear,' William reminded her with a smile which never failed to disarm Sarah. She saw the admiration in his dark eyes too.

'Och! I do hate it when we quarrel, William.' They were alone in the kitchen for once and she leaned her head briefly against his shoulder and clasped his arm. He bent his head and rubbed his cheek against the softness of her hair. 'You smell delightful, Sarah . . . of lilacs I think . . . Your hair is as dark as it was the day we were married . . .'

'William Fairly!' Sarah smiled up at him impudently. 'I do believe you are being flirtatious, and me an old married woman. Or are you just trying to take my mind away frae the question of Alex's future? I have never known you to be so stubborn before, but I canna bear to see Alex so unhappy.'

'I am only trying to do what is best for the boy . . .'

'Are you, William?' Sarah asked softly. 'Or is it your own schemes you wish to see flourishing?' William stepped away from her and his face darkened. Sarah's heart sank. She knew she had touched upon the truth. It was not Alex's future, or his happiness, which was uppermost in William's mind; he wanted to expand and he needed an intelligent young mind to train in the business of the Muircumwell Store.

'If only Billy had been the elder son, and old enough tae leave the school . . .' she sighed. 'He would spend all his time at the Store! Next year he'll be of age to leave school too. You'll have no place for him then though; he'll resent Alex being the elder son. They've aye been such good friends, for all they're so different. What trouble there will be. I shall have no peace in my home if my laddies quarrel.' She sighed softly, persuasively. William frowned, but Sarah saw a glitter of uncertainty amidst his anger.

'I could gang tae school as a part-timer!' an eager voice interrupted.

'Billy!' Sarah spun around startled. 'Where are you hiding Billy Fairly?' Her voice was stern.

William's eyes narrowed as his son crept out from under the table, yet he could never be really angry with his younger son and Billy was quick to see the tiny quirk at the corner of his father's mouth.

'You were listening!' Sarah accused angrily. 'Alex knows nothing of your grandfather's plans to move to the Mains, and if your brother canna be a part of them it is better that he should never hear!' she added bitterly. She could not resist a reproachful glance at William. 'It is wicked to hide! Listening in to private conversations! I'm ashamed of you, Billy Fairly. I'll leave your father to chastise you!' Sarah's fury was evident as she flounced out of the kitchen.

'Father, I could! I could gang tae school as a part-timer and work in the Store wi' Fred Clark in the afternoons,' Billy cried eagerly, as irrepressible as ever. 'I'd soon learn about the accounts and things then, and I ken all about the seeds and the mowers and ploughs and drills . . . Please! Please, Father . . .?' Billy's bright, dark eyes gazed up at William's frowning face. 'I didna mean tae listen. I'll tell Mother I'm sorry . . .'

'You were deceitful. It was a private conversation,' William said sternly. 'That is not the way to impress me. If you persist in acting like a schoolboy then you must stay at school until you learn manners and more good sense!'

'Father!' Billy clutched his father's sleeve as he turned to the door. The usual mischievous sparkle was momentarily absent from his dark eyes. 'Iain Graham only comes tae school part time, and he's only at Standard III in writing, reading and arithmetic! Maybe I'm no' as clever as Alex, but I'm at Standard IV, an' I wad work hard, honest I wad! Father . . .?'

William looked down into his son's eager face. A spasm of sadness swept over him. Billy reminded him painfully of Katie . . .

'Iain Graham's mother is a widow. She needs her son to work to keep his younger brothers. Your mama would never agree to let you leave school yet . . .'

'I dinna want tae leave, Father,' Billy persisted with barely concealed impatience. 'I just want tae be a part-timer, an' mother wad agree if ye let Alex gang with Grandfather Logan tae the Mains . . . and if I promise tae dae my lessons at night as weel. Alex hates the Store . . .' Billy saw his father's face darken. Young though he was, he knew his father could never understand people who did not share his own enthusiasms.

Billy did not share Alex's interest in the farm or the animals, but he could understand how much they meant to him. They had always been close friends as well as brothers. Billy wanted Alex to be happy, just as much as he wanted to be a part of Fairly and Guillyman's Agricultural Merchants.

'Please, Father . . .?'

Twenty-four

It was the end of November, 1896, when Alexander Logan went to live at Mains of Muir for the second time, but this time there was a difference. Abraham Sharpe had incurred further debts since his wife's funeral. Part of his agreement was that Sandy would use his remaining savings to settle the Mains's creditors. In exchange Sandy now owned three quarters of all the farm's horses and cattle, pigs and sheep, hens and ducks. Abraham Sharpe had handed over his responsibilities with a sigh of relief.

Although Sandy possessed almost as little money as he had more than thirty years earlier he was no longer a lowly horseman in desperate need of work and a roof over his head. As Abraham Sharpe's partner, he had been accepted as a tenant of Mains of Muir. Despite the neglect of recent years the land was potentially fertile, with the exception of a couple of fields of treacherous black moss at the lower end nearest the Solway Firth.

Sandy had once hoped the money he had saved from his work as factor, and from the breeding of his Clydesdales, would guarantee his independence during his old age; now he could only pray that God would grant him enough years to restore a little of the Mains's prosperity until he could leave everything in the hands of his grandson and namesake.

'I trust ye implicitly, Sandy,' Abraham Sharpe sighed with pathetic gratitude, as he and Sandy shared their first meal in the Mains's dining room. 'My only desire is tae end ma days here and I ken the Mains will prosper again now.'

'I hope so, God willing!' Sandy replied fervently. 'Though I dinna mind telling ye, I've wondered if I'm a fool. I dinna see many bright prospects ahead for farming folk. Yet I tell myself the townsfolk will aye need tae be fed, one way or anither. Even so I'll tell ye honestly Mr Sharpe, I wadna have taken such a chance at my age if it hadna been for young Alex. Captain Fothergill has promised tae take him on as a tenant if he can prove himsel' worthy by the time we're finished wi' the Mains.'

'The laddie's a welcome addition tae this household. He's eager tae learn everything.'

Abraham Sharpe repeated this remark to Betty Jamieson a few days later.

'He'll be as observant, aye, and as shrewd, as his Grandfather Logan one day, I reckon. And he doesna let his lameness hold him back much. Aye, it's grand tae have a young laddie about the hoose!'

Betty had been housekeeper at the Mains since the death of Abraham's wife. She welcomed Alex as though he were her own grandson. It grieved her that she had no grandchildren of her own; Agnes seemed content to remain unmarried at Fairlyden, and Beth, who had taken her own place as head dairymaid at the Mains, was already a widow and childless. Nick and Sally were Betty's only remaining hope but they had been married several years and there was still no sign of children.

Alex missed the gentle companionship of his sister, Ellen; he even missed Sadie's grumbles, and he felt life was certainly quieter without Billy's lively company, but he had settled easily into the varied routine at the Mains under his grandfather's firm but kindly guidance.

Billy was also content. He spent his mornings at school and his afternoons at Fairly and Guillyman's. He worked hard, and the dominie was both surprised and pleased by his sudden application to his lessons.

'Aah weel, I've guid reason tae want tae learn everything now!' Billy grinned at his mother.

Sarah had spoken to Dominie Donaldson while she was collecting her messages at Mr Jardine's shop and she had been delighted by his remarks on her younger son's improvement.

It was Sarah herself who regretted the changes. Fairlyden seemed so much quieter without Alex and Billy romping around, enjoying friendly squabbles. In the evenings she no longer had her father's company and she missed their discussions. William visited at least three local markets each week and he rarely left the Muircumwell Store until seven or eight in the evening. Billy usually waited for his father. She missed Alex and Billy's help with the afternoon feeding of the animals too, especially when Nick and Ewan and Thomas were busy in the fields.

'I'll feed all the hens in the coops, Mama,' Ellen offered eagerly when the first chicks began to hatch. Sarah spent a lot of time and care choosing the best broody hens to sit on the eggs and rear both the ducklings and chickens. Ewan had made several small chicken runs and coops so that she could protect them from the foxes but they were spread out in various grassy corners, in the rick yard and the orchard and in a nearby field. It took a lot of time to feed and water them all and she was glad of Ellen's help. Sadie, on the other hand, grumbled at the slightest task.

'I dinna want tae take the vegetable peelings tae the pigs!' she announced sullenly to Agnes.

'Och awa' wi' ye, you lazy bairn!' Agnes chivvied. 'There's bairns wad be glad tae eat the things we throw tae them pigs!'

Sadie pulled a face but she always took care not to let Agnes or her mother see.

Sarah had known every field and hedge on Fairlyden since she could walk and it was to her that Nick Jamieson turned with his problems and suggestions, now that her father had moved to the Mains and

William's interest had become increasingly confined to the affairs of Fairly and Guillyman's. Sarah began to enjoy her discussions with Nick, and making decisions about things besides chickens and eggs and butter. Once or twice, when she was uncertain about a problem, she had sent a note to her father inviting him and Alex to Fairlyden for their Sunday dinner after church.

These visits were becoming a regular routine every second Sunday as spring turned to summer and Sarah was delighted to find her family enjoying these gatherings; all except Sadie. It was becoming apparent to everyone that the youngest Fairly always found some reason to grumble.

Even Sadie, however, was affected by the excitement and the preparations to celebrate the Queen's Diamond Jubilee. The Reverend Mace unbent enough to hold a meeting of his elders and other men he considered influential. William was invited. His prestige had increased since the Minister had discovered his father had been an Earl. The Reverend Mace chose to ignore the more unsavoury rumours surrounding the late Earl of Strathtod.

'The Jubilee celebrations threaten to be far harder work than anything I do at Fairly and Guillyman's!' William chuckled one evening. 'Arguments have begun already!'

But Sarah knew he was secretly pleased that he had been invited to serve on the local committee. She wrote at once to tell Beatrice, and she was amazed and delighted by the swift response.

Highvale Farm
May1897

Dearest Sarah,

I was pleased to hear William has been selected to help on the Muircumwell Jubilee Celebration Committee. I can imagine all the bonfires on the hills round Fairlyden, especially Criffel. It will be seen for miles around on both sides of the Solway. Crispin Bradshaw called in today. He and his father are travelling up to Strathtod to join in the celebrations there. Crispin seemed disappointed that you and your family would be going to Muircumwell instead of joining them at Strathtod.

Sarah, I am so excited! The Bradshaws have suggested I should bring Meg and Richard to Scotland for the celebrations. Crispin is going to make arrangements for us to travel with them. I am sad of course because Dick cannot join us but you know the cows must be fed and milked. Everyone seems to be having a holiday that day and I feel very selfish, but Dick understands how I long to see you again, and your children. Can you accommodate us at Fairlyden?

I have had another surprise too, from my brother, Joe. He says Jamie Slater plans to come to England on business. He met someone in America recently who told him of the changes at Muircumwell Mill. The meeting has made James decide to take a look at his old home before he returns to America. He plans to spend the night of the Jubilee at the Crown and Thistle, so maybe I shall see him at the celebrations. Joe assures me Jamie is a good man, not at all like Wull.

I am so excited about seeing you all, but I fear you may find Meg a strange child, Sarah, at least until you are familiar with her ways. She seems to live in a world of her own, deriving pleasure from the strangest things. Things like the stars in the sky on a frosty night, and the moon, and dust dancing in the sunbeams during the church service. 'God's lights,' she calls them. Indeed she loves all kinds of lights and flames. She knows so many things, and yet – oh Sarah it grieves me to say it – but she hates to go to school! She has not learned to read or write. The other children make fun of her and that is another reason I am glad to be away from here during the games and sports which the village people are planning.

Sarah scanned quickly through the rest of Beattie's letter. She was delighted at the prospect of seeing her and her two children.

'Och, it'll be grand tae have visitors and tae see Miss Beattie again after all this time!' Agnes announced. 'How old are the weans noo?'

'Meg is nine, just a few months younger than Sadie. I think the two of them could sleep together and then Meg will not feel so strange.'

'And what about Miss Ellen?'

'Ellen willna mind giving up her bed. Perhaps she could sleep with you and Maggie. It is certainly the largest room in the house and Maggie has a bed big enough for two.'

'Aye, that wad be fine, and what about Richard?'

'He's seven. Mmm,' Sarah frowned. 'Billy had better keep his bed tae himself. He rises so early in the mornings to get to the Store. Richard can sleep with his mama, in our bed. The box bed in the kitchen will suffice for Master Fairly and me, I think.'

Excitement mounted as the twenty-second of June drew nearer.

'The bonfire on Criffel is to be guarded,' William announced on the Saturday evening a few days before the great celebrations were due to begin. 'There are fears that it might be set alight too early. It has cost seventy pounds to build! They plan to use eighty gallons of tar and forty gallons of petroleum to light it.'

'It must be huge, Papa!' Ellen declared with round eyes. 'Will our bonfire be big too?'

'Big enough!' William smiled at her. 'It will be on top of Avary Hill, behind the Hall. But there will be lots of surprises before that. There will be games and a picnic for the children in the afternoon, and tea in the hall for older people. Janet asked if you would bake some of your gingercakes and shortbread, Sarah? She is making some of her famous bread. Some of the other women are making potato scones and soda scones and sponge cakes and the good Lord knows what else!'

'William!' Sarah exclaimed reproachfully. 'Ellen dear, it is time you and Sadie were in bed.'

The two little girls went reluctantly and William turned to Sarah with a smile.

'Speaking seriously of the good Lord . . . the Churches have been commanded to hold a service to thank God for Queen Victoria's sixty years as monarch. Most of the Free Churches have volunteered to hold a service too, though I hear one or two are refusing to allow the National Anthem to be sung.'

'Surely the Reverend Mace will permit it? Oh William, I can hardly wait for Beatrice and her bairns to come!' Sarah declared. She felt almost as excited as the children.

'It is not long to wait until Monday! I believe you have missed Beatrice more than you would have missed your own husband.'

'I know what you're thinking, William.' Sarah flushed guiltily. 'But you're always so late! I dinna mean to fall asleep before you come to bed.'

'The Jubilee will soon be over. Then I shall be earlier.'

The intensity of William's dark gaze brought a very different flush to Sarah's cheeks this time. She had begun to wonder if William found her unattractive, or if he thought she was getting old now that she had reached her thirty-eighth birthday.

But I dinna feel old! I feel more alive that I've ever felt since the twins were born! She felt a stab of grief as she recalled Katie's rosy, merry little face. How she would have enjoyed the celebrations. Beattie would have loved her. But I must not think of Katie now. I mustna let my ain grief spoil anybody's pleasure.

'Tell me more about the plans for the Jubilee Day,' she said with forced brightness. 'Janet says the Minister intends to give a magic lantern show for the bairns.'

'Yes, his wife will explain the pictures of the Royal family at Windsor. I believe there are to be some comic ones too. Aferwards every child will receive a jubilee mug and an orange.'

'No wonder you've been preoccupied!' Sarah declared.

'Mmm, there will be dancing around the bonfire until midnight, but the Minister objected to the suggestion that a barrel of beer should be supplied. There will be sandwiches enough for everyone though. I shall have to be there most of the time. Do you mind driving the pony and trap yourself, Sarah? Or shall I ask Ewan to drive you and Beatrice and the girls?'

'Och, I'll manage the trap fine. Besides . . .' Sarah smiled, 'I think Ewan hopes to take Maggie. They'll want to stay for the dancing too . . .'

'Young Maggie?'

'Young Maggie!' Sarah scoffed. 'Maggie has been with us for almost eleven years, William Fairly! She's nearly twenty-four and Ewan has been casting shy sheep's eyes at her long enough! I know they are both saving every farthing they can spare. It would not surprise me if there's a wedding before long.'

'Well! I wonder why I never noticed,' William muttered incredulously.

'Because you're seldom here!' Sarah said a little acidly. 'You scarcely know what's happening at Fairlyden these days!'

Her smile softened the bitter edge of her words, but William realised with a shock that she was right. He had neglected his home and his family, and most of all his wife. Not only recently either; he had neglected Sarah ever since Elsa Guillyman's unexpected departure for America. He had intended to present her with a thriving and expanding business when she returned, though he had made no plans to pay out her husband's share.

William frowned. He was more upset than he cared to admit because Elsa had not written to him directly. He wanted to see her. He had ideas he could not share with anyone else, even Sarah. She would consider his schemes too ambitious, maybe even crazy. Yet in his own mind William was sure he could be a big merchant – not just selling to the farmers, but selling for them also.

Food was essential to the whole of the British workforce, yet half the labourers in the towns could not afford to buy enough, however cheaply the country folk sold it. The merchants who handled it charged too much. Farmers needed to be organised, to band together, to sell their own produce from a position of united strength. William had great visions of organising such a business, using his own railway carriages and carts, and having large stores in all the big Scottish towns, not just in Muircumwell, or Dumfries. But he needed capital. He was irritated by Mr Bogle's intransigence. Several times the lawyer had flatly refused to give him Elsa Guillyman's address. For the umpteenth time William pondered the reason for her sudden departure, and her subsequent secrecy . . .

'There you are again!' Sarah exclaimed in frustration. 'Awa' in a wee world of your own!'

William was startled out of his reverie. He glanced up at his wife and saw the twin flags of indignant colour on her high cheekbones.

'You're a fine looking woman when you're angry, Sarah!' he remarked involuntarily.

'Och away with your fine words, Master Fairly!' Sarah mocked, but she was pleased to know she could still attract her husband's attention.

When the Strathtod carriage drew up on Monday afternoon Ellen and Sadie watched in surprise as their usually calm mama ran eagerly along the stone-flagged passage, out of the door and into the yard to throw herself into the arms of the stranger standing beside Mr Bradshaw. Sarah's dark eyes were bright with unshed tears. Over Beatrice's shoulder she glanced up and surprised a look of infinite tenderness on

Crispin Bradshaw's lean face as he watched their fond reunion. Beatrice could not hide the tears which glistened in her blue eyes.

'It's so wonderful to be here, to see you again,' she murmured huskily as Sarah slowly drew herself away and held Beatrice's hands.

'You look very well, Beattie; lovelier than ever in fact. Your hair is still the colour of ripening corn.'

'Och, there's a few grey hairs here and there, and poor Dick is quite white now, you know. But you, Sarah, you scarcely look a day older than when I went away. Crispin told me you were still as slim and as light on your feet as a girl, and he really didn't exaggerate.'

Sarah was vexed with herself for blushing but she hastily averted her eyes from the disconcerting truth in Crispin's steady grey gaze.

'Where are little Meg and Richard, Beattie?' she asked a little breathlessly. 'I canna wait to see them!' Beatrice turned back to the carriage then, and Sarah saw two small fair-haired children sitting contentedly on either side of Bert Bradshaw, who was just finishing telling them a story.

'Come along you two and meet your Aunt Sarah!' Beattie called happily and the two children wriggled down from the seat obediently.

'Oh Beattie, what a beautiful child Meg is!' Sarah exclaimed involuntarily. Meg was the daintiest, loveliest little girl Sarah had ever seen. She was no taller than her brother despite being two years older. Her golden curls shone like purest gold, her skin was fair and her cheeks and lips looked as though they had been delicately painted, while her eyes were as blue as a cloudless summer sky. Yet as Sarah looked into those beautiful eyes a sudden shiver ran along her spine and her heart went cold. Meg showed not the faintest sign of acknowledgement as she looked beyond Sarah, beyond her children waiting patiently with Agnes and Maggie on the doorstep. She saw some distant world which belonged only to little Meg O'Connor.

'Say hello, Meg, and you too, Ricky!' Beattie chivvied them forward and in that moment the curtain of happiness was temporarily ripped from her eyes and Sarah glimpsed a deep heart-breaking sadness as Beattie looked down at her exquisite child. Then she was smiling again and Richard's lips curved in a happy grin which reminded Sarah of Alex when he was a small boy.

'You must all come in!' Sarah instructed gaily. 'You too, Mr Bradshaw! The kettle is boiling and I have some of your favourite gingercake ready.' For some reason she could not understand Sarah's eyes skimmed over Crispin. She could not meet his gaze but she muttered huskily, 'I canna thank you enough for bringing Beattie to see us again.'

'Eeh lass, it's a real pleasure. Y'both grand lasses. I wanted our Fanny and young Robert t'come up for t'celebrations but that 'usband uv 'ers wouldn't move from London. 'E thinks everything'll be better there – all glitter and fancy folks. But it's my brass 'e's spending,' he added with the first note of bitterness Sarah had ever heard him utter.

'Father . . .' Crispin intervened, 'Fanny couldn't come and leave Eric behind. It wouldn't be right, and we don't want to spoil Sarah's happy reunion with Beatrice, do we?'

'No lad, yer right. We'll not come in t'day, lass. You enjoy 'aving a right good gossip while y'ave a chance.' He lowered his voice and glanced to where Beatrice was shepherding the children into the house with Agnes and Maggie oo-ing and aah-ing. 'You'll 'ave t'watch t'little lass. I 'ope she makes friends with your bairns. It's what she needs if y'ask me, a bit uv cump'ny 'er own age.'

'I'm sure they'll get along fine,' Sarah smiled, 'but I wish you would come away in . . .?'

'Another time, Sarah.' It was Crispin who answered. 'I sent Mrs Bunnerby a wire so she is sure to have a good tea waiting for us.'

'Aye, she will that. We'd best get on, lass, but we'll see y'all tomorrow perhaps!' his father called cagerly.

Twenty-five

The weather for the Diamond Jubilee celebrations was disappointing but nothing could dampen the spirits of men, women and children determined to enjoy the sixtieth anniversary of Queen Victoria's eventful reign. It was a rare day of leisure and pleasure.

The magic lantern show was a surprise which many of the children would remember for the rest of their lives and it claimed even Meg's attention. Sarah spent the day helping with refreshments and chattering to Beatrice as familiar faces triggered off memories.

'Everybody has been sae kind and welcoming,' Beatrice marvelled, falling back into her old Scottish speech.

'They're all pleased to see you!' Sarah assured her. At the sports in the little field behind the manse they searched the crowd of spectators for her half-brother, James Slater.

'I'm not sae sure I would ken him!' she admitted. 'He was the youngest. He was only fourteen when he sailed across the Atlantic with the others. Joe says Bertie and Jamie have cleared and cultivated hundreds of acres o' prairie land since the two o' them moved tae America.'

'You must be looking forward to seeing him again, Beattie,' Sarah smiled gently, but Beatrice O'Connor looked apprehensive and her blue eyes were shadowed.

'Not if he's anything like Wull!' she said bitterly.

'You're quite safe with us at Fairlyden,' Sarah reassured her, sensing her nervousness. 'But I'm sure none of the Slater boys were ever as bad as Wull, even when they were young, and James has been away frae his father's influence for most o' his life remember. Joe has grown into a decent, God-fearing man, so why shouldn't James and Bert?'

'Aye,' Beatrice sighed. 'But Joe was more like Grandfather Miller than the rest, and he spent more time with him tae. James was only making a short visit. He has tae be back in Liverpool afore the ship sails. Maybe he'll no' come tae Muircumwell . . .?'

'Och, I'm sure he'll want a last look at his auld home!' Sarah smiled encouragingly. 'I wonder who he met in America that would know such a wee place?'

'I dinna ken, but it's a small world really. One of the auld drovers that works at the market in Yorkshire kenned Dick's father when they were wee bairns in Ireland!'

'Imagine that! You never mentioned that before,' Sarah exclaimed in amazement. 'Oh dear, it's time I found Agnes, and Maggie and Ewan. We must get back to do the milking. Would you mind keeping an eye on Sadie and Ellen for me, Beattie? I dinna want to drag them home and make them miss anything. Anyway Sadie and your wee Meg are getting on well together. It is good for both of them, don't you think? I thought Sadie might be jealous. Meg is such a pretty child.'

'Aye . . .' Beatrice sighed heavily. 'But if she was even half as clever as Sadie I wadna care if she was the ugliest bairn on earth. But I'm not going tae burden ye wi' ma worries, Sarah, 'specially not today!' she added brightly. 'We'll see ye up at the bonfire, shall we?'

'Yes, but dinna wait. I'll find you up there. The one on Criffel isna to be lit until half past ten. The younger bairns will be needing home to bed before then. Indeed if the mist doesna clear none o' us will see it.'

Sally and Nick had spent the day's holiday at Mains of Muir with Nick's mother and sister. Sarah guessed it hurt Sally to see all the other mothers with their small children at the games. They had just arrived back at Fairlyden when Sarah drove the trap into the yard.

'I'll bring in the kie while ye're changing intae yer milking aprons,' Ewan offered with a special smile for Maggie. The two had been together the whole day and Sarah guessed they were eager to be finished with the afternoon chores and get back to the evening celebrations.

'Mr Logan and Alex said they wad look for ye all at the bonfire on Avary Hill,' Sally told Sarah as they settled down to milk the first cows.

'Oh good. I knew Alex would not come for the races and wrestling, but I'm glad he'll not miss all the fun. There's to be a firework display tonight. I shall bring the bairns home as soon as it is over. I hope you and Nick enjoy the dancing afterwards, Sally. I've told Ewan he can take a horse and cart so you can all come home together when it's finished.'

A damp white mist enshrouded everything by the time Sarah climbed the hill behind Avary Hall so she was almost at the top before she saw the flames leaping into the air. The firework display had not started. There was a good crowd and she walked slowly, chatting with groups here and there. It was some time before she caught sight of Beatrice and the man sitting on a tree stump a little way from the circle of people. Meg was curled on her mother's lap. She was sound asleep, but Sadie and Richard were chasing each other round and round in circles and a few yards away Ellen was chattering to Janet Whiteley. None of them saw Sarah approaching and for a moment her footsteps slowed. She realised with a shock that the neatly dressed young man talking so animatedly to Beatrice must be James Slater. He had been a skinny lad the last time she had seen him. Now he was broad and thickset, as his father had been, but there the resemblance apparently ended, for as Sarah drew nearer she saw his clean fresh-skinned face, his dark brown hair curling crisply with the dampness of the clinging mist. Beatrice looked up, her face animated and eager.

'Sarah! I'm glad ye've come at last.'

'Have the bairns been a trial to you, Beattie . . .?'

'Och no! They've been good as gold and Janet helped me keep an eye on them. Sarah, this is James!'

Sarah looked up at the man who had risen to his feet. He held out a square hand with the same short stumpy fingers that she remembered on Edward Slater. For a split second she hesitated, suppressing an inward shudder, but as she held out her hand she felt his firm, cool clasp. She looked into his face. His twinkling grey eyes reminded her of his grandfather; she had always liked Joseph Miller, and respected him. Moreover there was no thick-lipped, sulky droop to James Slater's curling lips. His smile was slow and whimsical.

'I guess I would never have recognised you after all this time, Miss Sarah.'

Sarah grinned involuntarily. 'Why, you're American!'

'American! The folks back at the ranch think I'm as Scottish as they come.'

'James is travelling back to England tomorrow,' Beatrice said regretfully, 'but he's biding at the Crown and Thistle tonight.'

'Must you return to America so soon?' Sarah asked. 'Surely . . .?'

'I'm afraid so,' James said gravely. 'I had not expected to travel up to Scotland at all when I set out from the ranch.' His face shadowed and his mouth tightened briefly.

'Ye were just about tae tell me what made ye change your mind,' Beatrice reminded him.

'Aah yes. Well, there was this widow you see; she was visiting her cousin, a man named Forsythe. Whenever there's a new face from the old country the families for miles around gather to welcome them. Everybody has a real swell time. The women just long to hear about the fashions and the things back home of course.'

For a moment James's face was shadowed by something akin to grief, but when he looked up he was smiling a little.

'The Forsythes didn't hold a party when this cousin first arrived. She had suffered badly on the journey over, and what with her condition, and her being not long widowed . . .' He shrugged. 'Well I guess she wouldn't feel like celebrating.

'Of course when she had recovered and decided to settle in America permanently, the Forsythes made a real swell party. I was lodging in town after my journey from the ranch and the folks were keen to attend, so I went along with them.' Again the shadows of sadness lurked in James Slater's eyes, but he was determined not to burden Beatrice and her friends with his personal grief.

'Mr Forsythe knew I was travelling back to the old country, so he introduced me. He thought she might want to send some messages. Well you could have knocked me down when she said, "I have no messages to send. Avary Hall is closed. My home is here now." She smiled very politely and she would have turned away but I echoed, "Avary Hall! Surely that cannot be in Scotland? Near a village called Muircumwell?" She seemed surprised that I had heard of it, but I remembered that old Sir Thomas Guillyman owned most of the land round the village when I was at school. Do you re—?'

'Guillyman!' Sarah gasped, dragging her attention away from the children, who were becoming increasingly wild. The name and the connection registered belatedly in her brain.

'Yes. It is not a common name, is it?' James frowned. 'I don't remember her husband, Sir Simon Guillyman. I expect he would have been away at school. She said they had only lived at the Hall a few years . . .'

'Lady Guillyman!' Sarah breathed incredulously. 'I can scarcely believe it! Sir Simon Guillyman was my husband's partner . . .'

'Your husband, Miss Sarah?' James gave Sarah a puzzled look.

'Och, I havena had time tae gie ye all the news of everybody yet, James,' Beatrice laughed excitedly. 'I'm sure ye'll need tae stay a month to catch up.' James Slater shook his head regretfully.

'I can't do that, Beatrice, but I sure am glad we've met again. I hope you will write to Bertie and me and give us your news. Maybe one day you will visit us in America?'

'Oh no, not me!' Beatrice shuddered at the thought. 'But Sarah's husband has been tae America. I expect you and Mr Fairly wad hae quite a lot tae talk about if ye'd more time.'

'Mr Fairly!' James echoed incredulously and turned to stare at Sarah. 'You are Mistress . . . Fairly? Of course!' He whistled. 'Fairly and Guillyman's! I saw the name at the mill.'

'Aye. You seem surprised.' Sarah frowned.

'I guess I am . . .' He looked faintly troubled, Sarah thought and wondered why. 'So your husband owns the old mill now? The place they call the Agricultural Merchants' Store?' he mused.

His thoughts flew back to the christening in the little wooden church. It had preceded the big celebration at the Forsythes' own ranch, a sort of double celebration, a thanksgiving for the survival of the fatherless child. Simon F Guillyman. James hadn't paid too much attention to the name. His thoughts had been too sombre.

The christening had reminded him of his own young son's baptism – and Nellie's death less than a month later . . . That had been the real reason for his journey to the old country. He had promised to visit Nellie's parents, to let them see the son-in-law they had never met, the father of their only grandchild, whom they were never likely to see. They had been so grateful for his visit. They had eased his burden of grief.

'James . . .? Ye were miles away!' Beatrice laughed accusingly.

'Aw look, Mam, look!' Richard's excited cry interrupted further conversation as he ran to his sister, shaking her vigorously. 'Wake up, our Meg! Look at the fireworks! Aw, just look at that! That's better'n all them queer tales y'tell me, y'know, when yer staring into t'fire at 'ome, our Meg!'

All the children watched excitedly as the fireworks display proceeded, but Meg's blue eyes seemed to hold a wild, secret excitement as her gaze followed every single star and spark away into the misty realms of the night. Then, with her eyes still fixed on the sparkling lights as though she was bewitched, she wriggled from Beatrice's knee, stretched her arms up into the misty air and began to dance on the damp grass. Her child's body was as slender and graceful as a fairy's; her dainty feet barely touched the ground. Sarah felt she might fly away on one of the stars, she danced so lightly, engrossed in her own enchanted world.

At last the display was over, the fire still burned and sizzled. Someone tuned a fiddle, the wailing note echoing eerily into the white mist. Large baskets of sandwiches appeared as though from nowhere. For many the fun was just beginning but for the children and the elderly the day was over, the celebration ended. William came round from the other side of the fire as he caught sight of their little group.

'It was a magnificent display, William,' Sarah greeted him warmly, but she could not stifle a huge yawn. 'It is time the children were in bed. I think we must take them home now.'

'I'd like ye tae meet my brother, James Slater, before we all go back tae Fairlyden, Mr Fairly,' Beatrice said shyly. 'He's just over there. He met Sir Simon Guillyman's widow just before he left America . . .'

'He met Lady Guillyman!' William stared at Beatrice. 'Where is he?'

There was no doubting his interest, his sudden excitement, his eagerness . . . Sarah thought as William turned away from her. Sadie began to cry and Sarah went to comfort her.

'You're all tired. Ellen, come along now, we are going home; you too Richard,' she called briskly. It had been a long day since five that morning. She felt tired herself, and strangely dispirited. When the children were all gathered together she saw William still deep in conversation with James Slater.

'Mother,' Billy appeared out of the deepening mist. 'I'll ride hame behind the trap.'

'All right, if you're sure you dinna want to stay for the dancing, Billy?'

'Er . . . no, it doesna matter . . . It's getting mistier and wetter and Alex and Grandfather are going back tae the Mains now anyway.'

'Aye, I'll be glad to get home to bed myself,' Sarah smiled.

'Father willna be hame for a while then. I just heard him telling Mr Slater that he wad meet him at the Crown and Thistle later.'

'I see,' Sarah frowned. William had scarcely been near her or his children all day.

'Do you want to stay a while longer, Beattie, to talk to James?'

'No, I've just said goodbye.' Her voice wobbled slightly and she sighed. 'I'm deadly tired myself now, and as ready for bed as the bairnies. It's been a grand day though, seeing James again after all these years. He and your husband seem tae hae plenty tae say . . .' They both looked across to where the two men stood with their heads together in earnest conversation.

'Good night,' Sarah called. 'It was nice meeting you again, James.' William seemed to collect himself. He came striding to her side. In the flickering light Sarah saw his jaw clenched tensely, but there was a suppressed excitement in his dark eyes.

'I told Billy to see you safely back to Fairlyden, Sarah. You'll need to light the lantern on the trap, but I'm sure you will manage . . .?'

'I'm sure I shall.' Sarah's voice was flat. 'If you're not coming with us,' she added coolly. William was selfish. He had ordered Billy to leave the dancing because he did not want to leave himself. Yet all his duties were finished . . .

'I have scarcely had time to myself all day so I have invited Beatrice's brother to join me at the Crown and Thistle for a little talk – about America you know. Er . . . in fact, Sarah my dear, I think I will spemd the night at the inn. It would be late before I reached home. I don't want to disturb your sleep. I will go straight to the Store in the morning.'

'I see.' Sarah turned away abruptly. Was it James Slater's news of America, or of Lady Guillyman that had caught William's attention? Suddenly she felt cold and uncertain, and very weary.

It seemed a long walk from the top of Avary Hill to the old mill yard, and the drive back to Fairlyden seemed more like forty miles than four, at least to Sarah. Beatrice was preoccupied with her own thoughts.

Everyone was tired by the time they arrived home, everyone except Meg. She had slept earlier on her mother's knee. Billy volunteered to unyoke the trap and attend to both the ponies. Beatrice and Sarah did not waste any time in getting the younger children into bed, or themselves. Sarah was already snuggled into the box bed in the kitchen by the time Billy came from the stable.

'I gave Bo some hay and left him in the stable for tonight,' Billy yawned. 'He's not easy tae catch frae the field and I'll need him early in the morning if I'm tae get tae the Store afore Father.'

'Mmm,' Sarah yawned tiredly. 'You're a good laddie, Billy. Turn out the lamp on the table afore you go upstairs, would you? I left a wee stub of candle burning on the tall chest. It'll light you to bed.'

'Aye, good night, Mother.'

As Billy crept along the landing he heard Meg whisper, 'Please don't put the candle out, Billy! Sadie's asleep and I don't like the dark. Please, Billy . . .?'

'Are ye no' sleeping yet, young Meg?' Billy muttered wearily. 'Och, all right, I'll leave it a wee while until ye drop off . . .' It was only a stub and it would soon burn itself out anyway, he thought. He moved along the landing to his own room, scarcely needing the glimmer of light to find his way around his small familiar chamber.

The moment she heard his door shut, followed by the creak of the bed springs, Meg slipped lightly from beneath the bedcovers and crept out to the landing. Sadie did not hear her. Meg was wide awake and in her head she could still see the flames of the huge bonfire leaping and jumping and the blue and gold stars shooting into the air. She stood in front of the tall chest of drawers gazing up at the little candle. The yellow flame flickered in the faint draught, but it was not as exciting as the fireworks had been. Meg remembered how she had danced and how the flames had seemed to dance higher. Her heart had felt as though it was soaring into the misty night with the sparks and stars and shooting flames.

The upstairs landing at Fairlyden was little more than a shadowy alcove off the main passage from which all the bedrooms opened. On one side of the tall chest of drawers there was a sturdy wooden chair. Sarah had placed a spare blanket over it in case Beatrice felt cold. Meg laid her cheek against it for a moment. She loved the softness and warmth of the wool. She thought of her dog back at home in Yorkshire with Dada. She missed him. Then her attention was caught again by the flickering candle and she climbed lightly on to the chair. If she stretched on the tips of her toes – she – could – just – reach. Yes! Her thin fingers hooked around the loop on the shallow bowl of the candle stick. Sarah always kept this style of candle holder for the bedrooms. They were light and easy to grasp, it was almost impossible to tip them over accidently and the fluted tin saucers usually caught any overflowing candle wax.

Meg drew it to the edge of the tall chest. She lifted it and turned to look down. The floor seemed a long way from her perch on top of the chair. She could not see into the black depths. She moved the candle, peering down. The flame flickered and danced. Meg watched it with delight. She did a slow pirouette on the chair and the little flame danced with her. It tipped and dipped as she moved her slender arm. She was oblivious to the hot wax dripping on to Sarah's clean blanket. She bent awkwardly with the candle clutched in one small hand as she scrambled down from the chair. The candle flame tilted, singeing the soft dry wool, but Meg did not notice.

As soon as she felt the solid floor beneath her feet she began to dance, as she had danced at the bonfire, and this time the little candle flame really did dance with her. Meg was fascinated. She had no fear. Everyone else was sound asleep. The sounds of her light, dancing feet did not penetrate the thick wood of the bedroom doors.

Twenty-six

At the Crown and Thistle people had dispersed to their homes reluctantly. Only William Fairly and James Slater remained. William had already ordered a bottle of the best brandy and invited Beatrice's brother to join him. After a few short discussions on travel, America, people, farming, William could contain his impatience no longer. He refilled both his own brandy goblet and his companion's.

'So you were telling me earlier that you met my late partner's widow in America. Are you certain Lady Guillyman is not coming back to Avary Hall?' William forced himself to speak calmly, although his heart was beating far too fast for comfort. He had talked freely of his own experiences in America, summoning all his patience and conversational skills to put his companion at ease; they had laughed over shared difficulties and commiserated over misfortunes. Gradually James Slater relaxed, his tongue loosened by the brandy.

'I only met her for one afternoon,' he said slowly. 'I got the feeling she was reluctant to talk about the past, and I didn't blame her. It's not so very long since she lost her husband after all. Then again perhaps she was not pleased to make my acquaintance when she realised where I came from. Maybe she had heard tales of my father and his cheating, and his women . . .' James added with a touch of bitterness. He took a sip of brandy, then another. 'I had no plans to visit Scotland really, but the chance meeting, a few words . . . they awakened happy memories as well as bad ones. I'm glad I changed my mind. It was good to meet Beatrice again.'

'Yes, yes,' William interrupted impatiently. 'Where did you say Lady Guillyman was staying? Can you give me her address? Do you. . .?'

'She was staying with the Forsythes. I guess everybody knows Mr Forsythe, right across the territory. But I guess she'll build a house of her own. Maybe she'll take out a lease on some land now that she has a son to think of. I guess there's plenty of good men willing to manage for a—'

'A son! Did you say Lady Elsa Guillyman has a son?' William's face went white, and then a dull red colour suffused his lean cheeks before draining away again, leaving him pale and tense. 'When was he born? Lady Guillyman's . . . son?' His voice was hoarse. He leaned forward filling up the brandy goblet, his eyes fixed intently on James Slater's face.

Despite the brandy James's brain was alert enough to sense something of his inquisitor's sudden tension. James had inherited much of his

Grandfather Miller's trustworthy character, as well as his keen sense of justice. Also the small community he had left behind was intensely loyal to one another, and Elsa Guillyman – and her infant son – had now become a part of that community, however widely scattered their homesteads might be.

'I have no idea. I guess he was a weakly little fellow when he was born, probably on account of the sickness his mother suffered on the ship. It was a bad crossing, I understand.'

'But you must have some idea, man!' William's eyes narrowed as his brain made swift calculations. 'He couldn't have been born soon after she arrived . . .' he muttered to himself. 'I would have known . . .' He filled up the glasses again but James set his aside and his face was serious.

'It's no good thinking the drink will make me tell you any more, Mr Fairly,' he said stiffly. 'I scarcely know the woman and if she wants to leave her grief, or any other sort of trouble, behind her, who am I to interfere? I know what it's like to want to leave the past behind. If the lady's running away from something, I say good luck to her. Now I'll bid you good night. I have a long journey ahead of me and an early start.' James rose and moved towards the door but William was there before him.

'Surely you could just give me her address?' he pleaded. 'After all she is my partner's widow and I owe her quite a lot of money.'

'I guess if she wanted to contact you she would know where to write, and you said yourself you can write to her through her solicitor. Thanks for the drink. Good night, Mr Fairly.'

William stared at the closed door in angry frustration. He was almost certain Sir Simon Guillyman had been incapable of siring a child for several months before his death. Was it possible he was the father of Elsa's child?

William sat for a long time in contemplation, his head in his hands. If he had a son . . . surely he had a right to know? Maybe Elsa would need help? Advice? Maybe she was afraid to return to her own home in case he was angry . . . Besides, he wanted to talk to her about his plans. If they had a son maybe she would be glad to help him. He had a vision of Fairly and Guillyman's Agricultural Merchants stretching right across Scotland, and even into England . . . In that moment William made up his mind. He would go to America. Now that he knew the name of the man Forsythe, and the name of the small town where he lived, it should not be difficult to find Elsa herself. Further than that Wiliiam did not think; he did not consider Billy and Alex, nor even Sarah, his own wife.

Back at Fairlyden, Meg's little legs were tired of dancing and she did not care for the acrid smell which was beginning to fill her nostrils whenever she danced near the alcove with its chest, its chair and the woollen blanket. She crept lightly down the stairs. At the foot of the staircase the door opened into the kitchen. It was the largest room in the house, but Meg knew there would be no cheery fire in the middle of the night. She crept past the door, along the stone-flagged passage, holding the flickering candle to light the way, shielding it with her tiny hand as she had seen her mother do.

Next to the kitchen there was another door and Meg knew it led into the pantry where Aunt Sarah kept her jams and pickles. It smelled of apples and onions and there were hams in white cotton sacks hanging from large iron hooks in the ceiling. There were two stone tables where the little bowls of cream were set to wait for the morning porridge. Meg had no interest in entering the pantry now. At the end of the passage was a stout wooden door but it led into the yard and it would be cold outside. Meg's dainty feet were already cold and clammy from walking on the stone flags. Also at the end on the opposite side of the passage there was another door. It opened into the little parlour. Meg loved that room, though she was not allowed to play in it, not even with her new cousin Sadie. It had a piano and a cupboard with glass doors which was filled with books and pretty cups and two blue bowls. Best of all it had a large square carpet which covered most of the floor. It had once been red with a border of blue and green and gold. It was faded now but Meg thought it was lovely. She pushed the door wider and stepped inside, closing the door firmly behind her. The glow from her tiny candle made everything look warm and pretty. She set it down on the polished mahogany table beside the horsehair sofa. The flame jumped and flickered but Meg was too tired to dance any more. She lay down on the prickly sofa and tucked her cold little toes into her long flannel nightgown. She lay there, her curly head propped on one hand as she watched the yellow flame of the candle. Gradually her eyelids began to grow heavy. She pulled one of the four round velvet cushions closer and rested her cheek on it. She liked the silky feel of it. Slowly her eyes closed in sleep. The candle flame flickered and sputtered a little, and eventually it died away.

'Mama, Mama! I dinna like that smell!' Sarah heard her youngest daughter's whining voice through the heavy mists of sleep.

'Hush, Sadie. Away back to your bed or Meg'll miss you.'

'She's gone to sleep in her mama's bed! I'm cold tae, and I'm lonely.' The whine became a whimper in the darkness. 'I wish Katie hadna gone tae heaven without me. D'ye think she wad see the lights frae the bonfire if she was lookin' doon? Mama, I'm c-cold.'

'Och, come on in then!' Sarah sighed, half in tired exasperation, half in sympathy, for Katie had been much in her own thoughts during the day. She hauled Sadie into the box bed and tumbled her into the back, pulling the blankets up to her chin. 'Cuddle in now and go to sleep,' she whispered. 'It will soon be the morning.'

It seemed to Sarah that she had no sooner closed her eyes again than Agnes's voice was urging her to wake up, shaking her roughly.

'Oh Miss Sarah!' Agnes was beside herself.

'Agnes! What ails you? Are you all back frae the dance? Surely you werena at the whisky . . .?' Sarah muttered sleepily.

'Oh the guid Lord preserve us!' Agnes wailed. 'Get up! Get up! The hoose is on fire! Can ye no' smell the smoke?'

Sarah was suddenly wide awake and jumping out of bed before she knew it, hauling Sadie after her.

'I can smell it now!' She ran to the door leading to the staircase, yanking it open. Acrid smoke billowed into her face. 'Oh God help us! Beattie!' she shrieked. 'Beattie! The house is on fire. Come down quickly! Bring your bairns! Tell Billy. Sadie's safe with me.' She had groped her way half way up the stairs. The smoke made her cough. 'Beattie, can you hear me?'

'I'm coming.' Beattie appeared at the head of the stairs shaking a sleepy Richard, instructing him to get downstairs and outside. The little boy rubbed his eyes. He began to cough. Sarah grabbed him and ran down the stairs, expecting Beattie and Billy would follow. But Billy couldn't follow. The smouldering blanket had burst into flames with the draughts from the opening doors. Sheets of flame were already leaping into the air, blocking his way to the stairs.

'Shut the door, Billy.' Beatrice choked, covering her streaming eyes with her hands. 'I'll get ye a ladder tae the window!' she cried in alarm. 'Meg and Sadie are out already.'

Sarah was already frantically organising Ewan and Thomas. She had sent Maggie for Nick and Sally. They needed every pair of hands to carry water from the burn.

'Get a ladder!' Beatrice shouted frantically as she stumbled out of the house. 'The fire's at the back. Billy's trapped!' Sarah felt the colour drain from her face. Everything else was driven from her head.

'Oh dear God help us!' she whispered. I need you here, William! her heart cried silently.

Billy was white-faced but calm as he stared out into the misty darkness. The smoke was coming under the door and making him cough but he had rolled up a blanket and stuffed it at the crack. Now he struggled to open the window. It moved only a few inches and then stuck. Nothing would budge it! He saw the ladder coming against the sill, then Ewan's white face appearing out of the darkness.

'Get back, Ewan! I canna open the window. I-I'm going tae smash it!' Billy choked. Ewan saw him with his boot and scampered back down the ladder as glass splintered above. Billy hammered frantically at the wooden astricles which held the small window panes firmly in place. Then he was throwing out his boots and his breeches and scrambling after them, cutting his hand badly in the process. He saw his mother's white face as he reached the bottom of the ladder. She hugged him briefly, heedless of his blood staining her robe.

'Thank God!'

'It's bad, Mother! We need help! I'll take Bo!' Sarah hesitated for a split second.

'Strathtod then, it's nearer!' Billy nodded and sped towards the stable.

Sarah and Agnes hauled every possible bucket and container from the dairy, instructing Nick and Thomas, Maggie and Ewan to bring whatever water they could carry from the burn, but Sarah knew it was hopeless, unless Billy brought help quickly, very quickly. The damp mist had turned to a drizzle but it was not enough to prevent the fire spreading and destroying her beloved Fairlyden. A sob of despondency rose in her throat.

Why, oh why are you not here when I need you, William? she cried in silent anger as she sped towards the burn after the others. She was returning with her second load of precious water and already the muscles in her arms and calves and thighs were protesting, even her chest throbbed with the efforts of hurrying over the stony ground.

'Where are the bairns?' Beatrice shrieked across the yard.

'In the stable!'

'Ellen and Meg arena there!'

'Meg'll be with Sadie . . . Ellen! Oh dear God! Ellen!' Sarah's face turned a chalky white and she almost flung the pails of water into Agnes's outstretched hands.

'I forgot Ellen's in your room! Above the kitchen! I must get her!' she sobbed. 'I must go in!'

'No! Sarah no!' Beatrice almost screamed as she grabbed at Sarah's arm.

'I must get Ellen!' Sarah hissed. 'I f-forgot her.' Her voice cracked in a despairing sob as she broke away from Beatrice's clutching fingers. She dashed through the dairy and the scullery into the kitchen. She had closed the door to the stairs earlier, but still the choking smoke caught at her breath and stung her eyes.

'Ellen!' she screamed frantically as she ran to the wooden steps which led directly from the kitchen to the maids' room. Ellen had been sound asleep, exhausted after the day's celebrations, and undisturbed by the sounds in the main part of the house. She heard her name and recognised a fearful desperation in her mama's usually calm voice. Almost instantly she became aware of the horrid smell, and a stinging in her eyes. But it was dark and Agnes's large attic room was not so familiar as the little bedroom she shared with Sadie. She groped her way round the wall and had almost reached the door when Sarah flung it open. Ellen found herself grabbed in a swift, fierce embrace.

'Thank God!' Sarah muttered fervently. 'Oh, thank God!'

'What's wrong, Mama?' In answer Sarah grabbed a blanket from the bed, almost smothering Ellen as she threw it over her and hurried her bewildered child down the narrow stairs. Ellen was coughing now and gasping for breath, but Sarah dragged her through the darkness, heading instinctively for the scullery and the dairy, heedless for once of Ellen's bare feet on the cold floor.

Once in the yard Ellen saw the dark figures scurrying everywhere.

'Pull the blanket round you!' Sarah gave Ellen a little push. 'Run to the stable!' she gasped as a spasm of coughing overtook her.

Ellen ran across the yard obediently and was amazed when Aunt Beatrice suddenly appeared in her path and gave her another fierce hug, before running on to the house. Sarah's eyes were streaming and she could scarcely speak for coughing but she gasped the question uppermost in her mind.

'They're all safe now? Meg?'

'She's not with Sadie! I must go in there . . .'

'No, Beatrice!' Sarah found her croaking voice with an effort. 'She canna be upstairs!'

'Is everybody safe!' Crispin Bradshaw's deep voice barked the question urgently. Sarah and Beatrice blinked stupidly as they looked up at the lantern he held.

'Sarah! What have you done? There's blood on your shoulder!' Sarah glanced down and saw the dark stain.

'I'm all right. We canna find Meg!'

'She wasna in her bedroom!' Beatrice sobbed.

'Stand back, both of you. The men are making a chain from the burn. We must try to get the fire under control, then we'll search for Meg, if you're *sure* she is not upstairs?'

'She canna be!' Beatrice cried.

Sarah gasped as she saw the large number of men hurrying to form a line. 'Who . . .? Where . . .?'

'The dancing was just finishing. They all volunteered. Now tell me, where have you looked for Meg?'

'You organise t'men lad! I'll be lookin' round t'other side uv t'ouse!' Bert Bradshaw boomed behind him. 'T' little'uns in't stable don't know where she is. Must be 'iding somewhere.'

'Don't do anything stupid, Father!' Crispin called urgently after Bert Bradshaw's retreating figure, but he was already disappearing with his own lantern in the direction of the garden and the little closet. Suddenly Sarah had another idea as she realised his intention.

'I know the ground best of all,' she gasped. 'I'll find Meg if she's hiding. Please Beatrice, please see to the others. They're bound to be frightened.'

'Sarah!' Crispin grabbed her arm. She hesitated briefly, seeing the concern, and something more, in the grey eyes illuminated by the lantern he was holding up to see her own face. 'Be careful,' he muttered hoarsely.

'I will. I've just had an idea.' Crispin nodded but his fingers clenched briefly on her shoulder and she felt his anxiety in their pressure. Again the thought flitted through her mind, why is William not here when I need him so?

Sarah groped her way through the darkness after Bert Bradshaw. The rain was heavier now and she shivered in her wet nightclothes, but she was thankful; the rain would prevent the fire from spreading to the other buildings.

'She's not in't closet!' Bert Bradshaw announced disconsolately. He looked up at the black shape of the house with its smashed bedroom window where Billy had made his escape. Despite the rain the flames were flickering through the roof now and Sarah felt sick with worry.

'She must be in there!' she muttered hoarsely.

'Nay lass, her mother said she weren't upstairs!'

'Downstairs then! She loves the parlour . . .' Sarah was groping her way to the far end even as she spoke. Bert Bradshaw followed.

'Oh no!' Sarah groaned. 'I canna see in. I'd forgotten I'd barred the wooden shutters!'

'Where's t'nearest door, lass?'

'Round the corner, but—'

'No buts. If there's a chance she's in there I'm going t' look!'

'No! Not you! It's not your responsibility!' Sarah gasped, running after him.

'This it?' He turned the knob and the heavy door opened easily but a cloud of acrid smoke came swirling out and he shut it quickly. 'I 'ave t' try. Tell me which door. Don't argue. There's not much time!'

'The first door on the left, but—'

'I'm an old man. You've kiddies t' look after. Wait at t' window.' He disappeared inside, closing the door after him to stop the through draught which would fan the smouldering fire into an inferno. Suddenly Sarah bent double and was violently sick. She knew it was the shock, and the smoke. But what would Crispin say if anything happened to his father? She ran back to the window, hammering on the glass with her fists.

'Meg, oh Meg!' she shouted desperately. 'Are you in there? Answer me, oh please answer one of you!' It seemed an eternity before Sarah got any response but in fact it was not more than a few, choking, suffocating minutes.

'Stand back!' Bert Bradshaw gasped. The back of a mahogany chair sent the window panes and frame hurtling into the garden as Sarah jumped aside.

Bert Bradshaw's broad shoulders appeared. He coughed and spluttered helplessly as he drew fresh cold air into his burning lungs. In his arms he held Meg's slight, still figure.

'Here take her, lass!' He passed her through the jagged hole in the window and Sarah clasped her in her arms. Meg stirred but she did not open her eyes. At least she's alive, Sarah thought. Swiftly she groped her way to a patch of grass and laid her down gently, thankful for the glimmer of light from Bert Bradshaw's lantern. He passed it to her.

'Stand on the small table. It's solid. It'll help you over the sill!' Sarah instructed urgently. 'I'll help you!' The man obeyed instinctively. He was past thinking for himself now. His only thought was to get out before it was too late. Sarah helped him but he landed heavily on the path at her side and Sarah knew from the oath he uttered that he must have cut his hand on a jagged piece of glass. She guided him to the grassy patch and he fell to his knees, his breath coming in slow, painful gasps, far more alarming than his earlier spluttering. Sarah bent over him. He had no breath to speak but he waved her towards Meg and Sarah obeyed.

'I think she's all right. It's as though she's in a deep sleep.' She picked Meg up in her arms.

'Wake . . . her!' Bert rasped. 'Hit . . . her!' Sarah stared from him to Meg. He adored Beattie's pretty child.

'Make – 'er – 'owl!' he gasped. Sarah put Meg back on the grass and began to slap her back and then her face. Her blue eyes opened and Sarah turned her onto her stomach, not knowing what else to do. She knelt there massaging the thin little ribs. 'Make 'er . . . 'owl!' Bert Bradshaw gasped again and began to cough. 'She mun . . . breathe . . . fresh air!'

'Oh Meg!' Sarah almost sobbed in frustration. She slapped the cold little face hard and at last Meg began to whimper. Sarah slapped her again, and again – and then again as Bert Bradshaw nodded.

'Cruel t' be kind . . .' he muttered, but his own breathing was far from easy.

'Don't!' Meg cried in a small plaintive voice. 'Don't hit me, Aunt Sarah.'

'Oh Meg!' Sarah sighed with relief.

'I on'y borrowed t'little candle, t' dance. I'm sorry, Aunt Sarah . . .'

Sarah hugged the thin little body against her sodden chest and her tears fell on Meg's upturned face.

'You're going to be all right! Thank you, God!' Sarah murmured, raising her face unconsciously to the drenching rain. 'I'll take you to your poor mama. Stay there, Mr Bradshaw. I'll be back in a minute. This rain will help to dowse the fire, and at least we're all alive.'

Bert Bradshaw nodded but he hadn't the strength to reply. He felt as though his lungs were raw and his old heart was still pumping painfully . . .

As Sarah reached the corner of the house she saw Crispin near the head of the chain of men who were hauling bucket after bucket of water. Smoke belched upwards, and the increasing rain hissed on the smouldering oak beams of the roof; every now and again a persistent yellow tongue flared skyward. Sarah felt her head begin to spin as her dazed glance took in the scene.

'Is Meg all right?' Crispin called without breaking the rhythm of grasping and passing the buckets.

'Aye, I think so. I'm more worried about your father. He's inhaled a lot o' smoke. I've had to leave him lying on the wet grass.'

'We'll manage now, Mr Bradshaw,' Nick Jamieson suggested instantly. He was standing behind Crispin in the line.

'Thanks.' Crispin passed his bucket on and moved out of the line.

Nick stepped up a pace. The men closed ranks. 'I'll attend to my father.' Crispin strode to Sarah's side. 'I sent the women to the stable with the children. Beatrice is almost hysterical, but she'll be all right now Meg is safe. Sarah, you're soaked! And you're scratched everywhere!' His grey eyes reflected consternation.

'I'll be all right.' Sarah's voice shook as the full enormity of the disaster began to sink in. 'Fairlyden,' she whispered. 'It's been home to me all my life!'

'The rain is helping to control the fire. We may be able to salvage more than you think,' Crispin said gently.

'At least we're all safe, so long as your father doesna suffer any ill effects, Crispin. Billy had a nasty shock, but he acted like a real man!'

'Of course he did, Sarah. He's your son,' Crispin said quietly. 'Where is your husband?' he asked, his voice sharpening as he glanced towards the house.

It looks so much worse from this side, Sarah thought with a sickening lurch of her stomach. 'William knows nothing of this,' she muttered tightly. 'He hasna returned frae the day's celebrations. He— he's staying at the Crown and Thistle.' She was unaware of the hurt in her wide dark eyes as she stared up at Crispin's concerned face.

'Then you must let me take care of you all tonight. I will send my father back to the Tower House as well. I will stay and attend to everything here, at least until I'm satisfied the fire is well and truly under control.'

At the stable Beatrice wept with relief when she saw Meg almost asleep in Sarah's arms.

'Mr Bradshaw says she needs plenty o' fresh air into her lungs, before she sleeps. Crispin says we can all g-go to the Tower House f-for t-tonight.'

Amazingly it was Sally, quiet, diffident Sally, who led Sarah to a pile of straw just as her knees buckled beneath her. And it was Sally who took charge of everybody else too.

'Agnes and Maggie will come tae the cottage wi' Nick and me. It'll be milking time afore we ken where we are, Mistress Fairly, and ye're all in.' Her eyes and her voice were full of sympathy and Sarah felt her own eyes fill with tears. She blinked hastily.

'Agnes says her mother will look after the bairns and Mistress O'Connor at the Mains,' Sally went on soothingly. 'There's plenty o' room there, and it wad be better if they're out o' the way for a day or two until we see . . . well, until it's daylight. Billy's yoking the mare intae the cart now. We'll put a pile o' hay in tae keep them warm and we can cover them all with Ellen's blanket for the journey.'

'Ellen!' Sarah remembered her own daughter's narrow escape. She looked across at Ellen snuggled against the hay. Richard was cradled against her, his fair head on her lap, his thumb in his mouth. He was sound asleep. Sadie was whimpering and moaning on her other side. Ellen was talking softly, trying to pacify her younger sister. Sarah sighed.

'Ellen's such a good bairn. Almost a wee mother . . .' she muttered to herself.

Billy returned. His clothes were wet too, Sarah noticed.

'The cart's ready . . .' His eyes fell on Sarah and darted quickly to Beatrice pacing the floor with Meg still clutched in her arms. 'Are ye coming tae the Mains, Mother?'

'No,' Sarah swallowed hard and shook her head.

'Where will ye bide then?' he asked in concern, 'now that – now that we've nae hame . . .?' His voice was husky. Sarah thought it might be the effects of the smoke, but she guessed that beneath the manly bravado Billy was as upset as she was herself. Everything that was loved and familiar about the old house had probably been destroyed; all her small treasures, the blue bowl her mother had brought from her old home with such care; the grandfather clock which had whiled away even the grimmest hours with its comforting tick . . . Her eyes filled with tears.

'Take Aunt Beattie and the bairns to Mains of Muir.'

'But Mother . . .'

'Dinna argue, Billy,' Sarah's voice was sharper than she had intended. She summoned a wan smile. 'I'm sorry, laddie. At least the fire is under control. It might have spread to the rest of the buildings if you hadna been so brave, and brought help so quickly. But I'd like to stay a wee while longer, and it's time Meg was in bed. Mr Bradshaw's not so well. I'll wait to see how he is.'

Billy nodded. 'Maybe the bothy end o' the house willna be sae bad,' he said hopefully.

'We'll know better when it gets light. Meanwhile,' Sarah reminded, 'you're in for a long wet drive and you'll have to go steady with Aunt Beatrice and the four bairns as well as yourself.'

'Shall I stop at the Crown and Thistle tae tell Father?'

'No.' Sarah's lips firmed but she lowered her eyes, unwilling to let anyone glimpse the pain she felt at her husband's neglect. 'It's no good wakening the whole place until daylight. Nick and the rest of the men will make sure the fire is right out. There's nothing your father can do, n-not now.' Her voice shook, but she straightened her shoulders and stood up. 'I must see to Mr Bradshaw, Billy. Just tell your father when you go to the Store in the morning. I expect he'll close it up for the day and then you'll both be able to see if we can salvage anything. I'll have to find some wee corner to stay. I canna leave Fairlyden. There's all the animals and the milking, and butter and cheese to make.'

'Ye'll manage, Mother . . . won't ye?'

Sarah saw the apprehension lurking in the depths of his dark eyes. She sighed and patted his shoulder. 'You're a good laddie, Billy. Dinna worry, at least we're all safe.' She smiled. She was rewarded by a flicker of Billy's usual grin.

Bert Bradshaw was still kneeling on the grass where Sarah had left him. Crispin was at his side and he turned as Sarah approached.

'Could you drive my father back to Strathtod, Sarah . . .? In one of your carts perhaps? He is not fit to sit on his horse, and he's very wet . . . So are you!' He summoned a weary smile, but Sarah glimpsed his anxiety. She could not hide her own concern for the blunt kindly Yorkshireman who had proved himself such a friend. She did not know her brown eyes seemed enormous in her white, exhausted face.

'I'll bring the pony and trap tae the garden gate as soon as I can get him yoked.'

'Thank you. Some of the men will stay to make sure the fire is not smouldering anywhere. I will see that one of them boards up that window for tonight too, to stop the rain getting in. It may not be quite so bad as you fear, although all the bedrooms seem to have been gutted, I'm afraid. Anyway there's nothing more we can do tonight, and my father really ought to be in bed . . .'

'I'll be all right!' Bert Bradshaw muttered. His voice was hoarse. Sarah guessed his throat was even more raw than her own, and she dared not think what damage the hot smoke might have done to his lungs.

Twenty-seven

Mrs Bunnerby came hurrying to the door as Sarah drove Mr Bradshaw up to the Tower House. She stared in horror at Sarah's soaking garments, and Sarah knew she must present a terrible sight with her face and hair all streaked with mud and smoke. Mr Bradshaw was almost as bad and the little woman clucked anxiously over them both.

'I'll 'elp 'im up to 'is room, luv. Just you follow on and I'll show you where t'new bathroom is,' she added with a note of pride. 'That's what y'need, luv! What yer both need if yer ask me – a right good 'ot tubbing!'

'I just want t'get t' me bed!' Bert Bradshaw muttered, 'so don't fuss me, Mother Bunnerby! Not just now, any road,' he added wearily.

'All right, all right,' the little woman soothed. 'I've putten a hot pig in yer bed – even if it is June. As soon as yer dry and in, I'll bring an 'ot drink – just a medicinal now! No more'n that or Mr Crispin'll be after me.'

At the top of the stairs Mrs Bunnerby bid Sarah wait a moment while she escorted Mr Bradshaw into his room and made sure he had everything he needed; then she was back at Sarah's side, leading her to the far end of the long passage.

'T'new bathroom's at this end see, cos uv all t'pipes an' things they 'ad to put in and out and up an' down. Dear me, what a palaver it was! Mr Crispin says it's fair grand, but I wouldn't try it! That's 'is room, just across. You can 'ave this room next to t'bathroom. I'll 'ave a fire kindled up in a jiffy.'

'No, no. Please dinna go to any bother!' Sarah protested.

'Eeh lass, yer look all in an' it's not a bit uv bother. You wash yer 'air or whativer y'like. I'll 'elp you dry it. On'y . . . ' Mrs Bunnerby flushed and looked awkwardly at Sarah. 'My nighties'll make two uv you, but they're all I've got and yer'll need summat t' put on.'

'Oh Mrs Bunnerby, even a warm dry blanket would be wonderful!' Sarah assured the kindly little woman.

'That's all reet then!' she said with a relieved smile and went to fetch her best flannel nightgown and set it to warm around a hot stone bottle.

The hot bath seemed to Sarah the height of luxury. She marvelled that anyone could have a bath long enough to lie down in. She washed her hair and let it float on the water. Gradually some of her aching muscles began to relax and by the time she climbed out and towelled herself dry, some of her anxieties had lessened, or at least she was able to put them temporarily aside and concentrate on being warm and dry as she rubbed her hair before a huge blazing fire. Outside she could hear the rain pattering on the window. Soon it would be morning and she must return to Fairlyden, but for now the thought of a few hours' sleep in the big feather bed was bliss.

She smiled as she buttoned Mrs Bunnerby's best white nightgown up to her chin. It was far too wide and it only came down to the middle of her legs, for Sarah was tall for a woman and Mrs Bunnerby was quite short.

Sarah had just climbed into the big bed when there was a tap on the door.

'Come in, Mrs Bunnerby!' she called cheerfully, though she had already pleaded with the woman not to go to any more trouble.

'I've brought you something to help you sleep and keep the chill away,' Crispin Bradshaw announced from the doorway. 'Do you mind if I come in, Sarah? I wanted to reassure myself that you are unhurt . . .?'

'I-I'm f-fine.' Sarah knew she had blushed to the roots of her hair, and now she was stammering like a schoolgirl instead of a mature married woman. 'H-how is your father?'

'He's just had a nightcap too,' Crispin smiled wryly. 'He says if it can't cure him, then nothing will; though between you and me I was rather alarmed earlier.'

'Yes,' Sarah said anxiously. 'So was I. I shouldna have let him go into the house.'

'If he hadn't gone in, you would have tried to rescue young Meg, and as he says, he's lived his life and enjoyed a lot of it.'

'Dinna say that, Crispin!' Sarah shuddered.

He came closer to the bed then, holding out the little silver tray and the steaming glass. 'Drink this. It will warm you and help you to sleep.'

'What's in it?' Sarah sipped experimentally and eyed him over the rim of the glass.

'Some of your fine Scotch whisky, a little lemon, sugar. Nothing to do you any harm. Drink it up, there's a good lass.'

'Oh Crispin,' Sarah laughed shakily. 'You talk as though I'm a child.' Suddenly, without warning, her voice broke and her eyes filled with tears. 'Oh mercy!' she muttered, and tried to wipe them away with the back of her hand. 'I-I dinna k-ken wh-what's come over me,' she gulped.

'It's the shock – and exhaustion,' Crispin said grimly. 'You've come through a lot tonight, Sarah, and you were very brave. Why shouldn't you cry now that it is all over . . .?'

'B-but it's n-not all over!' Sarah sniffed. 'That's just the trouble. I darena think about tomorrow . . .' Her teeth chattered against the rim of the glass and her hand shook uncontrollably.

'Aah Sarah, my dear!' Crispin was beside her in an instant, perching on the edge of the bed, his long lean fingers holding the glass steady, putting it to her lips as though she were indeed a child. 'Drink it, my dear. It will help, I promise . . .'

Sarah obeyed, but slowly for the fiery liquid burned her throat. Crispin was right though, it did warm her, all the way to her toes. She summoned a wan smile.

'What a nuisance you must think me . . .' she sniffed apologetically. 'And I dinna know how I can ever th-thank you, or your father . . .'

'Oh, Sarah . . .' Crispin murmured gently, his mouth only inches from the top of her head, 'you must know I would never consider you a nuisance!'

'I needed help s-so badly, and y-you came,' Sarah stared up at him wide-eyed. 'I dinna want to think! The children . . . even Billy . . . th-they think I can make everything right again! B-but I k-keep seeing the house . . . without a r-roof! I-I've lived at Fairlyden all my life, Crispin. I've never slept anywhere else . . . I dinna think I can sleep . . . for all your Mrs Bunnerby has been so kind.'

'Hush Sarah, my love, you will . . . You will.' Crispin's voice was deep and husky. He began to smooth her long dark hair, his hands so gentle, so soothing.

It seemed the most natural thing in the world for Sarah to lean her head against his chest and for Crispin to hold her securely, his arm curving around her shoulders, instilling the warmth from his own body into hers. He held her as gently as he would have held a young child, but he had always been aware of Sarah as an attractive woman. Now for the first time he saw her with her newly washed hair curling almost to the middle of her back in a fragrant dark cloud; her skin was soft and smooth against the tips of his fingers. They seemed to move with a will of their own, slowly, almost hypnotically, over her neck, and round the tips of her neat little ears, finding the curve of her cheek, her throat . . .

'I dinna want to think about tomorrow,' she whispered huskily.

'I don't want to think about tomorrow either, my love,' Crispin murmured below his breath, yet Sarah heard, just as she heard the quickening rhythm of his heart beneath her cheek.

She tipped her head a little then and looked into his face; she saw the dark shadow of his lean jaw. He had bathed but he had not shaved. Her eyes moved upwards. His mouth was firm, serious . . . yet sensitive. Sarah remembered the hurt he must have suffered as a boy when he had lost his beloved mother. She knew of his vow; he would never marry. Yet Sarah was sure Crispin Bradshaw was a man with a wealth of love to give. He was a sensitive, caring man.

Her dark eyes continued on their slow upward journey, but she stopped short as she encountered Crispin's grey eyes watching her through their fringe of brown lashes. She felt a quiver of shock. There was a question there – not pleading, not demanding – but a simple, silent question. It was there in Crispin's steady grey gaze as it met, and held, her own. Sarah's breath caught in her throat. She knew she had only to lower her lashes; Crispin would rise from the bed and leave her, like the gentleman he was. But she didn't want to be left! She didn't want to be alone – not tonight! Her eyes darkened involuntarily and she heard Crispin catch his breath, but still the question hung between them.

It was no more than a fleeting second yet in that moment Sarah's resentment against her husband mounted. Why was William not with her now? She needed his strength, his support and comfort! Why had he stayed so long at the celebrations? Why had he not returned to her instead of blethering to James Slater? Her thoughts brought a stab of pain and resentment. Her wide brown eyes grew even darker; her lips trembled, full, soft, and so very appealing. She tipped her head, oh so slightly, against Crispin's shoulder. His breathing quickened. Sarah's dark eyes did not waver.

Crispin had his answer.

His lips were firm and cool against her own and Sarah responded to their pressure with an almost childish yearning to be loved, but as the pressure deepened passion flared within her. It was some time since William had taken trouble to rouse the passion in her as he had in the early days of their marriage.

Crispin was a caring and considerate man, and despite the desire, which he had suppressed for so long, he wanted Sarah to remember their time together. His touch was firm and sure, yet infinitely gentle; there was no boyish fumbling for Crispin Bradshaw. His nimble fingers were deliberately slow as he opened the row of buttons down the front of Mrs Bunnerby's voluminous white nightdress.

Sarah blushed like a young bride, but the response which Crispin's leisurely explorations aroused in her were those of a woman, a woman of passion – a woman in need of loving.

When Crispin could wait no longer, her breathing quickened with his own; he drew her with him to fulfilment.

A long sigh of ecstasy escaped Sarah's parted lips and she lay languidly in Crispin's arms, the trauma of the preceding hours temporarily forgotten. Crispin's fingers idly traced the blue veins in her wrist. Slowly her eyelids drooped, but even when she slept a little smile of happiness lingered on her lips.

Sarah had risen at five o'clock every morning for as long as she could remember and this morning was no exception, though it was barely an hour since she had fallen asleep. It was as though some inbuilt alarm had roused her. She stretched sleepily, unwilling to end a pleasant dream, yet already uncertain what the dream had been about. Suddenly memories came flooding back. The fire! The destruction! Her bairns . . . and little Meg! She moaned and turned her head restlessly as she forced her heavy eyelids to open. A lamp was still burning. Her eyes moved to the window. Rose-coloured curtains were still drawn across the long windows and the room had a cosy glow, but Sarah's heart was cold and fearful. She shivered. Immediately her hand was taken in a warm clasp. Slowly she turned her head.

'It was not a dream . . .?' Sarah's voice was croaky. Her throat felt parched and sore and she knew it was the effects of the smoke.

Crispin turned to the table beside the bed and poured her a glass of water.

'Drink this, Sarah. It will help your throat.'

Sarah accepted the water gratefully.

'Thank you.' She could not control the blush which rose in her cheeks as she raised her eyes to his face. 'Y-you think of everything. You are . . . very kind. I— I . . .'

'Hush, Sarah. I'm not "kind" and we both know it! I understand, so you needn't worry. You are William Fairly's wife, the mother of his children. I shall not forget, at least not after today . . .' He sighed. 'But last night you were mine, Sarah, and I'll never forget that either . . .'

Sarah bit her lip. Then she nodded, but her eyes were wide and troubled. 'I know it's wicked of me, but I'm glad . . .' she said softly. 'Glad you're still here.' She frowned suddenly. 'Did you sleep at all, Crispin?'

'My time with you was too short and too precious to waste in sleep, Sarah.' His grey eyes were filled with tenderness.

Sarah shook her head, not knowing what to say. Then she sighed.

'I'm sure it must be past five o'clock. I shall be late for the milking as it is, by the time I get back to— to Fairlyden.' Her voice shook as she thought of her beloved home. Then another thought struck her and her eyes widened in shock.

'I've nothing to wear! I've no clothes! Oh, dear God what am I to do . . .?' Her voice rose in panic.

'Hush my love . . .' Crispin soothed. 'It is too early for you to return to Fairlyden yet. Nick Jamieson can manage the milking without you for once.'

'Agnes and Maggie . . . they'll have no clothes either, save what they had on their backs! Oh Crispin . . . we've lost everything!'

'Listen to me, lass!' Crispin's voice was gruff, his accent broader, reminding her of his father, but the grave expression in his eyes compelled her to take heed. 'You've hardly had time t'sleep. When it gets really light you'll have a busy day, so rest a bit longer, while y'can. Everything will be black with smoke, and the water . . . We'll have to make sure it's safe to go in. So, you rest a bit longer, at least until Mrs Bunnerby gets up. Then I'll ask her to bring Fanny's clothes to you. She always leaves some of her gowns and shawls and things here . . .'

'But I canna take Fanny's clothes!'

'Of course you can. She would be the first to say so.' A wry smile curved his lips. 'Though they'll probably be far too short.' He ran a hand down the length of her body. Sarah gasped in surprise. Crispin chuckled, then sobered. 'You're a beautiful woman, Sarah Fairly!' His voice thickened.

'I-I'm just a . . .'

Crispin placed a gentle finger over her lips and shook his head. 'Don't Sarah . . .' He lowered his head and placed his lips where his fingers had been.

Sarah could not argue, even if she had wanted to, and suddenly she found she had no desire to argue anyway. Crispin was right. Soon the luxury of lying in a warm bed in a cosy room must end, and who could tell where she would sleep tonight? Her mouth trembled and Crispin's kiss deepened.

This time there was an urgency in their loving, a desperation in each touch, each kiss.

Afterwards Crispin lay with his head on Sarah's breast and it was her fingers which caressed and comforted, but eventually he raised himself on one elbow and gazed down into her face, as though memorising each separate feature.

'I shall always treasure the memory of these few hours with you, Sarah. Always.' His grey eyes were tender. Sarah opened her mouth to speak but he went on, 'I know, lass. It can never be repeated. Don't worry.' His mouth tightened briefly. 'I've been thinking while you were asleep. I'll have to stay away from you. I think I'll go back to Yorkshire tomorrow. Beatrice and her two children can travel back with my father . . . Later, when he has completely recovered, I've been thinking it's time somebody paid a visit to our wool merchants in Australia. Maybe it will do me good to get away from the factories . . .'

'You're going all the way to Australia, Crispin?'

'Mmm,' he gave a wry smile. 'I can't be tempted to catch a train to Strathtod from there, lass. I think it's best. My father will see to things in Yorkshire for a few months, and we've a good overseer. You'll be busy too, Sarah . . . rebuilding your home. It will be better if we don't see each other for a good while. Afterwards . . .' He shrugged, and Sarah could have wept for the unhappiness she saw in the depths of his grey eyes, despite the brave smile which curved his mouth.

'Oh, Crispin, I'm s-so sorry!'

'No! Don't be sorry, lass. I shall remember these few hours with you, even when I'm an old man! I shall never forget. Never. There's just one thing, Sarah; if ever you need a friend, think of me. You've only to say the word. I shall never take advantage, lass, you know that, don't you? Sarah . . .?' he prompted softly.

'Yes.' Sarah's voice was hoarse, and her eyes were bright with unshed tears. 'I have considered you my friend for a long time, Crispin. You're my very best friend.'

He leaned forward then and kissed her lightly on the lips. The next moment he was on his feet, pulling on his robe and stepping lightly to the door. As he opened it he looked back at her with his tender, kindly smile; then he was gone.

Sarah declined Mrs Bunnerby's offer to call the coachman to take her back to Fairlyden.

'Mr Crispin's already ridden off on 'is 'orse t'see if yer 'ouse is safe, then 'e's riding to t'Mains of Muir to enquire after t'children and Mrs O'Connor.'

'How is Mr Bradshaw?' Sarah asked anxiously and saw the smile fade from Mrs Bunnerby's rosy face.

'I'm that worried about 'im, Mrs Fairly,' she muttered, as though afraid he might hear and object. ' 'E's not breathin' easy. I took 'im a drink of tea and 'e drank it though.' She looked at Sarah, obviously seeking reassurance.

'He— he swallowed a lot of smoke. He was very brave, but I expect his throat is sore.'

'Well I could give 'im plenty of milk to soothe that . . . but it seemed t'me it was 'is lungs . . . the way 'e was breathin'. But 'e said I was just to leave 'im t'sleep. An' that's a sign 'e's not 'imself! Allus up early in't morning, 'e is.'

Sarah tried to offer reassurance, but she was worried herself. Bert Bradshaw was not a young man. She prayed the effects of the scorching, choking smoke had not caused any permanent injury.

The milking was finished by the time Sarah walked back to Fairlyden just after seven o'clock. Her heart beats quickened as she walked up the last stretch of grass above the burn and into the farmyard. The acrid smell of smoke hung in the morning air and Sarah thought it would linger in her nostrils for the rest of her life. Her heart filled with sick dismay as she stared at the blackened walls and gaping roof of her home.

'Fairlyden . . .' she murmured brokenly. For as long as she could remember the old house had given her shelter and security; she had loved every stone of its thick walls, every creaking door and shining window pane. A sob rose in her throat. Even the flags on the kitchen floor and the passage, which she had scrubbed so often, suddenly seemed dearer to her than the most ornate carpet. Tears blurred her eyes. She brushed them away hurriedly as Agnes and Maggie came out of the dairy.

'Sally's made porridge for all o' us,' Agnes announced. 'She said tae tell ye there wad be plenty if ye wanted some, Miss Sarah.' There was sympathy and concern in her tired face.

Sarah shook her head and summoned a wan smile. She had struggled to eat the bacon and egg Mrs Bunnerby had provided. She felt too sick at heart to think of food. She frowned and straightened her shoulders.

I canna give in. What's the use of crying anyway? she chided herself. Aloud she said, 'Eat your breakfast, Agnes, and the rest of you. I must see how bad it is.'

'Mr Crispin Bradshaw called in, just a wee while ago,' Agnes said. 'He's riding down tae the Mains, but he wanted tae be sure it was safe for ye tae gang inside.'

'I see.' Sarah felt the colour rise in her cheeks, and as swiftly ebb, leaving her pale.

'He's a kind man!' Agnes said fervently. 'He says the kitchen's safe, and most o' my things, and Maggie's, are all right, 'cept for smellin' o' smoke, but they'll wash. Mr Crispin said ye were not tae gang near the stairs. I was tae be sure an tell ye. They're no' safe.'

'Thanks, Agnes. I shall not take any risks.' She shuddered.
'Mr Crispin said the Master wad likely be sending a man tae see tae everything as soon as he hears the news frae Billy this morning!'
'Aye,' Sarah said shortly, but her mouth tightened. Would William understand how much the awful destruction meant to her? The loss of her small treasures, her home . . .? 'We shall all need something to wear.' She looked down at Fanny's blue woollen gown. It was much too fine for the work she had to do. Mrs Bunnerby had given her one of her own aprons though and it covered her almost completely, back and front.
'Mr Bradshaw said he wad call in on his way hame tae tell us how the bairns and Mistress O'Connor are faring at the Mains.'

It was neither Crispin nor William who came to Fairlyden that morning though. It was Alexander Logan and Alex.
'Aah, lassie, but I'm pleased tae see ye're all right,' Sandy breathed fervently as he caught Sarah to him in a fierce, brief hug.
Sarah felt the tears start to her eyes again and blinked them angrily away. She was not usually tearful.
'I'm fine,' she muttered huskily. 'How are Beatrice and wee Meg? And Ellen and Sadie?'
'They're fine tae. Well, considering the excitement and everything.'
'Thank God for that. Are William and Billy on their way . . .?' She sniffed and brushed away a stray tear impatiently.
'Och lassie,' Sandy murmured with concern. 'It's the reaction that's affecting ye. Beatrice and Billy . . . they said how calm and brave ye were. I'm glad Crispin took ye tae the Tower House, for ye'd no' hae found much rest here.' He peered into the smoke-blackened kitchen, which Agnes and Maggie were helping her to scrub, so he did not notice Sarah's guilty blush.
'The bothy and scullery are scarcely affected, and Agnes and Maggie will soon put their room back intae order. I expect the kitchen will be habitable by tonight, so we can use the box bed.' She sighed, 'I just dinna know where Billy and the girls are going to sleep, or Beatrice . . .?'
'Beatrice and her bairns are going back tae Yorkshire tomorrow with Crispin,' Sandy said. 'It will be better that way, I suppose. Young Meg has a bit of a cough, but Beatrice was making her a soothing potion. She reminded me o' my ain mother,' he mused. 'She was aye ready with some remedy or other, and the way she sets about it even. It's uncanny.' He turned and saw Sarah's white strained face. 'Are ye sure ye're all right, lassie? I dinna ken why William had tae gang away tae Dumfries this morning. He should hae been here, helping ye!' he added irritably.
'William has gone to Dumfries?' she asked incredulously. 'B-but why? And what is Billy doing? I thought they would have come to help, to see what we can salvage . . .'
'Aye, Crispin thought they wad be here by the time we arrived. Billy left the Mains at the crack o' dawn tae tell William what had happened,'

Sandy said slowly. 'But when we came by the Store Billy was still there. William told him tae stay and look after it and not to turn any customers away. I suppose all the money will be needed tae rebuild the hoose. Maybe I shouldna have been sae hasty, putting all my savings intae the Mains . . .'

'Oh, Father, we could not take any more of your money!' Sarah exclaimed with some distress. 'You've done more than enough for us, sharing the profits frae your horses to pay for the Fairlyden land we rent from Strathtod! William will manage.'

'Aye, Billy said we were tae tell ye his father has gone tae Dumfries tae see a Mr Blake about the insurance.' Sandy frowned, recalling the rest of Billy's words. 'But he hasna even been tae see Mother, or the damage! I reckon he had planned tae gang tae Dumfries this morning anyway! The insurance is jist an excuse. He was more interested in James Slater and his tales o' America!'

It was the first time Sandy had ever heard Billy breathe a word of criticism about his father. He had been too surprised to reprimand him. He knew Billy was shocked and tired and very worried by the night's events.

'There's Alex helping Ewan tae carry out the things that can be saved,' he said with forced cheerfulness. 'I'll see what I can dae tae help. Just sae long as ye're all right, lassie, that's all that matters.'

Sarah was consumed with guilt whenever she thought of the few hours she had spent at the Tower House with Crispin. But as the day wore on and her father and Alex had to return to Mains of Muir, and still William had not returned, her guilt changed to resentment at her husband's neglect.

It was late afternoon before William returned to Fairlyden but his greeting was no more than an absent-minded squeeze of Sarah's shoulders, with no sign of the comfort and concern and reassurance that his wife so badly needed.

'Surely Billy told you how bad it was?' Sarah demanded and she could not hide her hurt. 'I thought you would have come home immediately.'

William smiled ruefully and produced several lengths of material to make new clothes for herself and Ellen and Sadie, as well as some ready-made petticoats and a fine new shawl.

Sarah sighed and tried hard to control her irritation. It was not easy to show anger and disappointment to a husband who came bearing gifts, especially when she thought of her own secret guilt. But none of the material would be suitable for a good working dress. She would have to visit Janet at Mr Jardine's store tomorrow. William had sensed her vexation and he was anxious now to make amends, especially when his own plans had gone exceedingly well.

'I will build you a finer home than you have ever dreamed of, Sarah,' he promised with a beguiling smile.

'But I loved Fairlyden the way it was! It's the house where I was born! The only home I've ever known. I dinna want any changes . . .' Her voice trembled and trailed away. William would never understand how much the old house meant to her.

'It was a good enough house when my grandfather built it,' William conceded, 'but now we shall improve it. I will build the walls higher so that a man doesn't bump his head when he stands up straight in the bedrooms.' He grinned, but Sarah could not return his smile.

'Cheer up, Sarah! We shall have a proper bathing room too, with water that comes out of taps, instead of having to carry it all from the burn. You would like that, wouldn't you?'

'How could we possibly do all that?' Sarah stared at William. 'We canna afford such things.' She thought of the long iron bath on its four little feet in the bathroom at the Tower House, of the big brass taps gurgling and grunting, sending hot water spouting straight into the bath, and the plug in the bottom that let the water drain away without having to scoop it out with buckets; there was the toilet too, with its polished mahogany seat and a string that bought a great gush of water when you pulled it. Now that really was luxury! She did not realise that William was already perfectly familiar with all these things from his visits to Avary Hall.

'We could never afford such fine things,' she repeated.

'The insurance will pay for everything. You see, my dear Sarah, it was worthwhile after all, despite your doubts.'

'Surely the insurance company willna pay for a bathing room?' Sarah asked incredulously.

'Of course it will,' William answered with more confidence than actual knowledge.

'But how could we get water frae the burn to the top of the house . . .?'

'Aah! Now Sarah!' William wagged his finger in her face. 'That's where Fairly and Guillyman's comes in. And now that I think of it, this will be a splendid opportunity to demonstrate one of the new oil engines. We could sell lots of them after this! I will place an order for half a dozen at least. We might even pump water to a trough in the yard for the cattle. Yes indeed! It will be a good advertisement, far better than the local newspaper, though I see all manner of things advertised there these days. All the farmers round about will be demanding oil engines and water tanks when they see what can be done.'

'They might, if they can afford them,' Sarah reminded him doubtfully. 'Wheat is cheaper now than it was a century ago!'

'Farmers in this area don't depend on wheat for their living. I'm sure some of the big dairy farms must have piped water for their dairies. If they haven't, they soon will when they hear of Fairly and Guillyman's,' William declared jubilantly.

Sarah felt tired and depressed. Her husband's cheerfulness irritated her. He seemed almost glad that Fairlyden had been burned.

'You dinna realise, William, how hard everybody works, and still there's only enough money to buy food and clothes and pay the men and maids enough to do the same!' She didn't mention her latest worry which had been overshadowed by the excitement of Beatrice's visit and the Jubilee Celebrations. Two of the cows had given birth to dead calves, at least eight or ten weeks before they should have given birth at all. Neither of them would give any milk until they had another calf, and that would be more than nine months.

'Don't get angry, Sarah. I expect you are tired. It must have been a distressing day for you.'

'Yes it has! We've lost all our clothes, and . . . and, oh lots of things I treasured – like the grandfather clock in the hall, the one your Grandfather Fairly gave to his mistress – the first Sarah to live at Fairlyden! I dinna know yet what we can save frae the wee parlour either.' Her soft mouth trembled and she pressed her fingers hard against her lips. 'Crispin said it wasna safe to go in there until the ceiling was propped up. Did you call at the joiner's yard to tell Iain McKie we need him to mend the roof at once?'

'No.' William flushed. He had been too preoccupied with the news James Slater had given him to think about the joiner. 'I'll tell McKie tomorrow. He'll make sure things are safe until the man can come from Dumfries to draw up plans for our new house.'

'Surely Mr Carlyle can do the repairs to the walls and the roof if you tell him what you want?'

'Oh, he's just an ordinary village builder. We shall need a man who is skilled; a man who can understand the drawings . . .'

'But John Carlyle could do that. His uncle trained him and he was the best builder for miles around!' Sarah protested, but William just shook his head.

'You just leave such things to me, my dear. I shall see to everything.'

'But when? We need rooms for the children to sleep in!'

'They can sleep in the maids' attic for the time being. Agnes and Maggie can stay with Nick Jamieson and his wife.'

'I suppose Sally will manage with two extra for a few weeks, but there's only two small rooms at the cottage you know, William. What about Billy?'

'Aah yes . . . Billy.' William frowned. 'Perhaps he could sleep at the Mill House until Fairlyden is rebuilt. You could ask Janet if she would cook him a meal each day.'

'If Ray Jardine will allow her. He's her employer now remember. Anyway Billy wouldna have much comfort!' Sarah exclaimed uneasily. 'But I suppose the weather should be warm enough in July, and I suppose the town builder will be quick.'

That night Sarah slept beside William in the close confines of the kitchen box bed. It disturbed her that she could not find comfort in her husband's arms as she had done in Crispin Bradshaw's. She was plagued by guilt and angered because William had let her down when she needed him. Now his ideas for a fine house made her uneasy. All she wanted was a roof over their heads to keep out the wind and the rain, and the cold.

Twenty-eight

Sarah felt an instinctive dislike for the man who was accompanying William around the remains of her home when she looked up from inspecting the damage to her garden. She joined them reluctantly.

'This is Mr Crichton-Reid,' William announced with all the satisfaction of a conjuror producing a real white rabbit out of an empty hat. 'He has won acclaim for restoring several houses in the county, as well as one or two in Edinburgh.' The man had a curved beaky nose and his eyes were sharp and cold behind his steel-rimmed spectacles as he poked and prodded.

Sarah murmured politely but she was instantly aware of the man's condescension as he eyed her plain calico dress. She had bought the material at Mr Jardine's store and Janet had kindly offered to make it, knowing that Sarah was fully occupied with sewing and knitting new clothes for Sadie and Ellen, as well as making shirts and socks and underwear for Billy and William. Sarah was too proud to excuse her appearance. She had the impression that Mr Crichton-Reid considered it beneath his dignity to spend his time on a small, isolated farmhouse like Fairlyden. He made sketchy and impractical drawings on sheets of stiff paper.

'I could explain to John Carlyle exactly what I want him to build and he would build it!' Sarah said impatiently when he had departed, promising to send William some sketches as soon as they were ready. 'We have waited too long already, first for your insurance men, and then this— this architect . . .'

'I only want the best for you, Sarah. We must listen to the ideas of other people.'

'I dinna believe Mr Crichton-Reid knows anything about building a farmhouse. I'm sure he thought it was beneath his dignity even to look at it. Maybe he expected something like the Tower House at Strathtod!' William flushed and turned away. That was exactly what Crichton-Reid had expected when he heard the name Fairly. 'Anyway we canna afford his fancy ideas,' Sarah continued in aggrieved tones. 'What would I do with a glass conservatory leading into the garden? I would never have time to attend aspidistras and all those other things he talked about. It takes me all my time to grow enough of the peas and beans and sprouts and carrots you all like to eat, not to mention weeding the herb garden!'

'A conservatory was only a suggestion,' William said patiently.

'Aye, but your man was displeased when I said we didna want such a thing.'

'Well, he will send the plans soon for our approval.'

'So John Carlyle can start by next week?'

'Er, I'm afraid not, Sarah.' William frowned uncomfortably. 'Mr Crichton-Reid prefers to employ his own builders, from Dumfries.'

'But when will they come? It is the end of July already. If any more rain comes through frae upstairs we shall have no rooms at all to live in. The ceilings will come down altogether and there will be more expense.'

'Don't worry, Sarah! It was Mr Blake from the insurance company who recommended Crichton-Reid for the restoration. He assured me that his company will pay for all repairs.'

'We-ll, if you're sure . . .?'

'Of course I'm sure!' William snapped, exasperated by Sarah's doubts and questions. 'In fact it's time we had a decent house to live in, instead of eating all our meals with the servants, and sleeping in a room that is little more than an attic. We rarely have peace for a private conversation!'

Sarah's face went white. It had never occurred to her that William resented living at Fairlyden. She turned away so that he could not see the tears stinging her eyelids.

'Sarah . . .?' William sounded contrite, but it was too late. Now she knew how he really felt. 'I'm sorry, my dear . . .'

'I never knew . . . I-I thought you were happy to live at Fairlyden. Daniel Munro told me Lord Johnathan Fairly was happier here than he ever was at Strathtod, and he was your own grandfather . . .'

'He was happy because Fairlyden allowed him to be with the woman he loved. I came to Fairlyden because I loved you, Sarah, but it does not mean I don't want to improve it, especially since the fire has given us an opportunity. Now come to bed,' he urged, 'and forget everything else . . .'

Sarah obeyed but she lay awake long after William had gone to sleep. She recalled her parting from Beatrice at the railway station. She had found it impossible to convince Beattie that she did not blame Meg for the fire.

'I blame myself,' Sarah had said truthfully. 'Sadie told me there was a funny smell but I was tired; I thought it was just another of Sadie's ploys to get attention. Billy blames himself as well, because he didna blow out the candle. Let us just thank God we're all alive.' Now Sarah wondered what Beatrice would say if she knew William seemed almost glad the fire had occurred. It was a long time before she slept but she resolved not to interfere with William's plans when Mr Crichton-Reid came again.

As it happened Sarah was binding the first of the sheaves in the harvest field when the pompous little man presented his final drawings two weeks later and she was not sorry that he had to leave to catch his train before she returned to the house.

That night she was aware of William's suppressed excitement.

'You must be pleased with the drawings, William . . .?' she ventured, but he did not offer to show them to her. Indeed he did not bring up the subject of the house until they were lying in the darkness of the kitchen box bed.

'Crichton-Reid is going to send the builders from Dumfries next week.'

'Aah! I'm pleased to hear that!' Sarah declared with relief. 'I'd begun to think there'd still be no roof when winter comes. Where will the builders stay?'

'Mr Crichton-Reid says they will sleep in one of the lofts. There will just be one man and his apprentice, which is just as well since they will make extra mouths for you to feed, I'm afraid. Mr Crichton-Reid will travel from Dumfries once a week to see that the work is proceeding according to his instructions . . .'

'Once a week! How many weeks does he expect it to take? I remember when the cottage was built for Louis and Janet. It only took two weeks!'

'This is different. There will be pipes and plumbing for the water and the new bathroom. The walls will have to be built higher. There will be new doors and windows to make, and a new staircase. Mr Crichton-Reid has employed a very skilled joiner for that . . .'

'Oh,' Sarah said flatly.

'I want it to be the very best for you, my dear.'

'I know, William.' Sarah sighed. 'But I like Iain McKie. He and his father are good joiners and they could have done with the work, I'm sure. I dinna see why we need strangers coming all the way frae the town . . .'

'Mr Crichton-Reid knows them, and he will supervise their work.'

'Why should he need to supervise? I thought you . . .?'

'Er, no, Sarah. That is one of the reasons I wanted to have a man like Crichton-Reid, with proper plans which I have studied and approved.' He hesitated and cleared his throat. 'You see, Sarah, I know the house will be in a great upheaval until everything is finished, so . . . Well, the truth is I thought it would be a good time for me to be away, one person less for you to look after,' he added brightly, but Sarah sensed it was a false brightness. Even in the darkness she was suddenly aware of a new tension in him. He reminded her of Billy as a little boy, when he had done something he knew would displease her . . .

'Away?' she repeated warily. 'Where? For a whole week?'

'I have arranged my passage on a ship bound for America. I shall be—'

'America!' Sarah was incredulous.

'Quiet, my dear! You will waken the girls.'

'B-but America?' Sarah repeated in dismay. 'Why do you want to go to America, William, and at such a time as this?' Sarah knew her voice was harsh. William would avoid all the mess and upheaval; he was leaving her alone again, alone to deal with strangers.

'I need to see Lady Guillyman . . .'

'Aah! So you know where to find her now? James Slater told you? But why, William? It's so far!'

'I'm tired of communicating through that haughty old lawyer of hers!' That was the story William had resolved to tell Sarah.

'But what do you want to say to her? D'you need more money? Is—is Fairly and Guillyman's doing badly?'

'Badly? No, of course not! Whatever gave you that idea?'

'Billy says there isna much trade frae your new branch in Dumfries . . .'

'Billy has been looking into the Dumfries ledgers?' William did not sound pleased. 'He's too bright for his own good, that son of yours, Sarah!'

'He's your son too! Anyway you were proud that he was alert and bright and learning the business so fast. He says he has a lot more customers at Muircumwell than Fred Clark had. In fact I wonder at you paying the man to stay in Dumfries all week when most of the trade is done on Wednesdays when the farmers go to market.'

William was silent for several seconds and when he spoke he turned to her, reaching for her in the darkness of the box bed, surprising her by his warm embrace.

'Sarah Fairly, you're a very clever woman. No wonder we have a clever son . . .'

'We have two sons, and they are both clever,' Sarah reminded him shortly. 'Though I know you've aye been disappointed that Alex is your elder son and heir . . .'

William heard the hurt in her tone. 'I admit I was disappointed because Alex was born a cripple, but I know he is intelligent. I still think he should have joined me in the business of Fairly and Guillyman's. He'll never be anything better than an ordinary tenant farmer now, and a lame one at that.'

Sarah gasped indignantly, but before she could speak William went on, 'I shall take your advice and save money on lodgings for Fred Clark, at least until I return. Fred can go to Dumfries on market days. Billy can handle the Muircumwell Store in my absence. There will not be many orders for seeds during the winter and the boy deals with the machines and small tools as well as I could myself. Fred could take over my visits to Annan and Lockerbie markets, and maybe even Carlisle . . . Yes, Sarah my dear, you would have been an excellent organiser if you had been a man . . .'

Sarah sighed. All women need to be organisers to look after a man and his house and bairns! she thought indignantly, but aloud she persisted stubbornly, 'I still dinna see why you want to go to America . . . I wish you would bide at home. It's such a long way across the ocean. It frightens me, William . . .' She shuddered.

'There's no need to be afraid, Sarah,' William's voice was gentler than it had been for some time and he took her in his arms and kissed her tenderly. 'The steam ships are perfectly safe now, you know. They don't depend on the wind for their sails anymore, and I shall be back before you know it.'

'I hope so, I do hope so!' Sarah muttered fervently and kissed him with a passion that took William by surprise. He responded instantly.

A little while later Sarah realised they had not made love with such abandon, or with such satisfaction, for years – not since the twins were born in fact. William seemed to read her thoughts.

'You are still a witch of a woman, Sarah Fairly,' he whispered in her ear. 'I hope I shall not regret this night of passion. I was afraid I was going to lose you when the twins were born. Yet you drive me to distraction!'

'Well you needna worry, William. I'm thirty-eight! Too old to be having any more bairns . . .'

'Mmm, well I hope you're right. You were as loving as any new bride tonight. In fact you were somewhat shy and reserved when you were a new bride, as I recall.' Sarah could feel the teasing smile on his lips as his mouth hovered over her own.

Minutes later he was sound asleep, leaving her to consider the news of his proposed journey to America. Suddenly she stiffened. Her heart began to thump.

Surely I am right . . .? I am too old to bear more children! I must be! She trembled as she realised she hadn't given her bodily functions, or lack of them, any thought since the fire. There had been too much to do to pay attention to trivialities; but she had always had a regular monthly rhythm, ever since she was a schoolgirl. Could it be that she was really approaching old age then? I dinna feel old, she thought, in fact I've felt remarkably full o' life these past few weeks, considering the shock o' the fire, and all the work.

Sarah had not allowed her thoughts to dwell on Crispin Bradshaw, not even when Beattie wrote to say he had set out on his journey to Australia now that his father's health had improved. She had tried to block him out of her mind deliberately; she had committed the sin of adultery; she wanted to forget the guilt which weighed so heavily on her conscience. What right had she to deter William from going to America? From seeing Lady Elsa Guillyman again? She must not question his motives.

She moved her hands tentatively over her stomach. It was almost as flat now as it had been when she was a girl. She worked too hard to grow fat and her muscles were as firm and trim as they had always been. Nevertheless, now that the thought had occurred to her she began to count the weeks, seven, almost eight since the night of the fire, the night she had spent at the Tower House with Crispin Bradshaw . . .

William planned to set out for America early in September. Before he left, Ewan approached him.

'Maggie and me, well we hae plans tae marry in the spring. We thought we ought tae tell ye now, Mr Fairly. We wadna leave without giving ye a full term's notice.'

William had had little personal contact with Ewan since he hired him.

'We shall be sorry to lose you,' he acknowledged distantly.

'We dinna want tae leave Fairlyden.' Ewan sighed heavily. 'Maggie an' me, we've been happy here. But we'll need a wee hoose once we're married . . .'

William frowned. He guessed what was in Ewan's mind.

'Well I'm afraid I have no plans to build another cottage at Fairlyden, not at the present time, though I know Mistress Fairly will be sorry to lose Maggie too.'

'Aye, I understand, Mr Fairly,' Ewan acknowledged with quiet dignity. 'I'll tell Maggie. She'll be disappointed, but we ken ye'll need tae get Fairlyden intae order before the winter.'

'Aah, the rebuilding of the farmhouse is a different matter,' William declared with satisfaction. 'Fortunately I insisted on insuring the house and buildings so the work will be paid for. Of course it is a good opportunity to improve it while the repairs are being carried out.'

'I suppose sae,' Ewan nodded. He had seen the man, Crichton-Reid, strutting around measuring all sorts of places. 'I dinna ken about such things as insurance, Mr Fairly, but I'm glad everything will be all right afore the winter, for the Mistress's sake.' He turned then and walked away but William was aware of his disappointment and he knew Sarah would be doubly disappointed.

He had questioned the insurance agent more carefully after Sarah had expressed so many doubts. Mr Blake had been vague, but reassuring. Unknown to William the agent had listened to his plans for expanding Fairly and Guillyman's and envisaged prospects of increasing his own business. But despite his persuasive talk, William Fairly had not taken out any more insurances, not even on his own life, for all he was planning a long journey across the Atlantic. Blake regretted his initial rash statements, particularly since it was he who had instigated the engagement of Crichton-Reid and his flamboyant ideas.

Even William realised that the new bathroom, and the conversion of the bothy into a dining room could scarcely be regarded as repairs; he comforted himself with the knowledge that Fairly and Guillyman's would soon be expanding, especially if his reunion with Lady Elsa Guillyman went according to his expectations. He would need a fine house to entertain the merchants and other business associates then.

The prospect of losing both Ewan and Maggie saddened Sarah but her mind was preoccupied. She had hated saying goodbye to William, not knowing how many weeks it would be before he returned. His absence added to her uneasiness over the two builders who had arrived to begin the repairs to her home. Their presence meant two extra mouths to feed for six days out of every seven, and healthy appetites they had too.

'I would not mind if they worked as well as they eat!' she remarked bitterly to Agnes. 'Mr Crichton-Reid's plans say all the walls have to be built two feet higher, but it seems to take the men all day just dressing two stones!'

'Aye, I doubt Maggie and me will still be biding wi' Nick and Sally when Christmas comes at this rate! Mr Carlyle wad have had the roof on by now if the Master had brought him straight after the fire!'

Sarah nodded, but made no reply. She knew Agnes disapproved of the strangers even more than she did herself.

She was cheered by the prospect of a visit from Alex and her father the Sunday after William sailed for America. They had not been to Fairlyden for a Sunday visit since the fire.

As soon as the meal was over Alex and Billy set out for a walk round the Fairlyden fields.

'They miss each other's company,' Sandy remarked with a smile. 'They'll be exchanging their news, aye and views!'

'Maggie and Thomas have gone to visit Janet, Ewan too. He and Maggie are planning to marry come the spring, Father.'

'Weel, lassie, it's natural. They're a grand pair and they've waited patiently.'

'I hoped William would build another cottage so that they could stay here. I tried to persuade him to let them live in the bothy until we had enough money. After all they have their meals in the house anyway.' She did not add, 'He soon found money to pay his passage to America,' but the thought had niggled at the back of her mind; despite her efforts to dismiss it as unworthy and disloyal, it still persisted.

'We-ell, I suppose they could have managed in the bothy for a few months or so. Ye wad have found Thomas a bed in the house, once it's finished, I suppose?'

'William wouldna even discuss it. He said he had other plans for the bothy and that it had once been part o' the house.'

'Aye, so it was.' Sandy puffed at his pipe until it was going to his satisfaction, but Sarah knew it was his way of choosing his words. 'I wonder if William has any plans for the horses if Ewan's leaving? He's one o' the best young horsemen I've come across.'

'William didna mention the horses! We couldna keep the stallions without Ewan! I never thought of that. I know William willna want to bother with the horses when his time is so taken up with his own business at Fairly and Guillyman's, especially in the spring.'

'Mmm, that's what I thought. Well, lassie, if ye're sure ye canna keep Ewan, I could certainly find him a place at the Mains. Old Jake Brown is going tae live with his daughter o'er at Northbrae at the November term.'

'But Ewan would want a better job than old Jake's!'

'Aye, he would, but I've been thinking it wouldna be such a bad thing tae take the stallions to the Mains along wi' Ewan. It wad leave a lot less work and worry for ye at Fairlyden. Nick wad just hae the working horses tae look after. Anyway I miss my ain horses now I'm living at the Mains, but I didna want tae make too many changes, and I kenned they were in guid hands wi' Ewan. Alex is keen tae breed a stallion himself,' he added with quiet pride. 'Ye could ask William his opinion when ye write. I dinna want him thinking I'm making changes at Fairlyden while he's awa'. If he's agreeable, then ye can mention it tae Ewan and Maggie. They might not want tae come to the Mains.'

'I think they would. Ewan gets on well with Alex, and he cares for the horses as though they were his own. I suppose there would be work for Maggie in the dairy?'

'Oh aye. She might help a bit in the house tae.' He frowned thoughtfully and took another long puff at his pipe. 'Did Agnes tell ye her mother hasna been sae fit lately, lassie?'

'No! I canna imagine Betty Jamieson being ill.'

'Maybe it's just that she's not so young as she was. Anyway I reckon she would welcome a bit of help frae a grand lass like Maggie. I didna want tae grumble tae Mr Sharpe as soon as I moved in, but the twae maids in the hoose are idle beesoms.'

Sarah shoved the swey over the fire to boil the kettle for a quick cup of tea as soon as she heard her two sons returning with Ellen and Sadie at their side. It was almost time for Alex and her father to set out for the Mains again if they were to be back in time for the milking, but she loved to see her children together and so happy and healthy.

'We shall not have any cows to milk at Fairlyden soon!' Sarah remarked as she poured the tea.

'How's that, lassie?' Sandy asked, noting the anxiety in her brown eyes, despite her effort to smile.

'Another cow lost her calf two days ago. That's three in the last few months and all of them at least two months before their time. Nick will have to take this one to market and sell her for whatever we can get. We canna afford to feed them all winter when they've no milk, and not even a calf to rear after all these months of waiting.'

'Two of the cows Father brought had the same trouble last year, didn't they, Mother?' Alex asked, casting an anxious look at his grandfather. Sarah had turned away to fill up the tea pot and Sandy gave him a warning frown. Sarah had enough to worry about while William was away.

'Aye, but we thought it must have been due to rough drovers. We sold them again a month later. Your father lost ten pounds on that little deal.' Sarah returned the tea pot to its stand and covered it with the multicoloured cosy which Ellen had painstakingly knitted from some wool scraps. 'Why did you ask? Do you think we're neglecting our own cows or something, Alex? They get plenty of turnips and hay in the winter, as well as linseed cake and oats; beans too if we have them. We have good grass in the meadow.' She frowned. 'It just seems as though they canna carry their calves until they're ready to be born.

Nature being what it is, they dinna have any milk when there's no calf, so we dinna have any money.'

'Maybe the rest of the cows will be all right,' Sandy said, intending to comfort her.

'I should hope they will!' Sarah declared in alarm. 'We need all the milk we can get, if we're to make enough butter tae keep things going.'

'Aye, I'm sure things will be just fine,' Sandy said reassuringly. 'Now it's time we saddled the ponies and got on our way, young Alex, unless ye're wanting tae come back hame tae be spoiled by your mother . . .?' he teased.

Sarah and Billy smiled at the twinkle in his blue eyes. There was an answering flash in Alex's dark ones.

'Oh Grandfather, ye ken ye couldna dae without me at the Mains!' he responded with a cheery grin, and Sarah felt her spirits rise at their happy repartee.

Despite all her problems and the terrible upheaval caused by the workmen, Sarah had a strange feeling of confidence and well-being as the days passed.

Nevertheless she was considerably shaken when Mr Crichton-Reid called at Fairlyden the day after the walls had been built to his specified height.

'I hope the roof will soon be finished?' Sarah remarked. 'The weather has turned cold and the temporary coverings barely keep out the rain.'

'I shall send men to fix the slates as soon as you have paid me for the builder's work.' Crichton-Reid looked at her through his steel-rimmed spectacles and his eyes glinted coldly as he saw her dismay and watched the colour ebb from her face.

'I canna pay you until all the work is finished! We canna claim the insurance money until the house is wind and water proof again. Mr Blake sent some documents to that effect a few days ago. I read them carefully.'

'If you cannot pay for the builders the roof must wait until your husband returns.' Crichton-Reid sniffed disdainfully.

Sarah stared helplessly at his implacable expression. She had no money to pay. She had nothing to sell either. Even the diamond brooch, left to her by the Reverend Mackenzie, had been sold to help William with the Store. Her father had used all his savings to buy the Mains' stock, and he had done far too much for her and her family already. Sarah remembered how he had vowed never to have another loan from anyone. She could not ask him for help.

Sarah raised her eyes to Mr Crichton-Reid's. She saw contempt in his. An arrogant sneer curved his thin lips. She jerked her head high and looked at the man with pride.

'I shall pay you your money, if that is the way you conduct your business!' The scorn in her flashing eyes would have withered a softer man. She turned and left Crichton-Reid staring after her.

Sarah knew she had to have a roof on the house soon, but there was only one way to get the money. She had to have a loan until the insurance company would pay, and they would not pay until the roof was in place. That night she wrote a letter to William, telling him of her problems, hoping he would return soon, but she knew she had to pay the architect long before William would even receive her letter, much less send a reply.

The next morning Sarah drove to the station and took the train to Dumfries. She was unfamiliar with the bank but a black-coated clerk conducted her courteously into an office and bid her wait for the manager to see her.

'I shall require a letter from the insurance company stating that Fairlyden is indeed insured, Mistress Fairly, and that all payments are up to date.'

Sarah hurried out of the bank and found the offices of the insurance company only a few hundred yards further down the wide street. She obtained the required letter and returned to the bank.

'If our local builder had done the work he would not have taken any payment until the repairs were all completed,' she told the bank manager, half-apologetically, half-resenting the fact that the pompous architect had forced her to beg for money.

'Then what is the name of the builder, Mistress Fairly?' the bank manager asked in surprise.

'A man by the name of Alder under the engagement of Mr Crichton-Reid.'

The banker's eyebrows rose almost into his hair. 'Crichton-Reid? Indeed!' he exclaimed with a note of censure. 'He is not usually engaged on repairs to an ordinary farmhouse.' Sarah flushed.

'My husband arranged it all,' she explained defensively. 'Everything will be all right when he returns to deal with Mr Crichton-Reid himself.'

'Umph! Well I cannot allow you to borrow any more money after this. You must make sure the insurance company pays your claim without delay, as soon as the roof is repaired,' he advised stiffly.

Sarah thanked him but inwardly she was seething with anger. She marched out of the door and down the wide street leading to the river. It was here that Mr Crichton-Reid had his offices. A young clerk asked her business.

'I must see your employer at once!' Sarah summoned the precise pronunciation she had learned as a child from Daniel Munro, the man she had once believed to be her father. He had explained that it was essential to enunciate each word clearly so that her mother could understand the movements of her lips, even though she could not hear. Now she was glad of that early training as the young clerk hastened to show her into the inner sanctum of Mr Crichton-Reid's office.

He was almost lost behind a huge mahogany desk until he rose from his leather armchair. He did not offer Sarah a seat, nor did he extend a hand in greeting. Sarah's dark eyes flashed.

She put the envelope on the desk and as he reached – indeed almost grabbed at it – Sarah kept her hand on top of it and he had to withdraw his grasping fingers.

'I have brought the money for the builders. It is all there. But you will not receive another farthing until the work is finished! Is that clear?'

'My business is with your husband!' the man said coldly, drawing himself to his full height, which was still not as tall as Sarah herself.

'Then perhaps you should wait until he returns to demand payment!' Sarah retorted and took up the envelope.

'No!' He reached out but Sarah clutched the envelope out of reach of his short arms.

'You will have no roof for the winter if you cannot pay for the builders,' he declared venomously.

'Our local builders would have had the roof on by now!' Sarah fumed, 'and I have no doubt they would be pleased to do it still.'

'You cannot do that! Your husband signed a contract! I shall— I shall sue him for all the money whether my men do the job or not . . .'

Sarah frowned. Was he bluffing? Or had William really signed an agreement. 'I am sure the agreement would not allow you to take so long. If the roof is not completed by the end of next week I shall consult my husband's solicitor. Perhaps you will find you have taken so long that you are the one who is in breach of contract!' The man paled and Sarah watched him gobble soundlessly. 'Good day to you!'

She marched out of the room and through the clerk's room until she was outside. Only then did Sarah admit that her knees were shaking. She did not know a solicitor, but the thought that she might consult one had clearly shaken Mr Crichton-Reid out of his usual arrogance.

Sarah was still feeling weak by the time she descended from the train at Muircumwell station so she drove the pony and trap to the Store to see Billy. He made her a cup of tea on the fire in what had once been the Mill House kitchen and she sat at Billy's table and drank it gratefully as she told him of her encounter with the pompous little architect. Billy grinned back at her.

'I'm proud o' ye, Mama. D'ye think he's taken advantage, with Father being away? I dinna think he'll try such tricks again.'

Sarah breathed a sigh of relief when the roof at Fairlyden was completed within the week, but another worry was taking precedence over her problems with the house. She could no longer pretend, even to herself, that old age was responsible for her condition. She was thirty-eight and she was expecting another child. She had to face the truth.

The truth? That was the real problem. Was the child her husband's, or was it Crispin Bradshaw's?

Twenty-nine

William's journey across the Atlantic had been smooth and uneventful. Once ashore it had taken him some time to travel inland but eventually he had found Elsa Guillyman still living in her cousin's house. George Forsythe and his wife had given him a warm welcome, but there was no welcome in the eyes of the woman he had crossed half the world to see.

'He must be mine, Elsa! Before Sir Simon died you told me . . .'

'Hush! William, please . . . at least speak quietly. My cousin thinks we are discussing the business of Fairly and Guillyman's.'

'And aren't we?' William asked almost bitterly. Elsa looked wary, almost afraid.

'We are discussing . . . my . . . son.' Elsa set her lips firmly. 'I have told you, you can have the extra capital for the business at Muircumwell, William, but I do not want you to come here again – ever.'

'I know I am the father of your child,' William insisted stubbornly.

'You already have two sons. Simon always longed for a son.' Elsa's eyes were pleading.

'But I know Simon cannot be the father of your son,' William persisted.

'Supposing, just supposing, he was your son, William.' Elsa leaned towards him, speaking in a harsh strained whisper. 'What could you give him? You have two sons and two daughters already, and a wife! A good wife!'

'Elsa! I . . .'

'You could not give my child your name even!' There was contempt in Elsa's tone and her eyes were bright with anger. 'You are selfish, William Fairly. Do you think you can blackmail me into giving you more . . . and more . . . and more money for your business?'

'No!' William went white with shock. 'I would never . . .'

'Then listen to me! Hear what I have to say! As Simon Guillyman my child will inherit Avary Hall and eleven hundred and fifty acres of good land, as well as many of the cottages and shops in Muircumwell village, including the old mill, if he wants it. I have instructed Mr Bogle to put it in the hands of a good agent until Simon is old enough to decide for himself. There is money in trust until he comes of age. All of that would go to a distant cousin of my late husband. He left me sufficient money of my own to live in comfort. I have decided to make a new life, here in America and my cousin is already looking for a suitable ranch, not too far from civilisation. He will advise me, help me find a manager. I want to make a new life – with my son!'

'You are young, attractive, Elsa! You may marry again . . .?'

'I have no plans to marry, but even if I did, you surely cannot believe I would neglect my own son! Please William, don't stir up unnecessary trouble, for me, or for your wife and children.'

William was silent, staring morosely into space. Then he sighed heavily.

'Perhaps you are right.'

'I am, I know I am.' She smiled then, gratitude shining in her eyes as she clasped his fingers briefly. 'Now, I think my cousin is waiting to show you round the ranch. He has various friends with the kind of machines which interest you, though of course this is the wrong time of year to see them working.

William nodded. 'I would like to stay a while, now that I have come so far. I have a feeling I shall not return to America again, and I may take back some ideas for the Store.'

Nick Jamieson waited until Sarah was alone in the dairy and then followed her inside.

'Hello, Nick,' Sarah's smile slowly faded as she looked at Nick's worried face. 'What's wrong? You look . . . troubled?'

'Aye.' He hesitated, frowning. 'The truth is there's another cow lost her calf.'

'Oh no! Which one this time?' Sarah's face lost its happy glow. 'It's the blue roan, the one Maggie calls Bluey.'

'But she isna due to calve for weeks!'

'I ken. The calf – well ye couldna call it a calf really, it's just a wee slimy thing. I saw it lying behind her, or I wouldna hae kenned. That's what worries me!'

'You mean . . . if it happened in the fields . . .? To some of the other cows?'

'Aye . . . we wadna ken until their milk dries up.'

'You think it's a disease? That disease that's said to spread and affect most of the cows in the byre, don't you Nick?' Sarah muttered tensely.

'I dinna ken, Mistress Fairly. We've no ergot tae speak o' in the pastures, and we dinna mistreat the cows tae make them lose their unborn calves . . .' Nick looked anxiously at Sarah. 'What else could be the cause?'

'I don't know, but it seems it happened even before Christ's time on earth according to the Bible. I read something about it in the paper and the man who was writing thinks it's caused by germs. He reckons it will get less after two or three years . . .'

'But we'll have nae milk and nae calves by then!'

'I know, Nick. We have little enough milk already . . . this writer said we should keep the affected cows in separate places and disinfect the byre with blue stone. He also said it might help to feed a wee bit of carbolic to the cows when they come in for the winter.'

'Carbolic! They wadna take it.'

'It has to be mixed with crowdie and fed every two or three days until after the cows calve, but I dinna think the man was very sure whether it would work or not. We'll have to try something,' Sarah said in desperation. She did not tell Nick that the writer of the article had also said the trouble occurred more often when cattle were bought in from the markets. She was certain now that Alex had been right. The trouble had come with the cows William had brought to Fairlyden. Alex must have read about the germs which could not be seen with the human eyes.

'I didna mean tae worry ye,' Nick said anxiously. 'Is there no word o' the Master coming home?' His eyes travelled involuntarily over her thickening waist, before he hastily averted his gaze.

Sarah shook her head. William had not mentioned when he expected to return in either of his letters, nor had he mentioned her problems with Mr Crichton-Reid and his demands for money.

Sarah glimpsed the haggard look on Nick's lean face as he turned to leave. She frowned. 'What else is worrying you, Nick?'

'Nothing!' he said quickly, too quickly. Sarah eyed him keenly.

'Are you sure? I've thought you were a bit . . . tense and tired lately, even before this morning's trouble with Bluey. Is it too much worry for you with my father being at the Mains, and Master Fairly in America?'

'Oh, it's nothing tae dae wi' the farm!' Nick exclaimed.

'Is it your mother, Nick? I know she hasna been herself lately.'

'Mother isna well at all, but it's Sally I'm worried about . . .'

'Aah! I think I can guess what's wrong, Nick. Dinna worry, I'll talk to Sally myself. In fact I'll go down to the cottage as soon as I'm finished in here. It will be better if she's alone.'

'Aye . . . aye, it wad, I think.' Nick's expression was a strange mixture of relief, puzzlement and excitement.

About half an hour later Sarah knocked at Sally's cottage. Sally opened the door herself and her colour ebbed and flowed at the sight of Sarah.

'Mistress Fairly! Please, come in . . .' She led the way into the neat little kitchen. 'There's nothing wrong wi' Nick, is there?'

'No. Nick's fine, except that he's worried about you, Sally. I should have guessed it must be too much for you having Maggie and Agnes staying with you for so long. You've little enough room. I'm pleased to tell you the bedrooms are almost finished so Agnes and Maggie can move back . . . not that they'll have such a big room as they had before. Mr Crichton-Reid instructed the builders to knock a door in the wall frae the main landing and they've used half of the maids' room to make a new bathing room – if it ever gets finished! I'm sorry it's been such a burden to you. I hope it hasna caused a quarrel between you and Nick?'

'I dinna ken what ye mean, Mistress . . .?' Sally looked genuinely bewildered. 'Nick and me, we never quarrel . . . and I've fair enjoyed having company in the hoose, especially Maggie's.'

'Oh . . .' Sarah frowned. 'But why is Nick worried then?'

Sally went very pale, but she indicated that Sarah should take a seat. She pulled out a chair and leaned her elbows on the table, covering her cheeks with her palms.

'What is it, Sally?' Sarah asked gently and Sally's eyes filled with tears.

'Ye ken how much we wanted a bairn . . .' she began. 'Now I th-think I'm too old . . . ye ken what I mean, Mistress Fairly . . .? I-I havena had a sign for nine weeks now. Then . . . these past three weeks I've been sae sick . . . Nick has got it intae his head that I might be carrying a babe – after all these years! He'll be that disappointed when he kens he's wrong. . .'

'Will he, Sally? Are you sure it's not a baby? I mean you're never sick usually, are you?' Sarah watched as hope dawned in Sally's eyes.

'D'ye really think it's possible?' she asked breathlessly. 'Nick said ye wad ken about such things, b-but I thought I-I was just getting old . . .' She blushed furiously and looked at Sarah, then away again.

'And Nick reminded you that you're at least three years younger than I am, and I'm not too old to bear a child? Is that it, Sally?' Sarah asked with wry kindness.

Sally nodded. 'Aye,' she whispered. 'It's different for you though. Ye've had bairns before . . . Nick's so set on it being a bairn. I'm feart I shall let him down again . . .'

'Well I'm no expert, Sally. Would you like me to ask Doctor Kerr to call?'

'No!' Sally gasped and shrank into her chair. 'No, no! I dinna want any other man but Nick near me!'

'All right, dinna get upset. Do you feel ill then?'

'No. In fact I feel— I feel as though I hae a wee bubble o' happiness inside me, except when I get up in the mornings. Then I'm awful sick . . .'

Sarah smiled widely. 'It sounds to me as though it's a baby then, Sally. You'll know for certain in another month when your gown gets tight and you have to let the waist seams out!'

'Och, I wadna mind that, if ye really think it's possible, Mistress Fairly!' Sally's eyes were glowing with hope.

'I think we should celebrate with a cup of tea,' Sarah declared. 'I seem to have a craving for tea . . .'

'I'll make it right away,' Sally offered. 'But that's one thing I canna fancy these days . . .'

'Aah!' Sarah smiled. 'Let me see, Sally, nine weeks you said, so that would mean your baby would be born in the middle of June?'

'Oh, Mistress Fairly, I dae hope ye're right!' Sally said fervently. 'It's what Nick and me want more than anything in the world!'

* * *

Later that evening Sarah brought out her quill and ink and finished the letter she had started to William.

You asked about the improvements. I'm sorry to tell you they are not finished. The four bedrooms look much bigger now and each one has a fine new fireplace, which Mr Crichton-Reid describes as 'Adam style'. Billy says they look as though they have a row of square teeth beneath the mantelshelf. The windows are much bigger too and we get an even better view of the Solway Firth from the front. The doors are made of boards in a sort of yellowish pine but they fit very well and the new staircase is the same wood and nicely carved.

The slaters have made a good roof, but they insisted on having all new slates and they took a lot of carting up to Fairlyden so that is extra expense. The little stone porch over the front door will be very good for keeping out the draughts when winter winds come howling at the door.

Mr Crichton-Reid said you ordered the bathing room and a dining room. All sorts of queer-looking objects have been delivered and dumped upstairs. Now Mr Crichton-Reid says I must pay all that we owe before they can be installed. I told him you would settle the rest of his account when you return. I am so very worried, William, though I do not like to keep troubling you when you are so far away. I do wish you were home again with us. I cannot deal with strangers as well as I can with Iain McKie and John Carlyle. I know they would charge a fair price.

I have already paid Mr Crichton-Reid for the builders, as I told you, but now he is demanding far more money for the roof and the joiner's work, and for what he calls his 'professional fees'. I think he means taking a train ride to the country once a week, and hiring a pony and trap to bring him from the station up to Fairlyden. It is quite preposterous, and I am afraid I told him so. He is threatening to sue us for the rest of the money.

The insurance agent agreed to pay as soon as the roof was finished and he has kept his word, but it is such a small amount it does not even cover the loan from the bank which I had to pay for building up the walls. Mr Blake says insurance can only pay for repairs and he accused us of wanting to build a small mansion with the pennies other poor people pay to his company!

Billy says the six oil engines have arrived at Fairly and Guillyman's Store, and also the account for payment of them. We cannot fix one up here until the water tank is in place, and that will never be, unless we can find enough money to pay Mr Crichton-Reid.

Tomorrow Agnes is moving back into her room above the kitchen but she must now climb a small step ladder to go to bed and the room is only big enough for her. Maggie is staying with Sally until her marriage to Ewan next May. Also you will be surprised to hear that Nick and Sally are expecting a child at last. Sally is so slender and her bones are so finely made that she looks almost too delicate for such rigours, but they are both so very happy.

We all hoped you would be home for Christmas, William, but it will be almost here by the time this reaches you so I have decided it is time to tell you my own news. I would have liked to tell you in person. We are to have another child in the spring.

Sarah stopped and chewed her thumbnail. She was hurt and angry with William for staying away so long and leaving her to deal with the pompous Mr Crichton-Reid and his men. So far she had kept a tight rein on her feelings when she penned her weekly letter. The last time she had felt hurt by William's neglect she had turned to Crispin Bradshaw for comfort – comfort which he had been more than willing to give – but her own weakness appalled Sarah whenever she thought of the night she had spent at the Tower House. Even now she could scarcely believe the way she had responded to Crispin Bradshaw's gentleness, and his loving. The memory filled her with dismay. She realised how wise Crispin had been to go away, out of reach, but recently she had harboured a fear that her child might resemble Crispin Bradshaw. It was for this reason that she had not broken the news to her husband earlier. Neither had she told Beatrice. There was always a chance that she might mention the subject to Mr Bradshaw, and he in turn might mention her condition in one of his letters to Crispin. A guilty conscience was not an easy burden for a person of Sarah's integrity. She dipped the quill in the ink and continued her letter, avoiding all further mention of her unborn child.

Mr Sharpe died in his sleep ten days ago. My father had not expected him to die so soon and he is greatly saddened, though he is pleased the old man's last months were free from worry and his end was very peaceful. Father has an appointment with Captain Fothergill next week to discuss the transfer of the tenancy. Unfortunately Alex is still too young to be considered as a joint tenant, though the Captain had told Mr Sharpe that he thinks very highly of him.

Billy has saved every farthing he could earn to buy one of those machines called a bicycle. He even sold his pony, which was getting rather small anyway. He got the bicycle last week. It has rubber wheels with air inside. He only had it four days. He sold it to a fisherman and made a profit of one shilling and elevenpence. He is going to buy another and he wishes he had enough money to buy more to sell at the Store. He says even some of the ladies are riding them.

I told Billy about the ranchers making fences with barbed wire. He thinks it would hurt the cattle and the horses when they jump over while hunting the foxes. Some of the farmers have been asking if he can obtain a fertiliser called basic slag. They say it contains phosphorous as well as lime and that it encourages wild white clover to grow in the meadows. Billy tells me the slag is made when iron ore is smelted and lime is added to the molten ore. He is very knowledgeable despite his tender years, but I fear the responsibility will soon be too much for him. He seems worried because there is very little money in the Store's bank account. He also says Fred Clark has not taken many orders for grass or turnip seeds in readiness for the spring sowings. Most of the customers say they are waiting until they see you in person. Perhaps Fred is better as a storeman than a salesman? I have instructed Billy not to order anything else until you return. I am so worried about the money we owe.

Do please write soon. Tell us what we ought to do, dearest William. I long for your return. We all miss you.

Your loving wife,

Sarah.

Sarah knew William would not receive her letter until nearly Christmas for he had explained that it took at least two weeks to cross the ocean and then it had to be taken overland. So she was delighted when she received a reply at the end of the second week in January.

'Your father says he has written this as soon as he received my letter,' she told Billy. 'He has sent you instructions for the running of the Store. You are to order as much basic slag as you think the farmers will buy, and perhaps a few tons to spare, for those who wait to watch their neighbours before they order their own. Also you must order the same amount of turnip and barley seed as last year, from the same merchants. You are to do that at once, but he will order the grass seed himself when he returns . . .'

'When will that be? How are we tae pay for the orders? Does Father mention the bicycles?'

Sarah looked into her younger son's eager face. 'He says he will discuss the bicycles with you as soon as he returns as he has some new ideas of his own.' Sarah frowned. 'But he does not mention payment of the orders, nor the money we owe for the repairs to the house,' she added anxiously. 'He promises to come home as soon as he can get a passage on a ship, but he says much depends on the winter weather. I do hope he has enough money to pay for it. Maybe that is why the bank account for the Store is so low . . . Aah, he has added a postscript. He hopes to be home by February.'

'Hoorah!' Billy yelled, grinning from ear to ear.

'You sound more like a schoolboy than the man in charge of Fairly and Guillyman's Store!' Sarah teased suddenly.

'Aye, Mama, but ye look happier tae!' Billy retorted and Sarah smiled. 'You have just the same twinkle in your black eyes as your father, especially when he was a young man,' she added with a reminiscent sigh.

'Aah weel, it willna be long afore we see him again now. I'll awa' and tell Ellen and Sadie. I expect we'll see Grandfather and Alex at church on Sunday . . .'

'Yes indeed. We must get all the bedrooms into proper order before he comes. I do wish we could have had some of that patterned wallpaper for the front parlour, but it's no good wishing, not with yon Mr Crichton-Reid still demanding so much money!'

'Never mind, Mama, I'll bring ye some o' that coloured stuff tae distemper them when I gang tae Annan again on the train. Ye can get pink and green and blue . . . What wad ye like?'

'Pink for the bedrooms then, Billy. I think that would be nice. Agnes and Maggie should have them all finished by the time your father arrives. The weather is so mild it seems like springtime instead of January. I saw some snowdrops under the old walnut tree this morning.' Sarah sighed softly. 'I remember when your grandfather buried our wee dog there. Buff her name was. I planted the bulbs then . . .' Sarah looked round but Billy had already gone to tell his sisters the good news. He must have missed his father as much as she had herself.

Sarah was concerned about Sally Jamieson's health. There were many days when the morning sickness seemed to persist all day and even the patches of delicate colour which had always highlighted Sally's fine features seemed to fade.

'I think you should rest, Sally,' Sarah said one morning when Sally had made her third quick exit from the milking. 'You could take a spell away frae the milking, if it would help you.' Relief shone in Sally's blue eyes, but only for a moment.

'I canna dae that, Mistress Fairly! Ye're the one who should be resting.'

'Oh, Sally, I enjoy milking! It is a rest to me, sitting on my wee stool with my head against the warm flank of a cow. But then I've never been plagued with the sickness. Anyway it's a good time for you to take a rest from the milking. We've ten cows less now. And another two or three are almost dry,' Sarah added with an unconscious frown.

'Aye, Nick said there was a lot less butter tae take tae the market this winter. I ken he's worried tae. We— we understand what it means tae ye . . . and tae Fairlyden . . .' Sally murmured in her quiet voice.

Sarah smiled. 'Thank you Sally, I know you do, but the main thing is to take care of yourself and that precious babe. So take a rest frae the milking for a while, eh? Agnes and Maggie willna mind. They're both as pleased as I am about the bairn, and Ellen will milk a couple of cows in the afternoons when she comes frae school. She's a good wee milker.'

Sarah's thoughts were not so happy however as she absently watched the milk frothing into the pail. They could not afford to replace Ewan. Nick and Thomas would have to manage when Ewan and Maggie left at the May term. There were ten less cows and that meant ten fewer calves to rear both this year and next, and maybe much longer than that until they had enough replacement cows. More cows might become affected yet.

But it could take years to breed enough calves to replace the cows we have had to sell, Sarah pondered silently, and some of them were our best milkers too. Maybe we shall be able to hire some of the travelling Irish labourers for the turnip hoeing and the hay, her thoughts ran on anxiously. Then her heart gave a little skip of joy and relief. William would soon be home now. He would be sure to have some solution to the problems.

Thirty

Sarah had never seen a telegraph wire before and she accepted the yellow envelope wonderingly from Mr Braid's hand.

'Whatever can it be?' she muttered.

Agnes was in the dairy behind her, washing the pails they had just used at the milking. She was surprised to see the postmaster standing at the dairy door so early in the morning.

'Maybe it's frae the Master!' she exclaimed excitedly. 'Surely his ship hasna been delayed . . .?'

But as Sarah bent her head to tear open the envelope Agnes met Jim Braid's eyes and he gave an almost imperceptible shake of his greying head and his eyes were grave. Agnes's heart gave an unfamiliar bump and she moved towards her mistress instinctively, almost protectively.

Sarah scanned the white strips of paper stuck to the thin yellow sheet. The printed letters seemed to jump in front of her eyes.

'No . . .' she whispered. 'No, no, no!'

Ellen and Sadie came running across the yard. It was a Saturday morning and they had seen Mr Braid, the postmaster, coming up the track while they were feeding the hens.

'Is there a letter frae Papa?' Ellen asked eagerly. Mr Braid turned to face her and Ellen, ever sensitive to atmosphere, saw the anxiety in his blue eyes.

'Could ye put the kettle on, lassie? I could dae wi' a cup o' tea afore I walk all the way back tae Muircumwell . . .'

'Why, yes, of course . . .' Ellen looked puzzled. Mr Braid never asked for tea. He was too polite. Mama's face was so very white, even her lips seemed to have lost their bright colour. 'Come on, Sadie,' she added firmly, knowing they would hear whatever there was to hear in due course and sensing already that the news would not be good.

'Yes,' Sarah said hoarsely. 'We must make a cup of tea for Mr Braid.' She looked at the postman's anxious face but her eyes were stunned.

'Are ye . . . are ye all right, Mistress Sarah?' Agnes asked dubiously.

'It— it canna be true!' Sarah muttered. 'There's been a mistake . . .?' She looked pleadingly at the postmaster. He shook his head, twisting his cap in his hands, distressed that he had brought bad news.

'I think ye should sit down, Mistress. The bairns are making ye a cup o' tea.'

'They say he's dead, Agnes!' Sarah said numbly, almost like a bewildered child as she turned to the woman who had been her most loyal maid, aye and companion, since they were young girls.

'Whae's dead?' Agnes gasped fearfully.

'It's Master Fairly,' Jim Braid replied awkwardly. 'He— he died on board ship. I think we should gang intae the kitchen, have a seat maybe . . .? The shock . . .' He nodded at Sarah.

Agnes read his thoughts. Such a shock was bad for any woman, but especially for a woman in the Mistress's condition. Agnes took Sarah's arm and guided her through the scullery and into the kitchen. Jim Braid followed, wanting to help, yet afraid to touch Sarah. Her face was chalky white, but it was so still . . . so controlled. He knew the full implication of the news had not yet sunk in.

Sarah sat down obediently as the postmaster drew out a chair.

'The kettle's boiling,' Ellen said. 'Shall I make tea?'

'I'll make it, lassie,' Agnes said quietly. 'Maybe ye wad take Sadie tae feed the hens . . .?'

'We've fed them!' Sadie protested in her usual complaining whine.

Agnes glanced at her sharply, then back to Sarah, sitting so erectly at the table. Ellen followed her eyes. Mama looks like a marble statue, she thought and her young heart was filled with a nameless fear.

'Come on Sadie . . . Dinna argue!' she hissed and pulled her young sister protestingly out of the house.

'I'll no' stay for any tea, Agnes,' Jim Braid said, 'but if there's anything I can dae . . . and Mary said the same . . . anything at all, Mistress Fairly . . .?' Sarah's unnatural silence made him uneasy. She looked up at him but her dark eyes were blank. He frowned. 'Wad ye like me tae go tae the Mains . . .? Tell your father maybe . . .?' Sarah just stared at him dumbly, then she turned to Agnes and her voice shook.

'Buried at sea!' She smoothed out the crumbled telegram. 'They've put him in the ocean, Agnes. I'll never see him again! Never! They shouldna have done it! They . . .'

'There now! Drink this tea, Miss Sarah!' Agnes spoke as though her mistress was a child again.

'Why did they do it? Why?' Sarah shuddered. 'So cold! So cruel! We'll never see him again! It canna be true . . .' she whispered hoarsely. 'See! It says "More news to follow". It must be a mistake! It m-must be!'

Jim Baird shook his head anxiously.

'They have tae dae it that way, Mistress Fairly. Ye ken that. They couldna keep . . . they couldna wait . . . I-I . . .' He frowned and looked helplessly at Agnes. 'I'll gang tae the Mains . . .'

Agnes accompanied him to the door.

'Dinna forget ma sister says she'll help, if there's aught . . .'

Agnes nodded.

Sandy and Alex rode up to Fairlyden soon after midday, bringing Billy with them from the Store. Sarah was still sitting in her chair beside the table, as though waiting for someone. She had neither spoken nor eaten since Jim Braid left.

'Aah, Sarah lassie!' Sandy muttered gruffly. 'It's bad news ye've had this day.'

'Father? This isna Sunday . . .'

Sandy frowned and turned aside. Alex gazed at his mother anxiously and moved to her side.

'Dinna worry, Mother. I'll look after ye . . .' But Sarah made no response, even to Alex, and he raised his troubled gaze to his grandfather. Billy stared from one to the other, his brown eyes dark with stormy protest.

Sandy spoke softly to Agnes. 'I called in at Doctor Kerr's. He recommends a warm bed wi' a good hot drink o' milk, if she's still in a state o' shock by—'

'I'm not going to bed in the middle of the day!' Sarah spoke up almost angrily, surprising both Sandy and Agnes. 'I have far too many things to do. Have you forgotten it's the Sabbath tomorrow, Agnes?' she demanded sternly.

Agnes stared at her in hurt surprise, but Sandy patted her shoulder.

'Just dae whatever she says, Agnes,' he murmured softly. 'She's hiding frae the truth just now, but she'll need us badly when it hits her . . . Aye, she'll need us!' He turned to Alex.

'Have a bite tae eat, laddie. Then ye must go back tae the Mains. There's nothing ye can dae here today. I'll stay tonight . . .'

'But, Grandfather, I must look after Mother now! It's my duty as her elder son.'

Sandy shook his head sadly.

'We canna both stay. Ye ken as well as I dae what's tae be done at the Mains on a winter's day. And I need tae stay . . . Your mother is ma ain bairn, Alex. Ye'll hae plenty o' time tae comfort her when I'm gone, laddie, and right now I'm worried about her . . . It may be days afore she accepts the truth. It's aye worse when there's naebody tae be seen.'

Alex winced.

'Maybe ye'd call in at the manse. The Reverend Mace will need tae arrange a service. It might have helped if he'd been more like the Reverend Mackenzie. He wad hae kenned what tae dae tae comfort her.'

It was late in the evening when a pony and trap drove up the track from Strathtod. Sandy saw the flickering lantern when he was returning from the closet at the bottom of the garden. As it drew nearer he recognised the driver of the trap as the station master. His passenger was a young man of about twenty. He jumped out and cast a quick glance around the shadowy farmsteading before his eyes travelled slowly over the house.

Sandy opened the door and stood in its shelter for it was a cold night even for the end of February. He waited for the stranger to alight and state his business. Behind him Sandy realised the house was unnaturally silent. All day everyone had spoken in fearful whispers, if they spoke at all. Sarah's strange calm troubled him. How much longer could she hide from the truth, and what would it do to her when it finally penetrated? How long could she go without eating or sleeping, sitting in her chair like a petrified statuette?

'This is Fairlyden, I guess?' the young man asked diffidently.

'It is.' Sandy knew he sounded tense and strained but he could not welcome a stranger into the house at such a time.

'My name is Brad Leishman, from Massachusetts in the United States of America.'

'I see.' Sandy stared at the young man, his mind in a whirl. Then he collected himself and held out his hand. 'I am Alexander Logan. I am afraid this . . .'

Brad Leishman held up his hand. 'I understand, Mr Logan. It must be a mighty bad time for you, but I made a promise. I, er . . . would you know Mrs Fairly?'

'I am her . . .' Sandy hesitated. 'I am her father,' he declared firmly.

'Aah,' the young man looked relieved. 'Then I am pleased to meet you, Sir. I was with Mr William Fairly when he died.'

'Were ye now?' Sandy's surprise was evident.

'I was, and I promised that I would call upon Mrs Fairly. Indeed I have also brought his baggage. There it is in the trap. Shall I bring it in . . .?'

'Well!' Sandy was lost for words. 'I-I . . . Come awa' in! Ye'll need tae excuse such a poor welcome. My daughter hasna accepted the news yet. Maybe if ye talk tae her . . .?' Sandy looked uncertainly at the young man in the dim light from the trap's lantern. He seemed far too young for such a mission. 'I'll ask Agnes tae prepare a room for ye. Come, let me help ye with your boxes. Young McAllister will be wanting hame tae the fireside.'

'But I do not wish to be a nuisance! Surely there is an inn, or some other place to stay?'

'The least we can do is give ye a bed for tonight,' Sandy declared firmly. 'But I'm afraid it is a sad house and ye may not wish tae bide any longer.'

'Thank you. I shall be grateful, for it is getting late and I am a stranger in a strange land. Also the day has been a long one. I travelled by boat from Liverpool to Annan. I was fortunate to get a train to Strathtod.'

Sandy helped him carry the bags and boxes into the long passage and bid the station master's son good night.

'Come this way. It is the kitchen but it is warm, and there is no fire in the parlour.' Sandy eyed the young man steadily in the brighter light from the large oil lamp which hung from a hook in the centre beam of the ceiling. He was young, not more than twenty, Sandy guessed, but there was a sincerity in his blue-grey eyes and in his voice and manner. Agnes and Maggie were hovering at the door leading to the scullery, uncertain whether their services would be needed. Ellen and Sadie stared round-eyed and apprehensive from their places on the fender stool beside the fire.

'Sarah, we have a visitor,' Sandy said gently. 'This is Mr Leishman, Brad Leishman.' Sarah raised her head but her white face remained calm and impassive. Her eyes were twin pools of darkness, neither welcoming nor rejecting. 'He has travelled from America.'

'Good evening, Mr Leishman.' Sarah's voice was polite, but without expression.

'I-I'm sorry,' Sandy frowned. 'My daughter is still shocked by the news which came this morning.

'I understand,' Brad Leishman sympathised. 'The captain said he had wired a message. I guess that bit of paper with a few short words can tear out a heart in the most cruel way possible. That is why I—I wanted to come.'

'Aye, and I'm glad ye have, laddie!' Sandy said fervently. 'For something is needed, but first ye must eat and refresh yourself. Agnes, can ye make Mr Leishman a bite tae eat, maybe some soup if ye have any, for it's a cold night and he's had a long journey.'

'Aye, Mr Logan. There's soup and boiled bacon and bannock but we havena made fresh oatcakes or . . .'

'That sounds delicious . . . Agnes. What a fine Scottish name.' Brad Leishman smiled, and Agnes's wary heart was captured.

'Maggie, maybe ye could make up a bed for Mr Leishman, then ye can go tae Sally's. If Mistress Fairly needs anything I'll send for ye. Billy, can ye help with this chest, laddie? Mr Leishman, this is my grandson, Billy Fairly.'

'I'm real pleased to meet you, Billy,' Brad said earnestly as he shook Billy's hand firmly. 'Your father spoke about you.'

'Ye ken ma father?' Billy asked eagerly.

Even Sarah's dark eyes flickered and fixed intently on the young American's face.

'I shared a cabin with him on the ship. There were three of us, and an empty bunk. When your father became sick, the, er, the other passenger moved to another cabin. He just couldn't stand illness I guess . . .'

'Wh-what happened . . .?' Billy asked fearfully.

'I think ye should help Mr Leishman take his trunk upstairs and let him have a bite tae eat afore ye start asking questions,' Sandy reproved gently. He felt as though he had never been away from Fairlyden the way he was taking charge again, but someone had to see to things.

When Brad Leishman had eaten and Agnes and Maggie had left the kitchen Sandy allowed the girls to stay. He felt they too needed to know what had happened to their father and he knew instinctively that he could trust Brad to be tactful in his account. The young American reminded him a little of the Reverend Mackenzie in his manner and the way he had of looking a man in the eye and not shirking an unpleasant task.

'We had been at sea about four days when Mr Fairly became sick. The sea was not rough and he said he had travelled across the Atlantic, and back, already. He was a good sailor, so at first we did not worry too much . . .'

Sarah murmured a protest.

'You prefer not to hear, Mrs Fairly?' Brad asked with concern.

'Yes, yes . . .' Sarah whispered through white lips, and held out her hands across the table. Brad Leishman clasped them firmly in his and held them, as though trying to give Sarah strength and courage.

'Your husband never complained, but the sickness got worse. He grew very weak. Even a drink of water seemed to make him worse. There was a physician on board and the Captain sent him to our cabin. I did not want to leave him alone.' He frowned, remembering the harrowing scene in the cramped little cabin. 'He was very patient . . . very kind . . . the doctor. Believe me, Mrs Fairly, he tried everything he could to make your husband well again. But he became violently sick. The doctor said his heart was already weakened. Your husband told him he had recovered once from cholera and nothing could be as bad as that. He was determined to recover. But he became very hot. We could not cool him. I-I think he knew near the end that he was . . . dying.'

'No . . .' Sarah protested faintly.

'He was very brave, Mrs Fairly. He asked if I would come to you, to bring his gifts to you. Later his mind began to wander. The physician said it was the heat. He kept calling for Sarah . . . Sarah. Then suddenly, one night, his mind became perfectly clear. I thought he was getting better, although he was too weak to lift his head from the pillow. He talked of his family . . .' Brad Leishman looked towards the fireplace where Ellen sat with a comforting arm around Sadie's trembling shoulders. 'He told me he had a daughter called Ellen who would make a fine nurse one day. He talked of his sons too . . . but most of all he talked about the woman he loved . . . His thoughts moved back to his youth. The name that lingered on his lips was Sarah Munro . . . You would have been proud and happy to see the smile on his face, Mrs Fairly. You must remember, always, it was the thought of you which helped him to forget his illness . . . which helped him to die a happy man . . .'

'Oh no!' Sarah protested in a hoarse whisper, 'I wasna worthy of him . . . I— I . . .' She began to sob quietly, withdrawing her hands from Brad Leishman's gentle clasp and hiding her face, as though ashamed of her tears.

'It's all right, lassie . . . It's all right . . .' Sandy murmured soothingly, coming round the table to put his arm around her as though she were a child again. 'I think ye should go tae bed now. Ye've had a long day and kept your sorrow too long locked in your heart. Come on now, I'll help ye upstairs and bring ye a hot drink o' milk.'

'I'll make the drink, Grandfather,' Ellen offered quietly. 'I ken how, wi' milk and honey.'

'All right lassie, and then maybe ye'll get Sadie awa' tae bed, eh?'

Ellen nodded and smiled her child's sad smile.

Sandy helped Sarah to her feet. As she pushed her chair from the table and stood up, Brad Leishman saw her properly for the first time. He gasped audibly when he realised she was heavy with child.

'Dear God, help her!' he muttered under his breath as he watched her straighten and walk proudly to the stairs, holding back her tears with an iron will.

Alone at last in the darkness of her room, alone in the big bed she had shared with William, Sarah let the hot tears fall. Her heart had been frozen when she first read the telegram, her mind numbed. Now the full impact of William's death hit her.

'He's not coming back to me! Not now. Not ever . . . Dear God, forgive me!' Sarah moaned and hid her face in her hands while the tears of guilt and remorse trickled between her fingers.

'I didna mean to be angry . . . Oh, William forgive me . . .' she sobbed quietly. Later, when there seemed to be no more tears left in her, Sarah thought of Brad Leishman's story. Would William have fallen sick if he had waited for another ship? Was his death a punishment for her faithlessness? For her complaints about the house, her anxiety over the demands of Mr Crichton-Reid?

So Sarah tormented herself, blaming herself for William's death and grieving for the dark-eyed laughing young man she had married. She forgot the man he had become, the man who could neglect her and his children whenever he became obsessed with his own plans.

It was very dark when Sarah awoke. She was trembling violently, shaken by a terrible dream in which she had been tossed relentlessly in a cold and cruel sea. She saw William reaching out a hand for help and although she stretched her fingers out to him she could not clasp his; he sank away from her . . . away into the cold deep depths of the ocean. She called his name . . . she heard him answer 'Sar-aah, Sar-aah', but she could not see him . . . The sweat was trickling down her temples, dampening her hair, running between her breasts and down her back . . . She lay for a moment breathing hard as though she had been running, yet knowing it was only the effects of her nightmare. Gradually she grew calmer and her breathing eased. She lay on her back in the darkness. The pain took her by surprise. She caught her breath, almost overwhelmed by its intensity.

Then it eased and her breathing slowly returned to normal, but Sarah could not relax her tense muscles. She dreaded the pain coming again. The baby was not due for another month but she had experienced four labours already and she knew. When the pain came again Sarah was barely aware that it was her own voice which moaned in agony, but when it eased she became aware of Ellen groping her way through the darkness to her bedside.

'Mama, are ye . . . all right?' she asked timidly.

'Aah, Ellen!' Sarah strove for control. She brushed the damp hair back from her forehead. 'Can you put a match to the candle, lassie? It's on the wee table. Be careful . . .' But Ellen was a capable child and her little hands were neat and quick. The candle flared almost immediately and Ellen lifted it and peered anxiously at her mother's white, sweating face.

'Is it . . . is it the baby, Mama?' Sarah's eyes widened in astonishment, then she smiled wryly. Ellen had seen too many baby pigs born, and she was too intelligent not to understand . . .

'Aye, I think it is, lassie.'

'Ye will let me help ye nurse the baby, won't ye, Mama?' Ellen asked, her warm smile illuminating her young face.

'Aye. You're a grand bairn . . . I'll be glad of your help. Can you go to Agnes's room? Bring her here. You'll need the candle . . . but be careful.'

'I will, Mama.' Ellen smiled. 'I'm not like Meg ye ken.'

Sarah lay watching the shadows shoot up the wall and over the ceiling, before they disappeared as Ellen descended the stairs to the kitchen. The pain came again, not quite so severe this time. She gripped the mattress and screwed her eyes tightly shut as though she could keep it at bay. Her only thought now was for the safe delivery of the child.

Sandy had slept little in the box bed at Fairlyden and he saw the light of Ellen's candle approaching, then illuminating the kitchen. 'What's wrong, lassie?'

'It's Mama's baby,' Ellen said calmly. Sandy gasped at her childish assurance. 'I've tae waken Agnes.' She proceeded on her way to the short step ladder on the opposite side of the kitchen.

Sandy rose at once and pulled on his breeches. He lit the lamp and ascended the stairs to Sarah's room, just as the pain was receding.

'Shall I send Billy for Mistress Fletcher?' he asked urgently.

'Aye. He'll need the trap. Bring her back . . . Tell him . . . not to waste any time . . .'

While Billy dressed hastily, Sandy harnessed the pony and backed it into the little trap, and lit the lantern. He shivered in the cold morning air. It was the first day of March. Billy appeared, hastily fastening the buttons of his thick tweed jacket and pulling on his cap. His young face looked tired and pale in the flickering light of the lantern.

'Maybe ye'd best knock on Doctor Kerr's door tae, laddie,' Sandy advised anxiously. 'I think he'll be half expecting ye. The shock may have brought on the birth a mite early. He'll ken if he ought tae come or no'.'

Brad Leishman heard the noises and guessed that something was amiss. He lit his candle and washed the sleep from his eyes with cold water from the ewer, then he dressed and descended to the kitchen. Sandy had already stirred the fire into life and filled the kettle as well as a big black pot which Sarah usually used for cooking.

'Can I help?' Brad asked in his slow drawl. Sandy turned, his face lined and drawn and tired. He's aged ten years during the night! Brad thought with dismay.

'It's the shock, I expect. The bairn's coming.'

'I see.' Brad looked troubled. 'I must apologise if I am responsible.'

'No, laddie, it was the news.'

'I guess you would like me to leave the house now though . . . with this new trouble . . .?

'Ye canna leave yet. It's barely four in the morning and still dark. Besides ye'll need tae eat afore ye leave.'

'What can I do to help then? I assisted at two births on the ship . . .'

'Ye did?' Sandy looked in amazement. He was worried in case Billy did not bring the midwife in time. It was four miles to Muircumwell and four miles back, and it was dark.

Brad Leishman cursed himself for a fool.

'I am not a doctor!' he insisted hurriedly. 'At least not yet. As a matter of fact I had intended to be a preacher, until I met Mr Fairly. He studied to be . . . a minister? I guess that's what you call a man of God in Scotland?'

'Aye,' Sandy nodded. 'I hope William didna try tae persuade ye against the calling?' he ventured. 'Last night ye reminded me o' the best minister I ever knew.'

'No, Mr Fairly told me only that God's work was not for him. He also said I had what he called "the right way of it". I want to help people.'

'Then surely it would be a worthy calling?' Sandy murmured as he pulled the swey off the fire and hooked on the large pot.

'Not as worthy as healing the sick. I felt so . . . so helpless as I watched Mr Fairly grow weaker and weaker. There was nothing . . . nothing I could do to help! Don't you see, Mr Logan. I could pray! I could read my bible . . . but I had no knowledge of healing to assist my prayers . . . to carry out God's work to the full!'

'Aye, laddie,' Sandy looked at Brad Leishman's earnest face and he felt old and tired. 'Ye're young, and ye want tae make the world a better place, eh?' he sighed.

'Yes. I guess so. Is that so bad?'

'No. Tell me about the babes on the ship?'

The glow died in Brad Leishman's eyes. 'They died,' he admitted reluctantly. 'But they were premature . . .' he added quickly as Sandy's shoulders sagged visibly. 'The mothers survived. Their husbands were grateful for that.'

'Aye, they wad be,' Sandy muttered with feeling.

'My grandfather hoped I would attend a Scottish university. Now I hope to study at the University of Edinburgh. Doctor McIntyre has given me a letter to a professor there. I hope I shall become a doctor one day. We had many interesting discussions. Hygiene . . . cleanliness . . . He said they were the simple remedies that too many doctors forgot.'

He broke off at the sound of Agnes clattering hurriedly down the stairs. Her face was white and her eyes wide with panic.

'I've kindled the fire and put the clothes tae air. Now the babe's coming! Mistress Fletcher'll never be here in time!' she wailed. 'Oh God preserve us! I dinna ken what I ought tae dae next . . . and that lassie's in there! It isna right! There she sits as calm as an auld woman . . . holding her mother's hand!'

'Ye must stay with her, Agnes!' Sandy said in alarm. 'Dae ye want hot water? I have the kettle and the pot boiling.'

Agnes shuddered. 'What'll I dae with it?'

'Why, wash your hands of course! Indeed, scrub your hands!' Brad commanded. He looked from Agnes to Sandy in dismay.

'We aye had Mistress Johnstone, the auld midwife, here afore . . .' Agnes protested weakly.

'Mr Logan . . .? Do you think . . .?'

Brad frowned and turned abruptly to Agnes. 'Ask your Mistress if I can be of assistance?' Agnes's worried face flushed bright red as she stared at the young American. He sighed heavily.

'Tell Mistress Fairly I assisted the doctor on the ship with two births. Please come back and tell me if she requires my help – for the sake of the child!' Brad added impatiently as Agnes gaped at him.

Thirty-one

Sarah's son was small but his struggle into the world was aided by Brad Leishman's instinctive care. Doctor Kerr arrived shortly afterwards, explaining that Mistress Fletcher was already attending one of the fishermen's wives two miles on the other side of Muircumwell. He congratulated both Sarah and her self-appointed midwife.

'Now we must keep him warm and persuade him to feed. The laddie will likely be slow, but at least he is alive,' he added with profound relief. 'You will need patience, Mistress Fairly. Feed him often.'

'I'll try.' Sarah sighed wearily. She felt too exhausted to do more than agree. She had no swelling or tenderness, as she had had with her other babes, no sign at all that she would have milk to feed a healthy infant, even less one too weak to suckle.

'Perhaps I should call in at the manse and ask the Reverend Mace to baptise him . . .' Doctor Kerr mused, as much to himself as to Sarah but her eyes widened in alarm.

'Is— is he going to die, Doctor?'

'He seems healthy . . . but shock precipitated him into the world a little early. He may have less resistance to sickness. You must take care of yourself, and try not to worry. Your family needs you, Mistress Fairly.'

Sarah looked up into Doctor Kerr's concerned face and nodded.

Logan Brad Fairly was baptised later that day and the Reverend Mace prayed earnestly for his good health. Afterwards he congratulated Brad Leishman.

'Clearly you are a young man of intelligence, but Doctor Kerr tells me you showed surprising maturity and composure in such a crisis. Mistress Fairly has shown her appreciation by giving your name to her son.'

'Yeah! I'm real proud, indeed honoured, Mistress Fairly,' Brad Leishman beamed with boyish delight. 'I guess it will be the first thing I shall tell the folks back home when I write. They sure will be proud!'

'I'm grateful to you, Mr Leishman,' Sarah said simply. 'You saved my son's life.'

'I was guided by God, Mistress Fairly,' Brad Leishman said gravely. 'Now I know I must become a doctor.'

'Ellen is convinced you will be a fine doctor. She is grateful to you also for saving her baby brother's life.' She smiled at the young American, but her glance moved to her daughter, gently rocking the cradle. Sarah was grateful for her company. Despite her tender years there was something serene and soothing about Ellen's personality and her presence helped to dispel a little of the chilling loneliness which threatened to overwhelm her whenever she thought of William. It seemed a dreadful thing to become a widow and a mother at the same time. 'Ellen wants to be a nurse like Miss Nightingale,' Sarah told Brad Leishman, summoning a smile. 'Father thinks she is like my own mother.'

'I guess she will be a fine nurse one day!' Brad smiled. He found Mistress Fairly's eldest daughter a delightful child, and intelligent too. But her younger sister grumbled continually. It troubled him when he looked into those pale eyes for he saw jealousy and viciousness in them; yet her loving family seemed unaware of the flaw in her character. Brad recalled the way she had raged at her brother Billy.

'Why did Mama get another bairn? I wish he had died! She has Alex and you, and she has Ellen and me. I dinna want another brother! Already Ellen loves him better than me and she promised she would love me for ever and ever after Katie drowned.'

'Dinna be such a selfish creature!' Billy had snapped with unusual sharpness. 'Wee Logan will be a comfort tae Mama now that Alex and me are grown men.'

'Ye're no' a man!' Sadie scorned. 'Ye're only thirteen.' Billy glared at her, but he made no reply. His youth troubled him sorely. He knew Fred Clark and many of the customers at the Store would agree with Sadie for all he knew so much about the business at Fairly and Guillyman's.

During the two weeks following Logan Fairly's birth Sarah lived in an unreal world, shut away from the bustle of the household, from the whispers and anxious glances. She refused to let her mind dwell on William's death, or on the future. There were a few traumatic days when she almost gave up hope of being able to feed the tiny infant who seemed too weak and lethargic to suckle. But gradually it became apparent that her youngest child had inherited both stamina and determination.

Billy worried about the Store. He had ordered the seeds in readiness for the spring sowing as his father had instructed in his letter. Now he wondered if there would be enough customers to buy them all without his father to coax and chivvy. Already the accounts had arrived from the wholesale merchants, but there was no money in the Store account to pay them until some of the stock was sold. Many of the farmers seemed anxious about the poor prices they were receiving for their own produce. Two had declared they could not afford to buy new seeds. They were leaving the pastures unploughed and sowing their own oats on their ploughed land. When Billy tried to warn them of the consequences of sowing bad quality seeds with poor germination, one had snapped, 'Och laddie, ye're jist a bairn! What can ye ken about such things!' Another had jeered openly. Billy feared other customers would react in the same way. He prayed that his mother would soon be well again, but Grandfather Logan had warned them all that she must not be troubled.

Alex knew how eagerly his younger brother had awaited their father's return. He had thought Billy was eager to try out an idea of his own at the Store. Even he did not realise the full extent of Billy's anxiety.

'Mother will ken what can be done! Maybe she'll talk tae Mr Bogle,' Billy had remarked optimistically. But he knew his father had detested the dry old solicitor who conducted Lady Guillyman's affairs and his young heart was heavy.

Brad Leishman seemed reluctant to leave Fairlyden, but eventually he decided it was time to move on to Edinburgh.

'My parents will be disappointed in me,' he sighed when he came to say goodbye to Sarah. 'They dreamed of having a preacher son.'

'When they realise how much more you can help your fellow men – and women,' Sarah smiled, 'they will be proud of you.'

Brad Leishman still looked troubled. 'I am their only son . . .'

'Would it help if I wrote them a letter, Brad? If I told them how you saved my son's life? And— and brought peace and comfort to m-my husband, in his f-final hours.' Sarah's voice broke and suddenly she was weeping uncontrollably. She had a mental picture of William dying so far from home, from all who loved him. 'I— I'm truly thankful to know you were there . . . with him.' She sobbed quietly. Brad Leishman did not interrupt or offer comfort. Despite his youth he seemed to understand instinctively that her tears would heal the grief she had stored within her heart. At last Sarah gave a final sniff, and blew her nose and dried her eyes determinedly.

'I am s-sorry,' she gulped. 'I dinna know what came over me.'

Brad smiled. 'I guess I would have thought it strange if you had not wept at all. Mr Fairly told me that you were a woman with great character and fortitude, but I also know you have a kind and tender heart. Do not be ashamed. It cannot be weak to grieve for someone who was so dear to you. My own mother shed many tears the day I left; yet it was her wish that I should travel to her homeland, to finish my education.'

'You speak words of great wisdom for such a young man,' Sarah said wonderingly. 'You would make a fine minister. But Jesus healed people too. There is much suffering in the world; so many men and women who need help. I will write to your mother most willingly, and I shall tell her she has a fine son, whatever you decide. And Brad – you'll always find a welcome at Fairlyden.'

'Thank you, Mrs Fairly,' Brad said gravely. 'My mother will be comforted to know I have found such friends in her homeland.'

* * *

'The first thing we must do is to see Mr Bogle,' Sarah declared with troubled eyes, as she looked into Billy's earnest young face. Unknown to Fred Clark, he had brought home the order book and the account ledger from the store on Saturday evening.

'Mr Clark thinks he's the Master now that Father's gone,' Billy had announced bitterly. 'He thinks I'm just a bairn, but I know we have tae pay the accounts afore we can order more stock. He's had half o' the seeds sent tae the Dumfries Store and we dinna sell much frae there yet. Only last week he ordered a special kind o' seed for a new customer o' his ain.'

Sarah had known how badly Billy was missing his father but now she realised it was more than just his grief which had made him so uncharacteristically short-tempered. She sighed heavily.

'I canna see how we're going to keep the Store if these are all the orders, laddie. I'll have a talk with Mr Clark.'

'Three o' the regular customers cancelled their orders as soon as they heard about Father,' Billy said bitterly. 'And Fred Clark has only brought in half the usual orders frae the markets. We havena sold any o' the petrol engines either.'

'It is not your fault, Billy.' Sarah longed to comfort him, to rumple his curly dark hair as she had done when he was a small boy, but now he considered himself a man and he would be indignant. But he's still a boy, she thought unhappily. He shouldna have such burdens of business on his young shoulders. William should never have gone to America while his sons were still so young, she felt a little flash of her old anger. 'You've kept the books very well, laddie. I'm sure the dominie would have been proud of you,' she said aloud. It was the truth, but it was the only crumb of comfort she had to offer. 'I will write a letter today and ask Mr Bogle to come to Fairlyden, for I canna travel to Dumfries. I couldna leave wee Logan so long without a feed.'

The lawyer arrived the following Thursday morning and Sarah knew at once that there would be no easy solution. Mr Bogle looked grim and haughty and she remembered the difficulties William had encountered in his dealings with him.

'In my opinion, Mrs Fairly, your husband took unfair advantage of Lady Guillyman when she became a widow,' he announced pompously as he opened his leather case and spread papers over the table in the front parlour. Billy gasped angrily and twin patches of indignant colour stained Sarah's own cheeks.

'Mr Bogle,' she said coldly. 'You will kindly remember that my husband is dead. He cannot defend himself. Lady Guillyman offered to leave Sir Simon's money in the business! Do you understand? She offered. My husband did not beg!'

'Lady Guillyman was in a state of shock. She acted against my advice. She was misguided by her sympathetic heart and Mr William Fairly took advantage. He made no effort to repay her husband's share! Now my client is paying for her folly. The business of Fairly and Guillyman's appears to be deeply in debt. It seems there is not even sufficient money to pay the rent for the mill property to the Guillyman Trust.'

'Guillyman Trust . . .?' Sarah's brow wrinkled.

'Yes, Trust, Mistress Fairly,' the lawyer repeated impatiently. 'It was formed automatically as soon as Lady Guillyman gave birth to a living son. The Trust is in accordance with the wishes of the late Sir Gilbert Guillyman, the child's grandfather, because the heir to the estate is a minor. I had hoped that Lady Guillyman would return to the land of her birth now that—'

'Son? Did you say Lady Guillyman has a son, a *baby* son . . .?' Sarah stared at the lawyer in disbelief.

'I did,' Mr Bogle said stiffly.

'I see . . .' Sarah's heart began to thump and she knew the colour had drained from her face. She had been under the impression that Sir Simon Guillyman had been extremely ill during the last months of his life. She had assumed that he had been physically weak, as well as mentally ill . . . Suddenly she had a clear recollection of Lady Guillyman when she had come to say goodbye before she sailed for America . . . in early October. Sir Simon had died in March . . . yet his widow had shown no signs of advanced pregnancy . . . Even William had not known of her plans . . . She had gone while he was in Holland! She had not wanted him to know her address . . . Sarah's mind was seething with questions – questions she could never ask the lawyer.

'. . . So that is my recommendation. The business of Fairly and Guillymans's will be—'

'I— I beg your pardon . . .?' Sarah floundered. She had not been listening until the sharp movement of Billy's hand caught her attention and she saw his face go a sickly white.

'I shall put everything in writing!' Mr Bogle declared testily. 'Meanwhile it is imperative that all monies outstanding be collected. I shall appoint a suitable man to be put in charge of Fairly and Guillyman's until the business is wound up.'

'No!' Billy exclaimed.

The lawyer shot him an angry glance. 'Your son is too young to understand such matters, Mistress Fairly,' he snapped.

Sarah knew Billy was too young to have been left with so much responsibility, but he understood the situation all right.

'The debts are due to my husband's sudden and untimely death, not to Billy's mismanagement. If the Store must close then Billy and I will see to it.'

'You forget, Mistress Fairly. The rent due for the use of the premises is a relatively small item, but there is the value of Sir Simon Guillyman's share of the business at the time of his death. His widow allowed the capital to remain in Fairly and Guillyman's as a loan to your late husband, a loan which I believe Mr Fairly made no effort to repay. I have a duty to my client to see that the money is repaid in full, and without delay.'

Sarah's face showed signs of strain. She had forgotten that Lady Guillyman had left most of her husband's share of the capital in the Store until it began to prosper. Nevertheless she lifted her head proudly.

'The business of Fairly and Guillyman's will be conducted honourably,' she declared firmly. 'Your client will be paid in full – to the last farthing!' She rose to her feet, standing tall and straight.

Mr Bogle's eyes glinted angrily. He was being dismissed! He resented this ordinary widow who could act with such dignity in circumstances which would have shattered most women – and many men.

'You cannot possibly understand!' he protested. 'You will be responsible for the debts. Already Fairly and Guillyman's owes several hundred pounds to the wholesale seed merchants I believe. An official letter from my office would—'

'Would cost ten times as much as a letter from the firm of Fairly and Guillyman's,' Sarah nodded. 'Oh yes, Mr Bogle, you might get our money in, but you would certainly take most of it away again! My son and I will manage, but I should be obliged if you would leave me Lady Guillyman's address so that I might keep her informed directly.'

'I have undertaken to keep Lady Guillyman informed. I will not have my client pestered. You may send any communications to my office.'

'That will not be necessary.' Sarah's eyes smouldered with indignation. 'Billy, ask Ewan to drive Mr Bogle back to the station at once.' She swept out of Fairlyden's front parlour with all the dignity of a queen.

When the lawyer had gone Billy returned to the house to tell his mother he was proud of the way she had dealt with the lawyer. He was dismayed to find her sitting at the kitchen table with her head bowed dejectedly.

'Mama . . .?' Even to his own ears his voice sounded young and hesitant.

Sarah straightened immediately. She had not heard him return. She did not want him to guess how despondent she felt, and she would never let any of her children know of the suspicions which were tormenting her.

'Dinna look sae worried, laddie!' Sarah said briskly, dropping the careful diction she had summoned to aid her dealings with Mr Bogle. 'Ye're not tae blame for the failure of Fairly and Guillyman's.' She saw Billy wince at the word failure. Her lips tightened. She wondered what plans William had had in mind. Had he persuaded Lady Guillyman to lend him more capital? Well, she would never ask for help from William's . . . mistress . . .? The very thought of it made her feel physically sick, yet the more she considered the situation, the more certain she became that Lady Guillyman had fled to America to avoid a scandal. William must hae heard she had a son, she thought bitterly.

'But how shall we pay?' Billy asked anxiously.

'We'll do the best we can, laddie. Tomorrow you must tell Fred Clark to reduce the price o' the seeds. It is better to sell them at a loss than to have them standing in the store. According to the accounts the business didna make much profit last year, even with all the orders your father got at the markets. He bought the best seed frae the merchants, but not all the farmers can afford quality these days, Billy. Your father often forgot that. I suppose it was due to his upbringing as the son of the laird, instead of an ordinary farmer.' She sighed. 'There is also that great machine at the Store. It must be worth quite a lot of money . . .?'

'Ye mean the McCormick self-tying reaper?' Billy asked, his dark eyes glowing.

'If that's what you call it,' Sarah said dryly. 'The trouble is, Billy, Mr Bogle is right. The business of Fairly and Guillyman's is finished.

'B-but Mama! I've lots o' plans! What about the bicycles? And what am I tae dae? Father said . . .'

'Your father is dead, Billy!' Sarah's voice was harsher than she intended. She must not let Billy guess how alone she felt right now. 'Listen, laddie,' she added more gently, though her voice was firm. 'Whatever happens we must pay all your father's debts. I couldna bear to hear folks say he died in debt, or that he was like his half-brother. The late Earl of Strathtod was a dreadful creature! Your father was a good man, Billy,' she added loyally. 'He had fine plans for the Store, and I'm sure his ideas would have helped some of the farmers to improve their crops, and ease their labours, aye and he might have helped them join together to sell their own produce eventually – but the time isna ripe for such things right now.'

'But what am I tae dae if the Store closes?'

'You'll have work and food and a roof here at Fairlyden. When Ewan and Maggie get married next month I-I'll be glad to have a man like you about the place again.' Sarah prayed that Billy would not detect the small white lie. It did not win his support. She saw the anger and defiance flash in his brown eyes, then they were shuttered by his thick dark lashes. She watched his pale tense face.

'Ye ken I never wanted tae be a farmer!' he muttered vehemently. 'I like talking tae people! Learning about things – the seeds, the machinery. There's lots o' changes coming that ye wad never dream o', Mother!'

'Oh, I dream all right.' Sarah sighed. 'We all do that. Your Grandfather Logan had just as many dreams and bright ideas as you do, laddie. You ask him.'

'Grandfather Logan!' Billy exclaimed incredulously. 'But he loves farming.'

'Aye, but he knows there'll be changes one day. Maybe ye'll be able to do what you want then . . . but there's lots of things in life we all have to do that we wouldna choose, Billy.'

'Father said ye always see things more clearly than other folk,' Billy said glumly, 'but it doesna help me.' His young shoulders drooped as he moved to the door. He closed it quietly. Once he would have banged it in childish temper, Sarah thought sadly and her heart ached for the mischievous, bright-eyed boy he had been.

Billy did not appear for the evening meal. He had not returned when Sarah lit her candle and went to bed either. She was giving Logan his early morning feed when she heard him creeping past her door. She had not slept. The wind had risen earlier and the rain was lashing against her window. It sounded like a thousand demons out in the darkness of the night, but it was not the stormy elements which troubled her.

Her thoughts had gone round and round in circles. Their situation was even worse than Billy suspected. The work on the house had not been completed and it never would be now. She had to find the rest of the money Mr Crichton-Reid was demanding, as well as pay the debts from the Store. As she sat up in the big bed cradling her baby son to her breast and watching the first faint flush of a new day creep over the horizon, Sarah felt there could not possibly be any more troubles round the corner. Surely the good Lord would send her respite from the clouds which seemed to be hanging over her life.

The following morning the sky overhead was clear after the wild night. Scattered twigs and branches were the only evidence of the storm, but large pools still stood in many of the fields as a result of the deluge. It was just after midday when the station trap deposited Mr Crichton-Reid at Fairlyden. Sarah's heart sank instantly.

'Shall I show him intae the parlour?' Agnes asked gloomily.

Sarah nodded and went ahead, breathing deeply in an effort to keep calm and slow the rapid beating of her heart. She knew the visit would not be pleasant.

'I demand, yes demand, the money you owe me, Mrs Fairly,' the architect stated the moment he stepped into the room.

'And good day to you,' Sarah said dryly.

The man's eyes glinted behind his steel-rimmed spectacles. 'This is not a time for pleasantries!' he growled. 'I am told your husband has left nothing but debts and . . .'

'May I ask who has been spreading malicious gossip about a dead man who cannot speak for himself?' Sarah demanded, white to the lips.

'Gossip!' Crichton-Reid goggled at her. 'I believe it is the truth.'

'It is libelous! Perhaps you should remind your "friend" of that, though if by chance he is a lawyer . . .'

'I didn't say who . . .'

'No, you did not. As soon as my husband's affairs are in order you will be paid in full for the work you have already done. I give you my word on that.' Sarah was speaking quietly but the man could see the anger glinting in her dark eyes. 'As to the rest,' Sarah's lip curled in contempt, 'I would not have you, or any men belonging to you, in my home again.'

'B-but the bathroom . . . the water system . . .'

'Are unfinished on account of your petty demands!' Sarah said through gritted teeth. 'They will remain so! You can remove the iron bath, and everything else you have sent. I shall deduct them from your account. Now good day to you!'

Sarah did not believe anything else could add to her burdens until Billy arrived home earlier than usual, his young face white and strained. She was on her way to the milking but she paused, frowning.

'What is it, Billy?'

'It's the seeds, Mother!' Billy blinked and Sarah remembered that he was still just a boy when she saw the suspicion of moisture shining in his eyes.

'What seeds? What's wrong with them? Billy . . .?'

'The ones i' the wee store, at Dumfries. The— the river flooded last night with the storm—'

'No!' Sarah's face went white. 'No! Surely the seeds didna get damp?'

'The store's flooded. Fred Clark says the bags are soaked, ruined . . . A-and Mother . . .' Billy's voice cracked and he gulped hard. 'Fred went tae the insurance offices tae see Mr Blake. He— he says Father didna take out any more insurances, either on the Dumfries store, or— or on his ain life. We— we'll hae nothing, Mother.'

Sarah nodded. Her eyes held a faraway look that hid her desolation as she scanned the surrounding farmstead and the fields and hills beyond Fairlyden. Then she straightened and looked at Billy. She put an arm lightly round his shoulder.

'We'll manage, Billy. We'll pay somehow!' He looked up at her and nodded. Then he gave her the ghost of his former merry smile. Her heart ached for him.

'I-I'll try tae be a guid farmer,' he promised.

Sarah lay awake again that night mulling over the problems which were threatening to overwhelm her. She thought of Beatrice's letter, the genuine sorrow she had expressed at the news of William's death. Beattie had also conveyed her surprise at the news of Logan's birth. Sarah had detected a little of the veiled hurt she must have felt because she had not confided in her earlier.

Her thoughts winged back to the night of the fire and her promise to Crispin that she would always go to him, if ever she needed help. But she could never ask him for help now! Her pride forbade it. Already she fancied wee Logan bore a strong resemblance to Bert Bradshaw, Crispin's own father; it was there in his broad brow and wide-set grey eyes. Crispin was a confirmed bachelor and the last thing she wanted was to make him feel under an obligation to help her, and even less that she was angling for his support as a husband now that she was a widow. Sarah cringed at the very idea and her cheeks burned. Anyway he was still in Australia.

Eventually she reached a decision – a decision which she felt might break her heart – and her father's, if he ever found out what she intended to do.

Thirty-two

It was the first Sunday Sarah had ventured out in public since William's death and the birth of her child. She dressed carefully in her neat black dress and pinned a jet brooch at her throat. It had belonged to her mother and Sarah hoped it might give her a little of her mama's indomitable courage. She donned a fine black veil and glanced listlessly at her reflection. Her face was incredibly pale and her cheeks were hollow, but she could not help that and people would not expect to see her looking radiant at such a time. She clasped her bible in her hand and squared her slim shoulders. She would pray for further guidance, but in her heart she knew she had no alternative. All their debts must be paid. She owed that to William, and to their children. He had helped to buy Fairlyden for her, now it must be sold.

Sandy glanced sharply at Sarah's pinched white face as she took her place beside him in the family's pew with Ellen and Sadie, while Billy followed a few paces behind. Sandy wished the Reverend Mackenzie could have been in the pulpit to offer spiritual comfort. The Reverend Mace did his best but he was not an eloquent man at any time, and he lacked the sensitivity of his predecessor.

As soon as the service was over and they were outside once more Sandy drew Sarah aside.

'I didna expect tae see ye at the kirk, lassie. Alex and I had planned tae ride up to Fairlyden. Can ye be bothered with the twae o' us?'

'Of course we can, Father. You know there's always a good pot of broth on a Sunday, whatever else might be lacking.' Sarah made an effort to sound cheerful but her smile was wan.

After the meal was over the young Fairlys went about their own business and Sandy made himself comfortable in the wooden armchair which had always been his favourite.

'Can ye sit down for a bit, lassie? I'd like tae talk.'

Sarah's dark brows rose. 'I'll sit a while, but wee Logan will be wanting to be fed soon . . .' The truth was she felt uneasy when her father fixed his shrewd eyes on her.

'Billy came down tae the Mains the other night, tae talk tae Alex.' He puffed at his pipe but Sarah remained silent, waiting. 'He told us about Mr Bogle's visit.'

'Father, I know Billy is upset, but he had no right to come to the Mains and burden you with our problems.'

'Whist, lassie! He only came tae share his troubles wi' Alex, the way they've always done. Anyway, we're your family remember. If ye're having problems settling William's affairs I want tae help if I can.'

'Oh Father.' Sarah's voice trembled. 'I'm sorry I snapped at you . . .' She gulped, but she went on firmly. 'We shall manage. Billy and Fred Clark are selling as much of the stock at the Store as they can. The merchants will have to wait until then for their money.' Sarah made an effort to smile. She was aware of her father watching her through his sandy-brown eyelashes, for all he was supposed to be concentrating on puffing and poking at his pipe.

'Sarah,' he said at last, and his expression was grave. 'Ye ken ye mean more tae me than anything in the world. If ye need money I can give up the lease on the Mains. I'd have the stock tae sell then . . .'

'No!' Sarah exclaimed and her mouth set. 'You are happy there now, and so is Alex. It's a wonderful opportunity for him. It has scope; he can employ men to do the work he canna manage himself, you said so yourself; it's a lot bigger than Fairlyden.' She summoned a ghost of a grin. 'If we canna survive here we'll all come to the Mains and live with you!'

Sandy laughed. 'I ken ye'd never leave Fairlyden, lassie!' He did not see Sarah's face as she turned away abruptly. 'Anyway, ye ken I'm willing tae help, but ye're right about Alex. He's earned the respect o' the men at the Mains already. He doesna give in easily and most o' them wad dae anything tae help him now they ken he has sic spirit; they ken he understands a guid many things they'll never ken tae, for all he's still just a laddie.'

Sarah looked at her father's contented expression and she knew she could never ask him to sacrifice the Mains so that she could pay William's debts. She would stick to her decision. She would write a letter this very night, when everyone was in bed.

Despite her resolve Sarah chewed her thumbnail, as she always did when her thoughts were troubled, then she dipped the quill in the ink and proceeded to write to Bert Bradshaw. After several more pauses she continued reluctantly.

> Whatever your decision, Mr Bradshaw, I beg you not to tell anyone of my request. My father's dearest wish was to give me a secure home and he believes I have that at Fairlyden. He has worked so hard all his life and made so many sacrifices for me already. He even offered to give up the Mains, but he and Alex are so happy there and he has a secure lease for fifteen years; Alex is to take it over when he is old enough. I do not want anything to cloud my father's happiness, or to spoil Alex's chances.
>
> I shall understand if you refuse to buy Fairlyden, but I know it will be more valuable to you than to anyone else, when you own all the land round about it.

Again Sarah stopped and her gaze wandered round the familiar kitchen, then she finished her letter hurriedly with her best wishes for Bert Bradshaw's good health.

The reply from Bert Bradshaw came by return.

Dear Sarah,

I'm not much of a letter writer, lass. I like to talk to folk face to face. I can't come to Scotland for a bit though. There's no need to sell that little farm of yours and your fifty acres of land. I know how much it means to you. I could let you have two or three hundred pounds as a loan. I'd do that for you, lass, with a good heart.

If you still want me to buy Fairlyden though, I will. Nobody will know but you and me, and my lawyer.

Yours truly,
Bert Bradshaw.

Tears sprang to Sarah's eyes. Would Bert Bradshaw write so kindly, or so generously if he knew Logan could be his own grandson?

That night she took out her writing materials once more. She could not bring herself to tell Mr Bradshaw that even a loan of two or three hundred pounds would be far too small to cover their debts. In any case she had no hope of repaying him. Two more cows had lost their calves. The milk seemed to get less every day. Sarah gritted her teeth and asked him to purchase Fairlyden outright.

Then she wrote a letter to Beatrice.

I thought I was much too old to be a mother again, Beattie. I suppose I did not tell you because I felt a bit embarrassed, and ashamed in a way.

How true, Sarah thought grimly, but Beatrice must never suspect the real reason for her shame. Her guilt had lessened a little since she heard of the birth of Lady Guillyman's son. In her heart she was sure William must be the child's father. His infidelity could never excuse the way she had behaved, but Sarah knew that if her husband had been with her on the night of the fire she would never have sought comfort in the arms of any other man.

Now that Logan is here, and we are both so well, he is a great comfort to me, especially in the dark, lonely hours of the night. At first I feared I would not be able to feed him but now I have as much milk as I had when the twins were born and Logan is thriving and very contented.

I felt happier, and less selfish, when I knew Sally Jamieson was also to be blessed with a child. She and Nick have waited so long.

I shall be glad when it is safely delivered for Sally looks so very frail and she has not kept at all well these past months.

Sarah continued her letter as cheerfully as she could, mentioning nothing of her own troubles and asking after Dick and the children. She sighed and rubbed her tired eyes as she sealed the envelope.

Mr Bradshaw sent a draft for the purchase of Fairlyden by return with the promise that he would speak to his lawyer and ask him to draw up a lease which would give her security for the next fifteen years. He had written

By then your youngest will know what he wants to be about. Don't worry if you don't get the documents for a bit, lass. Mr Metcalf is a busy man and I don't feel like going up to his offices just yet. You know you can trust me, I hope.

Sarah did trust Bert Bradshaw. He had proved himself a true friend again. The money brought great relief. Fairly and Guillyman's Store had been emptied except for two items, one of which was the self-tying binder which no one in the area could afford to buy. Billy had pleaded with her to keep it at Fairlyden and Sarah had agreed, knowing she had little option.

Most of those who had made purchases had paid their debts in full despite Mr Bogle's gloomy predictions. Even so the business had made a substantial loss. Sarah had paid the merchants as soon as she could so that no smear could be attached to William's name. She had also paid Mr Crichton-Reid.

Meanwhile Maggie and Ewan had had a quiet, but very happy wedding and moved to Mains of Muir. Sarah missed Maggie's cheerful presence around the house and especially at the milking, but in her heart she knew things were settling down better than she had dared to hope when she first received the news of William's death. Sometimes she missed him dreadfully, but her life was hectic with her family and other responsibilities and there was little time to mope during the day. If she wept a few silent tears in the darkness of the night, no one was allowed to guess, or to suffer for her grief.

Billy tried to obey Nick's instructions but he was moody and his obvious discontent made Sarah unhappy. He lacked Alex's keen observation with the animals and Nick was uneasy when he had to criticise Billy's work.

Sally's baby was already overdue so it was no surprise to Sarah when Nick arrived in the dairy one morning before she and Agnes had started the milking.

'I'll need tae go for Mistress Fletcher,' he announced with a mixture of pride and anxiety.

'Is Sally all right, Nick?' Sarah enquired. 'Shall I send Agnes down to the cottage?'

'No, not yet.' He winked at Sarah behind his sister's back. Agnes had a way of organising Sally which could be irritating at times, although Agnes was kind and she meant well.

'I'll send Billy for Mistress Fletcher then, as soon as the milking and feeding are finished. He can take the pony and trap and bring her back. You stay with Sally, Nick. She will be pleased to have your company.'

'Thank ye, Mistress Fairly,' Nick accepted eagerly. 'I dinna like tae leave her on her ain, though she says it'll be a while yet.'

'Aye, first babes usually take their time,' Sarah agreed.

'And Sally's no sae young either!' Agnes added gloomily.

An anxious frown immediately creased Nick's brow and Sarah quickly ushered Agnes away to the byre to begin the milking.

It was almost time to begin the afternoon milking when Sarah saw Nick again and this time his face was white and strained. The midwife had been there for several hours.

'Is everything all right, Nick?' Sarah asked anxiously.

'I dinna ken. Mistress Fletcher says there's nought she can dae until the bairn's ready tae be born, but I'm worried about Sally.'

'She's stronger than she looks, Nick, and very brave,' Sarah comforted. 'Do you think she should have Doctor Kerr?'

'I'd be happier if she wad hae him, but Sally doesna want the doctor near her. She's aye been a modest lassie.' Nick flushed with embarrassment. He was used to dealing with cows and calves and all the other animals and their young. He knew all about their problems, but this was women's business. 'Mistress Fletcher says there's nothing any doctor can dae that she canna dae herself, but she's no very particular! Anyway she's spent maist o' her time drinking tea in the kitchen. I reckon she'll float soon.'

Sarah smiled at his apt description of the local midwife, but she was concerned too. 'I hope Sally insists she washes her hands regularly before she touches her? Mistress Johnstone was particular about that. Would you like me to look in at the cottage before I start the milking?'

'Oh aye, Mistress Fairly, I wad that!' Nick agreed gratefully, 'if ye've time tae spare . . .?'

Sarah felt instinctively that something was amiss when she saw Sally, despite Mistress Fletcher's placid assertion that these things took their own time. Sally always looked delicate but Sarah knew she possessed surprising stamina. Now she looked more than frail; her blue eyes were sunken and ringed with fatigue, her fair hair was dark with perspiration and matted against her scalp. She looked absolutely exhausted.

'Nick's very worried about you, Sally,' Sarah said gently.

'I'll be fine. Once the babe comes,' Sally whispered wearily. 'I just dinna seem tae make any progress, for all the pains keep coming.'

'Nick would like to send for Doctor Kerr.'

'No! I dinna want the doctor!' Sally's voice was stronger and she tried to sit up, only to slump back against her pillows as a spasm of pain gripped her.

'He wouldna charge much and . . .'

'It isna the money! I dinna want him! I wad be a puir weak woman if I canna bring my ain babe intae the world,' she gasped.

'Sally,' Sarah steeled herself to be firm and calm. 'Nick loves you. He wants the child as much as you do. How can you let foolish modesty harm the life of your unborn baby, and maybe even your own? You're not weak! You've suffered months o' discomfort without a word of complaint. Now Doctor Kerr will be able to help you.' Sarah was dismayed when Sally's eyes filled with tears.

'Ye're upsetting her, Mistress Fairly!' the midwife called from the door. 'I'll thank ye tae leave my patient alane!'

'I'm just going. What shall I tell Nick, Sally?'

'Ye ken best, Mistress Fairly. You tell Nick what tae dae,' she whispered and closed her eyes wearily. 'Thank ye for bothering wi' me.'

Sarah felt the tears prick her own eyelids at Sally's trust and humility.

Nick was waiting anxiously in the kitchen.

'I think Sally will see Doctor Kerr, Nick. She seems so exhausted. I'm not a doctor and I canna tell whether everything is all right or not. I've heard of first babies taking a long time, but I'd feel happier if Doctor Kerr came.'

'Aye, I ken fine what ye mean, Mistress Fairly.' Nick sounded almost relieved. 'I've the same notion. I'll gang for Doctor Kerr right awa'.'

'No, Nick. You sit with Sally. She needs you, even if she doesna talk much. I'll send Thomas for Doctor Kerr. Ellen will help Agnes and me with the milking as soon as she comes frae school. The horses and pigs can wait until Thomas gets back. He'll be pleased to help Sally. We're all very fond of her. Tell her that.'

Nick nodded. 'Thank ye, Mistress.' He swallowed hard. 'Ye've aye been guid tae Sally an' me, even wi' all yer ain troubles.'

Sarah smiled. 'Try not to worry. Doctor Kerr will soon have everything in order.'

Sarah genuinely believed the reassuring words she had uttered for Nick's benefit but there was still no news of Sally's baby when she went to bed that night and she slept badly. So she was delighted when Nick came to the house soon after dawn. She was raking out the ashes to kindle the fire before going to the dairy.

'Sally's had a wee lassie,' Nick announced with a smile.

'Oh Nick! I'm so pleased to hear that. I was getting worried when there was no news last night. Are they both all right?'

'The Doctor says Sally's exhausted, and weel she might be,' Nick answered with feeling, and Sarah glimpsed the anxiety in his shadowed eyes. 'She's asleep now. I'm no' tae waken her. The doctor is coming back later this morning.' He shuddered, remembering the bowls of bloody water and the instruments Mistress Fletcher had carried from the bedroom. 'He— he says he willna charge for his visit, Mistress Fairly, but it isna the money that worries me. We've aye managed tae save a shilling or twae in the years we've been at Fairlyden, but I'd gladly gie it all so long as Sally and the bairn are all right. Why dae ye think he's coming back, Mistress Fairly?'

'For the same reason that you go out at night to check up on the cows and the mares when they have had their own youngsters, Nick; because you care about them. Doctor Kerr is a good doctor. He will want to make sure his patient is all right, that's all. Now you get some sleep yourself. You look exhausted.'

'I canna dae that! There's the horses tae see tae and the turnip hoeing tae finish. If this good weather holds we'll need tae be scything the hay soon.'

'It will be worse if you're ill, Nick. Thomas will be finished and up at the turnips before long; and I have to admit that Billy makes a quick job of hoeing down the potatoes with that new-fangled machine. I went to the field to see them with him last night.'

'Aye, Billy's a grand lad wi' machines, and he's careful not tae disturb the young shoots o' the potatoes. He's really pleased that ye allowed him tae keep the self-binder for the corn tae. That should mak a difference tae the work at harvest time, especially now Ewan and Maggie are awa'.'

'Mmm,' Sarah pursed her lips. 'Well, we couldna sell it anyway, but that's enough talk, Nick. Get to bed and sleep until Doctor Kerr comes back. I'll send Agnes to mind the baby and see to the washing. You'll need her for the next two weeks until Sally's out of her bed again. Sadie can feed the hens and wash dishes. It's time she learned to help a bit, so dinna worry Nick. Everything will be fine once Sally gets her strength back. Have you given the babe a name yet?'

'Aye. Sally thinks we should call her Elizabeth after ma mother.' Nick bit his lip. 'I'm glad she's lived tae see her first grandbairn,' he added in a low voice.

Sarah nodded. 'Yes, my father believes the thought of it has kept her alive these past weeks. She will die happy now, especially when she hears you and Sally have given the babe her name.'

'Aye, we'll likely call her Beth though, like ma sister. Elizabeth seems such a mouthful for a wee mite.'

Despite Agnes's alternate coaxing and bullying Sally seemed to have no appetite for food of any kind and even her baby daughter could arouse no more than a fleeting interest. When Sarah saw Doctor Kerr's pony and trap at the cottage for the fourth time in three days her own concern grew. She visited the cottage again that afternoon, taking with her a light egg custard in the hope of tempting Sally to eat.

Sally was lying listlessly against a mound of pillows. Her lips were extraordinarily red and twin flags of colour seemed to burn on her high cheekbones.

'Thank ye for the custard, Mistress Fairly,' Sally roused herself from the terrible lethargy with an effort. 'I dinna seem tae be hungry, but I've a terrible thirst.'

'I expect that's nature's way of helping you produce milk for your bairn,' Sarah said matter of factly, though inwardly she felt a mounting concern at Sally's feverishly bright eyes. Most alarming of all was her lack of interest in her baby, the child she had longed for.

'Aye, maybe. The Doctor says she's a fine big baby.'

'Indeed she is, and a bonny wee thing too!' Sarah smiled, hoping to encourage Sally's flash of interest. 'Is she a good feeder?'

'Aye,' Sally's eyelids drooped. 'But she seems tae take for ever, and I get sae weary afore she's finished. All I want is tae drink and sleep.'

'Well, you've had a bad time, Sally. I'm sure you'll feel better in a few more days.' Sarah wished with all her heart that she could believe the comforting words she uttered. That night she prayed for Sally with all the faith and sincerity she could muster.

Thirty-three

Sarah never knew whether it was her own fervent prayers which had been answered or not, but Sally's fever reached a crisis the following morning. Although she was alarmingly frail afterwards, at least she was alive; and the long road to recovery had begun.

Sarah expressed her relief in a letter to Beatrice, for the childhood habit of sharing both joys and troubles had never really ceased, despite Sarah's reticence over Logan's birth.

> . . . So you and Dick will understand how greatly relieved we all are, but especially Nick.
>
> I know I should look upon Maggie and Ewan's marriage as a happy occasion, and indeed I do, but I miss both of them, and it will be even worse as far as the milking is concerned until Sally recovers, which I fear will be a long time. Apart from the fever, Doctor Kerr thinks the difficult birth has damaged her spine. It is too early for him to say how badly this might affect her.
>
> Agnes is doing her best to help. She feeds Beth on boiled cows' milk and honey diluted with water and uses one of those curved glass bottles with an india rubber teat. Billy brought it specially from the chemist in Annan. The poor wee mite is not at all content.
>
> Several times I have taken care of her myself to give Agnes a little respite; once or twice she has slept all night at Fairlyden. I put the babe to my own breast to comfort her and give her succour. Afterwards she sleeps as contentedly as a lamb, in the crib beside Logan. I feel a great tenderness for her, but I hope Sally will soon recover enough to care for Beth. She wanted her so badly. Also Agnes is growing possessively fond of her niece already.

It was the last week in August when Sandy and Alex rode over to Fairlyden to see Billy cutting a field of oats with the marvellous machine which could cut the corn and tie the sheaves with string. Sarah was helping to stook the sheaves with Nick, Ellen and Sadie. Thomas was fully occupied scything the outer rows of corn in the next field in readiness for Billy and his binder, and sharpening the pointed knives which fitted into the machine.

'It seems a big machine to drive, but Billy handles the two geldings well,' Sandy remarked.

'Aye.' Sarah sighed and wiped her brow with the back of her hand.

'It's a lot easier on the women now we dinna need to bind, as well as saving the men a lot of sweat over the scything. I dinna know how we would have managed with Agnes at the house minding the bairns, and neither Sally nor Maggie to help.' She sucked a finger and grimaced. 'I just wish there was a machine that would take away the thistles! I have two or three little daggers in my hand already and we've only just begun to stook!'

'I doubt there'll aye be thistles i' the corn, lassie,' Sandy sympathised. The others stopped work to gather round the basket of scones and bannock and buttermilk which Agnes had sent with him to the field.

Sandy and Sarah moved a little way away.

'Is it just the thistles, Sarah, or are ye worrying about something else? What's troubling ye?'

'You're far too observant!' Sarah sighed. 'As a matter of fact I was thinking about a letter I had frae Beatrice yesterday. She says Mr Bradshaw is ill. Have you heard frae him recently, Father?'

Sandy frowned. 'Not recently. He doesna like writing letters. I ken he wasna sae well after the fire, but he was better before Crispin went tae Australia. It's a while since he was up at Strathtod. It must be nearly a year.'

'It's more. Beatrice says he's had a chesty cough on and off since the fire. This time he's worse. Apparently he was very bad in the spring, but she thought I had enough troubles so she didna mention him then. She wrote to Crispin though. He's come home.'

Sarah did not mention the other comment in Beatrice's letter.

> Crispin came to thank me for informing him of his father's poor health. He is very glad to be back. He seemed concerned about you, and asked several times about wee Logan. Of course I couldn't tell him anything because you scarcely mention your youngest son. I expect that is because he reminds you of the tragic news which precipitated his birth.

Sarah had deliberately refrained from describing Logan in her letters to Yorkshire. She was convinced now that it was not just her imagination; Logan was developing a square jaw and a broad forehead which strongly resembled Bert Bradshaw's. It was true that two of her children had grey eyes of course, but Sadie's were pale, almost colourless, while Logan's had sparks of green and gold whenever he chuckled. His hair was like her own father's now that it was darkening to a coppery brown. Sarah knew it was her own feelings of guilt which made her so reluctant to mention her son. He was Crispin's son too, but she would never admit it, least of all to Crispin himself.

'Ye werena listening, Sarah!' Sandy interrupted her thoughts. 'I'm just saying ye canna worry about everybody's troubles. Bert Bradshaw told me some time ago, long before the fire, that he'd had a good life.

Crispin will see that he gets the best attention. Bert doesna need tae worry about the estate either now the new factor has settled in.'

'Mmm, speaking of the new factor,' Sarah changed the subject with some relief, 'he came to see Billy working the binder. I dinna like him much. Thomas goes down to the inn at Strathtod sometimes and he says Mr Reynolds isna very popular with any of the tenants.'

'Neither was I in the beginning!' Sandy reminded her wryly.

'Och, Mr Reynolds is different! He seems a cold fish; pompous too, dressing as though he's a gentleman and picking faults about the boundary fences.'

'Did he?' Sandy's brows rose. 'And is there anything wrong with the fences?'

'I dinna know yet.' Sarah frowned. 'I asked Nick to have a look but he forgot. He's forgotten several things since Sally has been so ill, and wee Beth not sleeping at nights.'

'Aye,' Sandy sighed, 'it's understandable, I suppose. Do ye want me tae have a word with him?'

'No,' Sarah said quietly. 'If he doesna improve soon, I'll remind him that I'm depending on him. I dinna think he'll let me down once things are settled again.' She sighed. 'Maybe William didna help me with Fairlyden much, but I miss his company, and his support with the bairns, especially Billy.'

'Aye.' Sandy sighed. 'Billy has taken it hard. William had the right ideas, but he was too soon with them. That machine is certainly a great benefit! Folks'll see that he was right some day . . .'

'Some day!' Sarah echoed bitterly.

'At least ye have Fairlyden and your ain bit o' land. William made sure ye had that, lassie. Ye could give up the lease on the acres ye rent, if they're too much o' a burden. The factor couldna interfere wi' ye at all then, whatever happens tae Strathtod when Bert Bradshaw is finished with it.'

'Finished with it?' Sarah echoed in alarm.

'Well, when a man's time is up he has tae go whether he wants or not, lassie . . . and since the government imposed death duties four years ago, ye canna be sure what might happen tae any o' the estates.'

'Surely Strathtod wadna be affected?' Sarah asked anxiously.

'I dinna ken. I suppose it wad depend whether Crispin wanted tae keep it, and whether he could pay the taxes. Bert reckoned his heart was always set on improving the factory and the houses for his workers, but I think he enjoys visiting Strathtod . . . Dinna look sae worried, Sarah. As I said, nothing can affect the part of Fairlyden you own. Anyway Bert Bradshaw willna give up that easily and maybe he's not as bad as Beatrice fears.'

'I do hope you're right, Father.'

'So dae I, lassie. Maybe I'll go tae Yorkshire and pay him a visit when we've finished the harvest at the Mains. I'd like tae see him again. Bert Bradshaw was a guid friend tae me when I needed one.'

And to me too! Sarah thought silently, but an unexpected shiver ran down her spine. She had not yet received the lease for Fairlyden. Had Mr Bradshaw been too ill even to see his lawyer about the promised lease?

Sandy did not manage to carry out his visit to Yorkshire. Ten days later both he and Sarah received ominous black-edged letters from Crispin Bradshaw informing them of his father's death.

Sarah was deeply distressed by the news. Apart from her anxiety over the lease for Fairlyden, she had grown genuinely fond of the blunt, kindly Yorkshireman who had come into their lives so unexpectedly and proved a worthy friend.

Sarah had almost dreaded a visit from Crispin when she first heard he had returned from Australia. The thought of him seeing Logan, and recognising any resemblance to himself or his family, had thrown her into a state of confusion. She scarcely knew whether she was relieved or disappointed by his silence. Now she must break that silence herself. She could not allow Bert Bradshaw's death to pass without expressing her sincere sympathy to Crispin, and to his sister Fanny. She received a formal acknowledgement of her condolences and she wondered if Crispin himself had ever seen her letter.

It was Beatrice who wrote of the large numbers of rich and poor who had assembled to pay their last respects to Cuthbert Benjamin Bradshaw.

> Fanny and her husband drove from London in a horseless carriage. Dick said it made noises like a gun and huffed and puffed in a most unseemly fashion on such a solemn occasion. To make matters worse they hurried back to the house almost before the vicar had completed his prayers at the graveside to avoid being drenched by the torrential rain.
>
> My poor Dick was soaked to the skin by the time he had made the journey home. He said that Crispin stood at his father's grave until everyone else had left, but many of the other mourners were very wet too. Few of them had as far to journey home as Dick. He was already suffering from a feverish cold and I almost wish I had not allowed him to go, for I fear he has caught another chill. Yet I think I could not have prevented him from paying his last respects to the fine man who risked his own life, and maybe shortened it, to rescue Meg from the fire.

Sarah was astonished when the postman brought yet another letter from Beatrice only two days later. It was very short and there was no doubt in Sarah's mind that Beatrice was distraught with worry. Her firm neat handwriting was shaky and near the end of the page was a watery blot. Sarah guessed it had been caused by a tear which had accidentally fallen on to the page. Her heart ached for Beatrice as she scanned the lines for the third time.

. . . So the doctor says the chill has developed into pneumonia. In a few hours my poor Dick will reach a crisis. He seems to be burning up, Sarah. I am sitting by his bed as I write and I have just bathed him with a cooling cloth. He lies as limply as a babe in my arms. He looks so ill! I think I cannot bear it, and yet I must be calm. If only you could be here with me. If only Meg could be depended upon. How I envy you your calm, sweet little Ellen at this time. Meg is ten years old now, yet if I send her to bring in the cows for milking I find her dreaming by the stream an hour later. What am I to do with her?

Dick is getting very restless. I dare not leave his side. I will seal my letter and bathe him again. I shall write more cheerfully when his dreadful illness is over, my dear Sarah. I am sorry to burden you with my troubles when you have so many of your own, but even writing to you brings me comfort.

Ever your affectionate friend and sister,
Beatrice.

It was the first time Beatrice had ever shown the slightest exasperation with her pretty empty-headed young daughter, and it was the first time she had signed herself as a sister. In her distress over Dick, Beatrice had revealed more of her private thoughts than was her habit and Sarah longed to be able to jump into the trap and drive to her home to bring her real help and comfort.

'I feel so helpless,' she confided to Agnes as she told her of Dick's illness. 'If only they had not moved so far away. I canna travel all the way to Yorkshire, with two bairns at Fairlyden and all the washing and cooking to do, as well as the milking and churning, and just the two of us now.'

'Aye, it's a sad business for the O'Connors, tae be sae far frae their ain friends at such a time,' Agnes agreed.

It was almost noon the following day when Jim Braid the postman came up the track to Fairlyden. Sarah's face paled at the sight of the yellow envelope and Jim Braid's troubled expression. Her hand shook.

'This is the second telegram in less than a year,' she muttered fearfully. 'Agnes, would you give Jim a drink of buttermilk in the kitchen. I—I would like to be alone, I think.'

She opened the envelope with trembling fingers and read the printed words.

15 September 1898 stop Dick died at dawn stop Beatrice exhausted. Letter following. Crispin Bradshaw.

Sarah read and re-read the printed words. Poor Beatrice. At least I had Father's support when William died, she thought, and trustworthy servants, Agnes, Nick, Ewan, Maggie . . . And I had little Logan . . .

Who would comfort Beatrice? Crispin was with her now, but he had grief and troubles enough, as well as a great responsibility with the factory and his workers. Beatrice needed her own family.

'And I canna go!' she moaned softly. Then she frowned. Father could go! she thought. He had intended to visit Mr Bradshaw . . . so why not Beatrice? He would go, if he knew . . .

As soon as the midday meal was eaten and cleared away and Logan and Beth had been fed and put down to sleep, Sarah harnessed the pony and set out for Mains of Muir.

'Give Logan one of Beth's bottles, or a sip of water, if I'm delayed, Agnes. And ask the girls to help with the milking as soon as they come home frae school. I wouldna leave you with so much to do if I could help it.'

'I ken that, Miss Sarah. We'll manage. Nae doubt Nick and Billy will be down frae the harvest field afore milking time. Nick said they were almost finished, sae dinna worry. Sally's improving tae, even if it is slow. She'd maybe keep an eye on the bairns while I'm at the milking.'

Sandy was surprised to see Sarah driving into the Mains yard. He was some distance away, crossing the home meadow on his way back from the field where the men were stooking corn. He waved his stick in acknowledgement and Sarah waved back, knowing his lame leg would not allow him to hurry. She released the pony from the trap and took off the bridle so that he could drink at the water trough, then she hitched him to one of the iron rings set firmly into the wall.

She crossed the yard and entered the house. She was dismayed at the sight of the untidy kitchen. Probably all the women, as well as the men, were helping with the harvest, but even so the grime on the windows and the cobwebs were not just one day's neglect, or even one week's. Sarah had only been in the Mains house twice and she knew things had deteriorated since Mistress Sharpe's death, and even more so since Agnes's mother had died. The fire was almost out and underneath the pit was full of ash so that it would scarcely draw when Sarah gave it an irritated poke. She turned as her father entered the kitchen.

'Aah, I see ye're putting the kettle on, lassie. I'm ready for a cup of tea and I'm sure ye will be. What . . .?'

'Father, things are an awful mess here! Why has Maggie not instructed the maids to clean? I thought it would make such a difference to your comfort, and Alex's, once Maggie and Ewan were here.'

'Aye,' Sandy frowned. 'Neither o' the maids can be trusted tae dae anything. Old Lizzie is as stubborn as a mule and she resents a young woman like Maggie coming in and criticising. I suspect she does the very opposite of what she says. As for Ivy, she's just a glaiket lassie, but she kens tae dae as little as possible whenever she can get awa' with it.'

'But I dinna understand it! Maggie was aye clean and tidy!'

'Aye, but Maggie doesna live in the hoose and she canna be here all the time. She's enough tae dae supervising the milking and making the butter, as weel as her ain wee hoose. This place had deteriorated before Maggie came. I dinna blame her. Anyway she's not been so well these past weeks.'

'Maggie's ill? What . . .?' Sarah stopped as she saw her father's eyes twinkle. 'I dinna ken what ails her for certain, but Maggie's pale and sickly and Ewan says they hope they'll be lucky enough tae have bairns afore they're as old as Sally and Nick.' He sighed. 'We really need a housekeeper tae look after us, Alex and me. We miss Fairlyden, I'll tell ye lassie. But ye didna drive nearly eight miles tae listen tae me grumbling. What brings ye here, Sarah? Surely nothing else can be wrong?'

Sarah bit her lip. How could she ask her father to travel to Yorkshire when his own household was in such disarray?

'Surely Agnes's sister, Beth, could take over the house now that she's on her own? I'm sure Maggie would be glad if she's not feeling well.'

'I asked Beth but she doesna want tae be tied tae responsibilities again, at least not here at the Mains.' Sandy frowned. 'She's not had an easy life and she's still a fine-looking woman for all she's been a widow for a guid while. The horseman frae Glenhaigh Farm has been calling on her this while back. She's asked him tae wait a wee while, but she's promised tae marry him. She only told me in confidence, mind, Sarah,' Sandy warned. 'Beth doesna want tae upset Agnes and Nick wi' talk o' her ain happiness when they're still in mourning for their mother.'

'No,' Sarah said slowly. 'I see that. But maybe she would agree to move into the house here and look after things for a wee while, if— if you were going to Yorkshire and leaving Alex on his own . . .?' Sarah was speaking her thoughts aloud and Sandy looked at her sharply.

'Why should I go to Yorkshire now that Bert Bradshaw is dead and buried? What is it, Sarah? What's wrong?'

'Oh Father, it's Dick. He caught a chill at the funeral and it turned to pneumonia. Crispin sent a wire this morning. He— Dick d-died in the early hours this morning.'

'Dick! Dick's dead?' Sandy stared at Sarah's white face incredulously. 'I canna believe it.'

'I know. Poor Dick, he worked so hard. I dinna know what Beatrice will do without him. They dinna have a man they can rely on. They never seemed to stay long. Beatrice said Dick worked as hard as two men and the hired men could never keep up with him, and most of them went to work in the pits.'

'And you thought I would go to Yorkshire, Sarah?' Sandy asked with a frown. 'I dinna think Beatrice would want me there at such a time. I'm not much guid for milking, or any other real work, these days.' He glanced bitterly at his crooked leg stretched out stiffly in front of him.

'But you would be company for Beatrice, and you could supervise the work . . .' Sarah shrugged. 'It would comfort her, I know it would. I would have gone myself, but I canna leave wee Logan, and I could never leave Agnes with so much work to do until Sally is better. Oh, Father, Beatrice needs somebody of her own just now. She's never really settled down there, for all Dick liked it so well. The Bradshaws were very kind to her, she always said that, but even Mr Bradshaw has gone now, and Crispin has his own troubles, as well as his business with the factories. Anyway he knows nothing about milking cows.'

'What about Joe Slater, Beatrice's brother. Surely he will go to her?'

'I expect he'll go for the funeral, but Joe has his own work, and he had six bairns to keep the last I heard. Anyway Joe wouldna know much about the farm, even if he could stay until Beattie pulls herself together. I dinna think Dick will have left much money. He was that keen to improve the farm . . .'

'I expect ye're right,' Sandy sympathised. 'A man's health is his greatest wealth if he makes his living frae the land, especially now; prices are barely enough tae keep things going. But, I canna see why ye think Beatrice would want me visiting her, and making another mouth tae feed, lassie?'

Sarah clenched her fists until her fingernails dug into her palms.

'I— I had you, when William died, Father. Beatrice needs her own flesh and blood too, at such a time as this,' Sarah said huskily. Then she raised her head and her dark eyes held Sandy's grey ones steadily. 'I always felt like a sister to Beatrice. Always.'

'Aye, well ye were guid friends even before the pair o' ye went tae school, but ye have your ain troubles, Sarah. Nobody understands that better than Beatrice.'

'But I was amidst my own folk, Father! Agnes and Maggie and Ewan and Nick. I had the boys and Ellen. I had *you*.'

Sandy frowned. 'It's nae guid getting upset for Beattie, lassie. I'd go tae Yorkshire tae please ye, if I thought Beatrice would want me, but I canna see why she should; I'm just a crippled old man.'

'Oh Father . . .' Sarah's voice trembled. She steadied it, but when she uttered the words which had echoed in her mind all the way to the Mains, it was no more than a hoarse whisper. 'Mistress Slater said you were Beatrice's father . . .'

At first Sarah thought he had not heard her. She looked up. She knew he had heard when she saw his white, shocked face.

'And ye believed her, Sarah?' He looked incredulous.

'Yes.'

'Jeannie Slater was a poor, demented woman.'

'She— she talked – more than I ever heard her talk before. It was after Slater fell; when she knew he was dead.'

'She must have been shocked. She couldna have known what she was saying – could she . . .?'

'I think she did, Father. I'm sure she believed it, because it upset her to— to tell me. She was clinging to the last shreds of her pride.

She begged me not to tell ye. Maybe she aye knew you would deny her . . . yet maybe she sensed that Beatrice might need help frae me, frae us, one day . . .?' Sarah finished on a pleading whisper.

Sandy rubbed his temples with the tips of his fingers, staring at Sarah in such a perplexed fashion that she almost wished she had never mentioned Jeannie Slater. 'Please, Father, forgive me. If it isna true, please forgive me!' She fell to her knees in front of him, her head bowed. She could not bear to hurt him, or to lose him. After a second or two Sarah felt her father's hand on her head, gently stroking her hair.

'Tell me everything, Sarah, everything Jeannie Miller, er, Mistress Slater, told ye . . .'

Sarah took a deep breath, struggling to remember every detail of that dreadful day at the mill. 'She said— she said you stayed at the Mill House, the night my mother married Daniel Munro.'

'That's right,' Sandy mused. 'I did. But . . .?'

'You were – she said you were very drunk.' Sarah paused and then went on haltingly, her head still bowed, unable to look her beloved father in the eye. 'She fancied herself in love with ye. She crept into your bed. You— you . . .' Sarah's face flamed with embarrassment, then drained of all colour. She could not raise her head to look at her father. 'Later you called out for Mama . . .'

'You mean I . . .?' Sandy moaned softly. 'Dear God forgive me!'

'She said you didna remember. The Captain's brandy had made you ill.' Sarah leaned back on her heels in front of him and looked into his face. It was creased in worried lines.

'I remember – the dream,' he said slowly, almost under his breath. He was as still as a statue, his narrowed eyes staring sightlessly as he struggled to recall the details of that fateful night. 'It seemed so real, I remember. Yet there was no one there. I felt deserted, desolate. Aye, I was ill, I remember that!' He grimaced with distaste. 'It's all so hazy, so long ago . . . And yet, and yet . . .?' Suddenly he gripped Sarah's shoulders so hard that she winced, but he didn't seem to notice as he stared into her face. 'Are ye absolutely sure o' this, Sarah? Did ye really think Jeannie Slater was telling ye the truth?'

'Yes, Father,' Sarah said quietly. Sandy released his grip on her and sat still, his hands hanging loosely between his knees as he stared into space. Sarah was afraid to move lest she disturbed his memories. 'So that's why I see sic an uncanny likeness tae my ain mother in Beatrice!' he muttered softly. 'And there's other things . . .'

Sarah did not reply. She knew he was not speaking to her. He was lost in memories of the past. He was not angry with her. She moved her cramped limbs and got quietly to her feet. The fire was burning cheerfully now and the kettle was beginning to sing. She warmed the teapot and reached for the caddy from the high mantelshelf. A little while later she poured two cups of strong tea and added a liberal amount of sugar. Then she went into the pantry in search of milk, frowning at the sour smell and the chaos which greeted her there.

Sandy accepted the tea almost absently, but he looked up at Sarah. 'I must go to her then, lassie.' He stood up. 'So many things fall intae place . . . Joseph Miller, I wonder if he knew?' He shook his head, answering his own question. 'But maybe he guessed.' Sarah watched as twin patches of guilty colour stained her father's ruddy cheeks. 'Does Beatrice ken?' he asked.

Sarah nodded. 'She was relieved. She hated Slater. I think she was glad it was you, Father, once she understood the – the circumstances,' Sarah said softly.

Sandy shook his head. 'I'm not worthy o' the twae o' ye. Ye're right, Sarah. I must go to Yorkshire!'

Sarah smiled her relief. 'Well sit down again and drink your tea. Ye canna go until tomorrow, but I'll send a wire as I go back through Muircumwell. I really must go home now, Father. Logan is a lusty child and he doesna like to miss a feed.' But Sandy still stood, almost in a trance. Sarah reached up suddenly and kissed his weathered cheek.

'I'm glad you know, and I'm glad you werena angry, and most of all I'm glad you're going to comfort Beatrice when she needs you.'

'Aye,' Sandy said absently, but he dragged himself back to the present as Sarah moved to the door. 'I'll harness up the pony for ye, lassie – and Sarah . . .'

'Yes, Father?'

'Thank ye, lass,' he said gruffly. 'For telling me, and for never uttering a word o' reproach.'

Sarah pulled a face. 'Remember the text the Reverend Mackenzie quoted so often? "Judge not, that ye be not judged".'

'Aye, he was a wise man,' Sandy sighed. 'But I'm a fortunate one, lassie. Take care now, and I'll see ye as soon as I come back frae Yorkshire.'

Thirty-four

It was Sunday, the first of January, 1899. Sarah was preparing to attend the morning service in the little church at Muircumwell. Thomas Whiteley would accompany them as usual, before joining his mother and youngest sister in their rooms above Ray Jardine's store.

'Somebody has tae mind the twae babes,' Agnes declared, adding candidly, 'and I'd rather listen tae their chuckles, aye and even their screams, than Mr Mace's sermons, if ye'll pardon me saying so, Mistress Sarah.'

'It isna my pardon you'll be needing, Agnes,' Sarah smiled with something of her old humour. 'Nor even the Reverend Mace's, but I'm sure God will forgive you when you've such patience with the bairns, and I know Sally still appreciates a wee bit of help with young Beth.'

'Aye,' Agnes murmured, her face creased in a smile as she glanced down at her niece, cradled in her arms. 'Nick said we could meet ye at the kirk, after he's finished looking o'er all the sows and watering the kie. We'll be there by the time ye come out.'

'That's fine then,' Sarah pulled on her gloves and drew her cloak more closely around her for the air had the seasonal tang of winter. 'We can drive on to Mains of Muir together. Your sister will be delighted to see her young namesake, Agnes. But I'll look after the babes myself next Sunday, while you attend the kirk remember,' she added firmly. 'I canna have the Minister thinking I'm making sinners of you all.'

A few hours later Sarah and her family were all assembled around the dining table at Mains of Muir, replete after an excellent meal.

'I'm glad ye've come tae look after Grandfather and Alex, Aunt Beattie. That was lovely, especially the stuffed lamb,' Ellen declared with youthful candour. 'Can we be excused frae the table now? Alex says he has twae white kittens tae show us before we set off home.'

Beatrice's pale cheeks flushed with pleasure at the sincere compliment. 'Of course, lassie. I expect Meg and Richard will want tae join ye.'

There was a mass exodus of children from the table, followed by Alex and Billy, who considered themselves too grown up to rush around like exuberant puppies now that they were fifteen and sixteen years old. But Sarah knew they were as eager to be together, and to inspect the kittens, as the younger children, and they were not above enjoying a wrestle in the hay either if the opportunity arose.

'One of the cows is near the calving. I'll just make sure she's all right,' Sandy announced, pushing back his chair. 'I'll maybe light up a pipe while I'm out. It will give the twae o' ye a wee bit o' peace tae chat.' He smiled down at them both.

'He looks happy,' Sarah said and sighed. 'I'm really pleased you agreed to come back to Scotland, Beattie. You've made such a difference here at the Mains already.' She looked around the firelit room. 'It seems like a proper home now. This house needs someone like you, and Father needed you too.'

'Well, he needed a housekeeper anyway,' Beatrice agreed with a small wry smile. 'But I'm glad he asked me. I would hae come straight away, but there was the lease, and I thought I owed it tae Dick tae try tae keep the farm on.' She bit her lip. 'I couldna manage like you do Sarah.'

'I'm fortunate to have two good men and Agnes, and Father gives advice, if I ask for it. These things are a help, when we're widowed.'

'Yes.' Beatrice sighed heavily. 'I'd naebody I could rely on tae help with the cows and the pigs.' She stared into space. Sarah thought she looked tired. Her fair hair was almost white and there were lines around her eyes and mouth. 'Richard loved the farm though and he didna want tae leave Yorkshire. The bairns at school mock him now for the way he speaks. He's had a few fights and I ken he hasna settled.'

'Oh, but he will soon. He's only been up here since the end of November. He'll soon forget.'

But Beatrice shook her head. 'He'll no' forget. Some o' the laddies taunted him about Dick being in jail,' she added bitterly. 'Anyway Richard has a mind o' his ain and he's stubborn as a mule. He says he's going back tae Yorkshire as soon as he's old enough tae leave school.'

'He'll change his mind, Beattie. He's only eight.'

'Aye, he is, but he's terribly determined for sic a young laddie.'

'And he's making you more miserable than ever,' Sarah observed shrewdly.

'Grandfather Miller once said my mother liked her ain way when she was young; he said she had a lot o' spirit. I never remember her being like that, but I think Richard must be a bit like her. Dick was such a canny man.' Tears sprang to her eyes and she brushed them away. 'Dinna think I'm not grateful tae your father, Sarah. I dinna ken what I would hae done if he hadna offered me a home, especially with Meg and Richard tae feed and clothe.'

'He's your father too, remember,' Sarah reminded gently.

'We talked about that. I always thought o' him as Mr Logan. I canna change now, Sarah. It doesna seem right somehow. Anyway it wad only lead tae a lot of questions and speculations if I started calling him "Father" after all these years. We've agreed that I'll just keep on with Mr Logan.'

'Well, whatever you call him, I know he's glad to have you here. Is Maggie keeping any better?'

'Och aye,' Beatrice smiled slightly. 'She's a grand help. It was just three months' sickness and she's pleased as can be that she's getting a bairn o' her ain tae cuddle. We've got a nice young maid called Emma as well. She comes frae o'er Lockerbie way. Her father has a farm there but there's a big family o' them and he doesna hae work tae keep them all. I told her she could go home because it's New Year's Day, but she'll be back tonight.'

Sarah nodded and sighed heavily. 'I know it's wicked to wish away time, but last night I felt truly glad to see the end of the year. It's been such a time of troubles and grief. I'd begun to dread each day dawning in case it brought bad news. Surely the new year canna be as bad . . .?'

'I certainly hope not!' Beatrice muttered fervently. 'Next year it will be more than a new year, it will be a new century. Imagine, Sarah, us living in the twentieth century! And our little Queen tae. I'm sure she never expected tae reign as long as this.'

'She's been very fortunate, yet she suffered great grief too when Prince Albert died. I think everyone believed she would never get over it.'

'Sometimes I wonder if I ever will . . .' Beatrice whispered. She blinked away her tears. 'I ken there's others in the same boat. Ye're all sae brave. I try tae think of ye all, but it doesna make me feel any better. I miss Dick so terribly.'

'We all feel that way sometimes,' Sarah said gently and covered Beatrice's hand with her own. 'I reckon Rabbie Burns understood our loss.

'. . . pleasures are like poppies spread,
You seize the flow'r, its bloom is shed!
Or like the snowfall in the river,
A moment white – then melts for ever:'

'Aye, I mind o' the lines,' Beatrice mused. 'We learned them at school.

'Or like the borealis race,
That flit ere you can point their place;
Or like the rainbow's lovely form,
Evanishing amid the storm . . .'

'He was right. Nae man can tether time or tide.'

'No, maybe not, but I'm glad you're back, Beattie,' Sarah murmured huskily, just as a loud wail disturbed their brief interlude. 'Ach, no more peace! That'll be Logan discovering he's wakened up in a strange place, and of course he'll be wanting his feed before we set off for Fairlyden again.'

'He's a fine boy, Sarah.' Beatrice summoned a wan smile. 'He must hae been a great comfort tae ye, though he's not a bit like Alex or Billy, is he? He's more like Sadie I suppose. With his grey eyes; he doesna have her narrow features though . . .'

'He's just one of his own kind,' Sarah said quickly, bending to lift her son and turn his baby frown into smiles.

Another wail accompanied an eruption of the older children into the Mains kitchen. Sarah's heart sank as the sound of Sadie's petulant voice reached them clearly.

'Meg made it scratch me! She did it!'

To Sarah's amazement it was Alex's voice that answered sharply.

'Meg didna touch the kitten, Sadie. Ye squeezed it too hard when it wanted tae escape. You've only yourself tae blame.' His deep voice sounded so like his father's that Sarah was momentarily shattered. A shiver ran down her spine. She could almost have believed William had come back from the cold grey ocean after all. But it was only a fleeting second before her own common sense reasserted itself and she began to move towards the door leading from the dining room into the large stone-flagged kitchen.

'There's nae peace when there's children,' Beattie murmured behind her, adding a little anxiously, 'I hope Meg hasna caused any trouble. Alex is so patient and kind to her. She worships him already.'

'Wherever Sadie is there's trouble,' Sarah admitted reluctantly. 'She's been worse since Logan was born. She's so dreadfully jealous, even of wee Beth Jamieson; she makes me ashamed sometimes. I hope she grows out of her whining soon.' Yet a part of her felt sympathy towards her younger daughter. Alex rarely criticised her as Billy did, in fact he was the one who usually soothed her ruffled feathers. Now she'll probably be eternally jealous of Beattie's pretty, scatter-brained bairn, she thought wearily.

The year passed relatively uneventfully for the folks at Fairlyden and Mains of Muir; courage and optimism resurfaced as the new century approached. Secretly Sarah was apprehensive about her future at Fairlyden. She had never received the lease which Bert Bradshaw had promised. She knew in her heart that the omission had probably been caused by his ill health and untimely death.

At least he sent the money, and I've managed to pay off all William's debts, she reminded herself whenever her misgivings threatened to destroy her hard won peace of mind. The first time she had sent the extra rent to Mr Metcalfe, the Yorkshire lawyer dealing with Bert Bradshaw's affairs, she had requested a copy of the promised lease. He had replied promptly, informing her that he was unaware of Mr Bradshaw's intention to purchase the house and buildings and fifty acres of land still belonging to her as owner of Fairlyden.

'I accept the extra rental and enclose a receipt, pending further investigation,' he had written. 'The papers appertaining to the transaction may be in a private deed box which will now be in the possession of his son, Crispin Bradshaw.'

Sarah's apprehension had increased. What if Crispin informed her father? But no, she calmed herself, Crispin was ever discreet. Surely he would not do that without consulting me? At first she had dreaded seeing Crispin when she knew he had returned to England, but as time passed she felt a little hurt that he had made no effort to contact her directly.

When a second rental payment was due Sarah again enquired about the lease for Fairlyden. This time Mr Metcalfe wrote a less formal letter, assuring her that she need have no fears for her future at Fairlyden, but still he did not send any documents to prove she was a legal tenant. He merely stated that the Bradshaw affairs were more complicated than had been anticipated and it would be a little while before any decisions could be made regarding his late client's estate. The statement did little to allay Sarah's apprehension and she could not confide in her father, or seek his advice as she was in the habit of doing on other matters.

Consequently she was too preoccupied to be fully aware of the shadows cast on the wider world by the outbreak of the Boer War. Only Sandy expressed his doubts as 1899 drew to a close. He still read widely and stories of British soldiers being held under siege by the Dutch troubled him greatly.

'I dinna think Britain's strength can be as great as we're led tae believe,' he remarked one Sunday while paying one of his regular visits to Fairlyden. He gave his pipe another thoughtful prod and a puff. 'The old Queen canna live forever.'

'Oh Grandfather,' Ellen reproached in her gentle way. 'Ye're awfully gloomy today. I thought ye were proud that the British Empire stretches tae all corners of the earth. Brad Leishman says we should be very proud that such a wee country has such a great influence on the world.'

'Umph, Brad Leishman does, does he? He still keeps in contact then?' Sandy raised his eyes to Sarah as he voiced the question.

'He writes quite regularly, but he is studying hard to be a doctor. Ellen asked so many questions about his work that I told her to write them down. Now he writes at length to Ellen, mostly of his studies. He always includes a note for me though!' she added with a wry smile. 'Ellen is right though, Father. You do seem unusually solemn. Are you keeping well enough?' Sarah looked at him closely. He was sixty-three but he didn't look it, she thought critically, except when he walked a lot and his lame leg troubled him.

'I'm fine. Beatrice looks after Alex and me as though we were royalty ourselves. Now young lady, what else does Brad Leishman say?' He turned his attention back to Ellen.

'He thinks women should be given the vote,' Ellen announced, watching her grandfather closely. 'Mother says ye think about such things. Do ye agree with Brad, Grandfather?'

'Weel, lassie,' Sandy heaved a sigh and blinked. 'I havena thought about that particular question, have you? After all ye'll soon be a woman.'

'Aye, I shall be fourteen next September. Mama says I can leave school at Easter if I get my certificate.'

Sandy smiled and shook his head. 'I suppose fourteen next year sounds better than being thirteen last September? What does the dominie say?'

'He says I can dae a lot o' my lessons better than most o' the boys. That makes me think that women should be able to vote because they must be able to think just as well as men, and they ken what's best for their children, don't they?'

'Aye, lassie, I suppose ye're right, but is that your ain thinking or is it Brad Leishman's?' he asked with a slight frown.

'Oh, that's what I think! That's why Brad likes me to keep writing because he says I write exactly what I think myself. He says it makes a change after all the empty-headed ladies he meets. Though they're not all empty-headed,' she added hastily. 'He met a lady called Doctor Inglis and he admires her, but he says most of the men doctors dinna think she should have been allowed to be a doctor. She went tae London and worked in a hospital for twenty-five pounds a year. That's as bad as making butter and feeding pigs, isn't it Mother?'

'Indeed it is!' Sarah smiled.

'She's come back tae Edinburgh now though. Brad says she's very indignant because women canna even have an operation tae save their ain lives unless their husbands give permission! Don't ye think that's wrong, Grandfather?'

'Well, I dinna ken . . . Maybe it's better than letting doctors dae whatever they like with their patients. I suppose the husbands always give their permission if the doctor's treatment is going tae make their wives well again.'

'They dinna *all* give their consent! Brad says one o' Doctor Inglis's patients had to go home without an operation. Her husband wouldna agree because he wanted her tae look after his children.'

'Umph . . .' Sandy frowned and cleared his throat.

Sarah chuckled. 'I think ye'd better let your grandfather have a wee bit peace, Ellen. After all this is the Sabbath remember.'

Ellen smiled and skipped away to the scullery to wash the dishes.

'Beatrice often wishes Meg had some of Ellen's and Sadie's good sense,' Sandy remarked when she had gone.

'Well, Meg seems happy enough. That's more than I can say for Sadie!' Sarah grimaced. 'Alex is very protective towards Meg these days though, I hear?' she added with a smile.

Sandy did not smile. 'Aye,' he said slowly and his brow creased. 'He's too protective. He thinks the world o' Meg. He says he kens what it's like tae be different to other bairns.'

Sarah stared. 'But I thought he'd got used to being different. I thought he didna mind so much now that he knows he can be a farmer and do most of the jobs that other men can do. Why you said yourself, Father, that he was as proud as a peacock at the harvest, after you bought the self-binder machine for him to work.'

'Oh aye, he made a good job, and he's considerate with the horses tae. Yon machine is hard on them, especially when that big driving wheel skids on the Mains' mossy ground. Alex changed his horses every couple o' hours tae give each pair a rest. I was proud o' him. He's a sensitive lad, but that's a bit o' the trouble, Sarah. He'll aye be sensitive about his ain affliction and the way he walks. Young Meg never seems tae notice that. She thinks he's a hero. I expect Alex likes that; he wadna be human if he didna like a bit o' admiration.'

'Oh well, Meg's just a bairn yet,' Sarah soothed. 'And she is his cousin after all . . .'

'Aye, but Alex doesna ken that and Meg will be a pretty woman before long. I wadna like the lad tae get hurt. Sometimes I think I should tell him . . .' He hesitated. 'Aye I think I ought tae tell him that Beatrice is my daughter tae.'

'What does Beatrice say?'

'I havena asked her. But now that I ken she's mine, Sarah, I'd like tae be sure she'll always have a roof over her head.'

'You know we would never see Beattie without a home, Father!'

'I ken *you* wadna, lassie, so long as ye're alive and well. It's a relief tae ken ye're secure here, at Fairlyden.'

He didn't see the colour drain from Sarah's face. She turned away swiftly knowing it would break his heart if he ever found out what she had done after all his own hard work and sacrifice. She made an effort to concentrate as Sandy went on.

'I canna make up tae Beatrice for all the years I never kenned she was mine, but I want tae dae something for her, and whatever I dae will affect Alex. Everything I hae is tied up in the Mains now. Maybe I should see a lawyer and make a Will? I told Alex it wad all be his one day if we managed tae make a success o' it. Well, we've paid for all the stock now, in spite o' the poor times we're having, but I couldna hae done it without Alex. His eyes are as sharp as needles when it comes tae the horses and cows, and he has a guid clear head on his shoulders. The men, aye and the maids, all respect him, young as he is. Captain Fothergill has given his word that he'll take Alex intae the lease for the Mains when he's twenty-one.'

'I dinna think Alex would resent Beatrice having a home at the Mains if she needs it, Father,' Sarah said slowly. 'And I'm glad you think so much of her. Maybe you could leave a letter for Alex, explaining why you're so concerned for her . . .?'

'Aye, maybe that wad be best. I'll think about it.'

When Sandy had gone Sarah sat staring into the fire. It was more than a year now since Mr Bradshaw had died but she had heard nothing from Crispin since the official notification of his father's death, and the formal acknowledgement of her condolences.

Surely he must know by now that his father bought Fairlyden? she thought anxiously. Had he disapproved of her seeking help from a sick man? Why has he never been to inspect his inheritance? He must know Fairlyden is part of Strathtod Estate again?

Yet the Strathtod Factor had not called to see her since the day he had made his unwarranted complaint about Fairlyden's boundary fences, shortly before Mr Bradshaw's death. She did not like Mr Reynolds, and she sensed that the feeling was mutual. She wondered if he resented her because of her friendship with the Bradshaws, or perhaps because her father had also been factor at Strathtod, and more popular with the smaller tenants? She knew he could make her own life as a Strathtod tenant very difficult, so she was both relieved and puzzled by his apparent oversight. Reynolds prided himself on his efficiency and he had a reputation for showing his authority. Sarah suspected he and Mr Bradshaw would not have seen eye to eye for very long if the Yorkshireman had had the strength to make his usual visits to the Tower House.

Sarah was at a loss to understand her own feelings regarding Crispin Bradshaw. She remembered his kindness on the night of the fire, his tenderness later, their shared passion . . . She wondered if Crispin ever thought of that night, or of her? Even if he had no wish to see her, why had he not visited his father's estate? Now that Beatrice had moved back to Scotland there was no one to pass on news of the Bradshaws. Fanny spent all her time in London with her son and her husband.

Sometimes Sarah called on Mrs Bunnerby at the Tower House but the kindly little Yorkshire woman knew little more than she did herself. Her wages were paid every six months and Crispin had written a letter soon after his father's death, assuring her that she would always have a roof over her head.

'But I do worry a bit,' she had confided to Sarah. 'You see, Mrs Fairly, it were Mr Crispin's dad that gave me t'job up 'ere in Scotland. I'd 'ad a bad time, eeh aye, a real bad time. All me troubles seemed t'come at once. Me 'usband and me eldest son were killed in an explosion down t'mine, y'see. That's where they worked. Me youngest son worked i' one uv Mr Bradshaw's factories. Well, 'e began working extra time, every chance 'e got. 'E was a good lad, our Brian. 'E wanted t'make up for 'is dad and 'is brother. I tried t'tell 'im 'e were killin' 'imself, but 'e wouldn't listen. Next thing I knew, they were bringing 'im 'ome on a cart! Maimed for life 'e were. Fell asleep at 'is machine 'e 'ad. Lived a year 'e did. Terrible it was t'see 'im sufferin' afore t'end.' Mrs Bunnerby's voice had quivered and she shed a few tears, then she sniffed and went on. 'While 'e were badly Mr Bradshaw came every single week and brought 'is pay, just like 'e was workin'. Eeh, I don't know 'ow we would 'ave managed without Mr Bradshaw. I really don't! Any road 'e sometimes stopped for a cup uv tea an' talked to our Brian. I started t'bake a cake or summat tasty when I thowt 'e'd be coming. That's 'ow 'e knew I could cook y'see. When Brian died though, I wanted t'die an' all. I wouldn't go out, couldn't eat.'

'I can understand that, Mrs Bunnerby,' Sarah said gently, 'and so would Mr Bradshaw.'

'Aye, 'e did. 'E came one day and said 'e needed me t' keep 'is 'ouse in Scotland. 'E said I owed 'im a debt and I ought t'come. Uv course it was just 'is way uv gettin' me going again, I know that now. Eeh, 'e were a kind man, 'e were that. I don't want t'go back t' them poky little 'ouses an' them dirty little streets. I want t'stay 'ere in Scotland an' it bothers me. Do y'think Mr Crispin'll think I'm an ungrateful old woman, Mrs Fairly? I know 'e's a good man an' all, just like 'is father, but in a different way. He cares about different things, if y'know what I mean?'

'I'm sure Crispin will carry out his father's wishes, Mrs Bunnerby.' Sarah had reassured the woman as far as she could, but her own doubts and worries were increasing as time passed and she still had no official proof that Bert Bradshaw had granted her the tenancy of Fairlyden for the next fifteen years. Without it she had no security at all.

It was the week before Logan's second birthday in March, 1900, when Sarah visited the Tower House again. Mrs Bunnerby answered the door herself. In fact she had seen Sarah coming from an upstairs window and hurried down to throw open the heavy door in welcome.

'Such a panic I've 'ad!' she declared breathlessly. 'T'letter came yesterday from Mrs Fanny t'say she's comin' up from Lundun in one uv them carriages without an 'orse.'

'Oh, then maybe I shouldna stay today,' Sarah began.

'Naw, naw, Mrs Fairly, you come in, do. I've gotten everythin' ready now and I've two young lasses comin' frum t'village t'elp at t'table, an' another for Mrs Fanny's bedroom, just as she instructed.' The bustling little woman led the way into the kitchen, indicating Sarah should have a seat beside the fire while she pushed the kettle on to boil, then she sat down heavily herself. Suddenly her face seemed to crumple.

'Mrs Fanny says this'll be 'er last visit t' Strathtod. Oh, Mrs Fairly,' her voice wobbled, 'Mr Reynolds says t'estate 'as t'be sold!'

'Sold? Strathtod is to be sold?' Sarah's face went white. 'It canna be true!' she whispered hoarsely.

'Mr Reynolds says it's true all right. There's death duties t'pay on t'land, 'e says. And 'e's lookin' for'ard to t'changes. Says some folks 'ave been 'ere too long an' it's time things were stirred up a bit.'

'B-but Mr Bradshaw willna sell the whole estate! Surely . . .?' Sarah muttered fearfully.

' 'E might, if 'e needed t'money for t'factories as well as these 'ere taxes. Mr Crispin's a great one for improvin' things for t'workers y'know lass. Made ever s'many windows in one uv 'is factories 'is father told me. Better for t'workers y'see luv. But what's t'appen up 'ere? Do y'think I'll be out uv 'ouse an' 'ome like Mr Reynolds said? Mr Crispin wouldn't do that would 'e, Mrs Fairly? I mean 'e's not that sort uv man is 'e?' she asked anxiously.

'No.' Sarah frowned. She felt as though the breath had been knocked right out of her, but she had to comfort the older woman. 'I'm sure

Crispin, er . . . that is Mr Crispin Bradshaw will let you know if he really plans to sell any of the estate, Mrs Bunnerby.'

'Ee, I do 'ope y'right. Mrs Fanny said Mr Crispin might come up with 'er t'ride in 'er new carriage. A motor car she calls it. Ee, I 'ope it's safe, an' I 'ope they don't bring that 'orrible 'flu with 'em. I've 'eard tell there's thousands uv folks died wi' it in Lundun town!'

Sarah did her best to allay all Mrs Bunnerby's fears but as she walked back to Fairlyden and stepped across the burn, she was filled with apprehension. How safe would her own future be at Fairlyden if Crispin did sell the estate? Would he draw up the lease his father had promised? Would it be secure with a new laird? How would she deal with the over-zealous factor? Why had Crispin never visited? A terrible feeling of depression settled upon her.

Thirty-five

The morning after Sarah's visit to the Tower House she discovered four young bullocks had broken from their shed and were galloping around the stack yard. She shouted for Thomas and Nick to help her chase them back into their pen. They had just managed to confine the spirited young beasts when a horseman rode into the yard from the Strathtod track. Sarah recognised Crispin Bradshaw immediately. Her thumping heart seemed to race harder than ever at the sight of him. She put up a hand in an effort to tidy the tendrils of hair which had escaped from her cap while she was chasing the cattle. She felt hot and dishevelled. She would have fled to the house if she had seen Crispin sooner, but it was too late to run away now. Sarah stood still, straightening her slim shoulders instinctively, but she could do nothing to control her breathing, and her cheeks were pink from her recent exertion.

Then Crispin was looking down at her from his saddle and she would have been blind not to recognise the incredulous admiration which flared momentarily in his grey eyes.

'My goodness, Sarah, you don't look a day older than the first time I saw you!' he exclaimed involuntarily. Then he blinked, gathered himself together and jumped lightly from his horse. Sarah, who would soon be forty-one, was cheered by this unexpected greeting, especially after such a long period of silence. Suddenly she relaxed her pursed lips. Crispin Bradshaw was more like his blunt-spoken father than she had thought. If he could be unconventionally frank, and flattering, then so could she.

'You're still pretty leish yourself.'

'Leish?' The grey eyes widened questioningly.

'Sprightly then,' she shrugged. 'The way you jumped frae your horse. Thomas!' she called, turning away from the bright, keen gaze which filled her with confusion. 'Would you come and take Mr Bradshaw's horse to the stable?' When she turned back to Crispin she had regained some of her composure. 'I dinna expect you're here with good news if the rumours are true . . .' her mouth tightened again, 'so I think we'll go into the house.'

Crispin fell into step beside her.

'Do you associate me with bad news then, Sarah, or have you had so much these past two years that you have grown to expect it?'

Sarah sighed. 'Both, I suppose.'

Crispin stopped and she was forced to stop too. She looked up at him questioningly and saw his frown, and the bleak look which had sprung into his eyes. Her cheeks had returned to their normal colour, but now they paled.

'Why didn't you ask *me* for help, as you promised, Sarah?' he asked coolly. 'Did you think I would bother you with my unwelcome attentions?' he added bitterly. 'I gave you my word that I would keep away, and I have. I wouldn't be here now except on business!'

Sarah swallowed hard. She had never seen Crispin so cold and angry before. She had probably imagined the look in his eyes earlier.

'Why did you ask my father for help instead of me?' he persisted. 'You must have been in desperate trouble to think of selling Fairlyden!'

'I was,' Sarah whispered.

Crispin pursed his lips.

'Perhaps we should go inside then, as you suggested. This time I hope you will be honest with me!'

He took her arm in a firm grip and escorted her into the house, but she felt more like a prisoner than his hostess. Agnes was churning butter in the dairy and Logan and Beth would be toddling around her skirts as usual; but Sarah did not pause in the kitchen. She led Crispin through to the front parlour and closed the door very firmly. There was no fire in here and the chilly air only added to Sarah's feeling of impending gloom.

'I'm to be treated as a formal visitor then?' Crispin remarked, looking round the neat, cold room. Sarah wondered if she imagined the pain which shadowed his grey eyes for a moment before they were hidden behind his thick lashes.

'It is a private conversation. No one else knows that I had to sell Fairlyden . . . that it is part of Strathtod again. It is better that Agnes should not overhear.'

'I see,' Crispin sighed. 'I believed Fairlyden meant more to you than anything else, except perhaps your family. Why did you insist my father should buy it, Sarah?' He seated himself directly opposite her so that he could watch her expressive face. 'I did not find the correspondence until some months after his death. It was in his private desk, also a letter from him . . . why did you sell? I gather he offered you a loan?'

'I needed money.'

'Well, I know farming prices have not been good, but you seemed to manage better than most . . .?'

'We did . . .' Sarah replied unwarily.

'Then why did you need so much money? Would a loan not have sufficed?'

'I knew I would never be able to repay him,' Sarah whispered hoarsely. She could never tell Crispin how much money she had needed to pay all the debts. She knew now that William had used money from the Store's account to pay his passage to America. Then there was the disease amongst the cows. Crispin would never understand the terrible effect it was still having on Fairlyden's fragile resources. 'I remembered what happened when my father had a loan!' she said aloud. 'And how troubled he was when he couldna repay it as he had planned. I thought it wiser to pay a rent. Your father promised to make a secure lease for me, but I havena received a copy yet. I— I suppose it's true? That you're selling Strathtod Estate?'

'Yes,' Crispin replied uncompromisingly.

'B-but your father loved it.'

'Owning Strathtod was the fulfilment of a dream for him. The ambition of a lifetime. Proof that he had really risen from the gutter. Now he is dead, Sarah.'

'But doesn't it mean anything to you?'

'Yes, it means finding a large sum of money for death duties,' he retorted harshly, then he sighed. 'Owning Strathtod would never fulfil my dreams,' he continued more gently and his grey eyes were fixed steadily on her face. Sarah's gaze fell. 'The lawyers have taken a long time to sort out my father's affairs. During his last few weeks he had finally accepted that I was unlikely to marry and provide him with the Bradshaw heir he yearned for. He felt a need to protect his factories, and his workers. He knew I would always care for them as long as I live, but he also made me a sort of trustee for Fanny's son, Robert. My father was a shrewd man and he was convinced her husband would squander everything he had worked for. He was probably right,' Crispin grimaced. 'Eric is disappointed with the allowance Fanny is to receive, although it is substantial. He tried to contest the Will. Consequently no real decisions could be taken until the lawyers had everything completely in order.'

'I see,' Sarah said slowly. 'I— I'm sorry you've had so much trouble.'

'Yes, well now I must raise money from Strathtod if I am to keep my promises. I must keep open the factories, and maybe improve some of the gloomy places where men and women spend their days working at the looms. If I paid the death duties and kept Strathtod, Sarah, I should be robbing hundreds of men and women of a chance to work. Did it occur to you that we have periods of poor trade in the woollen industry too?'

'N-no.' Sarah looked at him more closely then. She saw the lines of strain around his mouth and eyes. Crispin was a caring man, not a selfish industrialist.

'I have considered carefully, believe me. Strathtod must go.'

'I see,' Sarah repeated dully, and she did see, that was the trouble. Crispin had no reason to consider her, when scores of men and women could be without jobs, or homes.

'You haven't told me why you needed the money, if not to keep Fairlyden going?'

Sarah flushed. 'It was for Fairlyden in a way,' she said awkwardly. 'After the fire the . . . er, the repairs were more expensive than we expected. The insurance money was not enough.'

'Yes, I noticed you have raised the roof. The house looks much larger now; more impressive.'

Was he criticising her? Sarah wondered. 'I would have been content to keep Fairlyden the same!'

'But William wanted to improve it for you? Well I can't say I blame him, and having water from a tap, especially hot water, and drains to take it away, is a great benefit.' He gave a wry smile. 'One day I hope even the poorest of my workers will enjoy such luxuries. Maybe you will show me your improvements before I leave?'

Sarah's face flamed and she could not look Crispin in the eye. 'We dinna have a bathroom, or anything like that. Mr Crichton-Reid demanded such a lot of money for even the smallest jobs! I told him to stop after— after William died.'

'I see.' Crispin frowned. 'It must have been very hard for you then, dealing with such men, especially with a baby too.'

Sarah's colour flared and then ebbed at the mention of her youngest son. 'Aye, it was.'

'If only you had written to me.' Crispin sighed. 'I would have come sooner! I would have dealt with this Crichton-Reid for you! Surely the local tradesmen could have done the work?'

'I didna want any more debts.' Crispin's eyes widened.

'But surely you received the banker's draft from my father?'

'Yes,' Sarah mumbled uncomfortably. 'W-we had to close down the Store. There were debts to pay, for stock . . . Lady Guillyman had left her husband's share in the business too. I was determined to repay every last penny!' she said vehemently. 'No one could say William died in debt, like his half-brother. Anyway he paid off my father's loan to secure Fairlyden for me when we married. It was only right that I should pay his debts.'

'Oh my dear Sarah!' Crispin leaned forward and took her hands gently in his. 'Was it pride that kept you from writing to me for help?'

'Partly,' Sarah admitted honestly. 'Anyway I didna know where to write . . .'

'No, of course not. But my father would have sent on your letter. I would have returned . . .'

'Will my lease on Fairlyden still be secure when a new laird takes over? Y-you see, my father doesna know I've sold the house and the fifty-two acres of land he bought frae Lady Fairly.'

'I can understand that you would not wish to worry him. He has had his troubles. Now I believe he is helping Beatrice and her children?'

'Aye, but Beattie deserves his help after all these years. He has given Alex a fine chance too. That is enough for me. But how shall I keep the news frae him once there's a new laird, and the factor coming round to visit?'

'You do have another option, Sarah,' Crispin said gravely.

'What other option?' she asked despairingly. Crispin was silent for so long that Sarah raised her head to look at him. The coldness had gone from his grey eyes now; they were extraordinarily gentle. Even so she was unprepared for his answer.

'You could marry me.'

For a moment Sarah stared at him, thinking she could not have heard correctly, but his eyes held hers and she knew he meant exactly what he said. His gentle regard threatened to bring tears to Sarah's eyes. It seemed a long time since she had had anyone to care for her like that, someone who would be willing to share all her troubles.

'Oh, Crispin,' her voice was husky with unshed tears. 'You've always been kind, but I couldna accept such a proposal. I wouldna dream of burdening you. Why I have five bairns and . . .'

'I am aware of your family, Sarah.' Crispin's voice was quiet. 'I would welcome them as my own.' He hesitated as Sarah's face lost some of its colour, then he went on, 'I may be selling Strathtod, but I am not exactly a pauper. I have a large house. I can certainly keep you and your children, and life would be a great deal easier for you than it is right now, but . . .' he paused and Sarah waited tensely, her eyes never leaving his face. He meant this proposal. Suddenly she realised it was not a spur of the moment decision, it was something Crispin had considered maybe ever since he heard of William's death? 'As my wife you would live with me in Yorkshire. Your home, your place would be with me, at my side.'

Sarah's face lost all its remaining colour. She was silent. She could not answer. Her hands trembled in his and his clasp tightened momentarily. Her brown eyes were dark and troubled, but she faced him bravely. He held her gaze for several seconds, looking deep into her eyes as though trying to read her soul, then he sighed softly.

'I know your answer, Sarah. I think I have always known. Fairlyden is your first love, isn't it my dear . . .?' His eyes looked sad, yet resigned.

'I'm sorry . . . I do care for you, Crispin, I care very much, but I couldna tear up my roots now. I . . .' Her eyes travelled around the familiar little room, at the piano she could not play, left to her by the Reverend Mackenzie, the books in their bookcase, saved from the fire, the blue bowl her mother had brought from Nethertannoch . . . but it was not these things which troubled her; Crispin would have had them packed and moved to Yorkshire if she said the word. It was the thought of leaving Fairlyden itself – the house where she had been born, the fields and hills, the wood, the burn – the animals which demanded her attention . . . 'I just canna dae it, Crispin . . .' she whispered, 'not even for you.'

'I understand.'

'Do you, Crispin?' Sarah's eyes were pleading, she hated to hurt anyone as kind as Crispin Bradshaw.

'Yes, I do, better than you think, my dear. You see I have considered it a great deal, but I know I could not give up my work in Yorkshire, in the factories, all the things I hope to achieve there – not even for you, my dearest Sarah.'

Sarah stared into his eyes and she knew he was telling the truth, he really did understand.

'You're a good man, Crispin. I wish I could do as you ask, but I know it would make both of us unhappy in the end.'

He nodded. 'It would, my wise Sarah. However, there is one thing I can do for you, and I think you will find it easier to accept.' A wry smile curved his lips. 'My father did not have the deeds of Fairlyden incorporated back into the Strathtod Estate. That is why you have not received a lease yet. Also he was more ill than we knew. He did not have time to do all that he wanted to do . . .'

'B-but I've been paying a full rent to his lawyer since I received the draft for the purchase of Fairlyden . . .'

'Yes, I know. I needed time before I came to see you. We both did. I can still offer you a loan. The rent you have paid can be set against repayments. You can have the money for as long as you need it. Fairlyden can still be yours.'

For a moment or two Sarah's dark eyes shone with hope, then it died away. She lowered her thick lashes, unwilling to let Crispin see the tears she would not shed.

'I canna accept,' she whispered.

'Why not?'

'I see no way to repay you, Crispin. It takes all we make to keep the farm as it should be kept and buy the food and clothes and pay the wages . . .'

'You can have all the time it takes . . .'

'No! Thank you, Crispin, b-but I canna accept. I would always know I owed a debt. I— I . . . could you fix a fair rent, and make a lease for me, before you sell Strathtod? Could you make a lease that no other laird could break? J-just so that I know he couldna force me and my bairns to leave Fairlyden? Please, Crispin?'

'You're a very proud and independent woman, Sarah!' Crispin exclaimed with grudging admiration, as well as some frustration. 'You trusted my father. Do you trust me, now?'

'Yes. Yes, I do trust you, Crispin.'

'Very well, then I shall have my father's lawyer draw up a lease and fix a rent as you request, but I shall keep all of Fairlyden's one hundred and twenty acres, when I sell the rest of the Estate. You will be answerable to no one but me.'

'You, Crispin! B-but I thought you wanted to sever your ties with the Strathtod Estate . . . and with— with all of us . . .?'

'O-oh, I think owning Fairlyden and being your laird will have advantages. I shall have reason to return, if only to inspect my property. At least that way I shall know you have a home for as long as you need it. Oh,' he chuckled softly, 'I know how proud you are, Sarah, how you value your independence! I shall not interfere with the farm. I shall leave the entire running of Fairlyden in your hands. However, as the laird I shall pay for the repairs to the house and to the buildings.' For a moment Sarah thought she detected a fleeting sadness in his grey eyes, then he went on briskly. 'I hope you will never need help again, Sarah, but if you do, will you remember I am your friend, my dear – always?'

The tears really did spring to Sarah's eyes then. They were tears of gratitude for Crispin's kindness and above all his understanding. It was also a great relief to know that she would be able to spend the rest of her days at Fairlyden without harassment from a critical factor, without fear of eviction on the whim of a laird.

'You are kinder than I deserve, Crispin. I thank you from the bottom of my heart,' she whispered. Crispin stood up then and helped her to her feet. Slowly he bent his head and kissed first one hand and then the other. Sarah raised her face to his and her mouth trembled as their eyes met. Gently he cradled her face in his hands.

'One last kiss between friends?' he murmured huskily. It seemed to Sarah that it was a farewell kiss, and yet in her heart she knew it held a promise too. Crispin Bradshaw was her friend, and there had been many times in the past two years when she had needed him, she knew that now. He smiled down at her as he opened the door and stood aside for her to pass, but in the kitchen she turned to him.

'Mrs Bunnerby is very worried about her position too,' she said tentatively.

'She knows I shall take care of her. I told her so.'

'I know, but she doesna want to return to Yorkshire. She says it brings back too many sad memories.'

'Mmm,' Crispin frowned. 'That will present a problem then, when Strathtod is sold. The Tower House is a part of the Estate. I must give it some thought, but . . .'

'Mama! Mama!' Logan toddled through from the scullery with Beth waddling behind like a faithful little shadow. 'Ag'es has finished thurning,' he lisped. Then he caught sight of Crispin standing beside Sarah. His eyes travelled slowly up the long length of dark trousers, up and up until he saw Crispin's face.

'Man,' he announced cheerfully.

'Man,' Beth echoed faithfully.

'Hello, man.'

Again Beth echoed his words.

Crispin caught his breath as he stared down into Logan's round, cherubic face. He crouched down until his startled gaze was level with Logan's. He was looking at an infant miniature of his own father! Sarah's son! The boy was his son too! He was sure of it. He raised his head to look at Sarah, his eyes alight with a joy he had never imagined possible.

He's my son! The words on his lips remained unspoken.

Sarah was smiling tenderly at the two young children, her face soft with love, her brown eyes full of pride. Sarah must realise he was the father of her child! Crispin drew in his breath, but even as he rose to face her he knew he would be selfish to claim the child as his. Logan bore the name of Fairly, he had a kind and loving mother; indeed Sarah was the very best of mothers to all her children; Fairlyden was a happy home. The boy had space to grow here, good health, fresh air. No, Crispin thought silently, I cannot destroy such a wealth of happiness and security – yet maybe – just maybe, I can find a way to share a little, and even ease the burden. He was filled with an exhilaration he had never before experienced; a new gladness swelled in his heart.

Crispin bent down on his haunches again and held out a hand. Logan took it readily. He was a friendly child. Beth hung back shyly but she gave Crispin her sweet smile.

'What a lovely pair you are. What is your name?'

'Thogan.' The grey eyes lit with interest.

Sarah's heart fluttered nervously. Her son had never looked more like a Bradshaw than he did in that moment. His eyes were replicas of Crispin's own.

'He's Logan Brad Fairly,' Agnes chuckled behind them, 'but he canna get his wee tongue roon all that yet. And this is ma ain wee flower, Beth. Her proper name is Elizabeth Jamieson.' Agnes scooped up her golden-haired niece and Crispin stood up and caressed her soft cheek with a gentle finger.

'She's a beautiful child, Agnes. No wonder you are proud of her. How is Sally keeping now, and Nick and yourself?'

'Och, we're fine. Sally still has trouble with her back and she canna lift Beth, or a milk pail, but at least she's alive,' Agnes replied thankfully. 'Anyway wee Beth likes tae spend her time here, following wee Logan aroon'. I daursay they make the Mistress busier than she ought tae be though.'

Crispin glanced at Sarah but she smiled serenely. She felt as though a great weight had been lifted from her shoulders since Crispin rode into the yard less than an hour ago. Fairlyden was safe for her and the children.

'The bairns are no bother and hard work has never troubled me, so long as I have peace of mind. You've given me that today,' she said softly. Her gaze flickered involuntarily to Logan's baby face, then she met Crispin's grey gaze steadily. 'I hope you'll never do anything to destroy it.' Crispin caught his breath. Sarah knows he is my son, he thought, she may never admit it, but she knows. His eyes were gentle and understanding as they rested briefly on her face.

Agnes was unaware of the silent exchange as she set a wriggling Beth back on her feet so that she could follow Logan to the scullery again.

'They twae are hardly ever apart,' she declared with satisfaction. 'Happy as a pair o' wee linties they are.' Crispin dragged his gaze from Sarah's face.

'Linties?'

'Skylarks, Mr Bradshaw! Fancy anybody no' kenning that!'

'I learn something new every day,' Crispin smiled widely, 'and today has been a good day for lessons, I think. I'm glad to be back in Scotland again, even if it is only a short visit this time.' He turned to Sarah. 'I shall call again before I leave. I think I may have found a solution to Mrs Bunnerby's problem.'

'Thank you, Crispin,' Sarah smiled at him a little sadly. 'I can never repay you,' she added in a low voice as Agnes hurried after the children.

You already have, my dear, you already have, Crispin's heart sang as he cantered back to Strathtod.

The following morning Sarah delivered some of her dwindling supplies of butter to sell in Mr Jardine's shop, and collected her groceries.

'Ye look better than ye've looked for a long time, Mistress Sarah. Indeed ye look happy again this morning, and I'm pleased tae see it,' Janet said with the familiarity of long acquaintance. 'I ken it takes time tae get used tae being a widow, as weel as a' the problems o' fending alane . . .' She sighed. 'But life has tae go on, specially when we've bairns tae care for. They aye bring wee unexpected pleasures.'

'Yes, Janet,' Sarah smiled. 'I feel happier than I have done for some time. Maybe it's because it is spring again.' But in her heart Sarah knew it was not just the sparkling brightness of the spring morning which had lifted her spirits. It was the reassurance which Crispin Bradshaw had given her, and the renewed confidence and contentment his visit had brought.

She was thinking of Crispin as she drove the pony and trap past the manse grounds on her way home to Fairlyden.

'Good morning to you, Mistress Fairly!' She turned in surprise as Crispin himself rode up behind her.

'I was just thinking of you!' He breathed deeply in the clear air. Sarah noticed that the lines of strain on his face were less apparent than they had been yesterday. There was a new air of contentment in him, and it found an echo in her own heart.

'I'm glad we're friends again, Crispin,' she said impulsively.

His smile widened to a grin. 'In that case you'll not mind if I ride beside the trap?'

'Of course not, though I canna go very fast.'

'I was coming to Fairlyden anyway. I took an early morning ride to Mains of Muir. It is good to see Beatrice looking so much better, though I suspect she will always yearn for Dick. She has her hands full with young Meg. What a pretty girl she is!'

'Aye. She's a happy wee thing too.'

'Your father looks very fit, Sarah. I swear you and he have the secret of eternal youth. I wanted to discuss my plans with him.'

'Plans?' Sarah's face paled slightly.

'Trust me, Sarah!' Crispin chided softly. 'I have no wish to worry your father, but he would need to learn of my plans eventually and it was better that I should tell him myself. Anyway I needed his advice.'

He rode beside her until the track to Fairlyden narrowed and then he cantered on in front. A few hundred yards before they came to Nick and Sally's cottage he dismounted and turned to wait for her. She pulled the pony to a halt.

'Has your horse cast a shoe, Crispin?'

'No.' He held out his hand to help her down from the trap. 'If you are in agreement, I think I have found the ideal spot to build a cottage for Mrs Bunnerby. Your father agrees.'

Sarah blinked at him in surprise. He clasped her hand firmly and led her to the hedge.

'This spot will have a lovely view of the Solway Firth from the upstairs windows, and there's plenty of room for a garden and a small orchard.'

'Upstairs? Garden?' Sarah echoed. 'It sounds more like a house to me . . . Will Mrs Bunnerby want to live at Fairlyden?'

'Well, you were right about her not wanting to move back to Yorkshire. I gather she likes you, Sarah, and she's a motherly soul. She enjoys helping people, but she likes her privacy too, and so do I.'

'You, Crispin?' Sarah turned to look at him and found his grey eyes fixed on her intently.

'I shall have my own quarters here when I come to visit.'

'Visit? Will you still come to see us then, even when Strathtod is sold? You know you'd always be welcome to stay at Fairlyden . . .' Sarah issued the invitation with more warmth than she realised and for a moment Crispin paused.

'It is good to know I am welcome, Sarah,' he said slowly, 'but would it be wise? We have shared the same roof only once before . . .'

Sarah blushed at the memory of the one night she had spent in his arms and had found such comfort and tenderness.

'You're right.' She stared down at the grassy hedgerow. Crispin reached out and put a gentle finger under her chin, tilting her face so that she was forced to meet his eyes.

'I know I am, unless you have changed your mind about marrying me?' Sarah caught her breath.

'No,' she breathed. 'You know in your heart that marriage wouldna be right for us, Crispin. We're both too old to change our ways and our lives now . . . and yet— and yet I have to tell you, I value your friendship greatly, Crispin. I— I feel safe again since you came yesterday; yes, warm and safe – and happy. It's as though all my problems have suddenly melted away. But I dinna want to leave Fairlyden.' There was pleading in her brown eyes.

Crispin looked earnestly into her face, almost willing her to change her mind and marry him. Sarah was the first to look away. She looked around her at the budding hedgerows, the winter-brown grass already changing to green, the majestic hills in the distance and the shining waters of the Solway. Beyond the bend in the track was Nick's sturdy cottage; she had watched it being built, from the first stone to the last nail; beyond the cottage lay the farmsteading, and the house where she had been born, the burn where she had paddled, the fields where she had toiled. Yes, she had known grief, but she had known happiness too. 'I couldna leave Fairlyden,' she whispered.

'Then I shall build Mrs Bunnerby her cottage; she will be my housekeeper when I come to Scotland. One day Fanny's son will take over the factories. When that day comes, this is the place I shall call home.' He smiled down at her. 'You see, Sarah, I value your friendship too. I shall welcome the opportunity to see you, to help you if you need me, to watch Logan – Logan Brad? – Fairly,' he mused softly.

'He— he really was called after the young American who helped at his birth . . .'

'I believe you, Sarah,' Crispin said softly.

She looked up into his grey eyes with their dancing green and gold flecks. 'I— he . . .' she stammered.

Crispin laid a finger gently over her lips. 'I know you will be a good mother to him, Sarah. I shall never interfere in your life, or do anything to hurt you, or . . . our son. You have my word. All I ask is to know you are here, secure and happy at Fairlyden. I shall look forward to coming back to Scotland now, to staying with Mother Bunnerby, and to seeing Logan at Fairlyden as he grows from babyhood, to boyhood, and to manhood – God willing.'